# PRAISE FOR BRI

## *HER FINA*

"Labuskes skillfully ratchets up the suspense. Readers will eagerly await her next."

—*Publishers Weekly*

"Labuskes offers an intense mystery with an excellent character in Lucy, who methodically uncovers layers of deceit while trusting no one."

—*Library Journal*

## *GIRLS OF GLASS*

"Excellent . . . Readers who enjoy having their expectations upset will be richly rewarded."

—*Publishers Weekly* (starred review)

## *IT ENDS WITH HER*

"Once in a while a character comes along that gets under your skin and refuses to let go. This is the case with Brianna Labuskes's Clarke Sinclair—a cantankerous, rebellious, and somehow endearingly likable FBI agent with a troubled past. I was immediately pulled into Clarke's broken, shadow-filled world and her quest for justice and redemption. A stunning thriller, *It Ends with Her* is not to be missed."

—Heather Gudenkauf, *New York Times* bestselling author

"*It Ends with Her* is a gritty, riveting, roller-coaster ride of a book. Brianna Labuskes has created a layered, gripping story around a cast of characters that readers will cheer for. Her crisp prose and quick plot kept me reading with my heart in my throat. Highly recommended for fans of smart thrillers with captivating heroines."

—Nicole Baart, author of *Little Broken Things*

"An engrossing psychological thriller filled with twists and turns. I couldn't put it down! The characters were filled with emotional depth. An impressive debut!"

—Elizabeth Blackwell, author of *In the Shadow of Lakecrest*

# A
# FAMILIAR
# SIGHT

# OTHER TITLES BY BRIANNA LABUSKES

*Her Final Words*

*Black Rock Bay*

*Girls of Glass*

*It Ends with Her*

# A FAMILIAR SIGHT

## BRIANNA LABUSKES

Text copyright © 2021 by Brianna Labuskes
All rights reserved.

No part of this book may be reproduced, or stored in a retrieval system, or transmitted in any form or by any means, electronic, mechanical, photocopying, recording, or otherwise, without express written permission of the publisher.

Published by Thomas & Mercer, Seattle

www.apub.com

Amazon, the Amazon logo, and Thomas & Mercer are trademarks of Amazon.com, Inc., or its affiliates.

ISBN-13: 9781542027342
ISBN-10: 1542027349

Cover design by Rex Bonomelli

Printed in the United States of America

*To Abby Saul*
*For always telling me to write the book my heart wants*
*me to write and let you worry about the rest. Forever*
*grateful to have you in my corner as a tenacious agent,*
*a partner in celebration, a shoulder to melt down on,*
*and a dear friend.*

# PROLOGUE
## REED

The lace curtain created patterns of splattered light on the back of Reed Kent's hand as he held the wispy fabric away from the window, just far enough so that he had a clear view of the Porsche pulling to the curb.

When the woman stepped out of the little red sports car, she looked up directly at him, like she knew he was there, like she was meeting his eyes even though he was on the top floor of the town house.

Reed took a quick step back into the shadows, letting the curtain fall. It was insubstantial enough that he could still see her as she stared for a second longer. Then she nodded once, an acknowledgment, before heading toward the steps.

Reed shifted, pressed his spine to the wall, and sank to the floor, listening for the knock. It came, came again, and again . . .

A pause.

Reed's fingers tapped an echoing beat against the barrel of the gun cradled so carefully in his hands, his forehead dropping to rest on his upturned knees.

How had it come to this?

The door opened two floors below him.

The woman was smart. She knew he was done hiding. There was no need to bother with a lock. And she wasn't the type to worry about warrants.

The footsteps were tentative at first, and then quick and careful, the sharp staccato of high heels on marble pounding in his jaw. He could almost count the time it would take her to reach him.

Forty seconds maybe?

His lungs collapsed, his heart ripping at every vulnerable seam as he thought of the ways his life had led him to this exact moment.

Every mistake.

Every love.

Every tragedy. Every bruise, every laugh, every hesitation, every time he'd turned left instead of right.

Twenty seconds.

The glassy eye of one of Milo's stuffed animals watched him from where it was tangled up in Sebastian's bedding. Both the boys had insisted on bunk beds, and Reed hadn't been able to resist. They asked for so little, put up with so much.

A tiny whimper scraped at Reed's throat, one he'd be embarrassed by at any other time, and he reached for the animal—the bear that had once been so cherished. He buried his face in the worn fur of its belly and convinced himself that he could smell Milo on it still. Maybe even Sebastian. That he could smell childhood and innocence and silly giggles and overwrought tears.

Three seconds.

He dropped the stuffed animal to the ground and pushed to his feet, the gun pressed to the side of his leg, terrifying and powerful at once.

One second.

Reed breathed in.

The bedroom door opened.

# CHAPTER ONE

## GRETCHEN

*Three days earlier—*

Gretchen White couldn't deny that the shadows pooling in Lena Booker's bloodless hand fascinated her. As did the pale lips, and the way her friend's head lolled back against the couch cushions.

"Why am I not surprised to see you standing over a dead body?" came a Boston-drenched rumble from behind Gretchen.

"Because you think I'm a killer you just can't seem to catch," Gretchen answered, dry and honest, as she turned to find Detective Patrick Shaughnessy lurking just over her shoulder. Next to him stood a petite but curvy woman with inky-black hair and the big hazel eyes of a baby deer.

It had been an hour since Gretchen had found Lena cold and clammy, two since her friend had left that desperate voice mail on Gretchen's phone—the one Gretchen had no interest in telling Shaughnessy about.

*"I messed up, Gretch,"* Lena had said. Confessed.

"A killer I can't catch," Shaughnessy repeated, hiking up his trousers, the ones that always slipped down below the paunch of his belly, well fed as it was from a daily serving of pints and fried food. "Isn't that the truth."

The Bambi-eyed woman glanced between them. "You know each other?"

Gretchen bit back the cutting sarcasm that was her initial reaction. She'd long become an expert at swallowing her first response, and sometimes her second and third. In fact, she couldn't remember the last person with whom she didn't have to watch her words to some degree. Maybe Lena, when the woman was feeling vicious herself. "You've got yourself a true detective there, Shaughnessy."

It still came out meaner than was socially acceptable. But most people would excuse the tone, considering they were all standing over the body of Gretchen's friend.

Shaughnessy snorted at the jab. "Detective Lauren Marconi. Gretchen White."

Gretchen flicked him a look because he'd bypassed her honorific just to needle her. "Doctor."

"Dr. Gretchen White," Shaughnessy corrected with irritating emphasis. "Our resident sociopath."

The last bit was said as an aside to Detective Marconi, whose thick, unplucked eyebrows rose, creating wrinkles on her previously smooth forehead. Gretchen guessed the woman thought the comment was part of some schtick between them—the label of "sociopath" tossed around so cavalierly these days that it no longer carried any real weight. Marconi would learn soon enough that Shaughnessy wasn't joking.

Gretchen took the moment to study the woman, who she'd originally thought was in her late twenties. But the wrinkles at the corners of her eyes, at her mouth, suggested she'd hit her early thirties.

Marconi's lips twitched as she held still beneath Gretchen's scrutiny. She was in the uniform that most of Boston's female detectives seemed to have adopted—jeans, boots, a blazer, and then a button-down beneath that, as if the particular combination helped tilt it toward professional while still projecting a take-no-shit persona. There was not a trace of makeup on her face, but Gretchen was used to that—a rejection of femininity within the toxic old boys' club the city called a police department.

The detective presented as serious, tough, deferential to Shaughnessy—she'd positioned herself slightly behind his left shoulder. And even with all that effort she still couldn't mask her inherent beauty, the stunning kind that usually made Gretchen want to inflict pain on someone in creative ways.

Gretchen shifted her attention to Shaughnessy, eyes narrowed.

His lip twitched up. "Our resident sociopath . . . and a valued outside consultant for the department," he admitted. "She's helped solve dozens of cases, specializing in antisocial personality disorders and violent crimes."

"'Consultant' is shorthand for 'doing his job for him,'" Gretchen said in her own aside to Marconi. If Shaughnessy wanted to be petty this morning, she wouldn't hesitate to sink to his level. "I'm called in when the boys in blue here can't navigate out of whatever dead end they've driven themselves down."

"Called in from eating bonbons," Shaughnessy muttered under his breath, though it lacked any real heat. This was familiar, well-trodden ground, teasing almost, though Gretchen wasn't sure that was apparent to an outside observer. A look at Marconi's completely blank face revealed nothing.

"Your incompetence keeps me busy enough," Gretchen countered, though it wasn't quite true. There were only so many murders, even in a city the size of Boston, and while she had been called on by the FBI several times, they didn't use her for anything outside Massachusetts.

But it was enough. Her hefty trust fund supported her. The consulting work, more important, provided much-needed intellectual stimulation. Boredom had to be avoided at all costs—it tended to lead to self-destructive behaviors that were not compatible with the life she currently enjoyed.

The cases helped her scratch an itch, the dead bodies took care of that morbid fascination she could never quite shake. And the rest of the time she spent writing articles for academic journals that no one would read but that earned her respect in her field so that the cops would still be justified in calling her.

Gretchen refocused on the body sprawled on the ten-thousand-dollar custom couch Lena had dithered over buying for a solid two months.

"So what are you really doing here, Gretch?" Shaughnessy asked, stepping closer for a better view, his tone shifting to serious. Uniforms flowed in and out of the apartment like dark-blue water against Lena's perfectly neutral walls, but Gretchen and Shaughnessy ignored everyone else.

"I found her."

Shaughnessy huffed out one of his amused breaths. "For someone who's not a cop, you sure find a lot of dead bodies."

A truth she couldn't deny.

Gretchen's eyes strayed to Lena, finding and cataloging the very beginning symptoms of rigor mortis, the flush of chemicals working on her eyelids, her jaw, her neck. When Gretchen had burst into the apartment an hour earlier, there had been a moment when Lena had looked like she might be sleeping.

Now, there was no mistaking the reality of the situation.

"It was an overdose," Gretchen said. Lena had dabbled with pain-killers in the past, but she'd always had enough money to get the good stuff. Gretchen wondered if even the good stuff was cut with fentanyl these days. Or maybe Lena hadn't cared enough to be careful this time. Hadn't cared what the outcome would be.

"Overdose and not suicide?" Marconi asked, seeming to take her cue from Shaughnessy that Gretchen was allowed in on the investigation despite her lack of a badge. "I take it there's no note?"

Gretchen's urge to snarl at the inane question startled her into stepping away. It had been quite a long time since such a visceral throb of violence had nearly snuck past the iron wall she'd built within herself, a long time since she'd wanted to feel the snap of bone and the splash of fresh blood on her hands.

"Why are you here?" Gretchen asked Shaughnessy instead of answering Marconi. The best strategy she'd found for fighting those violent urges was to forcibly disengage and redirect her own attention. "Overdoses aren't exactly your wheelhouse."

Shaughnessy surveyed the scene, the one the paramedics had left intact.

"I'm on the Viola Kent case," he finally said.

Gretchen didn't roll her eyes, but she did turn her back on him. "I'm aware."

"Lena Booker was the lawyer defending Viola Kent," Shaughnessy continued, as if the details of the case hadn't made every front page in the city. As if Lena Booker wasn't the closest thing to what Gretchen could call a friend.

"Believe it or not, that had not escaped my attention," Gretchen drawled. She knew her expression gave nothing away. Not about the last voice mail Lena had left shortly before she'd died, not about the file that Gretchen had found lying beside Lena before the first responders had arrived. The one labeled KENT, VIOLA. "Is that why no one's moved the body yet?"

Shaughnessy lifted one shoulder. "Both the mayor and the commissioner want to make sure we're careful with this one. If there's even a hint of foul play, you know what a circus that will be."

A death connected to the most high-profile murder case in recent memory? "A circus" was probably an understatement.

The Kent case had been dissected down to the inanest details, and Gretchen guessed viewers were getting tired of the same old talking points.

Six months ago, nearly to the day, thirteen-year-old Viola Kent had stabbed her sleeping mother, Claire Kent, to death. When pressed, her father, Reed Kent, had admitted that Viola had violent tendencies and was regularly seeing a psychiatrist. It didn't take long for the gossipmongers to uncover the stories of animal bones found on the property, to dig up pictures of the brothers' broken little bodies, bruised and covered in scar tissue. It didn't take long for parents of Viola's classmates to come forward with stories of torture and manipulation.

It quickly became clear to everyone, including the Boston PD, that Viola Kent was a budding psychopath, even if she was technically too young to earn the diagnosis.

Everything about the murder looked exactly like what anyone could predict from such a situation—Viola Kent's bloodlust had escalated as her parents had always worried it would.

Despite the public's fascination with the story, there was nothing to suggest the case wasn't open and shut. And when Lena had been alive, she'd refused to answer any questions as to why she'd taken on a client that everyone in the city—everyone in the country—knew was guilty.

Now this. It wouldn't matter if Lena's death had nothing to do with the Kent family; talking about it would certainly help broadcasters keep their ratings up. Not to mention the amount of pressure that would be on the police department to make sure everything was handled aboveboard.

Even the mere suggestion of a scandal this close to the trial could drag them all down.

Lena's quiet sob, the damning hitch of breath right before her confession, echoed in Gretchen's chest.

*I messed up, Gretch.*

# CHAPTER TWO

## REED

*Three months after Claire Kent's death—*

Reed stared at the TV screen even after Ainsley turned it off and the screen went black.

"You've got to stop watching," his sister said as she tossed the remote onto the coffee table before sitting beside him.

Ainsley was right—Reed knew she was right. Yet he still found himself devouring the coverage, the early play-by-plays of Claire's murder, the features followed by more gossipy pieces as the weeks dragged on without any new updates for them all to feast upon.

"Sebastian and Milo?" Reed asked. He'd become neurotic about where the boys were, what they were doing. He'd said good night to his sons not twenty minutes ago, but he couldn't quiet the niggling fear that something had happened to them in that short amount of time, didn't think he would ever be able to now.

"Both went out like a light." Ainsley nudged his shoulder with hers. "You should go up, too."

Reed scratched at his knuckle, the one with the faint scars criss-crossing the raised bone. He shouldn't be irritated with Ainsley at the suggestion—his sister had dropped everything in her life to come help him with the boys while the details of Viola's trial were being worked out. But Ainsley had never learned when to leave him alone. It grated on him now, the way she was always trying to direct him. For his own good, of course.

"Not tired," he said, somehow managing to make it soft instead of bitter. Reed had no right to be anything but grateful for her support.

Still, he grabbed the remote, flipped the news back on. Ainsley sighed but didn't say anything more as Claire's delicate, beautiful face came up in the left corner, hovering above the anchor who wore the same serious expression that journalists always wore when speaking about Claire. Reed had it on mute so he couldn't tell what the woman was saying, but it didn't matter. He'd heard it all.

"Can't believe they're still covering this," Ainsley muttered beside him. "It's been three months since Claire died. You'd think there are more important things going on in the world."

Since Claire was *murdered*, Reed silently corrected. Ainsley had a way of doing that, framing Claire's death like it had been a car accident or a chronic disease instead of a brutal killing.

And anyway, Reed wasn't surprised by the unrelenting attention from the media, from the public. The case had all the makings of a sensational Lifetime movie. Rich family, troubled psychopath daughter, grieving-though-still-young-and-attractive widower.

Imagine if one of the reporters uncovered the rest of the story.

*"They won't,"* Lena had said when he'd voiced the concern weeks ago, when he hadn't been able to stop thinking about all the ways this could unravel. *"No one even suspects that we knew each other back then."*

That had been true. Some talking heads speculated as to why Lena Booker had taken the Viola Kent case, but no one had plucked at the threads of their backgrounds to find where they'd intertwined. No one knew that Reed Kent and Lena Booker were just two poor kids from Southie who'd made it out against all odds.

*"It's not exactly like you're proud of your roots,"* Lena had tacked on, a sharp elbow to the ribs that had landed.

At eighteen, Reed had met Claire, the only daughter of one of the city's richest, most established families. For some reason, she'd decided he was worth dating, worth sleeping with, worth marrying.

He still didn't know why.

But at the time he hadn't questioned it. His feet had been stuck in Southie concrete since birth. He hadn't spared a single glance back when Claire had offered him a way out.

Now, Claire's picture above the news anchor dissolved, only to be replaced by Viola's.

Ainsley stilled beside him, ready to calm a spooked animal, the reaction so common these days it barely registered.

Reed scratched at the scar on his knuckle as he watched the reporter's mouth move.

Was the woman giving a detailed account of all Viola's atrocities? Someone had recently let slip that there had been a padlock on the boys' bedroom door. A veritable field day had followed that tidbit.

Or was the woman instead talking about Claire's knife wounds, wondering without a hope of an answer if there had been a catalyst that had finally provoked Viola into killing her mother.

His own picture came up next, the anchor's head tipping in that sad, commiserating way everyone's did when they talked about Reed Kent these days.

Ainsley made an aborted attempt to grab the remote once more, but he held it away from her.

What would all those people, those people who watched him with some mix of pity and undisguised curiosity, say if they knew the truth?

Ainsley sighed, then patted Reed's thigh with a hand that wasn't quite steady. "Don't torture yourself too much longer, okay?"

Reed grunted, not an agreement but an acknowledgment.

He flipped through the channels until he found Claire's face once more.

If Ainsley really thought he needed news coverage to torture himself, she didn't know him as well as she thought she did.

# CHAPTER THREE

## GRETCHEN

*Now—*

Shaughnessy stood over Lena's body, his arms crossed. He looked up and met Gretchen's eyes. "If this weren't so obvious I'd assume it was your work."

Gretchen clenched her teeth until pain licked at her jaw. Then she counted to ten so the tension wouldn't bleed into her voice, so she would come off as lighthearted instead of antagonistic. A carefully crafted performance, just like most of the rest of her life. "Excuse you. I would never be this sloppy."

"I said 'if,'" Shaughnessy pointed out, amusement lurking in the corners of his mouth.

Marconi looked between them. "I honestly can't tell if you're joking."

"The detective doesn't have a sense of humor," Gretchen informed her. "We never joke."

"Okay," Marconi said, the intellect simply *dripping* from her contributions to the conversation. Gretchen walked away, bored and annoyed, which was by far the worst combination for her control. One thing she had learned in her life on the tightrope between the violent and nonviolent designations of her sociopathic diagnosis was that when she felt the need to remove herself from the situation, she had to heed the warning.

"So . . . she's a consultant? For real?" Marconi asked Shaughnessy behind Gretchen's back. Gretchen tuned out what she knew was Shaughnessy's rote answer. He'd been forced to give it enough times in her presence during the years they'd known each other that they both had it memorized now.

Dr. Gretchen White, who held advanced degrees in psychology, statistics, and criminology, had been tapped by Shaughnessy more than a decade ago to consult on a case where the suspect had reminded him of Gretchen. After that first successful investigation together, Shaughnessy had kept calling, slowly at first but then more often. And then other detectives had followed suit, until Gretchen was well known—though not always well liked—at Boston PD headquarters. During that decade or so, she had helped solve enough prominent cases that her own somewhat questionable past was often overlooked.

Because long before Gretchen was any of that, she had been the prime suspect in Detective Patrick Shaughnessy's first big case on the murder beat. It had been back in the early '90s when she'd been a child and when his belly hadn't poured over his waistband, his hair had been blond rather than nonexistent, and there'd been a gold band on his left ring finger.

The victim had been Rowan White, Gretchen's aunt. And the killer, in Shaughnessy's mind, had always been Gretchen.

He'd just never been able to actually pin it on her.

To be fair to Shaughnessy—not that she frequently had that urge—Gretchen had been found over the body, clutching the bloody knife that had turned out to be the murder weapon, her hand pressed to the gaping wound, not scared like any other child would have been but rather intrigued by the way the torn flesh had felt beneath her fingers.

The argument for her innocence hadn't been helped by the rumors even back then about how strange she was, how people in the neighborhood tended to cross the street and avoid her eyes despite that she'd been a mere slip of a girl.

Not that her age or looks had ever mattered. She'd learned when she was young that the normal people—the "empaths," as she'd learned to call them after they'd gleefully labeled her a "sociopath"—had an innate ability to recognize an outsider, a pretender, an empty void wearing the mask civilized society demanded of her.

As for Rowan's death, there had never been another viable suspect. Shaughnessy, though he seemed to have developed into a decent cop now, at the time had tunnel vision, blinded by his conviction that Gretchen had been the killer. Unwilling to think with a flexible mind that maybe there were other answers to be found.

The fact that Gretchen couldn't remember the night hadn't convinced Shaughnessy of anything other than that she was a believable liar to adults who didn't already suspect her of being evil.

Shaughnessy had seen the void from the start. And he never let Gretchen forget it.

Even as the case went cold, Shaughnessy hadn't been able to let it go. Gretchen would have found his obsession disturbing—albeit interesting—had she not understood so well the cruel grip of hyperfixations.

Since he hadn't been able to make an arrest stick, Shaughnessy had taken it upon himself to keep his eye on Gretchen from then on. It didn't matter how many times she explained to him that there was a subset of those with antisocial personality disorders who were nonviolent; to him she'd always be the girl with blank eyes who couldn't look away from her aunt's mutilated body.

When Viola Kent's case had hit the news, Gretchen had gone on a three-day bender, shocked at how startlingly familiar the murder was. A bloodied victim, a knife, a young girl who was the obvious suspect. There were differences, of course, but the similarities had been enough to keep her pestering Lena for details on the case. Details Lena had always refused to divulge.

*She's like you.*

It had been 4:00 a.m. when Lena had called, and Gretchen had slept through it, waking only to the beep of the voice mail.

At first, the message had been nothing but staticky silence. If it had been anyone else who'd left it, Gretchen would have stopped listening, thrown the phone across the room, gone back to sleep.

*When Lena spoke, her voice was small, broken. "I messed up, Gretch."*

*The words slurred together, even Gretchen's name coming out soft. Wine or pills of some kind had been Gretchen's guess.*

"She's like you," Lena murmured. "She's . . . she's like you."

"Who, darling?" *Gretchen asked, but quietly so that she didn't miss anything.*

"I messed up," *Lena said again, so hollow, so weak, so unlike Lena.* "You have to . . . you have to fix it for me, okay?"

*Gretchen's lips pressed into a thin line. Lena's voice trembled, her breathing going shallow.*

*What had Lena taken?*

*The silence dragged on so long Gretchen wondered if Lena had passed out with the phone still live. But then . . .* "You're always able to fix things."

"What do I have to fix?" *Gretchen asked, knowing it was pointless.*

"Viola Kent," *Lena said, almost like she'd heard Gretchen's question.* "Gretchen . . . Viola Kent is innocent."

And with that, Lena had ended the voice mail.

Gretchen had considered dialing 9-1-1, with how thready Lena's voice had sounded. But Lena would have killed her if it had been a false alarm—there would be no way to keep reports of that from being splashed all over the papers, especially with the Kent case on every front page. Instead, Gretchen had driven over to Lena's with the spare key her friend had given her.

As Gretchen had sped through Boston's nearly empty streets, she'd told herself Lena had just been drunk and not high and that's why she'd sounded so out of it.

But through the drive, through the race across the lobby and the interminable wait for the elevator, Gretchen hadn't been able to stop thinking of the little baggie she'd found a month ago in Lena's bathroom cupboard, tucked into an almost-empty tampon box.

It hadn't been Gretchen's business if Lena was seeking some relief from her high-pressure job, so she hadn't said anything at the time, had simply put the box back where she'd found it.

Gretchen wished she'd taken that bag, flushed the pills, pled ignorance if questioned. It wasn't like Gretchen had any qualms about lying.

Now, Gretchen crossed the threshold into Lena's bedroom. Save for an overflowing bookshelf that took up a good portion of one wall, it was nearly as spartan as the rest of the apartment.

Lena had a strong personality, but she hadn't ever been one to showcase it in her personal space. Gretchen had thought it odd behavior for an empath. She herself had always overcorrected in her apartment, filling it with things that she didn't care about so that it looked to any visitors like she had a rich inner life. Smoke and mirrors, always trying to hide the void.

Gretchen crossed to the one photo Lena had on her dresser—a picture of Lena and her grandmother at Lena's law school graduation—and gently touched Lena's face with the tip of her finger.

"I've been wondering something—it's been killing me actually," Shaughnessy said from the doorway. He seemed to have dropped the partner somewhere on the way from the living room.

Gretchen just waited, knowing he would tell her whether or not she asked.

"Why did Lena take the case?"

The question echoed closely enough to her own thoughts that it got Gretchen to turn to him, tipping her head to one side, considering. "Everyone thinks it's because of me."

"Because Viola Kent is apparently a . . ." He waved a hand in her general direction.

"A psychopath," Gretchen replied, somewhat amused by his hesitation. "You can say it. It won't summon her."

Shaughnessy snorted at that. "That's not why Lena took it?"

"No," Gretchen said, despite the ghost of Lena's voice. *She's like you.* "That reasoning ignores a crucial fact."

"Which is?"

"Viola Kent is a violent psychopath," Gretchen said.

"Right, we've established that." The words might have been impatient, but Shaughnessy's tone wasn't. Most of the time he was as hard to rile as she was easy. She hated that they were perhaps good for each other.

"I'm a nonviolent sociopath," Gretchen said. "Although you seem to be unable to grasp the fact that they are not the same beast, Lena knew they weren't."

"What's the difference?" It was Marconi who'd asked, stepping around Shaughnessy as she did.

Gretchen glanced at her, trying to decide if the woman would be around long enough to bother catering to her questions. It was pointless to try to learn anything beyond the names of the rotating cast of characters Shaughnessy took on as partners, but some responded to civility more so than others. She doubted Marconi was worth the effort, but Shaughnessy was watching Gretchen now, too, and she wanted to keep him in a benevolent mood.

"Think Ted Bundy versus . . ." Gretchen paused, nose wrinkling, annoyed at having to say such a ridiculous word. "Wall Street bro."

Marconi nodded. "Gotcha."

Shaughnessy hummed a little, though he'd heard that answer as many times as she'd heard him describing just who the lady wandering around a crime scene without a badge was.

"What are you thinking, Gretch?" Shaughnessy asked.

*I messed up.*

"There's no foul play here," Gretchen said slowly.

The thing about knowing someone for nearly three decades was that you could easily read the things they weren't saying in the silence they let hang between you.

"Right," Shaughnessy agreed easily. "But what aren't you saying?"

Her eyes swept the bedroom before landing back on Shaughnessy. Backlit as he was against the bright hallway, she couldn't decipher his expression.

Gretchen had a loose relationship with the truth, an even more relaxed one with lies of omission. There was no need for Shaughnessy to know all the details of her night, nor did she need to play him Lena's message. But she had to get him interested enough to let her investigate further.

It wasn't that Lena's message made Gretchen suddenly believe Viola was innocent. Any defense lawyer worth their degree would go to the grave swearing just that. Literally, in this instance. No, it was Lena's soft *I messed up, Gretch* combined with the Kent file lying out in the open that had Gretchen hooked, desperately needing answers. But until she knew what Lena had done—or hadn't done, for that matter—she wasn't about to tell Shaughnessy all that.

But she needed to dangle enough bait for him to bite. He was the lead detective on Viola Kent's case. Any hint that he might not have considered other suspects was a deep bruise she could press on, a reminder of her own case where he'd decided her guilt the minute he'd walked in the room.

Making allies often proved a challenge for Gretchen, but at times like these, she loved having them. Knowing someone, all their weaknesses, all their beautiful insecurities and vulnerabilities, all the ways to manipulate them—it gave her a high that she'd never been able to find even with the best drugs.

And she knew each and every one of Shaughnessy's pressure points.

"Lena called me," Gretchen said, crossing her arms over her chest as if she were comforting herself.

Shaughnessy's bushy eyebrows rose. She'd always found them a startling contrast to his slick, shiny dome. "What?"

That was Gretchen's least favorite word, and Shaughnessy knew it. She hated that it was imprecise, hated that it often made the askee repeat something that had already been communicated perfectly clearly, hated the very sound of it. She waited.

"What did she say?" Shaughnessy revised, because he was too curious not to break first.

"She told me why she took the case," Gretchen lied easily, meeting his eyes. It was important to create drama so that her revelation would be all the more impactful.

And she knew Shaughnessy was dying to hear the answer. Because Lena Booker defending Viola Kent had never made sense.

The thirteen-year-old girl had murdered her mother, had tortured her family for the months leading up to the death, hadn't demonstrated a moment of even faked remorse since being charged. If it had been anyone but Lena, Gretchen would have said it was the money, the publicity, the inevitable career boost even a losing conviction would bring.

But Lena had shunned the media, had turned down every credible journalist and every not-so-credible trash TV host who'd come begging for scraps they could use to feed a greedy audience.

On top of that, it was a well-known fact that Lena took only two types of cases. Her major employer was the mob, which accounted for the ten-thousand-dollar couch she'd so gracefully died upon.

The second was poor kids from Southie who would otherwise be stuck with an overworked public defender. And even then, the ones that Lena took interest in were few, far between, and usually for a particular reason.

Viola Kent—daughter of the fabulously wealthy Reed and Claire Kent—didn't fit either of those parameters.

The tension coiled in the air as both Shaughnessy and Marconi swayed forward. Gretchen had them exactly where she wanted them. The dramatics were all for show, all to get Shaughnessy to give Gretchen free rein here, but even as she said the words, she had a feeling there might be a kernel of truth lurking beneath.

"Lena thought Viola Kent was innocent," Gretchen finally said. She could already see the denial brewing in Shaughnessy's scrunched brows, hear it in Marconi's raspy inhale. "Which means, Detective, that once again you've gotten it wrong."

# CHAPTER FOUR

## REED

*One month after Claire's death—*

It took a month for Reed to plan the funeral. And even then, Ainsley had done much of the work.

A month might have been on the outskirts of what was acceptable, but Reed had found himself blessed with more leniency these days than he'd ever been granted before. All it had taken was a dead wife and a psychopath for a child. Add in two abused boys that everyone assured him he'd done a good job *trying* to protect, and Reed could probably get away with murder right now.

Inappropriate laughter caught in his throat, and he had to fake a coughing fit when Father Richards flinched at the strangled sound.

Reed made his excuses to the priest and weaved through the throng of people in the town house, all of them craning their necks as he walked by, doing their very best to pretend they weren't watching a car crash in motion.

Ainsley absently handed off a plate of cheap grocery store cake as he passed by, but she didn't even look to make sure he kept it. The purchase had been made on an emergency run after someone had realized that every gawker and acquaintance with even the slightest connection to the Kents had turned up at the wake. Claire would have hated that the tasteful designer cake had been devoured only to be replaced with the thick, oversweet icing, *Condolences* written over the top of the thing in a shaking, rushed scrawl.

Condolences for your dead wife. The one your daughter is in jail for murdering.

A panic attack coiled just beneath his sternum, and he rubbed at the spot with the heel of his hand as he tried to fend it off.

He'd been having them for years now, recognized easily the changes in his pulse, his breathing, his vision. Chatter chased him up the stairs, down the hallway, voices crashing through the floor, filling the empty spaces, filling every part of him until he was nothing except what people said he was.

When he blinked again, he found himself huddled in the corner of Viola's room. One hand curled around a porcelain unicorn, the horn digging an indent into the life line that ran along his palm. Claire had bought it for Viola on the girl's last birthday, an attempt at normalcy they all knew would fail.

*"At least I'm still trying,"* Claire had said, chin lifted, defiant, stubborn and broken all at the same time. *"You've just . . . given up."*

The accusation had struck, not just a slap across the face, but a burr beneath his skin that had caught, that had stayed, that had made its presence known every time he looked at Viola as if she would ruin them all.

There had been no handbook given out at birth on what to do when your daughter was a monster. No guidance offered other than psychiatrist after psychiatrist rubbing the space between their eyes as they doled out empty words and platitudes.

There was no fixing Viola.

There was only waiting—waiting until she did something so heinous as to be locked away.

The door opened, closed. Reed fought the desire to hurl the unicorn at whoever dared step into this room. Viola might be an abomination, but she was still *his*. And no one else had a right to be here.

But then Lena crouched in front of him, her hands resting gently on his knees.

"So," she drawled out, light and easy as if the past few months had never happened. As if the secrets they shared weren't heavy enough to bury them both. As if she hadn't dropped suddenly back into his life after two decades of silence only to rip it apart at every single seam. "I hear you're in need of a lawyer."

# CHAPTER FIVE

## GRETCHEN

*Now—*

"You need to rule Lena's death inconclusive," Gretchen told Shaughnessy. They were in Lena's kitchen, most of the rest of the uniforms long gone.

Lena had favored sleek and modern, so everything in the room was a bright, impersonal chrome that caught the overhead light and threw it back out twisted and distorted.

Shaughnessy ran a thick, pudgy hand over his worn face. "It's not, though."

"We both know that." This required a delicacy Gretchen wasn't always capable of. But there was a lot to work with here. She jerked her chin toward the living room, thinking of what Shaughnessy had said earlier, about why he was in the apartment in the first place. "But don't they want you to cross every t and dot all the i's?"

"Yes." Shaughnessy drew the agreement out, like he knew he was walking into a trap but couldn't help himself.

Political games were so easy to play. They were all about power, and Gretchen understood that better than most things. She didn't necessarily enjoy them, but when she played, she always won.

"Then tell them that's what you're doing." Gretchen smiled brightly. "With the best of the best on the case."

He squinted at her. "What's a couple days going to do? You know that's all you'll have."

"I don't know," Gretchen admitted, wondering if she should flat out beg. She would do so, if that would help, while also having the extra bonus of making Shaughnessy unbearably uncomfortable. Gretchen's pride was almost nonexistent when it came to getting things she wanted.

They both knew this was a big ask. With how the system worked, for Gretchen to be invited to consult with any of the detectives, the case needed to be open and active. A closed overdose investigation wasn't going to cut it. And if she wasn't officially working with the Boston PD, it would be a lot harder to get the doors she needed open to even crack a bit. "You know I'll be a pain in your ass if you don't do it."

"And that will be different how?" he asked, gruff laughter behind the question. He studied her for a quiet moment. "You really think Lena was onto something?"

*I messed up, Gretch.*

"No, but . . ." Gretchen blinked quickly, looked away. Sometimes Shaughnessy forgot who she was, forgot that she cried because she wanted him to bend to her will rather than because she was grief-stricken.

She shrugged. Almost defeated. "That was the last thing she said to me. That Viola Kent was innocent."

Like it mattered.

A voice chimed in from the doorway. "You won't have access to the Kent case. Even if we keep this one open."

The new partner. Detective Marconi.

Gretchen wondered what it would take to drive this one away. She hadn't been able to get a read on the woman yet, but what she'd seen she hadn't liked. When Gretchen didn't like Shaughnessy's partners, they didn't tend to last long.

"Who says I need access to the Kent case?"

Marconi didn't flinch beneath the stare Gretchen knew to be cold and calculating, one she'd practiced in the mirror along with a wide range of other expressions that had never come naturally to her.

"Because you think that's why she OD'd," Marconi said with a casual shrug.

The blunt assessment caught Gretchen off guard, impressed her, though perhaps it shouldn't have. This was Boston, and most people were straightforward to a fault. Gretchen tended to think she was born in just the right city for her special brand of brutal honesty.

"I don't need access," she said. "I just need the appearance of legitimacy."

"Legitimacy in the form of your attachment to the Boston PD?" Marconi asked, and Gretchen sighed at the tiresome questions. Wasn't that what she'd just said?

Gretchen turned her back on Marconi, shifting her attention to Shaughnessy. "A few days."

He studied her before his eyes flicked over her shoulder to where Marconi stood. "Fine."

Victory, sweet and addictive, flooded in, but it was tempered almost as quickly when he pointed a stubby finger in her direction. "But you need a babysitter."

The quiet groan from Marconi mirrored Gretchen's own, which she at least had the decency to swallow. "That's a waste of resources," Gretchen tried, though she knew the effort to be pointless.

At that Shaughnessy grinned. He was enjoying this. "Right, because you've always been so conscientious"—he rolled the word around in his mouth—"about our overstretched budget."

Gretchen pulled her shoulders back. "How do you know I won't kill her?"

That wiped the dopey, self-satisfied smile right from Shaughnessy's face as intended. "Marconi can take you."

With practiced deliberation, Gretchen let her eyes drag along Marconi's body, up and then down. Assessing. Then she shrugged. "I'd enjoy it if she tried."

Marconi's brows rose, but she didn't shoot back a rejoinder. It was disappointing. Gretchen enjoyed banter above most other things.

"A couple days, Gretch," Shaughnessy said from behind her, and she could almost detect a hint of something startlingly and unwelcomingly close to pity in his voice. "And then we gotta move on."

"More than enough time," Gretchen said smoothly, still watching Marconi. After that initial groan, the woman had kept any feeling about her new assignment from her face.

"God help us all," Shaughnessy muttered, nonsensically snapping his fingers at both of them in some kind of warning—though Gretchen for the life of her wouldn't be able to guess which one of them it was directed at. Then he left the room without another word.

"That was dramatic," Gretchen drawled, and Marconi snorted.

"That's Shaughnessy for you, right?" Marconi said.

*Interesting.* Was this the detective's way of trying to bond? In the past, Gretchen had discovered that a common enemy, or at least a common frustration, was an effective way to initiate a connection. She herself had employed the tactic plenty of times. "We need the Kent files."

Marconi rocked back on her heels. "I just said—"

"Indeed you did," Gretchen said, heading toward the living room. "We also need to talk to Reed Kent."

Gretchen's eyes lingered on the sprawl of Lena's lifeless body. Violent acts had never appealed to her personally; she far preferred devastation of the emotional and cerebral kind. But she was self-aware enough to know that she was drawn to the aftermath of such darkness. The pliant limbs, the empty eyes, the flesh when it was ripped, the bones when they were broken.

"He wasn't joking, huh?" Marconi said quietly from where she'd stopped behind her. "You are a sociopath."

Wrenching her attention from the sprawl of Lena's arms, Gretchen continued toward the door. "You know nothing about that word or about me."

"Then tell me," Marconi urged, falling into step beside her.

"That's not my job." She'd already done more than enough to help educate Marconi. Any more and Gretchen would surely grow bored enough to do something foolish and irrational. The feeling was always easy to predict, and thus avoid. It was a shame that no one could truly appreciate the restraint she employed. Nonviolent didn't mean she didn't have urges, ones that could so easily be let loose on an unsuspecting audience.

Shaughnessy was one of the few who realized it. She'd always liked that about him.

"What will the Kent files show you that you don't already know?" Marconi asked as they got in the building's elevator. "Every detail of that case has been covered by cable news. And your . . . friend . . . was handling the trial."

"Sociopaths have friends," Gretchen said, simultaneously irritated and amused by the pause. They quickly crossed the lobby and then stepped out on the street, where flashes of bright light popped with mindless urgency beyond the yellow crime scene tape. The vultures cawed, begging for comment, for even a glance in their direction. Both Gretchen and Marconi ignored them.

"How?" The question didn't come barbed, but rather smooth and curious.

Gretchen paused to study Marconi's face, but from what she could tell, there was no animosity hidden beneath some thin veneer.

Usually when feeling someone new out, Gretchen leaned toward lies. They were so malleable and easy to control, easy to retreat from if necessary. This time, she thought the truth might work better. She'd tested variations of this answer on other acquaintances and had found success.

"We need people in our lives who don't expect us to be anything but what we are," Gretchen said, and she could tell Marconi liked the poetic phrasing that made the sentiment seem prettier than it was. "The benefit I get from that is worth the cost of maintaining friendships."

Marconi's positive reaction was wiped clean as quick as it took to blink. Gretchen sighed, wishing it wasn't such a common occurrence in her life to go one step too far.

"Your car or mine?" Gretchen asked to get them away from this conversation. Always have an exit strategy, that was rule number one when interacting with normal people.

"Shaughnessy drove." Marconi let the rest of it drop without further comment, which Gretchen appreciated. There was nothing worse than an empath who couldn't leave well enough alone.

Gretchen turned the corner and then dipped down the alley where she'd parked her fire engine–red Porsche.

"You don't lock your doors?" was Marconi's only comment as she climbed into the passenger seat.

"I like to live dangerously," Gretchen purred, leaning into the cliché. They existed for a reason, shortcuts that everyone, especially she, understood and appreciated. When she tried to work up any fear over the car being stolen, there was nothing but an empty well to draw upon. The more interesting scenario was to test if someone would be so bold as to try to take her baby.

Marconi snorted, the same sound she'd made in the kitchen earlier. Gretchen slotted it into the mental file she'd started about Marconi's sense of humor.

"Tell me what you know about the Kent case," Marconi said, relaxed despite the fact that Gretchen had just barreled out of the alleyway without deferring to oncoming traffic.

From what Gretchen could tell, Marconi hadn't actually worked the case with Shaughnessy, but that didn't mean she wouldn't be well versed in the facts. Every person in the city had been riveted by the gruesome details over the past six months no matter how many times they'd heard them.

That meant Marconi's demand had more to do with getting Gretchen's spin on the killing than anything else. It wasn't a terrible strategy.

"About six months ago, Viola Kent, the only daughter of Reed and Claire Kent, stabbed her mother to death one evening when her father was out of the house," Gretchen recited.

"Motive?" Marconi pressed.

"Viola is a sadistic psychopath." The girl was technically still too young to actually be diagnosed, but Gretchen thought it silly to deny what was clear to anyone with even rudimentary knowledge of human behavior. "She doesn't need a motive. Well, beyond the fact that she wanted to see what her mother's blood looked like. Maybe her organs, too."

Gretchen had reviewed the file already. Despite Marconi's big talk about not giving over access to the official details, Gretchen thought she had most of them anyway. The photos from the scene would be disturbing if the viewer had a weaker stomach than she had.

Without reacting to Gretchen's shrugged-out diagnosis, Marconi simply asked, "Weapon?"

"Butcher knife from the kitchen," Gretchen said as they flew through a fresh red light. Horns followed in their wake, pissed-off drivers who could do nothing but slam their fists against their steering wheels. "For some illogical reason, Viola hid it in her sock drawer when she was done."

"Illogical?"

"As if anyone would suspect someone *other* than the sadistic psychopath of stabbing Claire to death," Gretchen said. Even now, with Lena's confession lingering in her head, Gretchen couldn't fathom how her friend had thought the girl innocent. Psychopaths killed. They tortured and they maimed and they killed. It was in their nature.

"Does that bias upset you?"

31

Gretchen laughed, actually very much amused by the question. "One, I'm a sociopath, as I've already said. Two—and please believe me when I say I am not being sarcastic here—of course it was Viola who stabbed Claire to death." Gretchen paused and then emphasized each word: "She is a sadistic psychopath."

"What about what you said to Shaughnessy?" Marconi pushed. "That he got the wrong guy."

And here was where manipulating someone who was actually paying attention could come back to bite you. So Gretchen hewed closely to the truth.

"Just because Lena might have thought Viola was innocent, for some asinine bleeding-heart reason, doesn't mean she was," Gretchen said. She was sure Lena had a reason to believe whatever she had believed. That didn't make it reality.

For psychopaths, it wasn't a question of *if* but *when.*

"Isn't that the perfect cover?" Marconi asked. "If someone wanted to kill Claire Kent? All the real murderer would have to do is shove the knife in the girl's drawer and, boom, no one asks another question."

Although Marconi's voice was more rhetorical than serious, Gretchen couldn't help but respond. "Are you trying to build a defense for Viola?"

"Just trying to figure out why Lena Booker *was.* Isn't that why we're doing this?" Marconi countered.

Gretchen snuck a glance at Marconi to see if there was something layered beneath that question, some suspicion that Gretchen wasn't telling her everything. There was nothing, though.

Maybe at some point Gretchen would tell Marconi more about Lena's last words. But for now, Gretchen would let her believe there was nothing more to it than a grieving friend who had enough connections to waste resources on a whim.

Marconi drummed her fingers on her jeans, oblivious. "Lena wasn't a sociopath by any chance, was she?"

Gretchen actually laughed at that. "The opposite, in fact."

"But why—" Marconi's mouth twisted, cutting off the rest of the question.

"Was she friends with me?" Gretchen guessed. So predictable. "As I said, a bleeding heart. Like magnets, they attract us."

"You sociopaths," Marconi said quietly, almost to herself. Then she soldiered on at normal volume. "The husband? You said he was out of the house?"

"Airtight alibi." Gretchen flipped a finger to the man behind her in a beat-up minivan who had seemed to take it personally that she'd cut him off. "He was at the Encore Casino in Boston Harbor the entire night."

Which meant his every move had been captured by the legion of security cameras that were mainstays at every casino ever built.

That seemed to catch Marconi's interest. "He was a gambler?"

"No."

"What?" It was only when Marconi's voice went sharp that Gretchen realized how relaxed her consonants had been before. Not from Boston, then. Not that it was worth noting. She was sure Marconi would be gone by the next case.

"There's no sign he was a gambler," Gretchen said precisely, repeating herself only because of Marconi's newly tense body language.

"Why was he at Encore then?"

At that Gretchen had to pause. She shot Marconi a speculative glance, her estimation of the detective rising slightly. "A boxing match. No one asked why he went that night, though."

Marconi huffed out a breath. "Why not? It's always the husband."

Gretchen braked in front of the elegant town house that she knew simply from catching glimpses of Lena's files. Then she turned to Marconi and grinned, flashing her incisors.

"Haven't you heard? Sadistic teenage psychopath beats out husband every time."

# CHAPTER SIX

## REED

*Three weeks before Claire's death—*

"Hi, Daddy."

Viola was sitting at the kitchen table, her back to the door, yet she'd known Reed was there, lingering in the hallway. The fine hairs on his arms rose as he realized she must have caught a flicker of his reflection in the butcher knife she was playing with.

"Where are your brothers?" Reed asked, trying not to betray any emotion. The stink of fear might as well be blood in the water for Viola.

Instead of lashing out, like Reed had expected, Viola just shrugged as she let the tip of the knife fall until it rested against the table. "Mommy is checking them."

Reed didn't ask, *For what?* Injuries, bruises, the like. So much pain could be inflicted on those little bodies, even when he tried to remain as vigilant as possible.

He crossed over to the counter where just enough coffee was left to splash into a mug. It didn't matter if he drank it or not; he just liked having something to do with his hands.

"How did the doctor's go?" Reed asked as he pulled out a chair across from Viola. She glanced up and lifted one shoulder. She was in an odd mood. Subdued, at least more so than usual. Normally, he would have expected her to scratch and claw at such a question.

"I don't like him," Viola said, not in a petulant, childish way, but nonchalantly. Because this was nothing new. Viola didn't like her psychiatrists. The only thing they offered her was a chance to toy with an adult, someone who knew how minds worked but never enough, seemingly, to keep a preteen girl from getting into their heads. "Mommy says I don't have to go anymore."

Reed suppressed any reaction. Claire had been reluctant to send Viola to professionals from the beginning.

She'd vetoed it when Viola was five and her little playmate had turned up in the hospital with burned skin that she refused to explain. She'd said it could wait when Sebastian had started crying anytime Viola got near him. Viola would peer up at them with her big, innocent eyes and protest that she'd never even touched him.

Even when teacher after teacher had expressed concern over the manipulation Viola deployed at will over the other students, Claire had insisted that the girl was a natural-born leader and others just couldn't handle her bold personality.

The only thing that had convinced Claire was that first big incident—when Reed had walked into the bathroom one day to find Viola holding Milo down in the bathtub, his limbs limp, his face lax. For one terrifying heartbeat, Reed had frozen, his brain unable to understand what was happening.

Then he'd shoved Viola, hard, so that her head had hit the edge of the cabinet under the sink. A thin sliver of blood had run down her temple, and she'd laughed and laughed and laughed as Reed dragged Milo out of the water.

*"Why did you do that?"* he'd asked later.

Viola had pouted. *"I wanted to see if his skin would turn blue."*

She'd been eight years old.

Looking back, Reed was actually surprised something bigger hadn't happened sooner. He carried around the sneaking suspicion that it had and he'd just missed the signs, caught up in his own problems, in his own stubborn conviction that Viola was just a kid. Kids were often cruel; that's just how they were.

It's why psychiatrists couldn't offer a diagnosis to those so young. But that didn't mean Reed and Claire could just let Viola hold their house hostage with her reign of terror.

*She likes hurting people, Claire.*

Claire didn't like that their friends and acquaintances would know, that their social circle would realize Viola had a weekly "doctor's appointment" and start asking questions. Nothing was more important to Claire than maintaining the carefully constructed facade she'd worked so hard to build. That need to control what others thought about them had blinded her to the fact that their friends and acquaintances already avoided their house so as not to have to look into Viola's empty eyes.

For a long time, Reed hadn't even blamed Claire for her reluctance. He willfully lived in denial, bought into the image of a perfect family and a perfect life, even when in pictures he always seemed to keep Milo and Sebastian to his right and Viola to his left, sandwiched between him and Claire.

*"Are we just going to drug her into a zombie?"* Claire had asked.

Reed hadn't responded because the option didn't sound so bad, and he knew that wasn't the right answer.

Love for your child should be unconditional. That was a truism that he'd never thought he'd have to confront. But when you looked at your child and saw nothing but darkness crawling beneath their skin, begging to be unleashed, how could you let that out into the world?

He'd already made peace with the knowledge that he would let Viola burn him and Claire to the ground if she ever wanted to set this place on fire. But he had to protect Milo and Sebastian as best as he could.

"You have to go to your appointments, Viola," Reed said now, bone-deep exhaustion leaking into his voice no matter how much he tried to keep it out. "We can find you a different doctor if you didn't like this one."

It would be her sixteenth.

Viola's eyes narrowed. "But Mommy says—"

A go-to tactic. Viola played him and Claire off each other with the ease of a master violinist fiddling around on an instrument for fun. It was kid-level stuff; even children who weren't Viola tried to find a way to exploit having two bosses with differing levels of discipline and empathy.

"What did you talk about today?" Reed cut her off before she could really go at that angle.

Viola's lips twisted before her face smoothed out, and Reed knew in that instant he wasn't going to like what was coming. She still hadn't learned to hide her reactions, the ones that gave away the game every time.

"About Mommy."

Reed's fingers flexed against his mug. This had been Viola's most successful tactic yet for manipulating her doctors, and any hopes that she'd abandon it were naive. Reed couldn't tell if he cared or not. He knew what she was about to say, but he asked anyway, couldn't help it. "What did he ask you about her?"

"If I wanted to hurt her," Viola said, her voice casual in a way that he knew was forced. She liked getting a reaction by saying outrageous things without emotional inflection. Thought it was funny. "Because I told him about her."

"What did you tell him?"

Viola shifted her attention to the knife she was now spinning on the table. "Did you know a high percentage of serial killers were abused as children?"

He did know that. The fact that he had pored over research on violent antisocial personality disorders was no secret to anyone in this house. And it was true. Genetics loaded the gun, environment pulled the trigger.

But this was also how she'd managed to get rid of at least four of her other psychiatrists. They'd watch Claire too closely when she sat in the waiting room, to the point that Claire would cancel the upcoming appointments, looking for a new psychiatrist. Reed had never told her about Viola's tactic, had never told her that she was dancing just like the puppet Viola saw her as. He wasn't proud of the choice. But maybe he was just tired of being the only one on the strings. "Did you tell him you want to hurt your mother?"

That was the salient bit. Reed knew Viola's true answer but was curious if she'd admitted it to a stranger. She would often pick truth and lies like shoes she was trying on for the day—whatever worked best for each situation. But what really mattered were the things other people knew, the things other people believed.

Viola nodded. "I described it. The ways I've thought about it."

Reed swallowed, looked away. "What did he say to that?"

"Don't tell me you're not curious about how I would do it," Viola taunted, and when he looked back, she was staring at him, her eyes devouring the light in the room. "I checked out an anatomy book at the library at school, you know."

Like they really needed her to learn more about ways to inflict pain. She smirked as if he'd said the thought out loud.

"There are a lot of ways you can cut someone to make her bleed just slow enough," Viola said, pressing the tip of the knife against the pad of her finger, her attention locked on the place where skin met blade, on the ruby-red droplet of blood pooling there.

Sometimes Viola could wear a mask well. She could play the normal kid, slightly mean because she was rich and spoiled and that was expected of her. She could lie with just the right amount of flush to her skin to be called on it. She could cry in quiet little hiccups as if she were trying to hide the tears, as if she were ashamed of them.

This right here was just as much of an act. This persona was probably closer to the real Viola, the one she would let loose if there weren't any consequences to her actions. It wasn't that she cared about being punished in and of itself, but she knew it would take away her access to certain things she didn't want to lose access to. Her brothers. The outside. School. These were her playgrounds, and being locked in her room wasn't outside the realm of possibility.

Reed often wondered what would happen when they could no longer physically contain her. When she realized she could leave for days and stay alive by hocking just an antique or two from their home. He didn't think she had fully conceptualized that she had the ability to do that yet, but the time wasn't far off.

Kids looked at their homes, at their parents, like this quasi prison was inevitable. Teenagers realized the mirage was just that, and the door could be opened from the inside.

"Tell me about it," Reed said instead of deflecting. Sometimes he would say things to try to shock Viola. She wasn't the only one who could play this game.

Her wolfish grin was the closest to pleased he'd seen her in a while.

When she was done laying out in excruciating detail just how she could flay a person alive, she drove the knife into the table so that it wobbled but stayed upright. They both stared at it, thrown there like a dare, before Viola leaned forward with a smug smile that was far scarier than her predatory victory of earlier.

"Don't worry," she said. "I didn't tell him that you've pictured it, too."

With that, she was up and off, quick footsteps on the stairs telling him she'd be Claire's problem soon enough.

For a long time he didn't move, just stared at the empty space where she'd been.

Then, numbly, he stood, walked around the table, and pulled the knife from where it was embedded, careful to touch only the blade. When he took it to the sink, he made sure to tilt the handle away from the water as he washed off the blood.

# CHAPTER SEVEN

## GRETCHEN

*Now—*

Marconi peered out the window of the Porsche for the first time since she'd gotten in the car and whistled low at the Kents' imposing Beacon Hill town house.

"You're going to inform Mr. Kent of Lena's death?" Marconi guessed, clearly putting the pieces together.

"No," Gretchen corrected, smoothing down her too-sunny smile. She was enjoying this, but showing that kind of glee less than a couple of hours after finding Lena wasn't empath appropriate. "You are."

To her credit, Marconi merely shrugged and hauled herself out of the bucket passenger seat. "Anything in particular you want me to say?"

Gretchen eyed her back, following her up the imposing stairs. "You need me to tell you how to do your job?"

Marconi flipped her off and then turned the gesture into a fist to knock on the door.

Reed Kent's face had been splashed up on TV screens across the city for months on end, but the pixelated version didn't do him justice. He was movie-star gorgeous, and Gretchen didn't think that of people lightly. She had high standards for beauty—in nature, in people, in things, in herself—that tended to borrow from the golden ratio.

Of course, Kent's perfectly spaced and symmetrical features lent themselves to that mathematical designation for attractiveness. His blond hair, stubble, and blue eyes, and his well-muscled yet lean body, also fit modern society's current preferences.

In addition to all that, he was magnetic in a way that went beyond the standard framework of beauty. It was a kind of charm that Gretchen recognized most frequently in fellow sociopaths.

"Can I help you?" Reed Kent asked.

Marconi dutifully held up her badge. "Mr. Kent? I'm Detective Lauren Marconi, with the Boston PD. And this is Dr. Gretchen White. She's consulting with us on a case."

"A case? My daughter's case?" The confusion, the slight worry, they were conveyed quite well. Delicate and not overwrought—not yet. If Reed were an actor, he'd be nailing this part.

"May we come in?" Marconi asked, but in that way cops did where she was already shifting her body into the entranceway, forcing Reed to step back before he even realized he'd done it.

In the next second, they were inside and Reed was closing the door behind him. A nifty little skill, that.

"Can I, uh . . ." Reed squeezed his eyes shut, and then seemed to shake off the hesitation. "Drinks? Can I get anyone water?"

"No, thank you." Marconi had now stepped into the sitting room off the entryway, leaving Gretchen and Reed to trail behind, the detective taking charge, but with a kind of subtlety that would likely skate under most people's radar. "Mr. Kent, perhaps you'd like to sit down."

"Tell me what happened." Reed's eyes darted between them, his hands on his hips. "Is it my daughter? Has something happened to her?"

Gretchen longed to dig into this man, grope around in his brain, rub at his emotions as they slid through her fingers. Would he really care if something had happened to Viola? Was this an act, or did his paternal instincts beat in his breast stronger than his love for his dead wife? And if that were the case, why couldn't he say Viola's name? Why "my daughter" only? That was a classic distancing strategy that Gretchen had seen utilized by victims and serial killers alike.

And what did he expect Marconi to say? What terrible news was he braced for? That Viola had figured out a way to kill herself? Or another girl in the facility in which she was being held? Would either surprise him having raised her for thirteen years?

"Nothing's happened to your daughter," Marconi said, falling into his speech patterns. Not naming the monster in the room. Gretchen thought it might have to do with Marconi finding Kent attractive and pleasing, and thus was subconsciously mirroring his behavior by avoiding Viola's name. It was a common practice for empaths. "Mr. Kent, if you'll sit down."

Reed started pacing. "Just tell me."

Marconi flung a quick glance toward Gretchen before finally ripping off the Band-Aid. "Lena Booker was found dead in her apartment today."

When some people reacted, it was an explosion—wild arms, wild eyes, wild curses.

But for others, it was an implosion. Everything folded in on itself, went quiet.

Reed fell into the latter category.

It was made more obvious because he'd been in motion since they'd arrived, his hands clenching, unclenching, swinging by his side, his fingers pinching the bridge of his nose, gripping his hips, his feet treading a clearly worn path over the gleaming hardwood. But when he heard about Lena's death, he stilled.

Gretchen could tell he didn't want to show them any emotion, but it was in the very nothingness he offered that she saw how much he cared about what they'd just told him.

"Found dead?" Reed finally asked, his voice well modulated, like when she'd heard him speak on TV. Guarded and careful. "What does that mean?"

It had been clever of Marconi to phrase it that way, and again Gretchen was impressed in spite of herself. Now they had Reed hooked, curious, and . . . possibly scared?

Gretchen's nails dug into her palms. She wanted nothing more than to scratch at his shellacked surface and peer into the swirling miasma beneath.

"An overdose," Marconi said after drawing out the silence for longer than socially acceptable.

Reed exhaled, a quiet release of tension. "I'm . . . That's terrible. But . . ." He looked between them. "Is this common practice? For the police to inform her clients?"

"You were her only client at the moment," Gretchen cut in. Reed stared at her without blinking, and Gretchen easily held his gaze. She always won staring contests, not feeling that same awkward throb of false intimacy that made others turn away.

As predicted, Reed looked down first, running his hand through his hair. "Still . . ."

"We didn't want you to hear it from the news," Marconi interjected smoothly. It didn't make any sense, but she said it with a finality that left no room for argument. At least not from someone who followed social niceties, which Reed Kent seemed to abide by.

He nodded, his gaze going a little distant as he lost himself to his thoughts. Marconi glanced over, and Gretchen jerked her head toward the door. She'd seen enough. For now.

Reed barely acknowledged their departure, taking Marconi's card with a tight smile and then showing them out with a simple goodbye.

Marconi paused next to Gretchen on the sidewalk, both of them staring back up at the town house.

"Did you get what you wanted?" Marconi asked.

"Of course." Gretchen grinned, quite pleased with herself. "I figured out the real reason why Lena took the case."

Marconi rocked on her heels, and Gretchen filed it under her reactions for "taken aback."

"What?" Marconi asked, then waved it away, seeming to have already picked up on the way that word bothered Gretchen. "Why?"

A curtain flickered on the third floor, but Gretchen couldn't make out the face of the person watching them.

"She took it because Reed Kent was in love with her," Gretchen said, absolutely confident in her own assessment. She'd spent many hours of her life watching videos, shows, interviews—anything recorded and available for public consumption—so that she could identify those complex emotions she'd never intrinsically grasped. Gretchen knew what grief looked like when someone you loved had died. "Now comes the interesting part."

"And that would be?"

Gretchen started toward the car. "Figuring out if she loved him back."

# CHAPTER EIGHT

## REED

*One month before Claire's death—*

Bostonians with a certain amount of wealth tended to flock together. Reed supposed that likely applied across the upper class anywhere in America, but in Boston it was almost a game.

There was new money and old money and older money—and it mattered very much which category you were sorted under.

It was probably why Reed hadn't run into Lena Booker in the past five years or so since she'd become successful. The money that sat in her bank account had been earned instead of inherited, and so she wasn't on the guest lists for the kinds of events Reed and Claire attended.

But tonight's event that Claire had dragged him along to was a Grogan & Company auction, a private gathering with three-hundred-dollar bottles of wine and appetizers too small to enjoy. The company was one of the rare few in town that didn't limit the guest list to old money. And so . . . there was a chance.

A chance that Lena might attend.

Claire brought his attention back to her when she squeezed his arm a shade too hard. Smiling was a reflex at this point, and he knew how to play his part. If nothing else, he was well trained.

"Yes, Reed has been struggling with what to do with his free time now that our youngest is in school," Claire said to the acquaintances gathered around them, her hand patting his arm like he was a 1950s housewife who couldn't quite see after himself. Two of the women nodded knowingly, while the three other men in their group eyed him with some combination of pity and disgust and boredom.

It was common knowledge he was the interloper here, and when at events like this with people like these, he'd never felt like anything but that Southie kid who'd scammed the heiress into marrying him. Reed had long resigned himself to the looks he was getting.

He touched the small of Claire's back and ignored the way she stiffened beneath his fingers. Leaning in, he stopped before his lips could brush the shell of her ear like he would have done in the early years of their marriage. "I'll get you a refill."

Her glass was barely half-empty. She nodded, and relaxed in the way they did these days when they were about to escape each other's presence.

He headed toward the bar, but instead of falling in line, he took a quick step to the left into the darkness offered by the lobby's dimmed lighting.

It took only a few wrong turns until he found a side exit that dumped out into an alleyway. When the door opened behind him, he wasn't even surprised that Lena stepped out, cigarette in hand. "Have a light?"

Reed buried his hands in his jacket pockets, leaning back against the brick wall as he did, shaking his head. "I gave up that particular bad habit a long time ago."

"But not all bad habits, right?" Lena asked, and with a sleight of hand the cigarette was gone. Like magic. Like Lena.

He didn't dare look at her. "No."

Lena didn't respond, but rather stepped closer. She was in a pantsuit with wide trouser legs and one of those tight vests with nothing but skin beneath it, in a deep-purple plum color that somehow made her hair look all the richer and her face look all the paler.

She was—and always had been—so different from Claire, who was dressed in an age-appropriate cocktail dress and the kind of shoes that had red bottoms and a fancy name that drew longing glances from her friends. Claire would never dream of turning up at a Grogan & Company auction in menswear.

And yet both were so similar to each other. Funny, smart, cold, calculating, strong, and loyal, both carrying vicious streaks a mile wide that were softened by the fire they felt toward anyone they loved. Reed had often wondered why they hadn't become fast friends when Claire had first stumbled into their lives that summer before college.

Then Tess Murphy, Lena's best friend and Reed's girlfriend, had disappeared, everything had gone to shit, and Reed had forgotten he'd ever thought Lena and Claire alike in the first place.

Reed had always told himself that he and Lena had drifted apart naturally, two childhood friends going in different directions. It was a common enough story that he'd almost been able to believe it.

But these past six months had made at least one thing clear—Lena's decision to cut him out of her life had been purposeful and merciless.

He wanted to blame Claire, as he liked to do with most things these days. She'd been just as relentless in slicing away any connections he had to his past as Lena was in ridding herself of him.

In this one thing, though, he knew the death of his and Lena's friendship was really his own fault. Reed had started dating Claire barely two weeks after Tess had disappeared, and he still remembered how Lena had looked at him when he'd told her about the new relationship. Still remembered the confusion, then the anger, the disgust, and finally, finally, the suspicion.

Reed hadn't realized at the time that it had been that moment, that conversation, when Lena had first started to think Reed had something to do with Tess's disappearance.

He realized it now, now after six months of Lena trying to insinuate herself into his life with the sole purpose of finding evidence to prove just that.

What he still couldn't figure out, though, after six months of these mind games, was why Lena had started digging into a past they'd both left far behind.

While Reed had well and truly erased his background—thanks in large part to Claire's powerful and wealthy family—Lena had used hers as part of her professional narrative to show how far she'd come in life. But she hadn't retained any actual connection to their neighborhood, nor to the people they'd grown up with.

So why stir things up when Tess Murphy was a ghost the world had forgotten about twenty years ago?

Although . . . that wasn't quite true. People did know about Tess Murphy. They knew her as now Congressman Declan Murphy's troubled sister, the long-lost runaway, the girl Declan featured in the campaign ads that focused on social service initiatives for young people in the poorer parts of the city.

What they didn't know was how she was connected to Reed Kent, who most people would assume couldn't find Southie on a map.

What they didn't know was that Lena Booker thought he had killed the girl and staged it to look like just another teenage runaway sob story.

What nobody knew except for him was what really happened twenty years ago.

He didn't know for how much longer that would be true. Lena was nothing if not relentless.

Now, Lena reached up with gentle fingers, her thumb brushing against the fading purple and green he knew lurked along one cheekbone. Most people would overlook it—how would Reed Kent have acquired a shiner?—instead seeing what they expected to see, a tired man with three kids and a beautiful wife to keep up with.

Lena always saw beyond what people expected to see.

"Viola?" she asked softly, something close to real concern in her voice, like she wasn't trying to tear his entire life apart.

In that moment, he remembered how they'd been when they were younger, remembered they'd loved each other like they were blood. Reed jerked his head back, away from the tender touch, worried that if he lingered in the bliss of it, he'd get too accustomed to gentleness.

"It's fine." The *back off* implied, even if he didn't go as far as to say it.

She took a jerky step away from him, her own walls coming up. "Of course."

"What do you want from me?" he asked, knowing his voice was too rough. He was tired of this game she seemed to be playing, tired of her lies, the manipulation. Maybe she didn't owe him anything, not after he'd left her behind twenty years ago, not after their friendship had dissolved beneath the weight of Tess's absence and Claire's influence. But he knew he didn't deserve everything Lena had put him through in the past six months as she'd hunted for ghosts and secrets, digging up a past that should have stayed buried.

Lena pressed her lips together and stared at a puddle of oil gathered in a pothole next to their feet. Then she looked up. "Do you love her?"

His thoughts had become so tangled, so disjointed that for a heartbeat Reed didn't know whom Lena was talking about.

*Her.*

Tess? She and Reed had dated that summer, the summer she'd disappeared. But it had been a weak, insubstantial thing born more of proximity and convenience than anything meaningful.

Lena had said "love," though, not "loved," as she would have for Tess. Because in Lena's mind, Tess was dead and Reed had killed her.

Viola, then? It was against nature for him not to love her, but did he? There was nothing but a pulsing darkness where love should live for his daughter, and he thought Lena would have been able to tell that by now no matter how he tried to keep it hidden. She had been back in his life for months, after all. She had recognized that his bruises could have been from the girl. Which left . . .

"Claire," Lena clarified. "Do you love her?"

His mouth was too used to lies to know how to form the truth. "She's my wife. How could I not?"

Lena looked away again, and he all but felt her retreat further, back through the door, back through the lobby, back out onto the street, away from this place, away from him.

Lena's chin jerked in an approximation of a nod, like she was telling herself something, convincing herself of it. When she met his eyes once more, her professional smile was in place, and she was a stranger, so far from his reach.

"My mistake," she said softly. And then she was gone.

Like magic, like Lena.

# CHAPTER NINE

## GRETCHEN

*Now—*

Marconi stashed her badge after she'd finished flashing it to the cop who'd caught Gretchen in a speed trap.

"Thanks, doll," Gretchen cooed, gunning the engine to scare the buff officer who'd pulled them over. He jumped, all flushed cheeks and stuttered apologies. Properly chastised.

"What do you usually do?" Marconi asked with a pointed eye roll for Gretchen's theatrics. "Flirt your way out of the ticket?"

"Or cry." Gretchen shrugged. "I'm conventionally attractive enough to get away with one or the other most times. Speaking of which . . ."

"Reed Kent?" Marconi finished the thought. Gretchen shot her an approving look, to which Marconi replied with a dry "I am a detective, you know."

"Yes, but sometimes you ask very stupid questions," Gretchen pointed out helpfully.

Marconi snorted. "Just because *you* don't understand why I'm asking them doesn't make them stupid."

Gretchen paused at that. It was close enough to one of her earlier thoughts that she tipped her head. She didn't enjoy the layered insult beneath, but she could overlook it. Perhaps Marconi could stick around longer than Shaughnessy's last partners. "Anyway, Reed Kent."

"Was he sleeping with Lena?" Marconi asked.

Not that Lena had told Gretchen. But for some reason Gretchen didn't want to admit that, in case it turned out that Lena had been having a little dalliance. Marconi already thought sociopaths incapable of having friends, and Gretchen was reluctant to provide any more fodder to feed those assumptions. Still, the rational course of action was to answer as honestly as possible even if she were later proven wrong. "No."

Marconi seemed to read some kind of hesitation in her answer anyway. "Was she the type?"

At that Gretchen clicked her tongue. "Anyone is the type."

"What do you mean?"

"You empaths and your stereotypes," Gretchen chided. "You think there's one rigid moral code—usually squarely centered around your own belief system. If someone follows it, she's 'good.' If she doesn't, she's 'bad.' As if that actually means anything at all, as if humans can be slotted into two permanent, unforgiving categories."

"Hey, I'm not judging anyone," Marconi protested, but it was weak, at least to Gretchen's ears. "I'm all for moral relativity."

"'Was she the type?'" Gretchen parroted back, glancing over. Marconi had the good sense to blush. Shame was such a powerful force it could easily be used to manipulate the desired response.

But Marconi didn't back down completely. "It's a necessary shortcut in this profession, Dr. White. You know them, you use them. For example . . ." Marconi waved to encompass the interior of the Porsche. They were dodging city traffic at sixty-five miles an hour now. "Sociopaths gravitate toward thrill-seeking behavior regardless of consequence."

"Ohhh," Gretchen crowed, delighted. "Do tell, Detective, when exactly did you have time to do research on me?"

"I have my ways," Marconi replied, her own smile smug. "Now come on, get off that high horse of yours. Lena—"

"Was she a home-wrecker?" Gretchen asked, tone dripping in exaggerated civility. "No. She barely dated anyone. Certainly no one fun, like a married man."

"Why was that?"

"Work," Gretchen answered easily, and then paused to think about it. "Actually, something had come up in the, I don't know, past year or so, maybe. She was more distracted than usual."

*Erratic* might be the better descriptor, but Gretchen knew what detectives would do with that word.

Plus there had been that baggie Gretchen had found. The one she should have flushed.

"And it wasn't a trial?" Marconi asked.

Gretchen ran the dates on the cases she knew Lena'd had on her docket. There had been three high-profile ones in that time span. But none of them felt relevant, other than the Kent case. "No, I think it was personal."

"You didn't ask?"

"Pry, you mean?" Gretchen countered. She was *not* defensive. Even if her tone suggested otherwise. She would soon grow tired of explaining that sociopaths could have friends, though they might not fall into the exacting standards of what others considered close confidantes.

"Right," Marconi agreed, and Gretchen could tell the woman was placating her. It made Gretchen grip the wheel a bit tighter, made her take the corner a bit wider, swinging into a lane of oncoming traffic. Marconi didn't so much as blink. "Whatever this personal 'thing' was, did it have to do with Reed Kent?"

"Don't you think I would have already said that if I thought so," Gretchen snapped, raw from the conversation. She got that way sometimes, could spot the warning signs of a fraying temper that wasn't the most controlled in the first place. She thought about Shaughnessy's cool stare, his wry humor, his insistence that she couldn't operate in normal society. She thought about Marconi's windpipe crushing beneath her palm, the way her pupils would dilate with fear.

The desire to prove Shaughnessy wrong won out. It usually did.

A pervasive myth had taken root that people like her lacked all control over their impulses. In actuality, a significant percentage of sociopaths passed for normal. Some didn't even realize why they never quite fit in, existing on the outskirts, maybe getting fired more often than their peers, maybe ruining a few more relationships than would generally be considered normal. But it was a leap for your average person to add all that up and diagnose themselves as a sociopath. After all, they'd probably never murdered anyone.

One man had even earned his fifteen minutes of fame when he'd stumbled over a brain scan that he'd noted was clearly that of a sociopath. In the next moment, he'd realized the brain scan was his own.

So it was true that sociopaths weren't all mindless killers. But they often needed an anchor, a line in the sand, something, something that would tether them to appropriate behavior to allow them to function in society.

For some, that was religion—a clear set of guidelines often proved extremely useful. For others, it was the penal code—racking up misdemeanors but steering clear of felonies.

It had taken a few years of trial and error—and a brief stint in what she now realized was a cult—for Gretchen to recognize that she kept coming back to one thing.

Shaughnessy.

She had no love for the man. Grudging respect would be as far as she went. Maybe on a good day an acknowledgment of their mutually beneficial relationship. But on most occasions when Gretchen's impulses had flared bright and big and almost impossible to put out, she'd seen Shaughnessy's face. The smugness that would come if he could ever arrest her for something. Anything.

Gretchen wondered idly what would happen when Shaughnessy's judgment was no longer around to offer that counterpoint to her urges.

There'd been only a few times in her life when the thought of him hadn't been enough to curb her violent tendencies. The worst had been at grad school, Columbia, a full-ride scholarship, though she hadn't needed it.

One day the dean had called her into his office, accused her of cheating. He'd sat back in his chair, legs splayed, eyes dropping to his crotch, in the worst cliché possible. Her fingers had dug into her purse, found the sharpened scissors at the bottom, had curled around the handles. She'd wanted to stab the blade into his groin to watch the blood spurt out as his heart pulsed with terror. Gretchen had gone so far as to stand, to take a step closer. The dean had licked his lips, thinking he'd won the little game. But then his secretary had knocked on the door.

It had been like a bucket of ice water on the flames of Gretchen's temper. She'd forced herself to drop the scissors back into the bag, had ducked her head, skirted around the secretary, and melted back into the crowds in the hallway outside his office.

Two weeks later the dean was gone, rumors flying about his firing. No one ever knew about the little investigation Gretchen had run and then submitted to the university's board. No one ever knew how close she'd come to killing that man, without a moment's hesitation. If she had gone through with it, not even Shaughnessy would have found out.

A loaded silence dragged on for all of three city blocks, and then Marconi's fingers started drumming on her thigh. When she spoke, there was nothing in her voice to acknowledge the tension. Maybe she'd been oblivious to it. Maybe she thought she could actually take Gretchen if it came to that. "What are you trying to accomplish?"

Gretchen didn't try to pretend she didn't understand.

She didn't care about Viola possibly being falsely imprisoned—if that was even what was happening here. The girl should be behind bars, no matter what sappy advocates might say about it. From what

Gretchen had observed through media coverage alone, Viola was destined to kill someone, and that she hadn't yet was nothing more than semantics.

Gretchen didn't care about Claire Kent's death, either, as much as she could attempt to pretend she did. If it came down to it, Gretchen would put on an act, but Marconi didn't seem like she needed that.

And since Lena had died of an accidental overdose, there was no need to pursue any kind of vengeance.

But she didn't make decisions based on justice or revenge or grief or love; she didn't even make decisions because she believed in the rule of law.

"I'm curious," Gretchen said with a shrug, because it was true enough. Truth adjacent, really. Lena may have asked her to "fix it," but Gretchen wouldn't have gotten involved if not for that base need of hers to untangle mysteries.

"Curious," Marconi said on a little laugh. "All right then."

In the silence that followed, Gretchen wondered if Marconi would keep pushing, but she seemed satisfied with that answer.

"Where are we headed?" Marconi asked.

Gretchen bit the flesh on the inside of her cheek, where she knew there were scars from years of such abuse. It was better than leaving scars on other people. "Lena's office."

"Did she talk to you about the Kent case?" Marconi asked, and there was no recrimination in her voice. The sharp exchange from earlier might as well not have happened. Not a grudge holder, then. Gretchen could appreciate that. She didn't hold them, either. That would involve an emotional investment that, quite frankly, she found herself incapable of having.

She just didn't care enough.

"Not often," Gretchen said, because it was safe to admit that without casting their friendship into doubt. Lena was a professional. It would be expected for her to keep the details of her cases close to her chest. "She found Viola to be disturbing."

Marconi shivered, a deliberate exaggeration of movement. "Girl's got spooky eyes."

"You've talked to her?" Gretchen asked, painfully curious. She'd been wanting to, but hadn't found a way in. Until now, she supposed. Perhaps she could get Marconi to convince Shaughnessy that it was imperative for them to interview the child.

"Just once," Marconi said. "The investigation was before I moved here, but we've done some follow-up interviews." She paused. "It was like staring down evil."

"Evil," Gretchen murmured, amused again. That word got bandied around with outright abandon, even though so few could define it. "I've never examined her myself, but from what I can tell, she's fairly high on the psychopathic spectrum. The Hare spectrum, that is."

"There are degrees of psychopathy?" Marconi asked.

"Most things exist on a spectrum," Gretchen replied. "Even if you people want to believe in black and white."

"Us people?"

"Empaths," Gretchen said, knowing a wealth of bitterness and fondness and several thousand varieties of emotion she couldn't even begin to understand were wrapped up in that word.

Marconi snorted again, but it was softer than that sound she made when she was amused. Another reaction to sort into Gretchen's mental file. "That makes us sound like superheroes or mutants or something."

"Sometimes it seems like you are," Gretchen said. "To me."

That admission earned her a steady look from Marconi that made her skin feel too tight against her bones. So instead of worrying about that, she continued, in lecture mode now: "The Hare spectrum is a twenty-item checklist. The top score is forty. For reference, Ted Bundy scored thirty-nine."

Neurotypical people loved talking about Ted Bundy. Gretchen knew this fact and used it often, despite not quite understanding the reasoning behind it. He had tortured and murdered so many women. But still everyone knew good ole Ted; everyone was fascinated by him. He would probably be quite happy about that.

"A checklist," Marconi mused. "The items. They're like . . . the desire to kill animals? Things of that nature."

"Not in and of itself, on this particular scale," Gretchen corrected. It was a common mistake and one she didn't hold against Marconi in the grand scheme of things. "You're thinking of what was once referred to as the 'homicidal triad.'" She held up her fingers as she counted them off. "Animal cruelty, fires, and bed-wetting."

"Yes," Marconi said, drumming her palm against her thigh. "Right, bed-wetting's a big one. Yeah."

"Further research has not validated that those traits are predictors for violent behaviors in adults," Gretchen said primly. Then she slid Marconi a look. "But let's be honest. At the very least, killing animals can be considered a marker."

"Then what else is on the Hare spectrum?"

"Lack of remorse or guilt, pathological lying, poor behavioral controls," Gretchen ticked off. "Failure to accept responsibility for one's own actions."

Marconi was quiet for a moment, before clearing her throat. "And that's different from you how?"

Gretchen shrugged, because that was fair. "It's not by much."

She'd scored on the lower end of the spectrum, barely clinical, just enough to be diagnosed. "They both fall under antisocial personality disorders. Psychopath is simply the more dangerous version, and neither are very technical terms."

They were easy for a layman to understand, though—far easier than the nuances that actually came with the diagnosis. So, despite her training, Gretchen had long ago found herself falling into colloquial terminology. Otherwise cops' eyes started glazing over fairly quickly.

"You said Viola was sadistic, too," Marconi said, a question beneath the statement.

"It's a stereotype that they go hand in hand, the two diagnoses," Gretchen said, wanting to put that out there. "Not everyone with an antisocial disorder is sadistic."

"Okay, but Viola . . . ?"

"Is, yes. I believe so, at least," Gretchen said. "To be fair, she's not my patient. I've simply studied her interviews."

"I think I'll trust your take for now," Marconi said, the corner of her mouth lifting in an amusement that Gretchen didn't understand. So she took the words at face value, as she was often forced to do when the complexities of normal conversation evaded her. "Tell me about sadists."

There was an ego-driven impulse to grandstand on everything she knew about the topic. But Gretchen also realized that wasn't an effective use of time. "At its simplest, sadists derive pleasure from hurting others."

"The 'S' in BDSM?" Marconi's voice went a little tight, a little high. Embarrassment, some distant part of Gretchen realized. It never failed to amuse her the way some people got uncomfortable around the subject of sex.

"Yes, but there are plenty of sane, safe, and consensual experience-seeking sadists out there," Gretchen said, hiding the enjoyment she got out of Marconi's unease. Perhaps Gretchen had a bit of emotional sadism in her.

Marconi relaxed enough to laugh, holding her hands up as she did.

"Hey, read all the Fifty Shades you want," Marconi said. She paused, seeming to gather herself. "So not all sadists are psychopaths, is what you're saying."

"They're two different disorders, and 'sexual sadist' is a label that's even more specific under that," Gretchen said. "But someone can be both a sadist and a psychopath. Ergo Viola Kent."

"I've seen the pictures," Marconi said quietly.

They all had. The images had been played on a loop right after Claire Kent's murder. The bruises on the two brothers, the cuts, the scar tissue, the gaunt frames, the looks in their eyes that even Gretchen could recognize as broken. That didn't even touch on the subject of the dogs and other animal bones that police had found buried in the backyard.

Viola had been terrorizing that household for some time before Claire Kent's death.

In a stroke of the good luck that always seemed to follow Gretchen around, a parking space opened in front of Lena's office just as they pulled up.

She didn't bother to lock the car as they climbed out and breezed into the building. Gretchen sailed by the impeccably dressed man at the desk in the front lobby. "Don't mind us, Hunter." When she noticed Marconi's hand in her jacket pocket, clearly reaching for her badge, she muttered, "Stop it. He doesn't care."

As if to prove Gretchen's point, Hunter flipped a page of the glossy magazine he was reading.

After the lobby came the elevator, and then well-polished glass with Lena's name on it in classy and understated silver lettering. Gretchen had a moment of doubt that the offices might be locked, but the doors swung open at the merest pressure.

"She had a partner," Gretchen told Marconi, who trailed behind her. "I wonder if he rushed out when he heard the news."

The place did have an abandoned feel to it, like in one of those apocalyptic zombie movies where the bagel was left half-eaten, the email half-read, the printer still running long after the world has ended.

Was that what Lena's death had meant to these people? The world ending?

Gretchen knew the place well enough to cross the white carpet to Lena's office and push through the door into the room without hesitation.

The desk was glass like the doors, in the modern style; the chair, dove gray with tufted fabric; the photos along the walls, impersonal black-and-white landscapes. Everything about the room was stylish, professional, and reassuring. Lena Booker made money, and she would keep you out of jail. That was the promise in the polished lines of every inch of the office.

It was that confidence that had made Gretchen seek out Lena Booker in the first place, back when Gretchen had started consulting with the Boston PD. Gretchen was a quick study and excellent at research, but there were weak spots that even she could admit to having. One of them was a thorough understanding of all the nuances of the legal system, especially when it came to minors.

Lena had charged her an obscene amount for her own consultation services, and Gretchen had taken to her immediately. Not in the sense that she'd *liked* Lena—she hadn't, that wasn't how Gretchen was wired. She remembered that quite clearly even through that rosy fog of grief that so often tinted relationships a prettier color than they were.

But Gretchen had always had an appreciation for women who knew their worth, knew how much they could ask from others, and then delivered. That had been Lena to a tee. Gretchen shouldn't have been surprised. Lena skyrocketed to notoriety in the city for defending mob bosses. A nonviolent sociopath had probably seemed almost harmless after that.

Lena hadn't been the only expert Gretchen relied on for cases, and if it had been up to Gretchen, they would never have interacted outside a professional capacity.

Then one evening about six months after Gretchen had first recruited Lena for help, she'd dropped by her office with a new case. She'd found the woman with puffy eyelids, smudged mascara, and a determined set to her mouth.

*"I'm getting sloshed, and you're joining me,"* Lena demanded.

*Gretchen waved toward Lena to signal Lena's clearly emotional state. "This is . . . not my forte."*

*Lena laughed long and hard at that. "Yeah, no shit." And then she poured them both outrageously expensive whiskey. "Don't need you to talk. Don't need you to listen. Just need you to sit there and drink."*

*"Well, that's my kind of evening." Gretchen tapped the rim of her glass to Lena's.*

"We need people in our lives who don't expect us to be anything but what we are" was what Gretchen had told Marconi when she'd asked how a sociopath could have a friend. And from that night when Gretchen and Lena had sat in silence for hours slowly killing the rest of the liquor, Gretchen had realized that maybe Lena had needed exactly that, too.

"Where does Lena even keep her files?" Marconi asked, interrupting Gretchen's thoughts. The detective looked distinctly uncomfortable, her hands in her jeans pockets as if she were in a museum or a china shop. Middle- or lower-class background, then.

The pale rose-gold file cabinet situated on the far side of the room blended in with the decor enough to be overlooked at first glance. Gretchen headed toward it.

"We're in luck," she said as she slid the drawer out, revealing its innards to the room. "It wasn't locked."

"What are you even looking for?" Marconi asked, now hovering by Gretchen's shoulder.

"I don't know yet," Gretchen said, quickly thumbing through and dismissing each of the files as irrelevant. When she made it through all of them, she shifted her attention to the bottom drawer and the hidden panel she knew was built into the case.

Her fingers traced over smooth metal until she felt the little hitch in continuity. Gretchen pushed. The faint yet audible pop was satisfying in the way sex must be to normal people. "And this."

Marconi's breath was hot against Gretchen's exposed neck, and Gretchen elbowed the woman back a step. Without missing a beat, Marconi just asked, "What is it?"

"Her finances," Gretchen answered, already flipping through the thick book, searching out the timeframe when Lena had started acting stranger than usual. If she were still alive, Lena would be furious if she knew Gretchen was rifling through her notes. But that was moot now. A transaction caught her eye. "Ah."

Marconi crowded back in close, seemingly immune to Gretchen's sharp elbow jabs. She whistled low and did that thing where she rocked on her heels. *Taken aback,* Gretchen's inner catalog helpfully supplied. "That's more than six months' salary. In one deposit."

"Right, which is why I said, 'Ah,'" Gretchen snapped. "Please keep up. It's a payment."

Marconi didn't bother to fight back. "One of two."

Gretchen pursed her lips while studying the numbers for a minute, hating that Marconi had figured out something Gretchen couldn't see. Finally, grudgingly, she gave in. "Why do you think that?"

A blunt, unpainted nail tapped the page. There was a scribble there that Gretchen couldn't make out. "Shorthand. You see it a lot with family accountants."

*Family.* The mob. Lena worked with them frequently, so it made sense she'd fallen into their patterns.

But it was interesting Marconi had spotted the shorthand. Had she been promoted to Homicide from Vice? If so, it must have been a nice change. Gretchen had a sneaking suspicion that at least some of the detectives who worked in Vice would land somewhere on the Hare spectrum, and another handful were likely dipping into the contraband themselves.

Even babysitting Gretchen was probably better than dealing with that lot.

Gretchen's eyes flicked up to the date on the deposit in Lena's records. A little over a year ago, long before Reed Kent would have hired Lena as Viola's lawyer.

Maybe this was irrelevant.

Idly, she flipped forward. Nothing else jumped out at her.

"Huh," Marconi said from still too close beside her.

Again, Gretchen swallowed an irritated "What?" and just waited. Loath as she was to admit it, Gretchen was beginning to appreciate the blasted word.

"It's just . . . ," Marconi started, then paused, shifted, leaning in so that her nose nearly touched the paper. Then she straightened and met Gretchen's eyes. "There's no two of two. Just the one of two marked."

Gretchen didn't have to flip through the dates to know she was right. "So whatever it was payment for . . ."

Marconi finished the thought. "Lena didn't hold up her end of the deal."

# CHAPTER TEN

## REED

*Two months before Claire's death—*

When Reed answered the knock on the town house door, he was greeted with a fist. It hit like a battering ram, sending him stumbling back into the hallway.

He was used to taking punches, and instinct had told him to lift his chin the minute he'd seen Declan Murphy standing on his stoop. The blow glanced off Reed's cheekbone just under his right eye, the shock enough that he didn't feel the pain at first. When it came, he welcomed it like a familiar friend.

Declan was panting, but it seemed from anger rather than exertion.

Reed didn't know why he hadn't expected this confrontation from the minute he'd realized Lena had suspicions that Reed had something to do with Tess's disappearance. Lena and Declan hadn't remained close, but it was a small city. What were the odds she hadn't at least spoken with the man about her investigation?

Especially since Reed knew Declan used the story to bolster his own congressional campaigns. Every time that Declan spoke of Tess in public, it was with the conviction that his sister had settled herself in a new and better life. Not once had he ever hinted that there might have been foul play involved.

Reed had never been close enough with him to ask why he never wondered why Tess hadn't contacted Declan in all this time.

"You killed her, didn't you?" Declan's accusation came on something close to a sob, confirming Reed's guess. "You sick bastard."

*Oh, Lena, what have you done? Why did you start all this?*

Why, why dig up this past? This hurt? These secrets?

Reed swallowed hard. Despite the fact that they were both standing there, perfectly still and upright, it felt like he was lying flat on his back, a bruise already forming on his whole body.

*I didn't kill Tess* is what he wanted to say. Instead what came out was, "But you think she's alive."

He should have seen the second punch coming, yet somehow this encounter had him so off-balance he didn't. This time he ended up crashing into the side table, the edge of it catching at the bottom of his ribs.

"You smug—" Declan advanced, pushed him, the brute strength of it finally sending Reed to the floor. "I should kill you."

Declan drew back his foot, the trajectory on a path to catch Reed at the already-tender spot on his side. Reed curled into a shivering ball.

*Protect your belly. The kidneys can take it. Protect . . .*

The kick lifted him, sent him skidding over smooth marble.

"Get up," Declan roared, his voice echoing, crashing over Reed so that he thought he might drown beneath it. "Get. Up."

Reed didn't move, didn't breathe.

"Fight like a man." Declan kicked him again, this time not quite as hard. A warning, an exclamation point.

Reed didn't move, didn't breathe.

"Get up." The demand when it came again was animalistic, guttural, and it crawled into the hollows of Reed's body and pressed outward until his skin, his bones, his spine ached to just give into it.

Reed didn't move, didn't breathe.

"Disgusting," Declan muttered, and then there was the rough sound, a drag of tongue and throat. The spit landed on the side of Reed's face, a hot glob that slid over the purple and green blooming on his cheekbone.

Reed wanted to wipe the saliva from his skin, but he knew it would never come off, a stain he'd have to live with forever.

Declan crouched, leaned in. "If I find one solid shred of evidence that you killed my sister, you won't have to worry about going away for life."

Then he stood and rested his boot exactly where it had caught Reed twice, where it had been bruised from the side table already. Declan pressed down. "Because I'll put you in the ground first."

Reed didn't move, didn't breathe.

The pain was easy to take, absorb, ignore.

The expectant silence weighed on Reed just like Declan's foot, the vise of Declan's contempt crushing his lungs. It was like Declan thought Reed at any minute was going to shake it off, get up, come out swinging, or come out protesting his own innocence. Because Declan didn't realize Reed had been broken long ago.

Maybe the courage that it took to survive this instead of fighting off the blows was lost on someone who didn't live under attack every day. But Reed was all that stood between his boys and death, torture, endless abuse. There was nothing he wouldn't do for them. Including play coward to a man whose honor was worth less than the spit on Reed's cheek.

When Reed stayed down, Declan swore, the condemnation clear in his voice.

And then he was gone, the door slamming behind him.

The high whine of sudden silence filled Reed's ears, and he held himself in his tight little ball, waiting for Declan to come back and finish it. Reed didn't know how much time had passed, but there was no cold barrel of a gun shoved against his temple, no steel-tipped boot catching him just right beneath his chin. No crushing blow to his skull.

Muscle by muscle, Reed relaxed. First his hands that were curled into fists, then his elbows where they were tucked up close to his head, then his backbone that had rounded in his body's effort to protect his soft, vulnerable underside.

Finally, he exhaled and shifted until he was lying flat on the floor, his eyes on the ceiling above him, concentrating on the new ways he hurt.

That was when he heard it.

A whimper.

*No.*

Slowly, so slowly, he turned just his head to track the sound.

And there, there was Sebastian watching him with watery eyes, sitting on the floor, crouched mostly out of sight in the entranceway to the den, his knees drawn up to his chest, his lower lip wavering with the effort to keep the sound inside.

Sebastian's near-silent anguish latched into Reed's belly, a fishhook that brutally yanked at the flesh there, so much more painful than anything Declan could have ever done to him.

At some point in his life, Reed had realized that being a good man, being tough, didn't always involve fists. Sometimes it involved staying down so you could get up later and protect those even more vulnerable than you.

At least that's what he'd told himself as he'd tried to protect Milo and Sebastian in a household too often defined by violence.

But maybe Declan was right about him. Maybe he really was weak.

Had he ever been a strong man? One with conviction and fortitude? Had he maybe had the potential and it had been leeched out? Was that giving himself too much credit? When he looked into Viola's eyes, he saw blackness, but when he looked into Milo's and Sebastian's, he saw every failure of his life laid out bare.

"Why didn't you fight back?" Sebastian asked into the damning silence.

Reed closed his eyes so he didn't have to look at his son's face any longer. It wasn't anguish there but disgust, the same as Declan's.

"I don't know, buddy," he finally said, his jaw sore from where he must have struck the marble. "Maybe it's time to start."

# CHAPTER ELEVEN

## GRETCHEN

*Now—*

Gretchen only looked up from where she sat among her scattered piles of Lena's files when Marconi stood and brushed her hands against her jeans.

"Well, I'm in for the night," Marconi said, stretching up so that her back popped audibly, just like that hidden panel. Gretchen nearly grinned at the thought, wondering what it would take to get Marconi to spill her innards out for Gretchen to play with like the cabinet had done.

"This is why no one believes me when I swear that the Boston PD really aren't the lazy so-and-sos everyone says they are," Gretchen said. But Marconi huffed out an amused breath. Empaths tended to think that Gretchen was teasing whenever she said what was on her mind. It was a nifty trick that she'd managed to hone over the years, injecting just the right twist to her words for them to come off as lighthearted instead of vicious.

She smiled to herself, pleased, and turned back to the files.

"Yeah, yeah," Marconi grumbled, but she hesitated, not leaving immediately. "Find anything?"

"Not of note," Gretchen said.

There was an uncertain pause. "Would you tell me even if you did?"

At that, Gretchen actually looked up. Most people working on police teams assumed their partner had the best interests of the case at heart. Gretchen offered no such promises, but she often relied on the presumed trust and was rarely called out on it beyond Shaughnessy's half-hearted attempts. So she answered honestly. "If it benefited me to tell you."

Marconi pursed her lips and then nodded, as if agreeing. "Makes sense."

And then she gave Gretchen a two-finger salute and headed toward the door without another word. Gretchen couldn't help herself: she watched Marconi go until she was out of sight.

For all that Gretchen had studied human behavior, human psychology, sociology, and an assortment of other fields, for all that she'd worked with the police department for years, consulting on everything from arson to murder, for all that she'd lived her life with the purpose of passing as normal, Gretchen didn't *get* Marconi.

And she liked that about the woman.

She supposed that Marconi wasn't actually invested in this case. No one thought Lena's death was anything other than an overdose, and no one thought Gretchen's presence was anything other than a veteran cop indulging a valued consultant's whim. No one seemed to be taking Lena's proclamations of Viola's innocence seriously, either.

If Marconi was a babysitter, she was a lax one. But why wouldn't she be? She had nothing to lose here, and a favor to gain out of it.

Still, Gretchen enjoyed studying her reactions, how she dealt with Gretchen, how she dealt with any situation. The truth of it surprised Gretchen. She'd been prepared to write the woman off, but she wasn't too stubborn to reverse course. Normal people so often relied on instinct when it came to that initial gut reaction about someone. First impressions might be important in this world made up of empaths, but relying on them was an absolutely foolish strategy.

Gretchen turned her attention back to the folder in her lap, the one that had been hidden along with Lena's financial documents. There was something off about it, but every time she looked too hard, the feeling flitted away, dancing out of reach.

The case was about a runaway girl from a poor Boston neighborhood. What followed seemed to have been a lackluster investigation where no one searching for the girl thought she wanted to be found.

It wasn't unusual for Lena to keep the police files, along with her own notes. But for this case, Lena didn't have an accompanying trial folder to go along with it. Gretchen didn't know if that meant this wasn't one of her actual clients or if Lena had hidden or destroyed the documents for good reason.

Gretchen touched the photo of the girl staring back at her.

Tess Murphy.

Pretty thing, she looked about seventeen and like she'd walked straight out of one of those teenage soap operas that were so popular these days.

Why had Lena kept her file hidden away? Why had Lena kept her file in the first place?

*Why are you important?*

The answer to that question wasn't going to come while she was sitting on Lena's office floor. Gretchen pushed to her feet and slid the file into her bag, leaving the others she'd been digging through scattered over the plush rug. Someone would pick them up eventually.

As she made her way back toward the elevator, she absently dialed Shaughnessy, her mind still stuck on the details of Tess Murphy's file.

Shaughnessy answered with a gruff "Did you kill Marconi?"

Gretchen rolled her eyes even though her intended audience wouldn't see it. She knew Shaughnessy would hear it anyway. "One of these days, my feelings are going to be hurt, you know."

He laughed. "You don't have feelings."

"Guilty," she drawled. It wasn't true. She had feelings, just not like empaths did. For her, tapping into them was more like tuning into a hard-to-find radio station, rather than the uncontrollable flood that seemed to be the norm for most everyone else. Still, she let Shaughnessy have that one. It was part of their dynamic, and she strove hard to maintain that dynamic. "Your little babysitter is tucked in for the night."

"Isn't that the reverse of what's supposed to happen?" Shaughnessy tossed out, but she could tell he wasn't invested in the conversation. If she had to guess from the ambient noises, he was packing up at his desk, getting ready to leave. "What's up, Gretch?"

She didn't bother beating around the bush. "I want to interview Viola."

That got his attention. "No."

"You can't deny you've been curious about how that would go," Gretchen tried. "Me facing off with a psychopath? Come on."

"Make a better argument," Shaughnessy said, but didn't deny it. Gretchen grinned. He would die before admitting it, but Gretchen knew Shaughnessy found her endlessly fascinating. He wouldn't have devoted a good chunk of his life to keeping an eye on her otherwise.

"No, you make it for me," Gretchen countered, and faked a loud yawn. "I'm just so tired from doing your work for you all day long."

He huffed out an annoyed breath. "My work was done at Lena Booker's apartment."

Gretchen waved at the guard in Lena's office and then stepped out into the cool night air. Her Porsche was still there because it always was. She slid behind the wheel.

"You've already agreed to this in your head, I can tell," she said, not even bluffing. Gretchen knew him well. "Be a doll and come up with a good argument for us, will you? I need my beauty rest. I'll expect a meeting arranged for the morning."

Without waiting for a response, Gretchen ended the call. She couldn't get away with that kind of behavior usually, not with Shaughnessy, who liked to make her life difficult when he could. But she also knew he wouldn't be able to resist watching her talk to Viola Kent.

Empaths liked to dress things up, but when it came down to it, everything was about the cost-benefit ratio. This would cost Shaughnessy little, and so he would make it happen.

He would grumble, but it would be done.

Gretchen navigated the streets on autopilot until she found herself back at Lena's apartment building. The cop cars and ambulances were long gone; the only reminder that they'd been there in the first place was a scrap of bright yellow crime scene tape caught in a bush near the steps. She plucked it free as she walked by.

As much as Gretchen might have been intrigued by a messy death, she would say she appreciated Lena's tidiness. When Gretchen stepped into the apartment, it was almost as if Lena had simply left for the day. Like the scene outside, almost nothing gave away the fact that there'd been a dead body there only hours earlier.

Gretchen crossed to the little bar discreetly situated in a corner of the living room, pulled out a glass, and uncorked the Merlot that Lena must have opened the night before. The dark cherry liquid was the closest thing to blood that the place had seen.

Cradling her generous pour, Gretchen moved toward the couch where she had found Lena. She sat in the slight indent and could almost feel the warmth there, though she knew that was impossible.

As the night deepened, Gretchen pulled up the voice mail Lena had left and hit play.

When it had finished, she hit it again, and then again, and then again, until Gretchen had devoured every nuance, every pause, every inhale and stutter.

*She's like you.*

The obvious takeaway from those softly murmured words was that Viola was like Gretchen. Innocent and framed, as Lena had always thought Gretchen had been.

Assumptions made the world go round. They were easy and frivolous and dangerous and essential to operating in a society where the vast majority of people seemed to intrinsically grasp the complexities of being human.

Gretchen let the smooth wine sit against her tongue, savoring it as she'd savored the shadows that had pooled in the hollows of Lena's body, and wondered if she was any different from everyone else. She heard the *she* and assumed Viola. The girl held the world's attention. Why wouldn't it be about her?

But it hadn't been Viola's case file that Gretchen had found stashed away in Lena's cabinet, a hidden secret that Lena clearly had played close to the chest. It had been Tess Murphy's, a runaway teenage girl from a poor neighborhood in Boston. A case that had been cold for decades.

*She's like you.*

So what if Gretchen was looking at it all wrong? What if the *she* wasn't Viola at all?

# CHAPTER TWELVE
## REED

*Three months before Claire's death—*

It wasn't on purpose that Reed started following Declan Murphy. The man just made it so easy.

He was campaigning for a public office, after all, so his schedule was plastered all over his website more often than not. Fundraisers, meet and greets, town halls.

Reed had been invited to that first event, when this had all started. Declan had shaken his hand, had made empty promises about getting drinks to talk more about Tess. And that had been that.

Reed hadn't meant to show up at Declan's rally three days later. He'd been out picking up a few random groceries the housekeeper had forgotten when he'd seen the signs, heard that booming voice. The recognition had wrapped around him like vines and tugged, pulling him closer. Not deep into the small knot of supporters, but enough to hover on the outskirts, enough to count as being there.

That next weekend, his running path had taken him into Declan's neighborhood. The following Wednesday, he'd happened to need to drop by the bookstore across from Declan's office.

By the third week, it had become a habit. Check Declan's schedule. If there wasn't a public event, he was still easy enough to find.

Viola and the boys had school, after all. And as Claire pointed out, it wasn't like Reed had much else to do now, not since he'd been let go from her father's company so many years ago. That had been a relief. He'd never wanted the position in the first place.

Reed didn't like to think about his actions too much these days—going down that path just tended to trigger his ever-increasing panic attacks—but he knew there was no reasonable explanation for tracking Declan. *Stalking* Declan, really. If he was being honest.

He told himself that if Lena was trying to pin Tess's disappearance on him, he had to keep track of all the players so he wasn't caught off guard should anything develop.

But that logic didn't really ring true. If that were the case, he would be following . . . tracking . . . *stalking* Lena instead.

He had picked up a few things from all that research he'd done into psychology when Viola had first started exhibiting her violent tendencies, though. And he thought maybe, if he was being charitable with himself, that this all had to do with control.

There was so very little he controlled about his life. More often than not it felt like all he could do was react to the chaos and violence that surrounded him and hope it didn't rip him to shreds in the process. Living like that frayed a person down to their most fragile of threads. And then Lena had come through with scissors, cutting with callous disregard to Reed's sanity.

Following Declan gave Reed a purpose, something to *do*, some way to feel like he once again had a grasp on his own life, no matter how weak or imaginary that grasp was.

If he tried following Lena, he knew she would spot him in a heartbeat. If he tried with Claire and she caught him, she'd make him pay for it.

So, Declan it was.

Declan's site finally loaded on Reed's phone. No public events today. Which was fine. That was fine.

He had to check on a pair of gloves he'd ordered at the shop on the corner of Declan's street anyway.

Slipping the phone back into his coat pocket, Reed then had just enough time to duck down behind a car when the gate at the side of Declan's town house opened.

Declan stepped out, dressed in well-fitted pants and a tight, white button-down that showed off the obscene curve of his chest and biceps. The man glanced at the thick watch on his wrist before closing the gate behind him.

He set off at a stroll with the confidence of someone used to being watched. He'd probably grown so desensitized to the feeling that he wouldn't notice Reed no matter how close Reed got.

They walked for a good ten or so blocks, and the neighborhood slowly bled from residential into commercial.

Once Declan took his final right turn, Reed knew where they were headed. The Liberty Hotel. Claire's favorite place.

Perhaps it was a coincidence.

Reed stopped just short of the circular driveway, finding it harder to blend in with his surroundings when there wasn't a flow of foot traffic like there was around the town houses.

But he wasn't worried about losing Declan now. Unless he'd rented a room for the night—unlikely given how high-profile the place was— then Declan was headed to the bar.

Reed gave it a few minutes and then casually followed. He hated that he was getting good at this sort of thing.

It was just past four, so the place wasn't crowded, but it wasn't empty, either. Nothing about the setup lent itself toward stealth; it was wide-open, with four floors and massive ceilings that spanned the entirety of the far walls. Throughout the expanse of the first floor there were plush seating arrangements clustered in groups of differing sizes.

The bar itself was tucked against one of the sides, all dark black wood and modern touches that rubbed Reed the wrong way.

Bars should be battered and worn, not sleek contraptions made for the rich.

But Declan looked right at home there, sidling up to one of the stools, ordering something that probably cost the same as a week's worth of groceries for the woman working the taps. It was funny. If Declan had married into this life, he would never receive the kind of stares Reed did when he went out with Claire. They were from the same background, the same neighborhood, yet Declan looked born to this lifestyle while Reed had not once felt like he fit into it.

Reed found a deep red velvet chair close to the bar, close enough to hear the murmur of Declan's voice, but not enough to distinguish the actual words.

He wasn't even surprised when Claire walked in.

The amber light washed over her striking features, turning her soft—whiskey-laced instead of frost-coated.

She wore a simple emerald-green dress that still somehow created the illusion of curves and valleys where Reed intimately knew there weren't any. When she walked into the room, it was with the sultry attitude of a panther on the hunt.

Reed ached in his chest, in his belly, in his groin as her hemline rose to reveal the hint of a delicate garter. That's what had always pulled him in, that mix of class, sophistication, and pure, unaltered lust. When he'd been a teenager, his brain had short-circuited from the combination. Even after all these years, he couldn't call himself immune to the attraction.

When Claire got to the bar, she ran a familiar hand along the straight line of Declan's shoulders, smiling in a way Reed couldn't remember seeing in a long time. She whispered something in Declan's ear, her lips brushing the shell of it, close enough that Reed could clearly tell this wasn't two old acquaintances meeting up to talk politics and policy.

Maybe Declan actually had rented a room in the Liberty.

Reed tried to probe at what he felt about that, like he would the bloody gap of a missing tooth. But instead of raw nerves, all he found was healed skin. If he and Claire had ever loved each other, it had long curdled into something unrecognizable. Now all he cared about was if the two of them were talking about Tess.

Because Claire knew that Lena was investigating the girl's disappearance. The only question that remained was if she would tell her lover. Tess's brother.

Luck was on Reed's side. Once Claire was handed her drink, they drifted away from the bar, settling into a set of chairs that had their backs to the rest of the room.

He waited a few seconds just to be careful. And then he ducked his head, stood, not suddenly, but slowly, and circled around until he could drop into the seat right behind them. Once there, he realized he needn't have bothered with the caution. They were fully lost in each other.

"I feel like I'm just . . . ," Claire was saying, her voice weak and trembling like he'd never heard before. "I'm at my wit's end, Declan."

Declan's soothing rumble was clear, and Reed, even with his back to them, could guess he'd probably laid a hand over Claire's. "Has he . . . has he hurt you?"

Claire laughed, though it was watery, not disbelieving. Reed forced himself to unclench the fists that had formed on the chair's armrests.

"He hit a wall," Claire said, quiet and almost scared. Like she didn't want to admit it.

Reed stared at the pink and puckered scar that ran across three of his knuckles and couldn't even deny the truth of it.

Declan inhaled, all indignation. "Claire . . ."

"No, no," Claire said, waving off his obvious concern. "It's fine. I just want this to be over."

"Your lawyer?"

"Says the prenup guarantees Reed money because we've been together for so long," Claire admitted.

He'd hated signing that thing when he'd been twenty and desperately in love. He'd wanted to toss it into a bonfire after spitting on it. The very notion that they weren't destined to be together and happy for life was repulsive. But he'd signed the papers because it was the only way he'd been able to be with Claire.

"It makes me nervous," Declan said. "You being in that house with him."

"He's not all bad," Claire said, almost gently.

"You're too nice," Declan decided, his voice rough.

"I don't want . . . Can we . . . can we just not talk about him?" Claire asked. Then immediately contradicted herself. "I'm worried he's going to take the boys and just run."

Declan made a small, startled sound. "He wouldn't."

"He knows that if this goes to court, I'll win custody," Claire said slowly. And Reed *did* know that was true. It was one of the few things that kept him tethered to his current life. Claire was the boys' mother, and to the court that meant she could raise them better than he.

"If he wants joint . . . ," Declan suggested, almost tentative, like he didn't want to piss her off.

"No." Claire's voice had gone hard and cold. And there was something else he knew. For Claire, there was no middle ground. She would never let him see his boys again if he tried to leave on his own. When Claire spoke, though, her tone had softened. "No. No, I . . . Declan, he punched a wall."

The back of Reed's throat burned. The implication was that he would turn his anger on the boys, despite the fact that she knew, *she knew* he'd die before he hurt either one of them.

Reality didn't matter, though. What mattered was what those cold, hard facts sounded like in court. Reed knew all those people in family law had heard that promise broken so many times it was almost an admission of guilt to utter it in the first place.

"All right," Declan said. "All right, you're right. Guys like that are powder kegs. But we have to be smart about this."

*We.* Reed nearly laughed. Oh, how easily they fell.

"I'm trying to be," Claire said. "He's just . . . he's so volatile these days. Running off, not telling me where he's going. He's been texting a lot, too. I think he's . . . I think he's been in contact with Lena Booker." A heavy pause. "She's a lawyer now. High-powered."

They all knew what Claire was implying. That Reed was trying to get ahead of the separation, trying to build his own legal team.

A small almost sob escaped from Claire, like she was desperately trying to hold herself together but wasn't able to stop the tearful little noise from spilling out.

"Oh, sweetheart," Declan murmured, and Reed wondered if he'd taken her hand or even shifted so that he was able to wrap an arm around her shoulder. "He won't take your kids."

"You don't know him anymore," Claire said, the words trembling masterfully. "He twists everything, makes them think . . . terrible things about me."

"Look, you know what he's trying to do now," Declan said. "You know he's gearing up for a fight. So you just have to be ready for one."

Claire murmured, "I will be," so softly Reed almost missed it.

They lingered for a bit, talking mutual acquaintances and social events, policy and Declan's campaign. Easy with each other in a way that he and Claire hadn't been in a long time.

When they stood up and headed toward the main lobby, Reed watched their knuckles brush against each other, knowing exactly where they were going.

Reed lost track of time after that, staring at the fake, flickering flame in the fireplace next to him.

Was it possible to recognize that you were the bad guy in a story? Reed hadn't thought he was, but how long could he deny that every person around him seemed to have cast him in that role?

The problem with accepting that fact was that if he started to believe them, he wasn't sure what would stop him from proving them right.

# CHAPTER THIRTEEN

## GRETCHEN

*Now—*

Viola Kent looked nothing like a monster.

Gretchen hadn't expected otherwise—it was empaths who thought evil manifested itself on the outside. She, on the other hand, knew better.

"Just a kid," Shaughnessy muttered beside Gretchen, his voice gravelly as if he'd stayed up all night arranging this little interview. Gretchen didn't care, nor would she thank him outright, but she liked his normal voice better so she handed over a throat lozenge that he took without a word.

"Just a kid who stabbed her mother thirteen times," Gretchen reminded him ruthlessly. Why did it matter that he was giving Viola the benefit of the doubt he'd never given Gretchen? It didn't.

He popped the lozenge in his mouth, his lips twitching as if he knew what she was thinking, as if he wanted to smile. She glared, but since his eyes were locked on Viola beyond the two-way mirror, her annoyance was lost on him. "You're wasting time."

"Well, good thing it's mine to waste then," Gretchen said. But then she paused, because she knew that positively acknowledging a favor usually was received better than ignoring it. "Thank you for arranging this."

Shaughnessy looked around. "Am I dying?"

Gretchen glared.

"Tell it to me straight, Doc." Shaughnessy tried to keep a serious face, but he was clearly too amused with his own perceived wit to do so. "That's the only reason I can imagine you being civil to me."

"Exactly how many cases have I solved for you?"

"And you got the paychecks to show for them," Shaughnessy shot back, like he always did. "How many times have you said thank you to me?"

Since she'd probably be able to count the number on one hand, she decided to ignore that.

"One of these days you're going to admit that you like me," Gretchen predicted, and then swooped out of the room without waiting for a rejoinder that he no doubt would consider funny and she irritating.

In the next moment, Gretchen stepped through the interrogation room's door and forgot about Shaughnessy completely.

There was nothing special about Viola Kent.

She had two pimples on her chin, greasy bangs, and lank dishwater-blonde hair. Her face was round and thin at the same time, her shoulders broad yet her frame delicate. The fluorescent lights did her no favors, but she wouldn't be remarkable even in the most flattering setting. The most notable thing about her were her eyes, which bent more toward silver than pale blue. But even the impact of the unique color faded quickly.

Viola was a thirteen-year-old girl in every way every other thirteen-year-old girl was.

And Gretchen could not be more pleased.

She knew what she looked like. Her own perfectly smooth blonde bob wasn't necessarily the flowing locks that celebrities favored these days, but it was more than acceptable in the Boston scene. Her skin was flawless, smooth and unblemished, rose-tinted milk. She was curvy, but not ambitiously so; short, but not remarkably so; well dressed, but not desperate. Women wanted to be her, men wanted to sleep with her, and thirteen-year-old girls dreamed of becoming her.

Gretchen could see it in Viola's eyes, even though she was sure the girl would be furious for being so obvious. In that moment, she was glad she'd worn her perfectly tailored dove-gray suit and heels. They made her feel all the more powerful as she slid into the seat across from Viola.

Without any introduction or preamble, Gretchen jumped in the deep end. "How did the blade feel going in?"

Viola blinked, three times, the flutter of lashes quick and startled. Then she seemed to compose herself. "Like butter."

Her voice was high and light. A girl. Just a girl.

"It didn't catch?" Gretchen asked, as if she knew anything about it. But this, this was her violence, her own knife sinking into someone else's psyche. She craved it like Viola must crave blood.

"On her lower ribs," Viola said, easily now, having sussed out the situation in a few seconds flat. Gretchen wasn't your ordinary detective or social worker, wasn't easily manipulated. "But the knife was sharp."

There was a psychiatrist who had been brought in on Gretchen's case all those years ago. He'd spoken in nasal tones and had decided that Gretchen had picked a knife because it was more personal, more intimate. She'd wanted to feel her aunt's soul leave her body.

He'd been a quack, that much had been clear even when Gretchen had been eight. But she could still remember the look on Shaughnessy's face when he'd heard that particular theory. The Gretchen of now would have played with them both; the Gretchen of then had thought she was about to be thrown in jail.

She wouldn't ask why Viola had chosen a knife. Because it likely had been the weapon that had been available to her. Not everything was Freudian.

"Why did you hide it?" Gretchen asked. It was the question she'd been dying to know.

Viola's lips parted, then pressed together, her eyes flicking just to the right of Gretchen's shoulder, then back to her face. Whatever was coming Gretchen guessed would be a lie.

"I wanted to see if they were stupid enough to be fooled."

Gretchen suppressed a smirk at what she was sure was Shaughnessy's outraged expression. Still, it was a good answer. Certainly believable. "Who?"

"The police," Viola said. Her eyes flicked over Gretchen. "You."

"You know who I am?" She wasn't anywhere close to celebrity status, but she wasn't unknown in Boston, either. If Viola'd had access to a computer while Lena was working with her, she might have come across mentions of Gretchen.

"No." A twitch of the hands. A lie.

"You've looked me up."

"I haven't," Viola protested, probably not realizing how young she sounded. The girl swallowed, immediately contradicted herself. "We have the internet here, you know." A pause. "They think you're so special."

It was such a childish thing to say, to deny knowledge of who Gretchen was and then pour out the bitterness that gave it away a heartbeat later. Gretchen couldn't help but feel a twinge of something that on her best days she might label "sympathy."

"Now everyone thinks you're special," Gretchen countered. At the praise, Viola preened like a flower opening up toward the sun. Narcissistic, Gretchen noted absently. "You killed your own mother."

Viola's body swayed toward Gretchen, eager and happy. "They'll talk about me."

She said it as a fact, not as a question. Gretchen found herself nodding anyway. "And how you treated your brothers."

There were those blinks again. Viola had careful control of her expressions, except for that. A flash of lashes against pale skin.

"They're so weak," Viola said, and sounded like she meant it. "Easy prey."

"Were they there that night?" Gretchen asked. "When you stabbed your mother to death?"

"Locked up," Viola muttered.

"What?" Gretchen hated the word, couldn't help but utter it anyway.

"The little lambs were safe in their room," Viola said, derision dripping from every syllable. She opened her mouth, shut it. Looked away. This was fertile ground. While psychopaths didn't feel any attachment to people, they still had *reactions*.

Gretchen pushed. "Were they kept there because of you?"

The bruises. The gaunt faces. Gretchen could picture them so well, the way that they'd been splashed over the news.

"There was a key," Viola said.

"Locked away from you," Gretchen repeated.

Amusement flickered across Viola's face. "What do you think?"

"Would you have killed them?" Gretchen made sure her voice came out flat, unaffected. It wasn't difficult. It's not that she wished the boys dead, but she just didn't care that they were alive.

Viola licked her lips. "Sebastian I would have gutted slowly."

"The older one?" Gretchen asked, intrigued despite herself. "Why Sebastian? Not Milo?"

"Like Mr. Peterson's dog," Viola said, ignoring the question, her eyes glazing over, then snapping back to Gretchen's. "Do you think Sebastian would have whimpered like that?"

Gretchen didn't flinch. "Did your mother?"

The tension in the room shattered as Viola's mouth twisted. "Mother would never beg."

"Did you ask her to?"

89

Viola tilted her head. "I killed her in her sleep."

Right. Gretchen knew that, yet she hadn't really put it together. "Why didn't you wake her up first?" Gretchen asked. "I would have wanted to hear her scream."

There was a surprised inhale that Gretchen knew Viola wouldn't have wanted her to hear.

"I was angry," Viola said, but some of the confidence had bled from her voice. A girl. Just a girl. "I didn't think."

Gretchen sat back in her chair, making sure everything about her body language could be easily read as *unimpressed*. "She didn't wake up at all during it?"

"Must have been dead right away." Viola shrugged. "Didn't matter to me. I just wanted to keep stabbing her."

"Where did you strike first?"

Viola's eyes narrowed. "You think I'm lying."

"I'm fairly certain that's a given anytime you open your mouth," Gretchen countered.

"No," Viola said. "You think I didn't kill Mommy." There was a long pause, where Gretchen could all but see Viola's clever little mind whirring.

"Are you here to save me, then?" Viola leaned forward with something that might have been glee. "Please, kind lady, tell me how I'm not actually evil."

"You know I'm not a kind lady," Gretchen said.

Viola sat back again. "I know you can recognize evil. Like looking in a mirror, perhaps?"

Gretchen snorted. "If you think my belief system in any way incorporates a good-versus-evil duality, you are not as smart as you look. You didn't answer the question."

"Her cold, dark heart," Viola spit out, somehow both furious and calculated at once. "That's where I aimed the blade."

"Poetic," Gretchen drawled. It was also wrong. But Gretchen didn't bother mentioning that. Viola could easily say she had been provoked into lying to get a reaction. "What was your final straw?"

"Do I need one?" Viola asked.

"No," Gretchen agreed. "But the way I see it, you didn't wake your mother up to torture her."

Viola's breath caught again, but she didn't flinch otherwise. "So?"

"So . . ." Gretchen pulled the word out, let it sit in the air between them. "That would suggest you were angry enough to react without really thinking about it."

"You're the only one who's asked me that," Viola said. "Not even that lawyer lady did."

For now, Gretchen ignored the mention of Lena.

"Then don't you want to answer?" Gretchen personally loved talking about why people had wronged her. It was one of her favorite topics. But here Viola was, buying time instead of spilling out the grudges she must have held against her mother. She didn't have a believable lie at the ready, if Gretchen had to guess. "Don't you want people to know what she did to you?"

A twitch of the lips, an almost smile.

"Well played," Viola said, tipping her head. "She wouldn't let me get a bunny."

"How could you have thought she would?" Gretchen asked, though the second she did, she realized it was a useless question. Psychopaths didn't reason like that.

"My friend got a bunny for her birthday," Viola said. "I wanted one."

"And your mother wouldn't let you." Gretchen decided she had little interest in pursuing that particular wish any further. Everyone in the room or watching the interview knew what Viola had wanted to do with the animal. "So you stabbed her."

"Yes."

Gretchen studied her closely, trying to decipher each facial twitch, each nonverbal cue, the way she relaxed, how she fidgeted and stilled. Gretchen had spent her life reading others' body language, like a zoologist studying the way wolves bared their throats and lions played. It had never come naturally to her like it did to others, but that hadn't mattered. She'd mastered the skill anyway.

Viola was trickier than most, and Gretchen was glad this conversation was being taped so she could watch it later.

"How was Mr. Peterson's dog discovered?" Gretchen finally asked after letting the silence hang for a significant amount of time.

That actually seemed to throw Viola—the quick blinks of earlier returning. "The basement flooded."

Gretchen tsk-tsked. "Bad luck. And the bird?" Everyone had heard about the bird.

"A car accidentally ran into the stone wall in our backyard," Viola said. She wasn't quite eager, but she was interested, engaged. She wanted to see where this was going. "It knocked everything loose. The bird was hidden in there."

"No one would have known about them if not for two freak occurrences," Gretchen summarized. Viola's gaze tracked up and to the side, like she was trying to beat Gretchen at her own thought process. Her eyes slid back to Gretchen's, her mouth slightly open. No longer gleeful, that was certain, when Gretchen continued with "Yet you hid the knife in your sock drawer."

This time, Gretchen didn't bother to conceal her smile. "Do you know what they would call you had you grown up to become the serial killer I know you're capable of being?"

"Evil," Viola tried, but it was weak, lacking the playful malevolence of a few moments ago.

Gretchen shook her head. "Organized."

And with that, she stood up. As entertaining as she found her conversation with Viola thus far, it was best to end with the upper hand.

"I killed her," Viola cried out, knowing exactly what Gretchen had meant. If Viola had really been the murderer, no one would have found the evidence as quickly as they had.

Gretchen placed her palms on the table, leaning in close so that their jaws nearly brushed. "No, you didn't," she whispered in Viola's ear. "But I won't say a word."

# CHAPTER FOURTEEN

## REED

*Four months before Claire's death—*

It had been a long time since Claire had surprised him with baseball tickets. It had always been their thing, even beyond those early years in the relationship when life had been magical rainbows and butterflies.

Reed didn't remember when they'd stopped going to the games, and he thought that was more depressing than anything.

When Claire dropped the tickets on the kitchen counter next to the coffeepot, Reed had been pleased, surprised, a little sad because that always seemed to be the case these days when remembering better times.

Claire had cleared her afternoon for the game, and Reed, at odds and ends anyway, just had to arrange to have Milo and Sebastian picked up from school and taken to their enrichment classes. That had been easy enough.

So, on a startlingly clear day, Reed and Claire voluntarily went somewhere fun together.

He brushed his knuckles against the back of her hand while they waited for hot dogs and beer, and she dipped her chin down, smiling softly to herself at the contact. Reed thought about lacing their fingers together but didn't want to startle Claire out of this rare good mood.

By unspoken agreement they didn't mention the kids the entire day. During the fourth inning, Claire whooped at a home run, sounding just like her eighteen-year-old self. They both jumped to their feet, and Reed couldn't help but lean in when she turned to grin at him. She tasted of hops and mustard and Claire, and it wasn't lust that pulsed in his belly but longing. Longing to go back to the days when he thought love really was as simple as this.

When they sat back down, Claire reached over and tangled their hands together, despite their sweaty palms, which he knew she hated.

It was the seventh inning when she finally asked.

"You've been . . . busy lately," Claire said, so casually that he nearly missed it entirely. He'd had three craft beers at that point, and his limbs, his tongue, his mind were all a bit loose. Claire had switched to water after that first drink.

Reed hummed, his eyes on the batter. Two outs, bases loaded. The stadium vibrated with the anticipation.

"Should I be worried?" Claire asked, jabbing her elbow into Reed's ribs lightly. Teasing—this was all teasing—is what that gesture tried to convey. Reed knew better.

He tore his attention from the game and shifted to get a better look at her. Claire had on a baseball cap with an endearingly straight brim over her sleek blonde hair, so he couldn't see her expression. If that had been calculated it was smart. Although who was he kidding? Now that the blinders were ripped off, he realized every part of this day was calculated. The bashfulness in line, the way she'd turned to him all but inviting the kiss, the ice cream she ate from a cone with tiny little kitten licks designed to distract and disarm.

Claire never ate ice cream. Reed should have known.

Once upon a time, he would have called himself crazy for jumping right into the worst-case scenario over a simple question. Once upon a time, he'd been young and foolish, though.

When he didn't say anything, his brain struggling to break out of his complacency, Claire tipped her head enough so that he could see she was watching him closely. "Was that Lena Booker I saw at the Weatherstons' gala?"

He swallowed the grunt that was nearly punched out of him. The question on its face might have seemed innocent, but he knew Claire better than that. She knew he'd been in contact with Lena again.

Had she known since that first encounter two months ago? When Lena had approached him in a Starbucks without ever once mentioning Tess? Or was it something more recent that had given it away?

Why had he ever thought Claire wouldn't notice? Just because she didn't seem to want to be around him most days didn't mean she didn't pay attention.

"Did you?" Reed asked. Pure denial might not be the smartest tack, but apparently it was the one his mouth decided to go with.

"She's made quite a name for herself these days, I suppose," Claire said, wiping her hands on a napkin.

"I think . . . a lawyer, right?" Reed nearly winced. He was bumbling this—he knew he was bumbling it—yet he couldn't seem to stop himself from bumbling it.

They both knew everyone in the city's upper echelon—by name and profession, if nothing else. It would be absurd to think Reed hadn't known what Lena had made of herself, especially when they'd once been so close.

"I ran into her getting coffee," Reed admitted. He'd learned coming clean was hard, but the alternative was harder. He left out the part where he suspected Lena had orchestrated that first accidental meeting.

"Oh really?" Claire said, but didn't sound surprised. "How is Lena these days?"

"Busy." Reed looked back toward the game, thankful for something to concentrate on other than Claire's watchful eyes. "We didn't get a chance to talk much."

"Curious," Claire said. The silence that followed perched on his shoulders, claws out, tracing gently against his skin, ready to dig in on command. "Someone said they saw you and Lena at Fiona Murphy's house a little while back."

A flush of heat crawled up the back of his neck. At first Lena had pretended to include him in the investigation into Tess's disappearance, he guessed to lull him into a sense of complacency, maybe to catch him in a lie when his guard was down.

She'd even proposed he come along to talk to Tess's aunt Fiona.

That had been back before he'd realized she was playing him.

Reed fumbled on his explanation. "Lena mentioned that she was planning on visiting her—"

"She mentioned this when you 'bumped into' each other at coffee?" Claire cut in to clarify.

He deliberately chose not to engage with her tone. "Yes. I hadn't seen Fiona in, God, decades probably. You remember her? Tess Murphy's aunt."

"Vaguely," Claire said with a refined shrug. "And you just . . . chatted about old times, did you?"

When he remained silent, Claire waved away the question. "Sorry," she said on a laugh. "Listen to me, I sound so accusatory. I'm sorry, I'm ruining this nice day."

Reed exhaled as she took his hand back, their fingers slotting together so easily still, their bodies remembering the good times even though their hearts had soured on them. "I'm sorry I didn't tell you," he said, because he knew his lines just as well as she did hers. "I honestly didn't think it was important enough to bring up."

Claire tensed for a second, and he remembered belatedly how much she hated the word "honestly"—believing no person who was actually acting honestly would need to say it. But she didn't push the matter, and a moment later she'd relaxed, cheering on a hit.

Reed had lost track of the game, and he doubted he'd be able to refocus to even figure out who won.

"We should have Lena over for dinner one night soon," Claire said, like it was an offhand thought.

"Sure," Reed agreed, trying to keep his voice steady, panic threatening to hijack his body as he ran through the ramifications of Claire *knowing*. Knowing that Lena was digging into Tess Murphy's life, trying to root out secrets that should stay comfortably in the past.

Through years of practice, Reed managed to smile, laugh at some weak joke over the loudspeaker, hand Claire some napkins with a little nudge toward the ice cream on her chin. But saliva pooled in his mouth, his lungs collapsing on themselves.

The numbers on the scoreboard blurred, and Reed wondered for a disconnected moment if he was just going to pass out right there.

But then . . .

A seed cracked open in the furthest, darkest corner of his mind, its rotted tendrils curling around all his worst intentions.

An idea, a plan. A way to solve all his problems.

Maybe not Lena and her questions and her silent accusations. But Lena didn't know as much as she thought she did.

The roots burrowed deeper, deeper into his mind as the bloodred flowers of this idea bloomed.

Perhaps it should have given him pause that the seed had come from the thought of Viola, of what his daughter would do in this situation.

But, as he'd said so many times before, Viola was his.

She'd come from him.

# CHAPTER FIFTEEN

## GRETCHEN

*Now—*

"What the hell was that?" Shaughnessy demanded as Gretchen stepped back into the small observation room after her interrogation with Viola.

Marconi was there as well, wearing what Gretchen was coming to realize was her standard neutral expression. At the sight of Gretchen, she rocked back a little on her heels, but otherwise telegraphed nothing else about what she was feeling.

"Don't worry your pretty little head about it," Gretchen murmured, crossing the space to retrieve her purse.

"You figured something out." Shaughnessy pointed a blunt finger in Gretchen's face, and she fought the urge to bite it off at the knuckle—after all, who knew where his hands had been? That wasn't something she wanted in her mouth.

She stepped around him easily. "Marconi."

Marconi hopped to it, well trained after only a day together. Gretchen was feeling more and more warmly about this partnership. She sensed more than heard the woman fall in behind her as they started down the long, sterile hallway of the detention facility.

Gretchen didn't fool herself into thinking Marconi was following for any reason other than that it was her job and she was as desperately curious as Shaughnessy had to be about what Viola had given away. But Gretchen didn't care about motives; she cared about behavior. Others put too much stock in affection-based loyalty, in friendships and partnerships built on the tenuous ties of emotion.

There was something Gretchen had that Marconi wanted. And so the woman would act accordingly. The cost-benefit ratio. That's what it always came down to.

"Where're we headed?" Marconi asked over Shaughnessy shouting Gretchen's name from behind them. He'd want to be careful with that. If Viola overheard, she'd understand the power structure in an instant.

Psychopaths read power the way empaths could read body language. Instinctually.

Gretchen didn't bother answering Marconi's question as she debated withholding the information she'd just gleaned. In the end, she decided it would be more helpful for Marconi to see the whole picture.

"Viola didn't kill Claire," Gretchen finally said as they stepped out of the facility and into the bright light of day. "Lena was right. But don't tell Shaughnessy."

Marconi stopped. "You already told him Lena suspected that. Why can't he know now?"

Gretchen headed toward her Porsche, not even checking to see if Marconi had brought a car this time. "I promised Viola I'd keep her secret. I don't break my word."

Marconi's sharp laugh was filled with too many nuances for Gretchen to pick up, and it rubbed along her raised hackles. But just as Gretchen paused in the act of sliding into the driver's seat, ready to rip flesh from bone, verbally speaking, Marconi raised her hands in a placating gesture.

"Honor between thieves," Marconi mused, and Gretchen couldn't tell if it was sarcastic, a joke, or an explanation for why she'd been amused. "I get it. But you told me, so technically you did break your word."

Gretchen considered holding on to her anger. But there wasn't time for that, so she settled in behind the wheel. "I don't actually care. Plus, you're not the detective on the case."

"You were about to skin me alive," Marconi pointed out, but there was no heat there.

"Yes, well, that's because you assumed that giving my word means nothing to me," Gretchen said, wondering why she had to explain that.

"I don't think I'm going to touch that logic," Marconi murmured with a little bit more of a bite than Gretchen had heard from her before. Before Gretchen could latch on to that, Marconi continued. "You don't think I'll tell Shaughnessy anyway?"

"You might."

Marconi sat with that for a second. "You're testing me."

Gretchen hummed a little agreement. "Some might call it that."

"Everyone would call it that," Marconi countered.

"I wanted to see if you rely on cost-benefit reasoning or emotions," Gretchen said, because Marconi wasn't wrong per se, but she wasn't exactly right.

"Ah." The corner of Marconi's mouth twitched up. "You're testing my sociopathic tendencies."

Gretchen neither confirmed nor denied that, but her silence likely did the job for her. It was obvious to anyone with two IQ points to rub together that Marconi wasn't a sociopath. But that left a lot of options when it came to how she approached life.

For some cops, loyalty came before anything else. They'd help their partner bury a body without blinking, and expect the same.

While Gretchen could see the benefits of having such a person feel that way toward her, it wasn't worth the energy pretending she would ever put herself out that much for someone else. Gretchen would quite willingly hurl someone under a bus if it served her purpose.

Some would say that made her a bad person, but considering that she was quite up-front with that aspect of herself, she tended to attract people who knew how to roll to avoid the wheels.

Since Gretchen didn't yet hate working with Marconi, she was hoping the woman was more rational than her predecessors. If she wanted information from Gretchen—which she clearly did—it would behoove her in the long run not to go tattling to Shaughnessy about every morsel she got.

It would be good to get this out of the way now before Gretchen got any more invested.

Marconi was nodding thoughtfully, still relaxed even as Gretchen tore through a red light. "Doesn't telling me you're studying my reactions ahead of time negate any results?"

"You would think, but no, I have not found that to be the case." Humans did tend to alter their behavior when they knew they were being watched, tended to perform as they thought they were expected to rather than how their nature compelled them. But Gretchen had run similar tests on Shaughnessy's other partners, and those traits would always out themselves. "Are you fighting the urge to tell Shaughnessy?"

Another lip twitch. "No."

"I didn't think so."

"Where are we headed?" Marconi asked again.

"I have a confession," Gretchen said instead of answering.

"Should I be scared?"

Gretchen grinned, a sharp flash of incisors that she knew looked predatory. "Always."

Marconi just rolled her eyes. "Does it have anything to do with the fact that you don't care that Viola might be innocent?"

In her surprise, Gretchen took a corner too tightly, sending a parked car's side mirror flying behind them. The thing was a junker so she didn't think twice about it. But she did stare a little too long at Marconi—who was clearly trying not to look smug—and had to slam on the brakes to avoid a pedestrian with a stroller. A tiny part of her wondered if the baby would go flipping through the air amusingly just like that side mirror had done.

"Close," Gretchen said, not willing to concede that Marconi had gotten it right. She gunned the Porsche, earning herself a nasty stink eye from the mother. "I don't particularly care who did kill Claire Kent."

"Because Viola's a psychopath, and the world's a lot safer with her behind bars?" Marconi guessed, not reveling in throwing Gretchen off.

"Whoever framed her had the right idea," Gretchen said. The murderer had likely killed two problems with one stone—or knife, rather.

"Do you think there's a possibility that she's not a psychopath?" Marconi asked. "Maybe that's a setup, too. To make the frame job stick."

"Oh, no," Gretchen said, though it wouldn't normally be a bad suggestion. In this case, there was no doubt. "She is most assuredly a psychopath. I would never say this in a professional capacity, but I would put good money on the fact that she'll kill someone someday if she's not behind bars the rest of her life."

"It sounds like there's another 'but' there," Marconi prodded.

"But, they're not mutually exclusive," Gretchen said. "She can be a psychopath and be the easy patsy. I would have absolutely done the same if I'd just killed Claire Kent."

"That scenario rings familiar, huh?" Marconi said, in what she probably thought was a subtle way. "Kid getting framed because they're not normal."

Gripping the wheel too tight, Gretchen bit at the inside of her cheek until she tasted copper. "I'm flattered," she finally said, coolly, "that you've studied my file so intently."

"Some light bedtime reading," Marconi said, again sounding amused, not frightened. Gretchen didn't like that, didn't like that Marconi didn't seem to realize how close Gretchen was to the edge of her limits, how quickly she could be pushed. She lived her life on a tightrope, knowing that a tiny step over, just a second where her wild impulses were let free, and Shaughnessy would win. He'd know she was the monster he thought she was.

But here Marconi was, poking at her bruises with a sharp stick, not a single thought to the consequences in sight.

"I wanted to see what her insides looked like," Gretchen said, going for shock value because it worked so well whenever her back was up against a wall. And Marconi needed a reminder that just because Gretchen had long ago honed her impeccable control didn't mean she was harmless.

"Doesn't mean you carved her open," Marconi countered easily.

Gretchen inhaled. It was the argument *she* had made in those early days, to Shaughnessy, and then later in her own mind. She didn't think her little eight-year-old self would have had it in her to kill her aunt Rowan, but as the decades slipped by and Shaughnessy continued watching her so closely, she had to wonder. Had the evidence really been strong enough to convince him so thoroughly but weak enough that she hadn't been arrested?

Gretchen had never looked at her case file. Even now, when she had enough clout to demand to at least examine the evidence. So much of her world was built upon the foundational premise that Shaughnessy thought her guilty of killing her aunt. If she disrupted that, she didn't know what her life would look like in the aftermath. And she liked her life.

"We're not talking about you," Marconi said. It was a white flag waved delicately, and maybe an acknowledgment that just because Gretchen wasn't tied to her emotions, that didn't mean she didn't bleed when she was cut. "Why is Viola taking the blame for Claire's murder?"

*They'll talk about me.*

"Highly narcissistic," Gretchen said. "She's not viewing it as taking the blame. She views it as getting credit."

Marconi digested that. "Couldn't you argue that's why the cops so easily found the knife?"

Gretchen dipped her head in acknowledgment. "I suppose. But why not stay with the body until it was found, then? She had plenty of time to play with Claire, yet she killed her immediately, stabbed her a few times to make it look excessive, then returned to her room to poorly hide the weapon and wait for the police to come? It doesn't track with her previous pattern of behavior, nor her psychopathy."

"She's a sadist," Marconi said. "If she was going to kill someone, she would have tortured them."

"There is no way that child would have killed Claire Kent without waking her up first," Gretchen agreed. "Apart from anything else, that's enough to convince me that she's not the real killer."

The only doubt Gretchen had was about Viola's motives for staying silent about it. Part of her thought the girl knew she wouldn't be believed if she argued her innocence. With the animal bones, the repeated torture of her brothers, the psychological reviews that had been done following the killing—there was a much stronger case against Viola than there had ever been against Gretchen. And still people thought Gretchen had gotten away with murder.

No way would Viola have been able to walk just on her own say-so.

The desire to be free, to wreak havoc, to have access to an unlimited number of victims would be strong. But Gretchen guessed that Viola was a resourceful enough psychopath to find targets wherever she was. Maybe being held in a secure facility presented a challenge that she even enjoyed.

"So where does Lena Booker come into this?" Marconi asked. "Isn't that what you're trying to figure out?"

Lena. Gretchen had almost forgotten about her. To be fair to herself, she did tend to get tunnel vision when working cases like this.

She still thought Lena's death was a clear-cut overdose. But that didn't mean it wasn't a ripple effect from this girl, this family, this murder.

*I messed up, Gretch.*

What that meant for Gretchen, she didn't know. Certainly, her curiosity had been piqued. Boredom was one of Gretchen's biggest fears. It was what caused most sociopaths to jump on the self-destruct button just to watch the explosion. Different people fed the need in different ways—drugs, crime, sex, and stocks were the big ones. Gretchen got her rocks off by investigating murders.

This case offered a puzzle that would keep her from sinking into the very worst of her impulses, if only for a few days. But that was all she could ever ask for, really. A few days, and then another dead body, another psychopath, another cold case.

She dragged her thoughts away from that, bored with herself for her wallowing.

*So where does Lena Booker come into this?*

"I don't know," Gretchen admitted as they pulled to a stop in front of the Kents' town house. "But if the thirteen-year-old psychopath has been ruled out as the killer . . . you know what they say."

Marconi didn't look at all surprised at their destination. "It's always the husband."

# CHAPTER SIXTEEN

## REED

*Five months before Claire's death—*

Reed knew that there were people out there who were convinced Tess Murphy was a murder victim rather than a runaway.

There'd been an investigation at the time, not that the cops involved had spent more than a half hour or so questioning Tess's family and neighbors. But the thin file just whetted the appetite of the people who got hooked by Declan's mentions of his missing sister over the years.

The man himself had never framed it as foul play, but that didn't stop conspiracy theorists' speculations.

Long ago, Reed had set up a Google Alert on his own name almost on a whim. But as he checked it now in the middle of the night in the darkened study, he realized he'd probably always known this would be a possibility. That Tess would haunt him for all the mistakes he'd made.

Some part of him almost thought it fair. Just.

He clicked into the site that Google had flagged for him and recognized the banner immediately. It was a popular crime-junkie blog that he'd always found particularly careless and crass in how they dug up any passing mention of a missing person.

The post itself wasn't about Reed or Tess, but there were dozens of comments to sort through. He found his name in a reply to one that called attention to the similarities between the girl who had gone missing and Tess's case from decades earlier. The commenter speculated that perhaps a serial killer had been involved, and suggested the blogger try to find other cases.

A handful of people had replied with derision, with the point that just because the victims were young and blonde and in the Northeast, that didn't mean they were connected. But one simple response caught his attention.

"Anyone ever looked into Reed Kent?" And then a link to a *Boston Globe* article.

Reed wiped his palms against his sweatpants. He and Claire were well known in Boston's upper circles, but they weren't famous. Usually any articles about them were linked to Claire's philanthropical work. Every once in a while there'd be a quick mention in a society or gossip column, but that was the extent Reed had ever really been in the public eye.

People didn't know him, didn't know much beyond his name and that he and Claire had met at Harvard. They—Reed, Claire, and, more important, her family—had all worked hard to make sure that was the case.

So where had this comment come from?

The response got a reply from the blogger. "I've heard about Kent a couple times recently. Are you making the rounds? Are you a troll?"

The questions had so far gone unanswered except for a few others weighing in that the person clearly didn't know what they were talking about.

Reed tried clicking on the profile of the commenter, but it took him to a dead page.

The rest of the commenters seemed to agree with the blogger's take on the situation. This was some random, anonymous person coming in to make trouble.

*A couple times recently. Are you making the rounds?*

Just because this blog shut down the suggestion didn't mean others had.

He tried googling his own name, in case the alerts had missed something. But he got nothing. If the person had been making the rounds, they'd done it in a way that wasn't picked up by the search algorithm. "Reed" and "Kent" weren't exactly unique keywords, after all.

Reed pressed his thumb against his knuckle, the skin still a little pink and raw, and gritted through the quick lick of pain that slid up his nerves.

There were threads of *something* here, he could tell. He tried to gather them as he finally clicked on the *Boston Globe* article the "troll" had included in their reply.

When the page loaded, Reed's pulse tripped, stuttered, raced.

He'd been expecting something about him, or Claire, or Declan, or even Lena, maybe. But what popped up was an old digitized article from the month Tess had disappeared, a local story about breaking ground on a playground at a large park just outside the city.

Reed didn't need the caption of the picture to tell him the name. World's End.

He and Tess had gone there plenty of times, when they'd just been friends and when they'd been more than that.

In the photo, bulldozers stood at the ready, shovels and other digging equipment scattered about. Reed knew what it looked like: an easy place to bury a body.

The threads tangled into each other, wove together until he could start to make out a pattern.

None of this was actually damning. None of this would make a cop reopen a twenty-year-old case about a poor girl who'd run away from home.

But he knew what groundwork looked like. This wasn't about convincing a single crime blogger—otherwise that profile would likely still be active. This was seeding, pure and simple.

Slightly numb, slightly breathless, he toggled back to the blog, back to the comment that had his name in it. Stared at the gray-faced box that accompanied the person's reply.

Was it Lena?

But what would be her goal with this? She was already investigating Tess's disappearance openly enough that she'd brought him in on it. Why start spreading rumors that could help build a case later?

Public opinion, maybe? If there was enough buzz, enough pressure to reopen the case, maybe the cops would be more willing to listen if Lena later on found anything substantial. That seemed far-fetched at best, though. Why would she do so much if she couldn't be sure she'd find any evidence against him?

Reed returned to the article, stared at the picture of the park, remembered that not fifty feet from that location was a bench that had his and Tess's initials carved into the wood.

What did a prosecutor need to build a murder case? Evidence of some kind. Maybe a weapon. DNA if the cops were lucky.

A body. That's what those crime shows always said, right? No body, no crime.

Maybe this strategy wasn't what he'd thought. Maybe this wasn't someone planting information that could be found by the police later or rile up enough of the crime junkies to get the public digging once more.

Maybe this really was a message just for him.

He pressed a blunt fingernail into his knuckle until the scab reopened, and wished desperately that he couldn't guess exactly what that message was.

# CHAPTER SEVENTEEN

## GRETCHEN

***Now—***

It wasn't Reed Kent who opened the door to Gretchen and Marconi but a woman who looked so much like him it threw Gretchen for a second.

The woman was as handsome as Reed, and though some might shift that descriptor to "pretty" instead, it wouldn't be accurate. She was statuesque, with thick, honey hair tied back in a ponytail. Her jaw was square and her shoulders broad, just like Viola's, the family connection written in the strong lines of her body.

Gretchen let Marconi handle the song and dance of introductions as she studied "Ainsley Kent, Reed's sister, here to help with the kids."

"Is Mr. Kent here?" Gretchen asked once they were shown in. Ainsley seemed friendly, if cautious. Nothing beyond what would be expected for someone in her current situation.

"Yes, he's up with the boys," Ainsley said, looking between Gretchen and Marconi. "I can go get him if you'd like?"

"No rush," Marconi cut in. "We just had a few more questions."

"He mentioned detectives had stopped by yesterday," Ainsley said, sinking into one of the seats across from the couch. "But he didn't say . . . Is this for Viola's case?"

"Tangentially," Marconi answered before Gretchen could reply. It was the most proactive she'd been yet, and Gretchen sat back, happy to play spectator if that was the role she'd been assigned. "Can I ask, do you know Viola's lawyer well?"

Ainsley's thick brows shot up. "Lena, you mean? Of course."

"'Of course'?" Marconi had leaned forward, her arms on her thighs. Ainsley glanced between them again, confusion evident, but she didn't seem defensive yet.

When Ainsley answered, she spoke slowly, like she suspected she was walking into a trap. "We all grew up together."

*Ah.*

"Who was 'we all'?" Marconi asked, her voice casual, like her entire attention wasn't locked on Ainsley's face.

"Lena, Reed." Ainsley paused. "Tess and Declan. Everyone drifted apart around college, but before that they were thick as thieves."

Gretchen couldn't stop herself even though it earned her a pinched look from Marconi. "Tess?"

"Tess Murphy," Ainsley said absently, clearly distracted. And that's when Gretchen heard it, too—footsteps.

"That's why Lena took Viola's case?" Marconi rushed to get the question in, probably hoping she could get an answer before Reed busted into their interview. "Because they were friends when they were younger?"

"No," Ainsley said, again not seeming to be fully present. And then it didn't matter anyway because Reed swept into the room. His expression was pleasant on the surface, but Gretchen could sense the thunderclouds lurking behind those eyes.

"Detectives," he greeted them.

"Doctor," Gretchen corrected with what she knew was a saccharine-sweet smile.

He ran a hand through his hair. "More questions about Lena?"

Gretchen hesitated. That hadn't been the purpose of their visit, but now with the information Ainsley had so carelessly dropped, she wondered if it should be. "You two were friends growing up?"

"We lived in the same neighborhood," Reed said after an awkward hesitation. "She offered to help with . . ."

He gestured toward the ceiling as if Claire and Viola were still in the house; then he dropped his gaze and shook his head.

"And Tess Murphy"—when Gretchen said the name, Reed's eyes snapped up to meet hers—"did she grow up in that same neighborhood, too?"

Is that why Lena had kept Tess's file? Because she'd been a childhood friend. Maybe that was all there was to it.

"Yes," Reed said, still cautious. "She and her brother. Declan Murphy. Congressman Murphy now, I suppose."

Gretchen could vaguely call up a handsome face and a too-white smile, but wasn't that all young politicians? "She disappeared when you were teenagers, isn't that right?"

Reed and Ainsley almost looked at each other but stopped themselves in time. Gretchen could still see the aborted movement in their stiff, twisted necks.

"'Disappeared' isn't quite the right way to put it. She was an adult and left town," Reed said in that measured, TV-interview voice. Gretchen recognized it for what it was, a brick wall slamming down between them. "I'm sorry, why are you here?"

Gretchen could push further, but that might backfire. If the two of them closed off completely, she might not get anything.

"Actually, I'm trying to get a clearer timeline on the night . . ." Gretchen trailed off delicately. "The night your wife was killed."

"Is that really necessary?" Ainsley stood almost before Gretchen had finished talking, her hand going to her brother's shoulder. "We've been through this many times. Months ago."

"Forgive me, I've been brought in as a new consultant on the case," Gretchen said. It was as good as any excuse for the repetitive questions. Marconi was back to playing the silent spectator, their roles switched as easily as if they'd planned it. Gretchen would have to give that some thought later. For now she carried on, laying it on thick. She'd had enough experience with interviews like this for the proper words to be well practiced and smooth. "I know this must be difficult, but it would be extremely helpful to hear it firsthand."

Gretchen wasn't above playing to her strengths, and so she peeked up at Reed Kent through lashes that she knew made her eyes look oh so inviting. She also knew with the way she was sitting that the very edge of the lace of her bra would be visible to him from where he loomed over her.

Reed reached up to pat Ainsley's hand. "It's all right, I want to be helpful."

Ainsley's expression shuttered, any and all animation wiped from her face.

The transformation gave Gretchen whiplash, and she didn't know what it meant beyond recognizing that it had happened. Sometimes when it came to body language, Gretchen could understand the words while the sentences remained gibberish.

"Can you walk us through what happened?" Gretchen asked as Ainsley sat back down and Reed crossed to the bookshelf at the far end of the room. He leaned his forearm against it, cutting a tragic figure whether on purpose or not.

"I can try," Reed said, gaze darting to Ainsley.

"Are you sure you want to be here for this?" Marconi asked gently. Three pairs of eyes shifted to her in varying degrees of surprise, but Marconi's own attention remained on Ainsley. Gretchen pressed a protest into the pocket of her cheek, where the flesh was scarred from the gnawing of her own teeth.

"Yes," Ainsley said with a decisive nod. "It's difficult to think about what Viola . . . what she's capable of. But Claire deserves justice."

Was it notable that the first Kent to say Viola's name in their presence was the aunt?

"Were you close with her?" Marconi asked.

"Detective," Reed protested, stepping away from the bookcase as if to throw himself on the tracks, despite the kid-glove questioning. *Protective.* Gretchen watched closely as Ainsley waved him off.

"I love Viola," Ainsley said, her jaw set, determined.

Love. No past tense. And it was interesting that she'd chosen to answer about her niece rather than her sister-in-law when given the flexibility of "her."

From the little sound Reed made but clearly tried to hide, he knew they'd find that choice notable.

What was going on here?

*Oh, Lena, darling. The messes you got yourself into.*

"And Claire," Marconi probed. "Were you close with her?"

Ainsley stilled as if she realized her misstep. Or . . . not her misstep but what she'd given away by thinking of Viola first. "We've known each other a long time."

Even Gretchen knew that nonanswer was a slap at a dead woman. "You didn't like her."

The room seemed to inhale, or maybe that was just Ainsley. Marconi rolled her eyes; Reed made some sort of half-realized gesture toward the lot of them. Gretchen watched calmly as everyone struggled to compose themselves. There were times when not giving two shits about societal norms paid off. Never once in her life had Gretchen felt awkward about asking a question that cut too close to the bone. She wasn't about to start now.

Ainsley licked her bottom lip, shifted, dropped her gaze to the floor. "Claire was under a lot of stress."

"Which isn't what I asked," Gretchen noted, trying to soften her voice so that it came off as prodding instead of antagonistic. From Marconi's look, she guessed she'd missed the mark.

By this point, Reed had crossed the room and had a comforting hand on Ainsley's shoulder.

"Look, I don't want to speak ill of Claire," Ainsley said. "We just disagreed on how best to handle Viola's unique situation."

That was quite the euphemism for *what to do with the violent, sadistic psychopath*. But Gretchen just nodded, like she understood. "And were you involved in those decisions?"

"I'm . . ." Ainsley glanced up at Reed. "I'm a nurse. A veteran now, but I was with the military for ten years. I work primarily with PTSD patients." Her fingers tangled on her lap. "Antisocial personality disorders aren't beyond me."

Gretchen straightened. An almost expert who had firsthand experience with Viola was certainly more than she could have asked for. "Were you the first to notice Viola's . . . tendencies?"

"She's too young to be diagnosed," Ainsley hedged. "But . . . yes. I couldn't help but see how she was with her brothers."

Just the subject Gretchen was curious about. Especially why Viola had focused on Sebastian rather than Milo. "She practiced on them?"

The rest of the room faded away as Ainsley met her eyes with a professional nod. "Much of her aggression was focused on Sebastian. He was the baby of the family until Milo came along, and you can imagine how she took that."

Normally older siblings acted out, regressed even. For a child with an antisocial personality disorder, it would be infuriating to have a younger, cuter, more vulnerable infant taking away attention.

"She was physical?"

"There were bruises," Ainsley said. "Reed only caught her in the act a few times."

Reed nodded, jaw tight. "We tried to keep them separated."

"A lock on their door," Gretchen said, thinking of what Viola had mentioned.

"Yes," Reed said, eyes wide and startled. "At night it's hard to monitor her."

Gretchen could imagine. The only way to prevent anything from happening would be to never sleep or . . . to lock the door. "But she still managed to get to them?"

The amount of scar tissue on their little bodies had been the stuff of trashy talk show hosts' dreams.

"My daughter is skilled with a knife," Reed said, without a trace of irony, considering how his wife was killed. Gretchen didn't know what that meant, but she didn't think it meant nothing.

"Viola particularly enjoyed forcing others to commit violent acts," Ainsley said, mouth set in a grim line, still reciting the facts in a professional tone. "The boys, on each other, for instance."

Beside Gretchen, Marconi inhaled, sharp and appalled. Gretchen wondered if she should echo the reaction, but she couldn't dredge up any surprise.

As appalling as the situation might appear, the satisfaction from the emotional violence of it all made sense to Gretchen. She and Viola *did* have that in common, it seemed.

Reed's fingers tightened on Ainsley's shoulder. Gretchen noticed how still he held himself beyond that small movement. Again Gretchen was struck with the overwhelming need to pry into his insides, to scoop out his psyche and dissect it on a sterile examining table. What must that have been like? To raise not only a psychopath but her siblings, too.

*Protective,* her mind supplied. How had Reed Kent reconciled that instinct with the need to protect his sons from the monster Viola's brain chemistry had created?

Gretchen imagined he'd felt helpless, trapped, cornered. That created unpredictable reactions, ones that didn't always make sense. Had that somehow led him to killing Claire?

It was the first time she really allowed herself to wander down that path. If it hadn't been Viola, Reed, of course, was the obvious suspect. But what about his airtight alibi? Which brought them back to . . .

"I'm sorry, I've taken us on a tangent," Gretchen said. "Can we walk it back? To the night of the killing?"

Reed grunted and moved away, back to his bookcase.

"Mr. Kent, you were at a casino that night," Gretchen prodded.

"A buddy had mentioned there was going to be a good fight on," Reed said. "I swung by to watch it."

"The whole night?"

"I had some drinks." Reed shrugged.

"And you were the one who found Claire?"

"I hadn't . . ." He shook his head. Everyone was silent, so silent they could hear him swallow, hear the click of his throat. "I hadn't even realized anything was wrong at first. The room was dark."

And that, that was horrifying even for Gretchen. The sheer shock of climbing into bed without realizing the person next to you was disemboweled far outweighed the intriguing lure of guts and blood on display. "What time was this?"

He flushed. "About four a.m."

Which was far beyond the window of when Viola supposedly took a knife to her mother.

"And that day, that evening before you left, had anything odd happened?" Gretchen asked, aiming for sensitive. "Anything with Viola perhaps? A fight between her and her mother."

Reed's eyes went a little distant like he was replaying something. When he focused again, it was with a curt shake of the head. "No, nothing."

"And you were home all day?" Gretchen asked. She tried to call up the timeline from Lena's file, but she couldn't remember what Reed had answered during the initial questioning.

A pause. But then he nodded. "Yes."

Gretchen didn't look away from his face. "You're certain about that?"

He met her eyes, his jaw set. "Yes."

"How did you get to the casino?"

Ainsley made a little sound, like she was about to protest. And Gretchen forced her mouth into a small smile. "Sorry, I'm just trying to get an idea of how the night played out."

Reed glanced at his sister, then back to Gretchen. "I took a cab."

"From here?" That would be easy enough to check. It would at least help establish the true window of time that Reed had an alibi.

"A few blocks away," Reed corrected. "They don't come down here much."

No, this was a neighborhood where the residents hired private cars. They weren't climbing in the backs of public taxis. It might be suspicious that Reed had chosen to take one over another option, but if he'd grown up in a poor neighborhood with Lena, then that could explain it.

"Had you ever been to that casino before?" Gretchen asked, and Ainsley shot to her feet once more. Reed sent her a quelling look, before he shook his head.

"No, the same person told me where I should go," Reed said calmly in the face of Ainsley's clear agitation.

"Who was this 'buddy'?"

"Uh." Reed looked between her and Marconi. Buying time? "Do you need to know that?"

Marconi was quick to step in even though she'd been the silent participant in this part of the interview. "Yes."

Reed chewed on his lip and looked about two seconds away from calling for a lawyer. Then he rolled his shoulders. "Declan Murphy."

Murphy. *Tess Murphy.* It kept coming back to one missing girl, didn't it?

"Reed," Ainsley breathed out—and there were layers in her voice Gretchen would never be able to decipher. It wasn't a question or surprise or admonishment, but something that borrowed a little from each of those.

Ainsley turned back to face them. "I think you should go."

"Ainsley," Reed said, almost pleading. But he didn't contradict the message.

"If you have any further questions for my brother, you can direct them to his lawyer," Ainsley said, and she had shifted her body enough that she was now standing in front of Reed.

Gretchen tried to catch Reed's eyes. But he was staring at the floor, fists clenched.

Beside Gretchen, Marconi stood. "We'll do that, Ms. Kent."

They were out on the sidewalk what felt like seconds later, the door slamming behind them.

"Well, that escalated quickly," Gretchen murmured, for some reason turning to look up at the curtain in the top level of the town house. It twitched again, just like the day before. But she couldn't make out the figure behind it. One of the boys? She couldn't imagine Reed dashing up the stairs just to watch them leave.

"Was it just me, or did she seem angrier at Claire than she did at Viola?" Marconi asked, shoving the tips of her fingers into her jeans' pockets and rocking back on her heels. Not taken aback, but thinking, Gretchen noted.

"I'm not getting the sense that she was brokenhearted over her sister-in-law's death," Gretchen agreed, and jerked her chin toward the Porsche.

"But she didn't panic until Reed mentioned Declan," Marconi said, dropping into the passenger seat. "And the casino."

Marconi didn't bother asking where they were headed next as Gretchen gunned it out into traffic. She simply dialed the station to get the address.

# CHAPTER EIGHTEEN

## REED

*Five months before Claire's death—*

When Ainsley arrived to visit for a few weeks, Reed didn't even ask her how she'd known she was needed. He just enjoyed the fact that she was there.

His sister didn't give anything away, simply announced that she'd missed the kids and was in between jobs anyway so it was the perfect time for a longer stay.

There was no talk about old ghosts or murder or girls who had disappeared decades ago.

Everyone in the household was on their best behavior, which made things almost disturbingly calm for a while.

Claire had insisted they maintain Sunday family dinners, despite the fact that it was torture for all involved. Except perhaps for Viola, who viewed it with the glee of a normal child discovering an unattended toy store.

She sat across from him, her hair braided in two neat plaits, wearing a pink sparkly T-shirt and striped leggings, looking for all the world like any other girl on the cusp of becoming a teenager.

Ainsley pressed her hand to the back of Viola's neck as she passed, tactile as she was with everyone, but especially his kids. She never moved quickly, never surprised them. But whenever she was visiting, she reminded them that touch could be good, welcome, normal. Sometimes they even stopped flinching by the last day of her visit.

Viola never flinched. But she didn't swat Ainsley's hand away, either. Didn't rebuff her aunt's attempt at treating her just like Sebastian and Milo. Reed didn't think that had anything to do with some sort of unprecedented fondness toward Ainsley. Instead he was inclined to tell Ainsley to start locking her doors at night.

For some reason, Viola seemed to view her aunt as a long game to be played, and was crafting the relationship with a patience otherwise unheard of from the impulsive girl. Reed thought it might be because Ainsley was the only adult in the household who had any sympathy left for Viola, and that kind of vulnerability might as well have been candy to her, sweet, delicious, and meant to be savored.

"How's the foundation, Claire?" Ainsley asked, like they were a real family sitting down to dinner and not just scraps of ripped and shredded souls going through the motions of civility.

Claire loved keeping up appearances. That's why she had the foundation. Her little kingdom. And when he'd suggested years ago that he might play a role there, she had laughed. The idea that he would be capable of fulfilling any position with competency was a joke to her.

"Very well, thank you." The answer may have been directed at Ainsley, but Claire was watching Reed. Whatever was coming next would land like a slap, he could tell. "We've just decided to officially endorse Declan Murphy for the House seat."

Ainsley glanced toward Reed, quick but damning. She seemed to realize her reaction wasn't helpful and turned back to Claire. "I didn't know your foundation got involved in politics."

"We do on occasion," Claire said. "When the matter is important enough."

Viola's eyes darted between the three adults, her infallible radar for drama clearly pinging off the charts. Milo and Sebastian stared at their plates.

"I wasn't aware Declan Murphy had any policies of import," Ainsley said, lingering on Declan's name like it was a rancid thing in her mouth.

Claire finally looked at her. "That's right, you two were involved, weren't you?"

"Oh, did you fuck him, Aunt Ainsley?" Viola asked, and no one reacted to the crude language. She'd been employing that tactic since she was old enough to speak.

"That was a long time ago," Ainsley said, calm as ever. He knew she wanted to unleash the full force of her temper on Claire. Had wanted to for a very long time.

He couldn't remember when the animosity had been born, or if it had always been there. Reed didn't remember Ainsley from when they were younger. Perhaps that was callous, but she was a placeholder in his memories labeled "sister." To him, she hadn't had a personality beyond annoying him, tagging along when he hadn't wanted her there, getting him in trouble.

He was fairly certain she would have bloodied her knuckles for him back then just as she was willing to do so now. He would have killed anyone who hurt her. But that had less to do with them liking each other and more to do with the culture in which they grew up. In their neighborhood, family came above all else, no matter how you felt about them.

*Knowing* her as a person unto herself was something he'd begun to do only in adulthood.

"You were friends with Declan's sister, weren't you, Claire?" Ainsley asked before taking a sip of her wine, holding Claire's gaze all the while. "Tess, wasn't it?"

Viola had scooched forward on her seat, elbows on the table, eyes wide.

"Boys, you can leave," Reed murmured. It was quiet. Effective. Practiced. Milo was gone almost before the words had left his mouth. But Sebastian stayed, his chin jutting out, the baby fat that had made his jaw soft gone now. He was getting stubborn.

Ainsley continued, not needing an answer from Claire. "Such good friends you snatched up her boyfriend before the sheets were cold."

"Oh, Mommy, you whore," Viola said, giddy with it.

"Viola," Claire snapped. It was telling that she acknowledged the remark. She had always been the one who insisted they not give Viola's bad behavior attention. Viola's expression went sly as she slumped back against her chair. The movement might have looked like defeat, but Reed knew his daughter. Claire turned to Ainsley, visibly composing herself. When she finally spoke, her voice was low, exhausted, the frost that had just coated it moments earlier melting. "That was a long time ago."

Beneath the expensive chandelier lighting, it was nearly impossible to see the lines around Claire's eyes, but Reed knew they were there. He had his own that were worn deep from constant worry. He forgot sometimes that she wasn't ice. Too often they slid into taunts and verbal jabs and passive-aggressive one-upmanship because if they didn't resort to petty tactics that helped them distance themselves from each other, they'd actually have to talk about Viola.

And that had never gone well.

So a pattern had been established, where they hurt each other because they both knew how to do that so well, and somehow it had become habit.

"Ainsley," Reed said, just as quietly as he'd murmured to the boys earlier. Just as easily understood.

Her mouth thinned, holding back the words she wanted to use like a whip to flay both him and Claire. Reed didn't think himself exempt from her anger. But unlike with Claire, Ainsley did care about him.

"Do you ever wonder where Tess got the notion to run away?" Ainsley wondered. "Just something I've been thinking about lately."

And with that parting shot, she pushed away from the table. Without even pausing, she pulled Sebastian from his chair, leaving only Claire, Reed, and Viola around the too-long dinner table, the full plates of food left behind a damning condemnation.

Into the silence, Viola asked, "Who's Tess?"

———

When Ainsley found him later, she handed Reed a glass of wine, the ruby-red liquid sliding up toward the rim as he took it from her gratefully. He was hiding in the room Claire referred to as his study in a way that he could practically see the air quotes in the aborted gestures of her hands.

Ainsley sat in the chair next to the sofa where he was sprawled, folding her long legs beneath her so that she was curled up, her chin resting on her hand as she studied him.

She broke the silence only after a good five minutes had passed. "What aren't you telling me?"

Reed scrubbed a hand over his face and then swallowed a hefty portion of the Merlot that came from a $150 bottle. It tasted like silk going down, and his younger self hated him for drinking it.

He wondered what Lena drank these days. Once upon a time they both guzzled dirt-cheap vodka and watery beer. They'd both come a long way from their teen years.

*What aren't you telling me?*

Everything. That's what he wanted to say. Something about the quiet and the shadows and the comforting click of the grandfather clock prodded at secrets. Something about Ainsley did, too.

"Why'd you show up out of nowhere?" Reed asked instead, and it came out harsher than it had lived in his head, the edges jagged where he'd thought them soft.

Still, Ainsley's calm demeanor didn't waver. "I'm just here to help, you know that, Reed."

Of course, of course she was. They needed all the reinforcements they could get now that Viola was getting older. Maybe Ainsley would finally move back to Boston now. That had to be easier than making all these long trips up here. He let his head drop back against the sofa. "I'm chasing a ghost."

"Who?"

A knock on the door interrupted them. It was gentle, tentative.

Milo.

"Come in, darling," Ainsley called when Reed just stared at the dark wood.

Milo's shaggy head popped through the crack, then the rest of him slipped through, a ghost in his own right. The way he moved, like a skittish animal, ripped something apart in Reed, just like it did every time he looked at his youngest.

The boy kept tight to the wall until he got close enough to dart toward the couch, ending up cuddled right up against Reed, his head buried beneath Reed's armpit, his arms clutching his beloved teddy bear.

Ainsley watched him, something like sorrow resting against the curved line of her shoulders. She was not old, yet she looked like she'd lived thousands of lifetimes and had felt each of them in her bones.

Then she blinked, and her expression smoothed into a tender smile. "And how was your day, Milo?"

He grunted, squirmed as if he could disappear into the cushions. Reed laid a hand on Milo's head, clearly telegraphing his movements so it wouldn't startle him. Milo sunk into the touch like he always did, desperate for gentleness.

When Reed met Ainsley's eyes, they were steely.

"This can't go on, Reed," she said.

Reed swallowed hard and kept his hand gentle as he combed through Milo's hair.

"No. It can't."

# CHAPTER NINETEEN

## GRETCHEN

*Now—*

Gretchen didn't like Declan Murphy, but that wasn't unusual when it came to meeting new people. He liked her, and that was what mattered.

He loomed over Gretchen and Marconi as he showed them into his office, using his imposing stature and muscular build to either peacock for her or intimidate Marconi—Gretchen wasn't sure which yet. Best guess was a combination of the two.

"You're here about the Kents, I take it," Declan said as he settled into the chair behind his desk. "Such a tragedy, that. My heart goes out to Reed. Losing his wife, having to take care of the kids."

He shook his head, grimacing in grief, though Gretchen couldn't tell if it was real or manufactured. She needed to get a better baseline on him, but politicians were notoriously hard for her to read, their masks as practiced as her own more often than not. That wasn't surprising, as most research suggested that sociopaths gravitated to such careers. The narcissistic rush, the power—those benefits compensated for how much they had to interact with the general public.

What she *could* see was that he angled himself toward her rather than Marconi, his eyes flicking up and down her body every so often, subtle enough that he probably didn't think she'd notice. What she could also see was that he wasn't wearing a wedding ring. It was unusual for someone of his age with his political ambitions not to have a partner to help manage those lofty goals. What she could see was the absence of any personal pictures, family, friends, or otherwise. That was also a strange choice as those little touches often warmed heartstrings and loosened wallets.

Gretchen didn't yet know how that information could be relevant, but she noted it like she cataloged most things around her.

"You knew Reed Kent growing up?" Gretchen asked.

"Yeah, yup." Declan nodded. "Southie boys made good."

"And you maintained that friendship into adulthood?"

"God no," Declan said on a bit of a disbelieving laugh. At Gretchen's raised brows, he held his hands out. "No offense to him. But we only saw each other at fundraisers every now and then."

"He and Claire were big donors to your previous campaigns," Marconi interjected, and Gretchen pretended not to be surprised at the information or at the fact that Marconi seemed to have an uncanny ability to do research on the fly.

Declan nodded easily, but his hands gripped the arms of his chair, like he was uncomfortable with this line of questioning. "Reed was always good with remembering his roots."

"Were you with Reed Kent the night of Claire's death?" Gretchen asked, hoping to catch him off guard even though she knew the answer was no. Reed Kent had been alone the entire time he'd been in the casino, according to the tapes.

Instead of going on the defense, Declan seemed confused. "What? No. I'm not sure I even know the exact date."

"But you know you weren't with him?"

A flush spread along Declan's cheeks. "This is going to make me sound like a jerk."

Gretchen nearly told him that it wouldn't take much. "Go on."

He looked away, his hands curling into fists and relaxing a few times, before he returned his attention to them. "The last time I talked to Reed was a few weeks before Claire's death."

"It sounds memorable," Gretchen drawled. Clearly from his reaction something had happened.

"Uh," Declan hedged and then sighed and slumped in his chair. "I punched him."

"Why?"

Declan rubbed a hand over his face. "If you're on Reed Kent's case . . . well, do you know about my sister's disappearance?"

"The bare bones," Gretchen said.

"My sister, Tess, Reed, and a woman named Lena Booker were best friends when we were younger," Declan said, and Gretchen guessed he didn't know her own connection to Lena from how he phrased it. "When Tess was eighteen, she ran away. Our parents fought a lot. Neither of us were bound for college or great things." He paused, his mouth twisting as he seemed to acknowledge where they sat. "Or we hadn't thought so at the time."

The details matched the ones in Lena's file but still didn't tell her much. "No one suspected foul play?"

"Uh, my crazy aunt." Declan shuffled through his phone, jotted down a number, and slipped it across to them. "Fiona Murphy. She'd be happy to talk to you. She has lots of conspiracy theories about Tess."

Gretchen slipped the piece of paper in her blazer pocket for later. "And you don't?"

"Fiona posts things online, goes to true-crime forums, stuff like that," Declan said, looking out the window once more. Nervous, fidgety. But not really defensive. If she had to guess, it was more fond irritation in his voice than anything else. "She gets people riled up. Gets people thinking they're going to have the next must-listen podcast or some such nonsense."

"So you mean true-crime junkies," Gretchen clarified. She was not ignorant of the phenomenon. In fact, the more gruesome shows helped her sleep at night, helped feed the unending need within her for violence and gore. At least she'd admit to the hungry darkness, the primal drive that consumed her at the first hint of blood spilled. Empaths seemed to dress the curiosity up with prettier words.

"Yeah, them, anyone who wants a slice of fame, really," Declan said, shifting his attention back to her. "The fact that I'm in the public eye doesn't help. But they soon realize there's nothing to really go on."

"There have been people who researched her disappearance?" Marconi cut in.

"Yup," Declan said, letting the word pop.

"And no one's found her yet?" Gretchen asked, because that seemed unlikely if Tess really was alive.

"Did you know there's hundreds of Tess Murphys out there?" Declan asked. "There's a sweet sixty-three-year-old grandma of five that I've become well acquainted with because she settled in Southie."

Considering how rabid true-crime junkies could be, that still didn't quite explain how no one had found anything. Bread crumbs, if nothing else. "So that's a no to my question?"

"They look at the report, they do some Google searching, and when that turns up nothing . . ." Declan trailed off, with an exaggerated *what can you do* expression.

But Gretchen was thinking about that deposit in Lena's ledger. What if a rich junkie had gotten far enough to figure out that there was history between Lena Booker, quasi-famous lawyer extraordinaire, and Tess Murphy, a politician's runaway sister? And, moreover, what if it wasn't just a podcast fanatic? What if it was someone who wanted dirt on Declan and thought this particular investigation would be fertile ground?

Gretchen was also thinking that Declan still hadn't straight-out answered the question. "You think she's alive?"

"She was a free spirit, our Tess." Declan's smile was caught somewhere between nostalgia and hope. "I like to picture her in San Francisco or an artists' colony somewhere in hippie country."

"That's a yes?" Gretchen pushed, knowing that if she had to talk to this man for much longer, she'd need to start fantasizing about peeling his skin from his bones to stop herself from doing any real bodily damage. Why didn't he want to be nailed down on such a simple question?

"You've been talking to Reed, huh?" Declan asked, looking between them, and Gretchen pinched the skin of her thigh through her pants.

"What do you mean?"

"He got obsessed with her again about, I don't know, a year ago?" Declan said with a careless shrug. "Was sniffing around asking me the same kinds of questions those crime-show fanatics asked."

"Is that why you punched him?" Marconi asked.

Declan licked his lower lip. "No. The first time he came to me, I gave him a bunch of her old stuff, her journals, some pictures, things like that. Didn't hear from him again after that."

They both waited for him to continue, and Gretchen wondered if it was media training that had Declan so easily dodging direct questions or if he had something in particular to hide.

"Right, the punch," Declan said as if he wasn't going on tangents on purpose. He rubbed his hand over his face. "Lena Booker, our mutual friend, well . . . she got in my head a little bit."

"How so?" Gretchen asked.

"Made me think it was all possible, that Reed really had killed Tess all those years ago," Declan said, shaking his head, the flush back. Gretchen wondered if he and Lena had been sleeping together, if that's how she'd convinced him that Reed had done something to Tess. Wondered if Lena had been sleeping with Reed, too. If he loved her like he seemed to. Wondered if Gretchen had really known the woman at all if the answer to either of those questions was still a mystery. Maybe

Marconi had been onto something. Maybe she and Lena hadn't been friends.

"What did she say?" Gretchen asked. "To convince you Reed killed Tess."

"It was more the alcohol she brought with her, to be honest." Declan's smirk was probably meant to be mischievous, but it made Gretchen want to lace his whiskey with cyanide. "And everyone stirring up all the old memories."

Gretchen pounced. "Everyone. You mean more than Reed and Lena?"

If she hadn't been watching closely, Gretchen would probably have missed the way Declan flinched. It wasn't big or obvious, but there in between blinks. "No, just them."

Lies were hard to detect. Gretchen could admit that freely. She'd ruthlessly taught herself body language, facial nuances, tone as best she could, mostly through watching hours upon hours of recorded inter-rogations. Power and emotion she could understand, the first because it was as natural as breathing, the second because she'd known she was lacking in that area. Lies drew on both in a way she could sometimes miss.

But she would put money on it that Declan had been thinking about someone else. Whom? The person who had possibly hired Lena to look into the disappearance in the first place?

Or had that been Declan himself who'd brought her into it? And the rest of this was just an act.

"Look, I apologized to Reed," Declan said. "It was water under the bridge. Offered him my box if he ever wanted to see a fight at Encore. Lena backed off, and a few weeks later Claire was dead. I haven't seen either of them since, and that's about what I can tell you."

"What about back then?" Gretchen pivoted. "Lena, Tess, and Reed were all friends in high school?"

"Yeah, and then Claire came along," Declan said, nodding as if this was common knowledge.

"Wait," Gretchen said. Beside her Marconi had gone perfectly still. "What do you mean 'Claire came along'?"

According to everything Gretchen had read, the Kents had met in college. Harvard, if she remembered correctly.

Declan glanced between them. "Claire met the three of them that summer. At a baseball game, I think."

Gretchen wasn't sure what this meant, but the fact that Claire and Reed had clearly done a damn good job at hiding that fact told her that it meant *something*.

"So Reed started seeing Claire before they went to college?" Gretchen asked slowly, searching for the right question, not sure if that was it.

"Well, I guess they didn't start at it until they were in college." Declan lifted a shoulder. "Reed was dating Tess at the time, so I don't think anything happened until after Tess ran away."

"I'm sorry," Marconi cut in. "Are you saying Reed was your sister's boyfriend, and once she disappeared he started dating Claire?"

Ordinarily, the question would have annoyed Gretchen, as anyone following the conversation wouldn't need those points repeated. But this was enough of a surprise that Gretchen couldn't even fault her for clarifying. If this was all true, that meant Reed Kent had dated two separate women who were now either missing or dead.

That wasn't exactly a tricky pattern to unravel.

"Almost immediately," Declan said with an unreadable expression. It wasn't quite anger and it wasn't quite admiration. But maybe a strange mix of the two.

"Not before Tess left, correct?" Marconi pressed.

Declan squinted, as if trying to jog his memory. He was far more relaxed talking about the past rather than the here and now.

"I don't think anything happened between them until Tess was gone." He leaned in a little. "To be honest, I think he was heartbroken and Claire was a rebound that went on a couple decades too long. Not to speak ill of the dead."

"Not a love-at-first-sight thing?" Gretchen asked, not that she necessarily trusted his take on the situation, biased as it must be.

"Ehh." He held out a hand tipped to one side and then the other. "They were older than me, you know? Maybe Reed was sleeping around on Tess. But . . ."

"But?"

"He didn't seem the type." Declan shrugged, and Gretchen gritted her teeth. That meant nothing. She thought back to Marconi asking a similar thing about Lena.

No one was unequivocally moral, flawless, mistake-free. And yet empaths always seemed blinded to the faults of those they were closest to, while unable to offer understanding to those they didn't know.

"Look," he said, reverting to his slick politician's tone, "if you're here because of Claire, it just . . . it's got nothing to do with Tess."

"You sound pretty sure of that," Gretchen noted, genuinely curious. She couldn't be positive, of course, that a decades-old case was somehow tied into Lena's and Claire's deaths, but it seemed odd to rule it out completely.

"Tess barely even knew Claire," Declan said.

"But she knew Reed and Lena," Gretchen pointed out. "You said Claire showed up that summer Tess disappeared . . ."

"Yeah. She . . . she was a rich girl they'd met," Declan said as if that explained something. "The girls invited her to a party. I think at first it started as a joke."

"A joke?" Marconi asked.

He grimaced. "Not the nicest joke in the world, but they were teenagers, you know?"

135

Gretchen didn't mention that teenagers often made more sense to her than adults. They reveled in their sociopathic tendencies, their cruelty, their base nature. "I still don't get it."

Marconi was actually the one who tried to answer. "It's . . . They wanted to mock her."

"How would they have accomplished that with an invite to a party?"

"She would be a . . ." Marconi glanced at Declan. It was moments like this that Gretchen felt most isolated. She didn't often sink into pity, as that wasn't productive, but there were things that others just seemed to understand that she could never grasp intuitively.

"Dancing monkey," Declan finished for Marconi, his tone not unkind. "They wanted her to be out of place, be uncomfortable, so they could feel better about themselves."

He said the last part with another wince, and at least that was universal. Whenever Gretchen made empaths explain a hard truth in careful detail, it rarely showed their fellow man in a good light.

"Was she?" Gretchen couldn't help but ask, recognizing the frustrating familiarity of being an outsider, unable to understand what she was doing wrong. "A joke, that is."

Declan smiled, almost to himself. Not mocking, but affectionate. Proud?

"Claire has never been a joke in her life."

Something about the way he said that had Gretchen staring at him. That didn't sound like derision, nor did it sound like a memory. That sounded like the admiration of a close partner. It had her circling back to a possible underlying cause for the altercation between Reed and Declan. Maybe Declan had just wanted a more blatant excuse to punch his lover's husband.

The Kent case may have dominated countless news cycles, but there wasn't much gossip about Reed and Claire's relationship. Some talking heads made a big to-do about the strength of their marriage in the face of Viola's disorder, but that kind of chatter tended to end up on morning shows where the hosts drank glasses of wine on air. What would the coverage have looked like if Viola hadn't been there to take the blame and the morbid fascination that came with it? Gretchen guessed the dirty laundry that was clearly piling up in their marriage would have been aired for everyone to see.

"Is that so?" Gretchen asked softly.

Declan straightened, fidgeted with a pen on his desk. "Yeah, she fit right in. She was a proper bitch, but they all were."

Beneath the collective weight of her and Marconi's eyes, Declan cleared his throat roughly, ran a hand through his hair again. "I just mean . . . they weren't overly concerned with being polite. Tess and Lena loved that about Claire. And Reed went along with everything."

"Did Lena and Reed ever date?" Marconi asked.

"Nah, nah, nah." Declan shook his head like the suggestion was personally offensive. "They were like siblings, those two. Everyone knew it."

In Gretchen's experience, saying "everyone knew it" was a red flag. It usually meant that the person holding that theory had no concept of the fact that his reality was not universal.

Gretchen thought back to the way Reed had reacted—or, better yet, had not reacted—to Lena's death. How she'd walked out of there convinced he was in love with her. She was wrong on occasion; she wasn't narcissistic enough not to realize that. But if that hadn't been romantic love she'd seen, the emotion had still been deep, rooted to the core of him.

*Oh, Lena. What have you gotten yourself into, darling?*

The question went unanswered, of course. Lena was on a medical examiner's slab somewhere cold and stark, where she would never be able to explain herself. But more and more, Gretchen wished she'd dropped some hints in the last year that this was going on. Gretchen refused to consider the fact that Lena might have and she'd missed them.

"How did Claire and Reed start dating, if your sister had just disappeared?" Gretchen asked. She didn't pretend to understand teenage melodrama. When she'd been that age, she'd been working on her first advanced degree, having eschewed the traditional public education once she'd realized everyone had thought her a killer who'd gotten away with cold-blooded murder. That was also before she'd started obsessively watching soap operas and sitcoms to better understand how people expected her to behave. To put it lightly, she had not been indulging in love triangles and dalliances the rest of her peers seemed to thrive on.

Declan shrugged. "At that point, I started drifting away from them. Didn't see much of them before Claire and Reed started showing up at fundraisers every once in a while. Like I said earlier."

"When did Lena Booker start showing interest in Tess's disappearance?" Marconi asked, shifting them back to the present.

Declan's mouth pinched in at the corners. "Around the same time as Reed, I think. I don't know."

"You didn't think that was odd?"

"Them both poking into closed cases?" Declan clarified. "Nah. Thought they were in on it together."

"And you didn't encourage them?" Gretchen pressed. "I would think they might actually be people you could trust to get answers."

"Once upon a time," Declan said, so quietly that Gretchen almost missed it. Then he shrugged. "I just . . . I don't need more people digging around into Tess's life."

That rang alarm bells like nothing else. "Why's that?"

"Hey, it's not like that," Declan said, clearly reading her immediate interest correctly. "Having cops get involved, start poking around, it will get Fiona riled, get people talking again for no good reason."

"And it might look bad when you're running for reelection," Marconi said, and, oh yes, he probably would care about that.

Gretchen turned back to him for his reaction to that accusation, and there was a blush riding along the ridges of his well-defined cheekbones.

"Family's more important than any election," Declan said in a curt, clipped voice. Abruptly he stood, a clear signal that the conversation was over. "I'm sorry, but I have a meeting. If I can do anything else for you, feel free to call my lawyer to set something up."

Gretchen startled a little but gamely pushed to her feet. "We'll be sure to do that."

They were almost at the door when Gretchen paused and turned, remembering something. "One more question before we go."

"Yes?"

"Have you ever asked your aunt who she thinks killed Tess?" Gretchen asked. She'd found that despite their penchant for being written off as crazy, people who devoted so much of their time to one killing often offered a perspective other people lacked.

Declan sighed and ran a hand over his face once. Then he lifted one shoulder in a tired shrug. "You know what they say."

It was Marconi who finished the thought. "It's always the boyfriend."

# CHAPTER TWENTY

## REED

*Five months before Claire's death—*

There was something inherently repulsive about reading a diary that wasn't yours.

It had been four days since Declan had finally called to tell Reed he could pick up the box of Tess's things. It hadn't taken much to convince the man who so clearly thought his sister had run off to a better life somewhere.

Declan Murphy used to be a scrappy kid with a blond, shaggy mop on his head, too many freckles on skin that was too pale, with a chip on his shoulder the size of Boston itself. There hadn't been a fistfight he'd ever sat out despite the fact that he'd been ninety pounds soaking wet, he'd known every curse in the dictionary by the time he'd been ten, and Southie blood had always run thick in his veins.

Now he'd become some jerk more concerned with poll numbers than with his sister, one who could barely make time for a meeting, even with one of his biggest donors.

During Reed's visit, neither of them had mentioned that Declan now used Tess's disappearance to fundraise for troubled-youth programs. The thing was, Tess had never really been all that troubled.

*"I know the odds are stacked against her being out there living a happy life . . . but I can hold on to the hope, can't I?"* Declan had said when Reed had asked about Tess.

It didn't matter. Reed had gotten what he'd wanted—Tess's things, a tangible reminder that the girl had lived, had felt, had wept and loved and danced and breathed.

Most of the box had been clutter—a few dust-coated trophies, two shirts, a platypus stuffed animal that was missing both an eye and a front paw, a porcelain cross Tess had gotten for First Communion.

And then there was the small book at the bottom, the flimsy lock dangling from the metal latch. Turtles and flowers crawled along the spine, Tess's name in loopy letters on the cover.

When he'd seen it, he'd recognized it, even though he'd forgotten he'd ever known of its existence. But it reminded him of Tess laughing, holding it close to her chest as he tried to pluck it from her. Of them both falling onto her bed, the journal tossed aside, a mere ploy that had let him get close enough to bring her down into the comforter with him.

Had he wanted to read it back then? He supposed so, though now it felt foreign to want to pry into someone's intimate thoughts, their opinions, their reality that inevitably was so far removed from his own.

Youth had a way of making secrets seem delectable rather than the rotting things age helped you see that they were.

*"You know all my secrets anyway, Reed,"* Tess said as he brushed his nose *against her temple. Her shampoo was bright and sweet and fruity, and he buried his fingers in the mass of her hair. "We've known each other since we were, what, five years old?"*

*Her calves wrapped loosely around Reed's, her thumb brushing the scar on his collarbone when he pulled back to grin at her. The flirtation died in his mouth as he noticed her expression. Fond, loving. Devoted. He tried not to flinch away from the depth of her feelings so blatantly on display, but it took all his willpower.*

"You got this scar sledding on that hill at the park," she whispered, like it was her own secret. Perhaps it was. That she remembered something so inconsequential about him.

Had she always looked at him like this? Had he just not noticed?

When he met her eyes once more, hers were big, like she was expecting a similar revelation from him. He scrambled to find one. There was a scar on her elbow. But he couldn't remember where she'd gotten it from. There was one above her eye that cut into her brow and was noticeable only from close up. Had they come from the same accident?

Shouldn't he know this?

Panic rushed in, held him locked in its grip, his mind emptying even further so that any little tidbit he'd ever collected about Tess was suddenly gone. In its space was a smile from Claire as she explained how she ate strawberries only in the month of July because otherwise she thought it was bad luck.

Did Tess even like strawberries?

His tongue felt heavy, clumsy, poised to unleash words he wouldn't be able to take back.

He loved Tess, he did. Just maybe not like she loved him. And when had that become the worst realization of his life?

The expectation had long dropped from her expression. It was replaced by a curious head tilt and eyes that he could no longer read.

"I need to go," he somehow managed to get out.

She didn't stop him.

Reed pressed the pad of his finger into the sharp edge of Tess's diary and wondered why she'd left it behind. Almost by definition, runaways had to travel light, but weren't hidden thoughts like this a teenage girl's hoarded treasure? Wouldn't she have destroyed them before letting them fall into the wrong hands?

Like his.

The Tess he'd known back then wouldn't have wanted him to read this right now.

Reed flipped to the first page.

His name, Lena's, they both made frequent appearances. That was no surprise. The three of them had been inseparable since birth practically, had lived in each other's pockets always, but that summer in particular.

Because that's when he and Tess had gotten together.

*The college party was Lena's idea. She was always the boldest of the three of them, the wildest, despite her impeccable grades and extracurriculars that she was using to build flawless applications to the best schools in the country. Lena always claimed you could be good for only so long before you had to be a little bad. Otherwise, once you got a taste of something other than perfection, you'd never want to go back.*

*Reed drank beer and smoked an odd cigarette or two. Nothing like some of the boys his age in the neighborhood. He had no delusions of grandeur—he was hoping for a construction job with a friend of his uncle's after graduation.*

*Tess was a good girl through and through. No drugs, no sex, only a rare drink on occasion. Sometimes Reed wondered why she bothered to spend time with them. But then Lena would say something outrageous and biting and clever, and Tess would toss her head back and laugh, and Reed thought that maybe he didn't really understand her at all.*

*She watched him that night more than normal. He wasn't exactly on the prowl, though he was trying to keep an eye on Lena, who'd cornered a scared and excited frat boy. Tess was hanging out with Reed in the kitchen, a plastic cup in her hand. Sometimes if someone passed too close by, she pressed up against him, like she was making space for the other person and somehow just accidentally was forced to brush her breasts against his chest.*

*Her cheeks were flushed, her temples a little sweaty. And Reed wanted to kiss her because she looked like she was in the middle of foreplay and he wasn't with anyone else at the time.*

*That would be a disaster. Tess was one of his best friends. They'd seen each other puke, seen each other cry, seen each other at their worst, most humiliating, and most disgusting. Maybe some people thought that made a good foundation to a relationship, but Reed didn't think so.*

*There was no mystery with him and Tess, no passion. She might as well be his sister.*

*So he put it out of his mind until they were walking home. Lena had stayed with her conquest, and so it was just him and Tess, who was gently swaying and giggling with each step she took.*

*"You're drunk." He laughed, almost incredulous. Tess didn't get drunk.*

*"Liquid courage." She said each word with a triumphant punch in the air. And then she stopped, and he knew what was coming. He knew it.*

*And he didn't stop it.*

*Tess pressed her lips against his, hers still slightly sticky from the too-sugary drink, his chapped and probably tasting of hops. The world didn't shake; there were no fireworks. But when she pulled away, her expression was a bit dreamy.*

*"I think you're my boyfriend now," she slurred and then lurched toward the bushes. Reed held her hair back because he loved her and would always hold her hair back.*

Following that night, everything about their little group shifted.

Not a lot. Enough, though.

Later, Tess had admitted that Lena had been the one to convince her she should go for it with Reed and stop pining. *Shit or get off the pot* had been the exact wording.

Reed had just laughed because he'd realized it wasn't so bad, being in a relationship. Even though Tess drew the line at sex, they made out plenty.

And he'd loved her, he really had.

The diary started a week or so into their relationship. And like a weary historian he trudged on, passing events that acted as mile markers on his path to Claire.

Where the kiss between him and Tess had been a barely noticed ripple in their lives, Claire had been an earthquake.

And if that particular catastrophic event had an epicenter, it would be Fenway Park.

None of them had been baseball fans, but there was a beer vendor who'd been lax about checking IDs, and hanging around the stadium for the length of the game let them escape their parents' nagging about getting shitty minimum-wage jobs. So they'd shelled out ten dollars for nosebleed seats a few times a week and tried to forget the world outside those green walls.

A teenage Claire, on the other hand, had loved stadiums. Not baseball, but the places themselves—*modern-day amphitheaters, the pleasure palaces of their times* is what she always said. They were where the rigid class structure that existed everywhere else dissolved like the blue and pink cotton candy that bobbed through the crowds.

Never mind that while Reed and the others baked under a hot sun, barely able to see if there were players on the field, Claire had access to season tickets in an air-conditioned VIP box with all the champagne and high-class finger food she could want.

She'd been a stranger then, dressed in crisp white clothes with a baseball hat whose brim hadn't been bent in the slightest. She'd been lecturing the poor friend she'd dragged along with her while standing in a line for hot dogs—because that was part of the experience, she told the girl, who had heaved a long-suffering sigh. Reed had laughed at her. Obnoxiously, derisively. He hadn't been able to stop himself because he'd been a rude teenage boy who'd wanted her attention and didn't know how to go about it otherwise, so he made fun of everything that was so easy to make fun of about her.

Reed paused on the entry for that day, hesitated, skimmed it. Came back, read it word for word.

Claire hadn't even been mentioned, despite the fact that she and her friend had trailed him back to his seats, had met Lena and

Tess, had been invited to a party that weekend, and had garnered a few snide remarks from Lena once they'd left to return to their air-conditioning.

Wasn't that funny? How one person's earthquake went undetected by someone who should have felt the shaking the most?

# CHAPTER TWENTY-ONE

## GRETCHEN

*Now—*

"I'm starving—do you eat?" Gretchen asked as they stepped out of Declan Murphy's office. She waved away her own question. "Of course you eat."

"Most people do." Marconi's voice was dry as dust.

"Yes, but you especially eat," Gretchen said, not sure why she had to spell it out. "Italian."

"I would find that offensive," Marconi said slowly. "But . . . you're not wrong."

"I rarely am," Gretchen assured her, as she took stock of their surroundings. Marconi followed when Gretchen started down the block.

"So what's your guess on all this?" Marconi asked. "Oh wise one."

Gretchen slid her a glance from the side. Usually something like that from one of Shaughnessy's partners would be laced with bitterness. But Marconi had the start of a small smile tucked into the dimples of her cheeks as she stared at the ground.

They turned the corner, and Gretchen put off answering in favor of swinging through the door of her favorite restaurant in the neighborhood they were in.

A little man rushed toward them in greeting.

Maks kissed both of Gretchen's cheeks. "Dr. White, so good to have you in today."

"There's space?" Gretchen asked the birdlike maître d' despite the fact that the tables were all empty. That wasn't what mattered.

"For you, always," Maks assured her with a somewhat cheeky wink. It seemed almost out of place in his old-world face, but Gretchen had always found that assuming anything about Maks was a mistake.

The man was the maître d' for a Russian restaurant that was a front for the mob. Lena had insisted that she didn't draw a distinction between the Russians and the Irish, and she was so good she didn't need to. Both factions pretended that she represented only them. It was probably the only peaceful—if tacit—agreement in decades between the two organizations.

He showed them to a small table in the back corner covered with a thick ivory tablecloth lined with lace. For a tense moment, Maks watched Marconi—who carried herself in such a way that anyone in a ten-mile radius could tell she was a cop—but then he smiled wide at them both, bowed a little, and scuttled off without bothering to give them menus.

Marconi raised her brows in a silent question.

"They order for you," Gretchen said, and accepted the small glass of vodka being thrust into her hands by a nervous waiter. Marconi took one, too, but set it aside. Gretchen downed hers in one swallow, earning her an appreciative look from the young boy, who couldn't have been more than nineteen. She grinned and slipped him a card that already had her number written on the back. He flushed prettily before scampering off.

"I think cops have been shot for less than busting into a mob head-quarters like this," Marconi said, though she smartly pitched her voice low even as she was complaining.

"What's life without a little danger?" Gretchen asked, and snatched up the vodka she knew Marconi wouldn't touch while she was on the job. The liquor was gorgeous, went down without any kind of pro-test, and deserved to be consumed instead of ignored. Gretchen was happy to do her part. When she'd finished, she jerked her head toward Marconi's phone. "Pull up some sites for those crime-junkie crazies."

"I think that is the official name they go by, yes," Marconi mur-mured, but was already typing away. Like Shaughnessy, Marconi didn't seem one to cut off her nose to spite her face. Good detectives liked solving crimes, and Gretchen's commentary wasn't enough to put them off that single-minded pursuit. At least not the smart ones. The rest could rot for all she cared.

Marconi wrinkled her nose as she scrolled through whatever she'd found. "This is nothing."

"I find it hard to believe that no one has discovered anything on the girl," Gretchen said. It made her wonder again if there was really any mystery behind the disappearance. Had Lena really thought there was, or did she just miss her old friend?

Was Tess Murphy really important at all? Or was Gretchen finding ghosts where none actually existed.

*I messed up, Gretch. You have to fix it.*

Had Lena messed up with Tess Murphy's disappearance? Or the investigation into Claire Kent's murder?

If she took Lena's last call at face value, then nothing would point back to Tess Murphy.

But Gretchen still couldn't get over the connections, the thin lines that ran between people who had clearly tried to hide over the past six months that they knew each other at all while the press tore apart the Kents' life. That must have taken an effort, must have been deliberate.

"It seems like anyone digging into the case would have incentive to really try to find something," Marconi agreed, and began typing away again. "Congressman brother and all that."

"Conspiracy theories play into humans' worst instincts," Gretchen commented idly as she watched for any signs of their food.

When Marconi glanced up with a small smirk, Gretchen narrowed her eyes. "What?"

"The way you call us humans," Marconi said, amusement thick in her voice. Then she shook her head and went back to scrolling. "It's like you're not a part of that group."

Gretchen swallowed, her throat dry all of a sudden. She would die before acknowledging that Marconi was right, that she didn't think she fit in with the rest of them. The moment in Declan Murphy's office where she hadn't understood what both of them had so clearly grasped was a sharp memory against her skin. "Well, clearly I'm superior to all that."

"Clearly," Marconi agreed, and it didn't sound mean. Not that Gretchen could always tell. But . . . she didn't think it sounded mean.

She sighed in relief as the kitchen door swung open. Two burly men emerged, both bearing trays loaded down with food.

Marconi stashed her phone as she took in the feast. Once the waiters retreated, Marconi predictably went for the pierogi first.

"Looks like everything on those forums is hearsay at best," Marconi said, around her first bite. "Maybe there really isn't anything suspicious going on."

"But wouldn't she have been found?" Gretchen asked, stuck on that for reasons she couldn't explain.

Marconi raised one shoulder. "People both overestimate and underestimate how easy it is to disappear."

"Oh, that's so very helpful," Gretchen drawled. "The taxpayers are doling out the big bucks for that insight, are they?"

Marconi muttered some choice phrases, but her voice didn't carry any heat. In fact the message was completely undermined by the sauce running down her chin and wrist. She tried to lick it up, but Gretchen could have told her it was a lost battle.

"Not only did Lena keep Tess Murphy's file, but she kept it hidden away in the same secret compartment that she kept her financial records," Gretchen said, offering the tidbit in the hopes of keeping Marconi interested and engaged—at least to a point. "Why would she do that if she didn't think there was foul play involved?"

"I don't know, Dr. White," Marconi said, voice dry. "Maybe I'd have an answer to that question if I'd known about it for longer than the last ten seconds."

Gretchen waved away the implied criticism that she'd been withholding important information. Marconi would have to get used to that. "And here I thought you detectives prided yourself on your ability to think on your feet."

Marconi looked like she was waging a battle with herself, and Gretchen decidedly did not smirk. If Marconi argued further, she'd come off like she couldn't handle unexpected information.

After a minute of tense silence, Marconi sighed, a resigned exhale that sounded like victory to Gretchen. It was these little wins in life that kept her going.

"Lena could have kept it because of the personal connection," Marconi said.

"Possibly," Gretchen admitted.

"It's strange that they're all tangled up," Marconi said as she stuffed the remainder of a pierogi into her mouth. It was a close-enough echo to Gretchen's own thoughts that she tipped her head in acknowledgment.

"And then the wife dies," Gretchen said.

They both paused as another round of plates was brought out. Marconi huffed, staring down at the spread, then shrugged and dived in for more.

"Tell me about conspiracy theories, Doc," Marconi said as she pulled the bowl of borscht closer to her. "Pretend I know nothing about it."

"That won't be hard," Gretchen said.

"Too easy," Marconi chided, and Gretchen had to agree.

"There are brains that are more prone to illusory pattern perception," Gretchen said instead of acknowledging it. "More prone to finding connections in unrelated data. They're simply wired that way."

"All right, so what brains are prone?"

"People who have an excess of dopamine pumping through their gray matter," Gretchen said, popping a slice of decadent duck into her mouth. "It's the reverse of low dopamine in addicts. That deficit makes them think that nothing matters. For someone with high dopamine levels, they think *everything* matters."

"So they see conspiracies where it's just happenstance," Marconi said.

Gretchen nodded, eyeing what was left on the plates.

"That's not everyone, though?" Marconi pressed. "I mean most people believe at least one wild theory, right? JFK, Pearl Harbor, Tupac Shakur still being alive, etcetera. They don't all have excess dopamine levels."

"Pareidolia," Gretchen said easily, snagging the last pierogi without shame. "That's a fancy word for humans' tendency to find significance in something where there is none. Like kids finding shapes in clouds. We do that a lot. And that technically is a subset of apophenia, which is the tendency to find connections where they don't exist." Gretchen paused, looked up, studied Marconi for a moment. "Are you lost yet?"

"Just don't give me a quiz at the end," Marconi drawled. "So why are humans prone to . . . those things?"

"Survival," Gretchen said with a shrug, not calling Marconi on the fact that she'd already forgotten the scientific names.

So many people thought they were in full control of their actions, but much of human behavior was hardwired through evolution. People couldn't change it if they wanted to. "If a man is walking through the forest and he hears a noise . . . if he assumes it's a tiger and runs away, he's more likely to survive than the man who hears a noise and guesses it could be anything. The man who survives has kids who have the gene to be suspicious of random noises and make connections even if they don't exist."

Marconi huffed. "Okay, I guess that makes sense."

"It's also why people see religious faces in inanimate objects," Gretchen said, digging the tines of her fork into a particularly succulent piece of sausage. "And why you can hear your name called in a noisy crowd." Gretchen pointed her fork at Marconi. "You probably are on the higher end of the spectrum for those tendencies."

"I can't tell if that's a compliment or not," Marconi said.

"A compliment and a rare one, so be grateful," Gretchen said. "You see patterns where others might miss them. Just watch out. Schizophrenia is where it starts becoming a diagnosis."

"Well, so are we seeing patterns in this case where none exist?" Marconi asked, masterfully bringing them back on topic. Gretchen held back any noise of approval, in case Marconi was getting too confident in their partnership. "Are we falling in that trap?"

"Almost certainly," Gretchen said, gracefully accepting the dessert from the young boy who'd taken her card. She threw him a wink, and he tripped as he retreated. "But that hasn't stopped anyone else. Why should it stop us?"

# CHAPTER
# TWENTY-TWO

## REED

*Five months before Claire's death—*

Reed and Lena met at a hot dog cart near Faneuil Hall. No one Claire associated with would be caught dead in that area, let alone ordering from a street vendor.

Lena loaded on the mustard as she always had and smiled to herself just before taking a bite. It reminded Reed of the way he felt when he indulged in something silly and obscurely pleasurable. He didn't tease her about it, just dumped a spoonful of relish on his own dog.

"Tell me why you think Tess was murdered," he finally said after they'd walked a few blocks. There had to have been a catalyst to drag all this up again. There had to be a reason.

Lena didn't answer, simply stared lovingly at the last bite of her hot dog before finishing it off. If this was Lena being cagey, Reed didn't blame her. Tess had always been, would always be, a sore subject.

The two girls had been so different and yet so close from the start. Tess was air, was light, was too good for this world sometimes. She'd volunteered at soup kitchens on weekends, and not so she could add it to her application letters like Lena. College had never been in Tess's plans, though both Reed and Lena had worked to make sure she knew she was smart enough to go.

She would just laugh and ask who exactly was paying that bill. That always shut them up. Lena had been counting on a scholarship, and though Tess had earned decent grades, they hadn't been good enough for that kind of help.

Lena had always been the one who'd been scared their little trio would fall apart once they were separated by experience. What she'd really meant was that she'd been scared she'd get cut out. How could they relate to someone going to Harvard? What did that person know of the daily lives, the hurts, the struggles, the humor and pain of the people they'd left behind?

Maybe all this digging around in the past had to do with some kind of lingering guilt?

"I got an email," Lena said, her husky voice going quiet despite the fact that surely nobody around them would be able to overhear her. "Someone looking to hire me."

"You gonna tell me who it was?" Reed asked, expecting—

"Nope," Lena said with a charming little smile to soothe the sting.

"That can't be it, though," Reed pressed. "You got an email? That's what you're basing all of this on?"

Lena kept her attention straight ahead. "It was a convincing email. Hey," she said, stopping abruptly, and grabbing his arm. "Do you remember your last conversation with Tess?"

Reed sensed the trap but couldn't quite stop himself from stepping into it. The lie came easily. "Coney Island."

"What?"

He ducked his head, as if bashful. "She'd always wanted to go. We were planning a trip."

"Hmm," Lena hummed, but didn't meet his eyes, and he wondered what that email had said.

"Hey." Reed couldn't help himself. "If you think Tess was murdered, who do you think killed her?"

When Lena looked up at him, her pupils were pinpricks, her eyes deep green and watchful. Her tongue darted out, wetting her lower lip. "I don't know."

He shoved his hands into his pockets so that she wouldn't be able to see the tremors in his fingers.

Lena had always been able to read the thoughts he didn't say. But here was another truth: he'd always been able to do the same with her.

And in the space between those flimsy words, he heard what she really believed.

Who do you think killed Tess?

*You.*

———

Days later Reed put his fist through a wall still thinking about the accusation in Lena's eyes. He'd assumed the worst that would happen was he'd leave a hole in the plaster, but instead he'd hit brick behind a thin veneer of plaster and paint.

It had taken him to his knees.

The hydrogen peroxide splashed against his ripped, raw, flayed knuckles, the sharp sting of pain almost welcome against the dull throb that suggested he'd broken a bone with his careless punch.

Streaks of red were smeared against the porcelain of the bathroom sink. So much blood, far more than he'd sustained from his careless swing.

Reed wiped at his nose with the back of his wrist. It came away wet.

The neat, white perfection of the room had been destroyed. There was blood on the tiled floor, on the counter, on the petals of the fresh-cut white roses Claire kept in there at all times despite the fact that only family used this bath.

The doorknob rattled, and Reed stumbled back, eyes on the flimsy lock. Would it hold?

It did, it did, it did . . .

Reed didn't realize everything had stilled until his thigh muscle twinged. He was on the floor in the small gap between the toilet and the wall, arms wrapped around his legs, holding them close to his chest. How long had he been down there? He didn't remember folding himself into the tight space, didn't remember the light fading where it spilled in from the window. Had it been hours that he'd been locked in here? Locked inside his own mind.

He exhaled and realized his cheeks were damp, this time from tears rather than blood. Swiping at them furiously, he tried not to let the anxiety that was threading through his chest gather into a knot that he wouldn't be able to swallow around.

The pain of his already-broken knuckles smashing into the toilet's porcelain bowl held off the panic attack.

He fumbled for his phone. His vision went dark, and he gripped the edge of consciousness with the very tips of his fingers. Without letting himself hesitate, he found the number he was looking for.

"Who hired you?" Reed asked as soon as Lena answered.

The shuffling, the background noise on the other side of the line dropped to nothing. When Lena spoke again, he could tell she'd moved to somewhere private. "Reed, are you all right? Do you need help?"

He pressed his lips together, knowing she wasn't going to answer. That question or the one that came next: "What do you want from me?"

Lena was quiet. He knew her, could all but see her, sitting in a fancy chair, with her fancy clothes, every inch a rich lady she would have thrown names at in a different lifetime.

"Tess hated Coney Island," Lena said, and it took a moment for the words to make sense. When they did, he nearly swore. "You said that was your last conversation with her. That she wanted to go to Coney

Island. But when she was little, her aunt took her there and she got lost for most of the night."

Of course, now he remembered. There had been a reason he'd always thought of Tess when he thought of that place. "Lena . . ."

Lena charged on. "So you can see where that had me wondering, Reed."

He stared at the blood on the tile.

"Do you just not remember?" Lena continued, soft as anything. "Or can you not tell me?"

Reed pulled the phone away from his ear, and ended the call.

# CHAPTER
# TWENTY-THREE

## GRETCHEN

*Now—*

Fiona Murphy invited Gretchen over almost before Gretchen could tell her why she was calling. That was the silver lining with these obsessed family members. They *wanted* to talk to the cops. Especially since Fiona had been ignored by them for decades.

Or so she informed Gretchen and Marconi as she served them off-brand Oreo-like cookies that tasted like cardboard and disappointment. Gretchen just glared when Fiona tried to foist some more of the things onto her plate. But Marconi took one for the team with a smile on her face. Another benefit of having a partner who bent to the dictates of politeness.

"Ms. Murphy," Gretchen said, interrupting Fiona's rant about the way she was always forwarded to the records department whenever she called the police station these days. "We spoke to your nephew."

Fiona's eyes tightened at the corners, but she didn't quite scowl at the mention of Declan. Gretchen got the sense that she wanted to. "That must have been nice."

The tone was bitter enough to confirm Gretchen's guess. "Do you not talk to him anymore?"

"Boy has gotten too big for his britches," Fiona muttered into her teacup. "Thinks I'm delusional. Wants to keep me out of the press. But if I could just talk to a reporter . . ."

She trailed off, her mouth working but not making any noise. Her thin gray hair was scraggly around her face, a smear of lipstick running into the cracks of her mouth. A pair of glasses hung around her neck, but another pair sat on top of her head, and still yet another pair was hooked onto the collar of her blouse. When she spoke, spittle flew out to fall onto the tabletop between them.

There was no question as to why Declan kept her hidden away. One interview with this Fiona Murphy would have his opponents giddy.

"What would you tell them?" Gretchen asked. If Tess hadn't been found yet, or come forward, after all this time, would an article in the *Boston Globe* really do anything?

"I'd tell them about the incompetence of the very men who are supposed to be protecting us," Fiona said, eyes wide and a little wild. Then she sat back as she seemed to realize whom she was talking to. "Oh."

"I'm sorry your concerns have been dismissed, Ms. Murphy," Marconi said with seemingly genuine sincerity. "I'm sorry you've been treated so poorly."

Fiona straightened at that, her chest expanding, her papery cheeks going pink with pleasure. If that's all it had taken to smooth things over, Gretchen didn't know why some dispatcher hadn't tried it in the first place. Though maybe Gretchen shouldn't be surprised. Sometimes it felt like Shaughnessy was the only halfway decent cop in that place.

She slid her eyes to Marconi. Maybe there were two. But that was it.

"Well," Fiona said, fussing with a button on her blouse, clearly overwhelmed by a bit of kindness. She would be so easy to manipulate, desperate as she seemed for acknowledgment. Gretchen tried to remind herself that she wasn't here to play mind games with a paranoid old lady, tempting though it might be.

"Can you tell us why you think Tess was murdered and didn't just run away?" Gretchen asked, trying to get them somewhat back on track.

"My Tess loved me," Fiona said with the conviction of someone who would never be contradicted by a living relative. "She would have gotten in contact with me if she were alive."

"But when you were interviewed by police back then, you already seemed convinced she'd been killed," Gretchen pushed. "That would have been before you could have reasonably assumed she would have contacted you."

Fiona opened her mouth, closed it. "Huh."

"So," Gretchen said, trying to keep any annoyance out of her voice, trying to keep it gentle, the same way Marconi had when she'd apologized for something that was in no way her fault. "What made you suspect that it was foul play twenty-four hours after she'd gone missing?"

"I just knew that Reed Kent boy had something to do with it," Fiona said, her eyes narrowing into slits. "Lena thought so, too, she told me."

Gretchen tried not to pounce. "Lena thought Reed had killed Tess?"

That was what Declan had said, too. Did that make it true?

"Well." Fiona patted her hair, looking a little less certain in the span of a few seconds. "She didn't say it in so many words, but she might as well have."

"And this was recently?"

Fiona squinted. "A year ago? She came to see me a couple times— brought that boy once."

"You let him in your house?" Marconi asked and sounded surprised. Gretchen glanced over, not sure why that was her question, but Marconi was watching Fiona.

Fiona leaned forward like she was about to tell them a secret. "Lena asked me to. Asked me a lot of things, actually."

"Like what?" Gretchen asked, keeping her voice as gentle as possible, not wanting to startle Fiona out of spilling everything she knew.

"She had me show him something," Fiona said, patting her pockets absently as if she were carrying around whatever it had been. "Wanted to see his reaction, she said. Wanted me to play along with a little script she'd written."

Neither Gretchen nor Marconi shifted even a centimeter. "What did you show him?"

The air of distraction sloughed off Fiona's shoulders like she'd shrugged out of a coat. Now her eyes were sharp and focused. "Lena also told me not to tell anyone else. Swore me to secrecy."

Gretchen gnawed on the skin inside her cheek, did the square roots of the largest numbers she knew, pictured digging her thumbs into Fiona's eye sockets until the white-hot anger dissipated as quickly as it had come. She exhaled. "She was a good friend of mine, actually. I think she would have wanted me to see it."

Fiona's lips pursed as she studied them, her eyes lingering on Marconi, on the pocket that held her badge. "Nope, she said no one."

Then she mimed zipping her lips and throwing away the key. Gretchen sat back against the couch so she wouldn't do anything so foolish as to lunge across the small coffee table.

"Did she say why?" Marconi stepped in, like she had every time Gretchen had been pushed to her limits.

"No, but Lena was a dear," Fiona said. "She was the only one who still stopped by to talk with me."

"Why did you think it was Reed who killed Tess?" Gretchen asked, not sure what to make of the information on Lena. Had she wanted to watch Reed react to the pressure? And if Lena really did think Reed had killed Tess, why would she later work with him? Why take his daughter's case? Why did it seem like Reed had loved her, at least like a sister if nothing else?

Why did this seem so much more tangled than a quick glance would lead someone to believe?

"Tess was always sneaking off with him," Fiona said with a little sniff. "He was going to get her in trouble one way or another." Her eyes lit up. "Maybe that's why he killed her. She found out she was pregnant, and he didn't want to step up and take responsibility."

"She was pregnant?" Gretchen asked.

"Not that I know of," Fiona said, like she was talking to someone who was lagging far behind in the conversation. "But it could be a motive."

Gretchen sighed. This woman had no idea what had happened to Tess. Marconi shifted beside her, and one glance at her expression— carefully composed as it was—hinted that she was reaching that conclusion as well.

"Were Lena and Tess quite close growing up?" Gretchen asked, pivoting slightly. There was still something about the dynamics of their little group that had Gretchen wanting to dig deeper to find the messiness buried beneath the surface.

"Oh yes, like sisters." Fiona nodded earnestly. "Those girls were attached at the hip."

"And Claire . . ." Gretchen paused, realizing she didn't know Claire's maiden name. A misstep she'd have to rectify when she could. "Reed's wife. Did you ever meet her?"

Fiona's scraggly eyebrows met in a tight vee. "Tess knew that girl was after Reed."

"Did she confront her about it?" Gretchen asked.

"No, Tess was so gentle," Fiona said, her voice going a little dreamy. "She would never yell at anyone."

But she might have run away from her problems. A broken family life, a boyfriend who had his head turned by a pretty girl. What had been keeping Tess here? Maybe she had just taken off like everyone thought.

Gretchen stood, unwilling to waste any more time. "Thank you, Ms. Murphy. I appreciate you talking to us."

Fiona's shoulders slumped. "You sound like the rest of them."

Marconi made a little sympathetic sound but got to her feet. "We'll look into this further, I promise."

That got Fiona's attention, and she looked at Marconi like she'd just come down from heaven. Then she was up and bustling them to the door. "And you tell that Detective Shaughnessy that just because Kent is a widower doesn't mean he should stop investigating him."

Gretchen stopped, one foot on the stoop, one foot inside. She shifted until she was facing Fiona again. "Detective Shaughnessy?"

Fiona nodded. "Yes, he took over the case years ago."

Gretchen smothered a grin. "Well, isn't that convenient?"

# CHAPTER TWENTY-FOUR

## REED

*Six months before Claire's death—*

When Reed came to a stop at the address Lena had sent him, he couldn't shake the golden warmth that set up shop in the hollows of his chest. *Southie.*

The house was split in two, a duplex where you could probably hear every flush of your neighbor's toilet. An old, hunched man watched him from across the street, his Red Sox hat tipped down to cover his face.

Reed didn't jump when knuckles tapped against the glass of the passenger-side window of his SUV.

"Ms. Murphy's going to call the police on you," Lena said as she climbed into the SUV. "She probably thinks you're the mob."

They both glanced toward the house. No one was at the window, but that didn't mean Ms. Murphy wasn't watching them with her eagle eyes.

"She'll have recognized you," he said. Lena looked more like her teenage self today than she had in that Starbucks a week ago—her hair pulled back into a low ponytail, dressed in jeans and flannel. He could even see the light dusting of freckles across the bridge of her nose.

Reed looked away as Lena laughed.

"Yeah, and think I'm cavorting with drug dealers."

"I thought the mob?" Reed said, his lips twitching. It had been a while since he'd been amused by anything.

"I changed my mind—the car's too new for the mob," Lena countered, flipping her hair in a way that was so Lena he nearly wept with the grief of having been separated for so long. Before Claire, before Tess, before anything had happened with anyone, there had been Lena. His first friend since they were five, playing beneath forts made of sheets as their moms drank coffee in the kitchen.

He shook his head, cleared his throat. "She knows we're coming, right?"

Lena nodded. "We've been talking by phone. I told her you were coming." She paused. "She's, uh . . ."

"Not fond of me," he finished, amused. "She caught me sneaking in the window one night when Tess was staying here."

"And how did that end up for you?"

"On my back on the grass, staring down the barrel of her shotgun," he said, exaggerating only slightly.

Lena's grin was quick. "I want to be Ms. Murphy when I grow up."

"*I* want to be Ms. Murphy when I grow up," Reed agreed, flipping the engine off. It was so easy to fall back into the rhythms of talking to Lena when she looked like this instead of the sleek stranger he didn't know. He paused just before closing his door behind him, wondering if she'd dressed down for that very reason. To put Ms. Murphy at ease, to get her to talk.

From what he'd heard, Lena was quite good at her job. She would know how to convince people to let down their guard, even if they didn't want to, without them realizing it.

He shook off the thought. It didn't matter. His walls were so thick it would take more than whatever Lena had up her sleeve to break through them. And that's all that he cared about—keeping his secrets safe.

"So where does your better half think you are?" Lena asked as they started toward the door.

Reed hesitated, wondering why she was asking. And then he chided himself for being paranoid. "She doesn't think anything. She's at a charity luncheon."

"And . . . the kids?"

That was almost funny, the way she said "the kids" just like he and Claire did when they were trying not to single out Viola. In another life, he wondered what would have happened if Claire hadn't come along, if Tess hadn't disappeared. Would Reed have broken up with her anyway and eventually ended up with Lena? His childhood best friend and teenage confidante.

What would their lives have looked like? Would he have gotten her pregnant at eighteen like what happened to a bunch of their peers from high school? Would they have been living down the street in a house just like the one they were about to visit? Would they have loved or hated each other? Reed imagined the latter. Lena had always been too smart to tie herself to him. He'd known that at thirteen and sixteen and eighteen, and he knew it now.

They would never have worked. But maybe if he'd chosen that path, Viola, and her endless complexities and challenges, would never have been born. Would avoiding that fate be worth watching his friendship with Lena curdle, just like his relationship with Claire had?

Perhaps he really was the common denominator here, the problem, just like Claire said.

"School," he said shortly.

"Right, of course," Lena said, shaking her head and laughing a little at herself. Lena didn't have kids, didn't have her world revolve around anyone else but herself. For one breathless moment, Reed wished with everything he had that he could say the same for himself.

Lena tugged on his arm, and they continued up the steps.

Fiona greeted Lena with a fierce hug, her chubby arms holding on tight for too long, pink-smeared lips landing on Lena's cheeks no less than three times.

Reed was spared a look and a nod and that was it before Fiona hustled them both into her living room.

It was as familiar as the outside of the house, and he smiled when he sat down, the sofa's plastic wrap crackling beneath him. He and Tess had never been able to fool around on it, even if Fiona hadn't been watching from the kitchen, pretending not to.

"I don't know what I can tell you," Fiona said. "I've tried to get the police to do something. Still call them up every year on the anniversary."

"You always said . . . you were always so certain Tess hadn't simply left town," Lena said. Her voice gentled when she continued. "What do you think happened to her?"

Fiona's eyes slid to Reed. They were dark brown and beady, and just like that, he was sixteen years old again, staring down Aunt Fiona's gun. "I just don't think Tess would leave like that."

If that was her justification, Reed understood why she hadn't been able to get through to the cops. They had bodies floating in their harbor on the daily, and here was an aunt who didn't want to believe her niece was a runaway.

"I've been called foolish and worse than that, so whatever you're thinking, I've heard it," Fiona said gruffly. "Tess stayed at my house that night, the night she disappeared."

That in itself wasn't surprising. Tess's parents had always scrapped at each other, but those summers when she was in high school had been the worst. She used to stay in his bed—just to sleep—when she couldn't take the yelling anymore. Her aunt's place must have been her other refuge.

"She snuck out," Fiona said. "That night. I heard her, didn't try to stop her. I'd been young once, too, if you can imagine."

"You think she was meeting someone?" Lena pressed.

Again Fiona's eyes flicked to him. "It wasn't unusual," she said instead of answering, *Yes, that boy,* like she clearly wanted to. "I didn't want to stop her. Didn't want her to think I was policing her. Then she'd have nowhere to go when that father and mother of hers . . ." The venom dripped from her voice.

"I remember they divorced after she disappeared," Lena said. "Left town."

"Good riddance," Fiona said, and Reed had a sneaking suspicion she would spit if it wouldn't ruin her pristine carpet. "Danny's in the morgue. That woman is somewhere in Palm Beach shopping for her fourth or fifth husband."

"Do you think their fighting had anything to do with Tess leaving?" Lena asked.

Fiona's lips pursed. "She didn't leave. She would have contacted me by now."

Little by little, Reed's muscles loosened. This was irrational emotion speaking. Not facts. Not some hidden evidence that had somehow resurfaced after twenty years.

Everyone but a few die-hard obsessives knew that Tess had been a typical teenager, tired of living in a volatile home. She'd looked around, seen nothing to keep her there, and taken off for parts unknown.

Fiona zeroed in on him just as he had the thought.

"You weren't enough for her to stick around," Fiona said. "You've never wondered about that? That she didn't find it worth it to say good-bye to you."

Reed swallowed, didn't say anything, couldn't.

"Makes a person question just how much you loved that girl," Fiona said, in a way that reminded him of a snake pulling back before the bite. "Makes a person question if the despondent boyfriend was ever really despondent at all."

There had been talk among his friends, among their parents, when Claire and he had started dating not long after Tess had left town. But here it was, on display, decades later. Lena was watching him, too, her head cocked just to the side. Like she was remembering that she hadn't been around to see it.

The thing was, Reed was ashamed. He'd been a young, stupid teenager, distracted by a pretty face, and he'd ended up hurting a girl who'd been his friend for so many years they didn't bother to keep track anymore. It was one more thing in a long list of shitty things he'd done in his life.

At the time, Claire had felt impossible. Like she didn't exist and that if he didn't grab hold and do everything he could to keep her, she would disappear as if she'd never been there in the first place. Serotonin was a powerful chemical, especially in idiot boys who hadn't had sex yet despite having a girlfriend all summer.

He wasn't proud of his actions; he almost wished Tess were there to give him hell for being such a jackass.

But normally he'd wear a mask, fake an understanding smile, smooth it over. Instead he dropped his chin, scratched his nose, rounded his shoulders so that his regret could be read clearly in the lines of his body—an apology neither of them would be out of line to ignore.

"She really didn't say anything to you, Reed?" Lena asked. "No grand plans she'd been scheming up for weeks? Didn't mention hoarding money, or anything?"

"No." He tangled his fingers together in his lap, pressing his thumb into the hard point of his knuckle.

"Not sure he was paying too close attention at that point," Fiona muttered ruthlessly. "The thing is, Tess snuck out that night—that wasn't unusual. But she didn't take anything with her."

Both Reed and Lena looked over at that. Lena found her voice first. "Nothing?"

"Just what she was wearing and her purse," Fiona said. "Watched her from the window to make sure she'd made it to the ground okay."

Lena's foot tapped out an uneven rhythm. "That doesn't make any sense."

"That's what I've been *saying*," Fiona said with exaggerated emphasis. "But that's not the worst bit."

"There's more?" Lena's eyebrows rose.

Fiona nodded and levered herself up to her feet, sliding on reading glasses as she did.

Reed kept scratching at his knuckle, a ringing in his ears. He didn't know why he was braced for a blow, but he'd taken enough to know the way his body prepared.

When Fiona shuffled back toward them, she held a plastic ziplock bag with a scrap of paper inside. "Found that on the desk in the room she'd stayed in when she was here."

Lena took it almost reverently, and a part of Reed remembered how close the girls had been, neither of them jealous of the other, despite Tess ending up with Reed. Lena had loved Tess like a sister, would have taken a bullet for her if necessary.

Now, she inhaled as she read the short message. When she went to hand it over to him, she paused, her eyes tracing over his face, before she held it out all the way. His hands didn't shake because he'd spent years making sure they didn't give him away.

On the carefully preserved ripped notebook page was his own familiar scrawl.

*Meet me at our place at 10 tonight.*

# CHAPTER
# TWENTY-FIVE

## GRETCHEN

*Now—*

"Tess Murphy," Gretchen said as they walked into Shaughnessy's office. There was someone standing at Shaughnessy's desk, a folder in his hand, clearly cut off midsentence by their entrance. But the kid scampered off like a good boy after one pointed look from Gretchen.

"Who, what, now?" Shaughnessy shot back.

"Tess. Murphy," Gretchen repeated with exaggerated emphasis.

"Sweetheart, I've worked in Boston for decades," Shaughnessy said, gesturing for both her and Marconi to sit. "If you think the name Tess Murphy means anything to me, I have a few Irish neighborhoods to introduce you to."

"Fair," Marconi muttered, and shrugged when Gretchen glared.

"You bleeding hearts act like everyone you come in contact with is the most worthwhile person you've ever met, and you don't remember a seventeen-year-old girl who turned into a cold case?" Gretchen asked, going deliberately for shame and guilt. They were both solid manipulation tactics.

But Shaughnessy was onto her, and by this point Gretchen guessed Marconi was, too. That pleased her for reasons she would look into later but suspected had something to do with the fact that her closest friend had just died, and that took the number of people who understood her down to a tragically low number.

"Dismount from your high horse, if you please," Shaughnessy said, and Gretchen laughed. When he waved a hand, she turned over the file.

She watched his face closely, but he gave little away as he scanned the picture and details, his fingers tracing over and over the place on his own face where a mustache would live if he had one.

After a few minutes, he tossed the folder onto the desk between them. "I gotta be honest, the thing I remember most about this case is that the aunt calls in every once in a while."

"There was nothing that screamed foul play?" Gretchen asked. "Nothing that made you think it wasn't your run-of-the-mill runaway?"

"Nope." Shaughnessy sat back, crossing his hands over his belly. "These cases are a dime a dozen. Families want to believe their kid couldn't be a runaway, so you gotta go through the motions. But there was never any evidence she was anything other than a troubled kid who wanted to get out."

Even Marconi was nodding along.

"No inkling that this was murder, then?" Gretchen clarified.

"Eh." Shaughnessy lifted a shoulder. "No, not that I remember. The aunt was convinced the boyfriend had killed her. But we never found a body. Teenage boys? Not exactly known for being tidy."

Gretchen guessed that in his quick scan, Shaughnessy had missed a key name. "What if I told you that very boyfriend was Reed Kent?"

Shaughnessy sat up so suddenly his chair yowled in protest. He leaned on his desk, his eyes intense. "He's been connected to two different murders?"

Once a coincidence . . .

Marconi piped up. "Over the span of two decades."

"How many civilians have even encountered one?" Gretchen said, and Shaughnessy nodded.

"True," Marconi conceded. "So, what are we thinking? That Reed Kent killed his high school sweetheart and then killed his wife?"

Shaughnessy's body lurched forward. "Wait, wait, wait."

Gretchen wanted to slam her forehead into the desk.

"Who said anything about Kent murdering his wife?" Shaughnessy asked.

Marconi winced and Gretchen just rolled her eyes, consigning her promise to Viola to hell. "If you want to bury your head in the sand and blame the girl, fine. But you can't deny there's something strange going on here. Ordinary people don't end up connected to separate murders."

"And at least three deaths if you count Lena Booker," Marconi added.

"Okay, just for the moment I'm going to ignore the Claire Kent thing," Shaughnessy said, though he paused as if he wasn't really going to leave the topic. Then he shook himself like a dog and refocused. "I dug around the kid's—God, Reed Kent's—life back then when I first got handed the case. Beyond the aunt, no one really thought he was a killer. They just didn't have another viable suspect."

*Another viable suspect.* The words might as well be branded into Gretchen's skin for how familiar they were. That's what they'd always said about her aunt Rowan's case.

Couldn't find *another viable suspect*, so it must have been the eight-year-old. Never mind that the assumption had burdened said eight-year-old with a lifetime of suspicion and a reputation that she had never been quite able to shake no matter how upstanding a citizen she'd proven herself to be.

Shaughnessy must have read the tension in her face, because he exhaled, loud and exasperated. "Look, even if he was somehow involved in the high school girlfriend's disappearance, you have to admit he has a solid alibi for his wife's murder."

"That he or Declan Murphy or a combination of them orchestrated," Gretchen said.

That got Shaughnessy's attention. "What?"

"The reason Reed Kent was at the casino that night was because the brother of that disappeared high school sweetheart told Reed to go there," Gretchen informed him while trying not to gloat about the ace card she'd just played.

"Well, he gave him his box to use anytime," Marconi qualified and ignored Gretchen's disgruntled glare. "Reed Kent could have just seized upon a convenient alibi, and Declan might not have been involved at all."

"Seems a little too convenient to be coincidence, doesn't it?" Gretchen drawled.

Shaughnessy plucked at his lower lip. "Draw me a picture. What's happening here?"

The problem was that Gretchen couldn't quite make it come into focus even for herself yet. But she was as good as the next person at spinning bullshit until it sounded convincing. "What if Claire Kent found out something about the old case?" she started, without an end in sight. "Something about Tess's . . . murder, if it was a murder."

"They were friends back in the day," Marconi said slowly.

"Who was?" Shaughnessy interrupted.

"The whole cast of players." Marconi waved a hand as if to encompass them. "But Tess Murphy, Lena Booker, and Reed Kent seemed to be the linchpins."

"Claire came in late in the game. Declan Murphy and Ainsley Kent were the younger siblings," Gretchen noted. "But that doesn't mean they didn't play a role in whatever happened."

"You're making it more suspicious than it is," Shaughnessy said. "So Kent remained friends with Declan Murphy. That doesn't make either of them guilty of anything."

Gretchen jumped on that. "They hadn't. The Kents were sporadic donors at best. That's it. Not friends."

"And Declan got squirrelly when we pushed too hard about why he didn't want us reopening the case," Marconi pointed out.

"That's right," Gretchen said. "That's when he lawyered up."

"He brought in a lawyer?" Shaughnessy sat up a little straighter at that.

"Well, he politely suggested we contact his," Gretchen said. "But half a dozen one way."

"And he was talking freely before that?" Shaughnessy checked.

Marconi tipped her hand back and forth and Gretchen lifted one shoulder. "I'm not certain he wasn't lying out of his you-know-what, but for the most part he didn't seem to be trying to shut us down."

"Lying?" Shaughnessy asked.

"I had the feeling that he and the late Mrs. Kent were a bit more friendly than he was with Reed," Marconi said, picking her words carefully.

"They were screwing?" Shaughnessy said, his pure Boston accent seeping through.

Gretchen grinned. "I had the same impression."

"Affair gone wrong?"

"I don't know," Gretchen said. "Declan and Reed got in a fistfight about two months before Claire died. Could have something to do with it."

Shaughnessy whistled. "Well, now, that's interesting."

"He claims it was because Lena had convinced him that Reed killed Tess all those years ago," Gretchen said.

What Gretchen desperately wished she'd had was Lena's reasoning for making Declan think that Reed was guilty. Gretchen remained convinced that Lena had, at the very least, been important to Reed Kent. So what had convinced Lena to turn on him? The evidence must have been strong. And why the act with Fiona Murphy? Gretchen guessed whatever the woman had shown Reed was evidence that could make him feel guilty if he was the killer. What happened between that visit and Lena taking Viola's case?

"So, Lena Booker and Reed Kent both start poking into the disappearance of their friend from twenty years ago and then Reed's wife ends up dead," Marconi said, laying it out. "And everyone's lying to us about it."

"Ainsley Kent essentially showed us the door when Declan was mentioned," Gretchen said.

"And that's Reed Kent's sister?" Shaughnessy asked.

"She's staying with him to help with the kids," Marconi said. "Or so she says."

They sat with that for a second, before Gretchen jerked her chin toward Shaughnessy's computer. "Do you have the coroner's report on Claire Kent?"

"If I dig for it, yeah," Shaughnessy said, already tapping the mouse. "What are you thinking?"

"Was there any amount of time in the TOD window where Reed Kent was unaccounted for?" Gretchen asked.

The office fell silent as Shaughnessy typed away. "All right, time of death was somewhere between ten p.m. and two a.m."

"And the first time Kent is caught on tape?"

The keyboard clattered beneath Shaughnessy's clumsy fingers. "10:06 p.m."

"Windows are called windows for a reason," Marconi ventured, but it was weak.

"Let's game it out," Gretchen said. "Let's say the coroner was a half hour off, which is plausible."

"Not likely," Shaughnessy muttered.

"But plausible," Gretchen said, stressing the words and waiting for his begrudging nod of acknowledgment before continuing. "Reed said he caught a cab a few blocks from home. The casino is how far from the Kents' town house?"

"Twenty minutes or so, but with traffic . . ." Shaughnessy shrugged.

"He would have had to stab her, run down the stairs, chase down a taxi, and have everything work in his favor to hit that time stamp," Gretchen summed up. "That's risky."

And bloody. From those stab wounds, Reed would have had enough spatter he'd have to change and hide his clothes, maybe even scrub down enough to be passable.

"If he had it planned out, maybe that's part of his strategy," Marconi suggested. "Making the window look so implausible that no one would even think to question it."

"Well, it is implausible," Shaughnessy pointed out.

"But not impossible," Gretchen murmured. Though it seemed much tighter than she would have thought it would be. "Did you confirm with the taxi company?"

Shaughnessy shot her a disgruntled look, and she just shrugged.

"Timeline matches up with the driver's logs," Shaughnessy said by way of an answer.

The taxi could be part of the plan, to extend the alibi as much as possible. But why take that chance when the Kents kept a car in their garage? That would have been a far safer choice than interacting with someone who would surely be interviewed by the cops. "He was at home until that?"

"That's what he says," Shaughnessy said, holding up his hands. "No reason to doubt that."

Gretchen swallowed the harsh reprimand that probably would have slipped out ten years ago. She had better control these days, but she let herself silently vent. Even in an open-and-shut case like this, not getting a corroborated timeline from the husband of the victim was just sheer laziness. Gretchen exhaled, counted backward from twenty, and then rolled her shoulders. "All right, that leaves two options, beyond the obvious."

"That the sadistic psychopath actually did kill the mother?" Shaughnessy said, a little twist to his words. "I'm all ears for the others."

"Organized sadistic psychopath," Gretchen felt compelled to say. Maybe Viola had gotten sloppy, unable to process the overwhelming rush that had come with actually taking a life—not just any life but her mother's at that. But Gretchen sincerely doubted it. Organized psychopaths didn't break their patterns, even young ones. "One, Reed Kent had an accomplice."

"Believable," Marconi said.

"Or Declan Murphy wanted Reed out of the house to do it himself."

Shaughnessy's lips pursed, and she could tell he was intrigued by that one. "Motive?"

"Like you said, affair gone wrong," Marconi suggested. "Claire wouldn't leave her husband for him. Declan gets jealous and arranges for Reed to be out of the house."

It would explain why Ainsley had tensed at the mention of Declan, if she'd known about the infidelity. And why Declan had lawyered up when he sensed them circling around his connection to Reed Kent.

"Maybe," Gretchen said. "Would he have known that Viola would be an easy patsy?"

Because it seemed like the Kents had put their energy into making sure no one else knew about Viola's disorder. Would Claire really have told her lover about Viola's violent tendencies? Would Declan have thought to take advantage of that? "The cops knew to look in Viola's drawer."

"Right," Marconi said, seeming to catch up to Gretchen's thought process. "Who told the uniforms on the scene?"

They both looked toward Shaughnessy, who was chewing on his lip. "Must have been Reed Kent."

That seemed to close the door on whether Reed was completely innocent. If he hadn't been involved in the murder, why would he have told them to search his daughter's room for evidence? Gretchen was fairly convinced the girl had been framed. She would guess that if Reed was the one telling cops to search his daughter's room, he was the one who had done it.

But he also had a nearly airtight alibi.

"I guess we've landed on the accomplice option," Marconi summed up.

Shaughnessy coughed, shifted in his seat, glanced at Marconi as if Gretchen didn't know exactly what he was thinking. Still, she wasn't going to help him say it.

*I messed up, Gretch.*

The conclusion was an obvious one.

After longer than she would have thought, he finally spit out, "So where does Lena Booker come into this?"

Because now, with this new information, what her death looked like was self-medicated *guilt*.

And if they were searching for Reed's accomplice, there was one logical choice.

"Get me in with Viola again," Gretchen said, pushing to her feet, not waiting for a response. What she needed right now was a wild card. And she knew just where to find it.

Marconi stood, but Gretchen shook her head. "I'm taking the rest of the day off."

Shaughnessy and Marconi exchanged a skeptical glance that Gretchen ignored.

"If you try to follow me, I'll slash your tires," Gretchen sang out cheerily as she sailed out the door.

She heard Shaughnessy sigh behind her. "Don't test her. She's done it before."

# CHAPTER TWENTY-SIX

## REED

*Six months before Claire's death—*

Reed knew that women liked looking at him. Their interest tended to wane after they'd slept with him, but he'd be a hypocrite to want them to fall in love, so he didn't mind. Few were deterred by the gold ring on his left hand.

He didn't know why he'd thought Lena Booker would be.

Two weeks after Lena had come back into his life during a chance encounter at Starbucks, she slid into a booth across from him at his favorite guilty-pleasure diner.

Reed kept watching her face, not the one across from him but the one plastered all over the TV that hung on the far wall. He didn't want Lena hitting on him, and he couldn't say exactly why. It wasn't that he was faithful to Claire—that ship had sailed a long time ago. But his memories of Lena Booker were tinged with innocence, with friendship. For some reason, he found himself reluctant to taint them.

A bell rang, and a moment later buttery eggs and bacon were shoved under his nose. He smiled his thanks to Mellie, who rolled her eyes.

There was something refreshing about someone who could withstand the charm that came so easily to him.

"Just coffee," Lena said, speaking for the first time since she'd sat down.

"Look, I . . ." Reed didn't know what to say. He was pretty sure *I'm flattered* would get him slapped. He ran a hand over his face, too tired for this.

Lena's disbelieving laugh rang sharp and clear. "My God, the arrogance on you. I forgot about that."

Reed dropped his palm to the table once more. "I'm sorry?"

"I'm not stalking you," Lena said, and took a sip of the black coffee Mellie had just delivered. "To throw myself at you."

Amusement, derision, and something that might creep close to fondness slid into the words, and Reed huffed out an embarrassed breath. "Do you blame me? I haven't seen you in twenty years and then twice in two weeks?"

Lena watched him over the rim of her mug. "All right, fine. I need your help."

Reed paused at that, fork halfway to his mouth. It had been a long time since someone looked to him for help. "For what?"

"Tess Murphy," Lena said, and there was a hint of something there in her voice that he couldn't place. "You remember her, right?"

If it had been anyone else, Reed would have said the question was caustic. But Lena softened it with a muted version of that smile that had been on the TV screens. It gave him a moment to recover from hearing the name. "Uh, yeah."

Lena scrunched her nose at his nonreaction and looked away, her arm slung over the back of the booth. "I'm pretty sure she was murdered."

Reed didn't flinch, didn't pause in shoveling the food into his mouth, no matter that it no longer tasted of anything but dust. He nodded in the right places, hummed sympathetically in others while

Lena told him how she was investigating the disappearance. Just poking around a little, nothing serious. Maybe he could help?

Reed could feel the heavy weight of her eyes on him throughout. He hadn't managed to meet hers since she'd said Tess's name.

His body ached with holding still, holding rigid, holding his placid expression in place as Lena filled him in on what she'd found—not much yet—and whom she planned to talk to next.

The relief that came with her departure nearly winded him.

Even Mellie swung by. "You okay, hon?"

Reed imagined he answered yes, thought he left money on the table as he stood up. But everything blurred and shaded into black and white as panic laced his bloodstream.

He didn't remember how he got back to the town house, but it felt like in the next blink he was kneeling on the dusty floorboards in the attic, bloodless fingers pushing aside quilts and photobooks in search of . . . in search of . . . in search of . . .

Ah.

His hand closed around the box, pulled it out. He let the momentum propel him back onto his ass, scooting across the floor until his spine pressed up against an exposed beam.

The air was thin around him, or maybe that was just his lungs. Still, he forced himself to open the box that he never thought would see the light of day again.

And all he could do was blink down at the empty space where a bracelet used to be.

# CHAPTER TWENTY-SEVEN

## GRETCHEN

*Now—*

The passenger-side door of the Porsche opened just as Gretchen was about to slam on the gas.

Gretchen silently repeated her *I'll slash your tires* threat with a single raised eyebrow.

Marconi's mouth tilted up as she settled into the seat. "I don't own a car."

The little . . .

Gretchen absolutely did not grin as she gunned it out of the police station's parking lot.

"Do you trust me?" Gretchen eventually asked Marconi as she took a sharp left that had them careening over the sidewalk's curb a block from their destination.

"Absolutely not even a little bit," Marconi responded as the car righted itself.

"Fantastic," Gretchen said, all bright and cheery, as if she'd heard only Marconi's first word.

She didn't explain as she headed deep into Southie, didn't explain how she knew the streets so well, either. Just pulled to a stop outside a pub so Irish it didn't even need a name. It just needed the flag and a neon shamrock sign so people knew what kind of place it was.

"You're not even locking it here?" Marconi asked as she climbed out of the Porsche, glancing around at some of the battered front porches, the cardboard in the windows. People thought because Gretchen was raised in wealth she didn't know about this side of town. But she did, too well.

And she knew no one here would touch her baby.

Gretchen didn't bother wasting breath explaining that to Marconi. She simply pulled her bag out of the back and started digging inside. The first thing to go was the blazer—that was obvious. She shucked her professional blouse, right there in the street. Marconi made some kind of sound, but Gretchen was already sliding the stretchy black tee over her head to cover her bra. "Prude."

"Uh, cop, more like it," Marconi said, her back to Gretchen now. "Ever heard of indecent exposure?"

"Not worse than a bathing suit," Gretchen countered as she used a bit of the gel she always traveled with to slick her hair back away from her face. With her faded jeans, she was pretty confident she nailed the look. She shoved everything into her bag, tossed it into the back seat, and headed for the pub's door.

"Who are you and what have you done with Dr. Gretchen White?" Marconi murmured behind her, and Gretchen turned to flash her a bright smile.

"You've never heard of adapting to your surroundings?" she asked as she used her butt to push through the door.

Marconi's response was lost to the surge of noise, the jukebox that blared Billy Joel just like she knew it would, the clack of pool sticks on balls, the high buzz of waitresses' voices calling out orders, the rowdy laughter of some boys in the corner watching some game, the clink of beer pints on wood.

Gretchen took a quick glance around for Shaughnessy's minions, who could be found there at least three nights of the week along with him. It was all clear, so she turned her attention to finding her real target.

And there, there he was. In the back, in a booth, poring over what she knew would be horse racing charts. Ryan Kelly had a weakness, and it could be exploited. But she wasn't about to press on that sore spot tonight. No, Kelly would give over his information easily if she simply paid for his round.

"Did you miss me?" Gretchen asked as she slid into the bench seat across from him.

"Desperately, darling," Ryan Kelly purred back, the hint of Irish in his voice distant. She knew it got thicker the more pints he'd put away, and she was a little disappointed that he wasn't further along on his nightly pursuit of sailing three sheets to the wind.

His eyes shifted to Marconi, and there was something predatory about the way he looked at her that Gretchen found displeasing. She snapped in his face. "Not for you."

"Aw, Gretch, you know you're the only woman I want," Kelly said, a bald-faced lie that was fun to play around with.

"Detective Lauren Marconi." Marconi leaned heavy on the honorific.

Kelly held his hands up like he was the very picture of innocence. "Whatever Gretchen told you I did, I'm innocent, I swear."

It was funny because Kelly had probably not stepped a toe out of line his whole entire life. His only weaknesses were the booze and the gambling, and, really, who couldn't forgive him those vices in this hard, hard life?

Marconi didn't say anything, and Gretchen realized that was her MO when faced with a situation she didn't quite fully grasp. Silent observation. It wasn't Gretchen's preferred method, but she couldn't deny it was probably effective.

"Kelly, your glass looks empty," Gretchen said, despite the fact that there was half a Guinness left in it. His mouth twitched in that way of his, and he downed the dark liquid in one swallow.

"You always had a fine eye for things, Gretch," Kelly said, slamming the heavy glass back on the table and motioning to a waitress. "Bridget dear, when you get a moment?"

The waitress rolled her eyes but nodded as she went to take the orders of the college boys who'd just commandeered a booth at the front of the dark, little pub.

Kelly sighed a little morosely at his racing charts, but then folded up the paper and shoved it under his butt. "What can I do you ladies for?"

Ryan Kelly was an everyman kind of handsome. Pleasing but not attention catching, with dark hair and dark eyes, a square chin, and a patrician nose. He had a lean, wiry build that spoke of too much caffeine and too many skipped lunches, and his fingers shook when he wasn't actively playing with something. Right now, it was the saltshaker as he eyed them both.

"Marconi, this is Ryan Kelly of the *Boston Crier,*" Gretchen said. Marconi's eyes widened slightly at the mention of the most infamous and trashy tabloid the city had to offer.

"Charmed, I'm sure." Kelly gladly accepted the new Guinness that was thrust into his hands and didn't even blink as the beer sloshed over his wrist.

Gretchen had met Kelly years ago, when he'd been fresh out of journalism school and thinking he was going to do big things and take down big names. Then he'd realized the *Crier* was nothing but a soap opera in print, and the shine was gone. Gretchen found his complete lack of giving a shit endearing, and he found her brutal honesty hilarious. A match made in heaven, practically.

Like everything else in this town and Gretchen's life really, the relationship was parasitic. Gretchen gave Kelly tips before other reporters, and Kelly gave her the gossip on the street for the low, low price of alcohol.

It had proven a very successful friendship.

"You're covering Claire Kent's death?" Gretchen asked.

Kelly laughed as he wiped away the tail end of a foam mustache. "I think there's a statue of her in the *Crier's* lobby these days."

"Or Viola," Gretchen suggested.

Kelly touched his nose and then pointed at her like she'd gotten it right in one. "Fair point, Gretch. Like always."

"Is there any chatter about the death being anything other than it seems?" Gretchen asked, knowing that Kelly had a wealth of information they could tap but also knowing she had to ask the right questions to get it.

"You mean not the thirteen-year-old psycho?" Kelly asked. "Nah, everyone's pinned it on her. She sells well."

Gretchen nodded and wondered what the coverage of Rowan's death must have been like back then.

"Any talk of any . . . extramarital activities with the Kents?" Gretchen tried, as delicately as she knew how.

But Kelly's eyes went wide in such a way that she figured she'd missed the boat on subtle. "That dirty bastard. He was cheating on her?" Then his face lit up. "Or, God, was she cheating on him? People would eat that up."

"Neither that I know of," Gretchen admitted, finding herself wanting to give in to the drama of it. "But I take it there's no gossip on them?"

"Harvard sweethearts turned tragedy," Kelly said. "And a husband that isn't the killer? TV producers are practically setting up camp outside his door to sign him for the next season of *The Bachelor*."

When neither Gretchen nor Marconi laughed, he muttered into his glass something about being underappreciated among cultural snobs.

"What about Declan Murphy?" Marconi asked.

"Did he kill a prostitute?" Kelly asked with avid interest, his eyes ping-ponging between them, his forearms on the table. "I'd make twenty bucks if he did."

"Why do you have money on him killing a sex worker?" Gretchen asked. Declan had struck her as nonviolent—even on the off chance he was a sociopath. She predicted he was going to have a long career in Congress if he wasn't involved with this case in some way.

"No one's that perfect, right?" Kelly lifted a shoulder. "I'm just waiting for his skeletons to be unearthed."

"So you have no new information for me whatsoever?" Gretchen asked.

"Now, did I say that?" Kelly asked with an obnoxious wink. He knew he could get away with it because she wanted something from him. But Gretchen plotted ways to make him pay for the audacity later. "Anyway, even if I didn't, you came to me, lady. I wasn't out there soliciting your favors."

Gretchen couldn't deny he was right. There was always a chance he wouldn't have anything, but more often than not he had a bead on the gossip that wouldn't make it to any cop's ear.

Instead of admitting that, Gretchen leaned forward, knowing what it did to the front of her stretchy black T-shirt. More specifically, she knew that it provided a peek at the lace of her bra, at the shadows that hinted at something more. Gretchen looked up at him through her eyelashes and pouted. She thought she heard Marconi make some strangled noise that probably would have sounded like a scoff if she hadn't covered it with a cough.

"And if you were out there soliciting?" Gretchen teased, voice drenched in innuendo. "What would you tell me in exchange for a . . . favor."

"Oh my God," Marconi said under her breath.

Kelly didn't take his eyes off Gretchen. "I'd say that pretty little lawyer friend of yours had dinner with Reed Kent the night of his wife's death."

That surprised Gretchen enough that she dropped the act. "Lena?"

"Yup," Kelly said with a nod, back to his normal cocky grin. The air of expectation that had woven around them completely dissipated. Though they'd slept together a time or two, they hardly needed these tiresome games to initiate it. That could be done with a text message. "I've got eyes and ears out on the family's known associates. A mention of it got dropped in a normal report—didn't think much of it until she took the case a few months later and everyone was out there acting like she didn't have a connection to the Kents. The cops never followed it up, though, so I figured it was a dead end."

"Christ," Marconi breathed out and banged her head gently against the wall. "Who missed that on the timeline?"

"Guess it wasn't so much a dead end as a missed turn, huh?" Kelly was watching them with those greedy eyes of his, the ones that made him her go-to, the ones that kept him in good beer and nice ties—another weakness of his, though that probably didn't really count as one. She eyed the red-and-black tie he wore now and made a mental note to send him something special for this nugget. The information, even as good as it had been, certainly wasn't worth the kind of favor she'd suggested.

"Do you remember the name of the restaurant?" Gretchen asked. Kelly was good with those sorts of details, good enough that she suspected he had some kind of eidetic memory, either auditory or visual, though he'd never confirmed that.

"La Mer," he said with an arrogant little smile, because he knew he was good at this, and that she owed him big. She was pretty sure La Mer was somewhat near the Kents' town house. She could almost picture driving by it just a few hours earlier.

Gretchen snagged the wrist of the passing waitress. "Bridget, the rest of the night his drinks are on my tab."

"Lucky you," Bridget said, but nodded, taking Gretchen's card as she did.

"But there was no talk of infidelity?" Gretchen checked again. If someone had made her repeat something she'd already confirmed, she would have walked away from the conversation, but she found others didn't have her hair trigger when it came to things like that. They were more lenient toward inanity, and so why not take advantage of that?

"The dinner wasn't on the down low," Kelly said, sizing up the last quarter of his beer before downing it in one go. He smiled big and toothy when Bridget came back with both Gretchen's card and a refill. "Those things only get noticed if everyone's being sneaky about it. You know that."

He'd pointed one of his long fingers almost into Gretchen's face. And she took the moment to remind him that she didn't tolerate such behavior. Kelly jerked his hand out of the way just before her teeth would have dug into skin.

"Naughty kitty," he scolded.

"Gross," Marconi said with a slight shove at Gretchen's hip. Gretchen took the hint and stood. Marconi was quick to follow.

"Don't be jealous," Kelly crooned up at Marconi. "You can join in, too, gorgeous."

In the next instant, Marconi had her hand pressed into Kelly's throat, snug up against his jaw in the perfect position to cut off his air supply. Gretchen leaned to the side to get a better view, giddy at this new development.

"If you ever make me think about your dick again, I'll rip your balls off," Marconi said, in a perfectly calm voice, which made it all the more effective. "Got it?"

"Yes, ma'am," Kelly choked out in a tone that suggested he wasn't so much scared as turned on by the situation.

Marconi pressed in tighter with the curve of her hand until he nodded, this time without the extra attitude. Then Marconi turned and walked past Gretchen without another word. Gretchen resisted applauding, but only just.

Kelly rubbed at his throat, his smile back in force. "I'm only giving you this because you're about to pay for quite the binge."

"Yes," Gretchen said. "What?"

"Talk to Penny Langford," Kelly said, a little hoarsely. "She was Claire Kent's number two at that foundation of hers. If anyone has anything . . ."

"It's her," Gretchen murmured.

When she started for the door, Kelly stopped her.

"Hey, Gretch." He waited until she turned toward him. "I like your new babysitter."

Gretchen rolled her eyes. "Try not to drink yourself into a stupor."

She didn't mention the part where she thought she might agree with him.

# CHAPTER TWENTY-EIGHT

## REED

*Six months before Claire's death—*

Reed flinched when the hand landed on his biceps. It was a gentle touch, but his body always seemed braced for a hit these days. He fumbled with the coins in his hand.

The owner of the hand laughed out a soft apology, the kind Reed knew well. The kind that was surprised at his surprise. The kind that carried pity in its wake.

"I'm sorry, I just . . . Reed?" The voice, the melodic yet husky timbre of it, was familiar first before the face, before the name. "Reed Kent, right? I thought that was you."

*Lena.*

He turned, slapping on a smile that felt slightly less fake than the ones he usually wore these days. "Lena Booker."

She was slick nowadays, that's all he could think. Sleek like a panther, worlds different from the Southie tomboy he'd known once upon a time, the one with frizzy hair who'd worn her mud stains and bloody scrapes as badges of honor.

Still beautiful. Always had been. Her strawberry-blonde hair had deepened—whether through age or a salon—into a tangled mess of auburn and purple and cherry that fell in loose curls down her back. Her heart-shaped face was as pale as always, though the sprinkle of freckles he'd always found endearing were nowhere to be seen.

As Reed took her in, Lena's body swayed toward his as it always had, then visibly stilled, like she was stopping herself from hugging him, uncertainty flitting over her face only to be snuffed into a non-expression. Because he'd flinched before, because he'd been such a goddamn—weak, pitiful, fragile—coward that he couldn't handle being touched unexpectedly in public.

He refused to let the tension settle, not with Lena Booker. He would have possibly broken down and cried if they were stiff with each other now. Instead, he gathered her in his arms, in an embrace that was far more familiar and casual than warranted from two childhood friends who hadn't seen each other since they were teenagers. But he couldn't resist pressing in close, as if she could offer a blessed port in a storm—right in the middle of this crowded Starbucks.

"Reed," she murmured, her hand cupping the nape of his neck, her thumb brushing against the fine hair there. "It's good to see you."

He swallowed. He nodded. And then he stepped back.

Even after all these years he could read her concern clearly in the way her tongue touched the corner of her lips, in how her fingers toyed with one of the buttons on her well-fitted blouse.

She didn't pry. "How are you?"

Before he could respond—a lie, because he couldn't remember the last time he'd given an honest answer to that particular question—the barista cleared her throat.

As he shuffled into place in front of the cashier, he tipped his head toward the menu, his eyes still on Lena. "Can I get you something?"

She let him buy her coffee, stood, and made small talk as they waited for their orders. Somehow without him realizing how he'd accomplished it, she allowed him to direct her into a two-person table in the far corner of the crowded store.

Reed sat with his back to the wall and wondered if the choice had been as obvious to her as it seemed to him.

"How are you?" Lena asked again. She reached out, brushing his knuckles. His hand stilled beneath the gentle touch. "Reed. How are you, really?"

There were words he could pull out, empty and meaningless; expressions he could don, practiced and shallow. Most people bought them, didn't bother to look any further to the darkness beneath. But Lena had always been able to see his darkness.

Maybe because it matched her own.

His lips twisted, his tongue heavy. He hadn't done anything but weave false stories for years now. What did honesty taste like?

"Is it Claire?" Lena asked, soft despite the bitterness that must have lingered there. Neither of them had talked about it, but their friendship had withered about the time Claire had come into his life. Lena had to realize that hadn't been a coincidence.

He shook his head. "No."

Reed stared down at the well-manicured fingers still resting on top of his. So much like Claire's. So much like all the women in his life. Impeccably maintained.

"Your job?"

Laughing beneath his breath, Reed shook his head. She wasn't going to be able to guess. Who would ever be able to guess?

When he met her eyes, he almost let it spill out, every terrible thing that pressed into his skin like bruises, that dug into his flesh and scraped at his bones. But he'd been careful, so careful, for too long to risk it now.

The lie came almost as easy as breathing. "It's my daughter. Viola."

# CHAPTER TWENTY-NINE

## GRETCHEN

*Now—*

Penny Langford looked like the type of woman who you'd want to hand over the keys of the world to in the midst of a crisis.

She was tall, whip thin, with a buzz cut she wore with the confidence of a military general. Her deep-brown eyes were a shade darker than her skin, and everything about her, from the way she stood to the way she watched them to the way her mouth pursed just slightly when she looked at Gretchen, screamed competence.

Gretchen hated women like Penny Langford because they tended to see through any performance she put on. While Gretchen knew that most things about herself were smoke and mirrors, she didn't particularly enjoy it when other people noticed.

Marconi seemed to take to her immediately, and Gretchen wasn't surprised, but she was annoyed and jealous, and feeling petty about both. It made her want to seduce Penny into liking her more than Marconi, but Gretchen knew through painful trial and error that would be a terrible move.

So instead she hung back a little, toned down the charisma that was usually her go-to when meeting intimidating people, and let Marconi take the lead making introductions.

They settled into Penny's corner office, the view of the harbor impressive for a charitable foundation.

"Claire never wanted to sacrifice aesthetics if she didn't have to," Penny said. There was a complicated blend of emotions in her voice that Gretchen couldn't decipher. But a hint of grief lay underneath it, and Gretchen decided that Penny had, at the very least, been sad her boss had died.

"Will the foundation continue?" Gretchen asked, and Penny shot her a thoughtful look. "With Claire gone?"

"Claire was our primary funder, and Mr. Kent has not expressed any interest in continuing that support," Penny answered, and Gretchen gave her points for her diplomacy. "While our trust has other generous donors, we may not be able to keep on at the level we had been."

"She didn't set any safeguards in the event of her death?"

"We had talked about it," Penny said, seeming hesitant to admit it for some reason. "But had never gotten around to finalizing the paperwork."

"Which would have done what?"

"Left a sizable portion of her vast fortune to the trust," Penny said, her eyes flicking to Marconi before coming back to Gretchen.

Everyone seemed to think the badge made Marconi the more dangerous of the two of them. That was fine with Gretchen.

"But since she didn't go through with it, that money went to . . ." Gretchen let it dangle, wanting Penny to actually be the one who said it.

"Her husband." Penny's voice was neutral, and Gretchen guessed that's why she was being so careful with her words. That answer alone could be—at least implicitly—a serious accusation.

"Did anyone ever interview you after Claire was killed?" Gretchen asked, and she could almost feel the whisper of one thin layer of suspicion dropping from the wall Penny had put up around herself.

"No, they did not."

This case truly was a study in confirmation bias. Once the idea had been planted that Viola was the guilty party, a vicious cycle churned until it had become almost impossible to think that anyone other than Viola could have killed Claire. Assumptions had become reality.

Marconi looked like she was about to start in on some gentle probing to work them around to any suspicions Penny might have had about Reed Kent, but now that some of Gretchen's nerves had calmed, she could read the room better.

Despite her caution, Penny seemed like a take-no-prisoners kind of woman who wouldn't be thrown by tough questions.

"What do you think happened that night?" Gretchen asked just as Marconi had been about to speak. "The night Claire died."

Penny stared at her for a long time. "You mean the night she was murdered."

Gretchen nodded at the correction and took a chance. "You don't think it was Viola."

It was only when Penny sat back in her chair that Gretchen realized how tense the woman had been, how much she'd clearly been braced for battle. That complicated blend of emotion that Gretchen had heard in her voice fluttered in quick succession over her face. When the neutral mask was back in place, Penny sighed.

"No," Penny said, finally. "I do think the girl is capable of it. I've met her."

They all shared a look.

Then Penny held up a hand stopping the next question. "But I don't think Reed Kent had the guts to do it, either."

"Why do you say that?"

Penny tilted her head. "Have you talked to him?"

"Briefly."

She chewed on her bottom lip, looking like she was trying to figure out the best way to put it. "He likes playing the victim."

That hadn't been what Gretchen had expected. "How so?"

"Claire would hate that I was talking about this," Penny said more to herself than to them. Then she straightened a bit. "But Claire's dead."

Gretchen and Marconi both nodded despite the fact that the statement needed no verification.

"She didn't talk about him much toward the end," Penny continued, more determined now. "But we'd drink a glass of wine or two when we got stuck here late. And she'd rant a little."

"About Reed?"

"I know I was only getting one side of the story," Penny prefaced her answer. "But yes. She asked him to do marriage counseling, especially once Viola started acting out more. Asked him to do couples retreats or vacations. Asked him to do *something*. He just refused to work on their marriage even though they both knew they had problems."

"Did she offer him an ultimatum?"

"She hadn't, no," Penny said. "But I was guessing it wasn't far off."

"So you would say their marriage was troubled?" This on top of Declan's tone when talking about Claire made Gretchen all the more curious how rumors of a shaky relationship hadn't been on the front page of every tabloid in the city.

"He just seemed to have a different version of reality than her," Penny said with a little shrug. "Everything that came out of her mouth he took as an insult, didn't ever give her the benefit of the doubt, things like that. He started getting real moody and quiet toward the end there." She paused but didn't wait to be prodded. "Claire thought it might be an affair at first."

"It wasn't?"

"She shut down whenever I pried," Penny said. "Embarrassed, I think. I wish I'd been more insistent."

Gretchen thought someone with a higher emotional intellect than she might murmur soothing platitudes here, but she knew they'd come off just slightly wrong enough to be jarring if she attempted such a thing.

"But you don't think he's the one who killed her," Gretchen clarified.

Penny considered it, then shook her head. "Reed's the type of person who stays down when he gets hit and hopes pity saves him from a beating."

From the way Penny said it, Gretchen could tell that the assessment was about the worst thing Penny would say about someone.

"Do you know him well?" Gretchen asked.

Penny inclined her head like she was acknowledging a point. "I suppose not."

"Just what Claire's said about him, then?"

"I've known both of them for years," Penny said, and Gretchen couldn't tell if she was arguing a point or conceding one. "I've spent time with him, just not much outside fundraisers and parties. But I've watched it happen. The way Claire would say something offhand and Reed would get that kicked-puppy look about him."

Penny clearly had no sympathy for anyone she considered weak. Had Gretchen been friends with her, and wanted Penny on her side, she would play that aspect up, drop hints about how spineless her husband was, things like that. If she kept it up consistently enough, even someone as quick as Penny would start looking at him differently, each interaction shaded by a belief that had been built brick by brick into something unshakable and solid.

Letting confirmation bias strike again.

It happened all the time. Gretchen was just a little more . . . active about it than others tended to be.

"Was there anything else going on with Claire in those last months?" Gretchen asked.

"No," Penny said, and then, "oh."

"You remember something?"

"I don't know if it will help you, but it might give you someone to talk to," Penny said, and Gretchen wished sometimes people would just answer instead of qualifying so much ahead of time. "But there were a few months before Claire's death that Reed's sister, Ainsley, was staying with them."

"A few months?" Marconi interjected. Ainsley Kent had made it seem like she'd just popped up to help with the kids recently.

Penny nodded, seeming to gain steam. "Apparently she and Claire had never gotten along."

"Did Claire ever say why?" Gretchen asked. "Is Ainsley like Reed? Does she like playing the victim card?"

"The opposite in fact," Penny corrected. "I think she'd always been his protector."

"Then why . . . ?"

"Claire met Reed when they were still teenagers," Penny said with a shrug in her voice. "I think Ainsley just always rubbed her the wrong way."

Gretchen made a sound that probably read like agreement, but wasn't. "Do you know why Ainsley stayed with them so long?"

"I just assumed, well . . ." Penny looked between them. "That she was helping with Viola. She is a nurse."

"And this was a few months before Claire's death, you said?" Marconi had a notebook and pen out.

Penny's gaze went a little distant, and then she inhaled sharply. "I think it was right before, actually. I can't swear to that . . . but, yeah, Claire was still complaining about her the week before she died."

Marconi scribbled something as the answer hung in the air between them, ripe with implication.

Then Gretchen pivoted. "Have you ever heard of Tess Murphy?"

"Congressman Murphy's sister?" Penny asked, and all Gretchen saw in her expression was confusion. "Of course. But I didn't know her personally, if that's what you mean."

"Claire never talked about her?"

"No," Penny said, and it sounded honest and interested.

Gretchen nodded and then gestured to Marconi.

But instead of getting to her feet, Marconi leaned forward, her notebook put away and her eyes intent. "So who do you think killed Claire?"

Penny's gaze drifted to the view of the harbor for a long, contemplative moment. "I don't know," she said slowly. "But my money? It's on someone who bought tickets to Reed's pity party."

# CHAPTER THIRTY
## REED

*Two years before Claire's death—*

Reed rarely left Boston these days. He had to keep an eye on the kids, and Claire couldn't manage Viola by herself now that the girl was taller, stronger than she had been when they could so easily control her.

On the few trips out of state he'd made, he sometimes would wonder on the way back if everyone would be alive when he got home.

But Ainsley had asked him to help her move into her new house months ago. Backing out would have simply given her more ammunition to lecture him about, well, everything. He'd already heard it all, the voice in his own head was as relentless as she was. Brutal, too.

At the end of a long, sweaty day, they sat on the floor, surrounded by boxes. Ainsley snapped her fingers and pushed to her feet. When she returned, she was holding a bottle of cheap gin.

Reed laughed because he hadn't even seen that brand since he'd been sixteen and thought all alcohol was essentially the same, meant for one purpose—getting drunk.

Ainsley waggled the bottle at him, which he took, downing a swallow and cringing at the roughness of it. He was used to silky wine and vodka that tasted like money. Still, there was something to be said about passing some bad liquor back and forth after a day of hard labor.

He missed this. He would die before saying that out loud, but he missed being someone other than Reed Kent, Claire Kent's husband. One half of a power couple so rich they could buy half of Boston and still not work another day in their lives.

And more than that, he missed Ainsley. She and Claire were not fans of each other to say the least, and so getting Ainsley to visit took much bribing and cute pictures of the kids.

He bumped her shoulder with his as he handed over the bottle. "You did good, kid."

She bristled at the "kid" just like he'd expected her to, and was about to fly into some impassioned lecture about being a grown-ass woman when she must have caught sight of his twitching lips.

"Jerk," she cried, shoving him. He let himself go with it and ended up flat on his back, staring at the ceiling.

The sound of waves crashing against the beach drifted in through the open window, and the fan above them frantically tried to battle the humid air. South Carolina nights, even in the fall, clung to the heat, refusing to let it go, refusing to give in to the cool darkness in ways Reed had never understood.

"Why'd you pick here?" Reed asked, tipping his head just enough so that he could take another swallow.

"It's different, isn't it?" Ainsley mused, like she'd read his thoughts. Different from Boston, different from the city that had been their home, that was still his home. A small part of him ached that she could leave it—leave him—behind so easily. They were friends these days, after all. He didn't have many of those.

"Anyone I have to give the shovel talk to?" he asked, thrusting the gin back in her general direction.

Ainsley took the bottle but laughed so hard she ended up sprawled on the floor right next to him, a tear trickling along her temple and into her hairline. "Oh, thank you, I needed that," she said between pants, holding her stomach.

"Screw you," Reed muttered without any heat. Despite his height and build, his demeanor wasn't exactly threatening. He liked to tell himself he could play the role of protective older brother, but they both knew if anyone was going to threaten a potential partner to treat his sister right, it would be Ainsley herself.

He started laughing, too, his amusement getting Ainsley going all over again.

By the time they both quieted into gentle, sporadic giggles, Reed realized he hadn't laughed that hard in years. Muscles that had atrophied tugged in the most pleasant way, his belly and cheeks sore. The thought sobered him quickly.

Ainsley didn't glance over, but she must have sensed his mood shift, because she was already nudging the drink back toward him. "You really don't think Claire will give you a divorce?"

Reed sighed, wished they could go back to ten seconds ago, ten minutes ago, ten years ago, when he didn't have to answer this question. "Oh, she'll give me one."

"But never let you see the kids," Ainsley finished the thought grimly. Her jaw was locked, her eyes on the ceiling, her free hand curling into a fist. "What a controlling—"

"Ainsley," he murmured, before she could spit the venom that sat on her tongue.

She wrinkled her nose. "You've thought far worse."

There was no denying that. Still, Claire was the mother of his children. "When did you start hating her?"

Because Ainsley hated Claire. There was no sugarcoating that. Claire rarely mentioned Ainsley in return, and when she did it was cordial. But Claire hated Ainsley right back, as often was the case. He did wonder which one started it.

"You know I never liked her," Ainsley said. "I was rooting for you and Lena."

That got his attention. "What?"

"I know you were dating Tess, but she was too much of a people pleaser for you," Ainsley said, a shrug in her voice. "I figured you'd get the blonde out of your system and then settle down with Lena. She was always the one, wasn't she?"

*Lena Booker.* Honestly, he hadn't thought about her in years. But if pressed, he would admit that his eyes sometimes drifted around crowded galas or auctions, searching for someone. Not anyone in particular, he'd always told himself. But someone.

*She was always the one, wasn't she?*

That wasn't true. Claire had been. Even if he sometimes despised her now, Claire had always been the person who'd been able to see him and then lift him up or destroy him. His soul mate, his twin flame. He shouldn't be surprised now that his life was consumed by fire. Their love always had been.

But Ainsley, since the day she'd been born, thought she knew him better than he knew himself. Thought he wanted the *best* for himself— which of course would have been Lena—and not what *fit* with him. Too often, she treated Reed as if he were the younger sibling, and she had to map out his life because he just didn't know better.

He knew better. He knew Claire had been the wrong choice. But he'd made it with eyes wide-open. And Ainsley couldn't take that away from him.

Life wasn't always about making the right choices. Sometimes it was about making the wrong ones just to see what would happen.

"When did you start hating Claire?" Reed prompted again. He knew better than to ask this question, just like he knew better about a lot of things. That would never stop him from asking. Claire was a raw, pus-filled wound at the moment, and there was nothing more satisfying than picking at it to watch it ooze.

"One day when Viola was about five or six, she gouged the eyeballs out of all her dolls with those blunt kiddie scissors that barely cut paper," Ainsley said. Though it wasn't even close to the most horrific thing his daughter had done, Reed still exhaled, quick and fast like he'd been punched in the gut.

"I didn't know."

"I know," Ainsley said, her voice flat. "Viola lined them up on my bed. There were seven or eight of them, all mutilated."

"You told Claire?" Reed asked, despite already knowing what the answer would be.

"She said all girls cut their dolls' hair," Ainsley said. "Can you believe that? All girls cut their dolls' hair."

Reed waited for more that didn't come. "That's it? That's what did it?"

He'd imagined some big fight, some confrontation, a verbal barb that had burrowed too deep and stuck. Maybe even a slap.

Ainsley laughed without humor. "I knew right in that moment that she didn't give a shit about Viola. And yes, that was it. Right there."

There was a long silence, and then Ainsley nudged his foot with her own. "When did you start hating her?"

He didn't ask how she knew he did. "From the moment I met her."

"Bullshit," Ainsley said, before taking a swig and passing it over.

"Love and hate, it's two sides of the same coin, isn't it?" Reed said, before dumping the rest of the liquor down his throat. It burned so good. "Loved her from the moment I met her, too."

Ainsley huffed out something that sounded like *men* under her breath but didn't push it.

But he wasn't lying. From that first time he and Claire had met, Reed had known this one, *this one*—well, they would burn each other to the ground.

# CHAPTER THIRTY-ONE

## GRETCHEN

*Now—*

"We need to check if Ainsley Kent has an alibi for the night of Claire's murder," Gretchen said as they got back into the Porsche. "I'm assuming it hasn't been done already."

"I'll have Shaughnessy send someone over." Marconi was already dialing.

"Tell him I'm tired of saving his incompetent—" Gretchen heard Shaughnessy through the tinny speakers yelling back at her, and she nearly smiled.

Once Marconi was done relaying the conversation they'd had with Penny, she hung up and stared at the phone, her mind clearly elsewhere.

"I'd offer a penny for your thoughts, but I'm not yet sure they're worth anything," Gretchen said.

"They're not yet," Marconi said quietly. "Maybe later."

Gretchen could relate. Something was starting to form in the fog, but she couldn't quite make out the shape of it yet.

"I wish Lena had told you more," Marconi said, mostly to herself. "Just that Viola was innocent, and that was it?"

For a split second, Gretchen started composing yet another lecture on friendships and sociopathy, but then something jostled in her memory.

About a month before Lena died, she'd sent Gretchen an email. The subject had been "Break glass in case of emergency," and the body of the message had been a quote.

Gretchen had sent back a string of question marks that had gone unanswered, and then had googled the vaguely familiar-sounding quote. Lena had pretended the whole thing hadn't happened when Gretchen had asked her about it later, and Gretchen wrote it off as Lena drinking too many glasses of wine one night.

But Lena rarely did anything without purpose.

Now, Gretchen cursed, loud and vulgar.

"I'm an idiot," Gretchen muttered. Then she paused, not quite willing to take all the blame for such an opaque message. "Lena and I are both idiots."

Well, that would be past tense for Lena. But the judgment stood.

Gretchen gunned the engine, making an illegal U-turn to head in the opposite direction. Two oncoming cars had to veer and slam on their brakes, but they didn't hit her, and really that was all that ever mattered.

"Wait," Marconi said, looking a little dumbfounded. "I think I need you to say that again. I wasn't recording it."

Gretchen flipped her off. "It's a once-in-a-century admission. It won't ever be happening again."

Marconi laughed and didn't bother with any more questions. She probably had guessed she'd find out soon enough, and she didn't seem surprised when Gretchen pulled up to Lena's apartment.

Normally, Gretchen would have chafed at her presence by now. They'd been together most of their waking hours over the past two days. But Marconi had stopped feeling like a babysitter and had started feeling like a partner, and Gretchen couldn't pinpoint exactly when that had happened. She wasn't always good at recognizing her feelings in the moment.

Gretchen guessed that Marconi would find some new and spectacular way to irritate her before the day was done, but for now, she was proving herself worth keeping around.

Using her spare key to let them into Lena's tidy apartment, Gretchen took a moment to appreciate once again how anal Lena had been. Then she headed directly to the bedroom.

When Marconi didn't follow immediately, Gretchen turned to see what had caught her attention. Marconi was bent over a massive pile of files Lena had stacked on her desk in the corner of the living room.

"There's nothing interesting in there," Gretchen told her.

Marconi shrugged, not even bothering to look over. "How do you know?"

That was a good point that Gretchen didn't want to give her credit for. It was unlikely that someone had carefully sifted through them.

So Gretchen just rolled her eyes and continued toward where she knew Lena's bookshelf stood. The rest of the apartment was spartan enough that you could doubt someone lived there in the first place, but here, here was Lena's personality. And, if Gretchen was lucky, her secrets, as well.

While Gretchen started searching for the right title, Marconi leaned in the doorway. "Does it bother you?"

Gretchen didn't like wasting time on asking someone to clarify their questions, which Marconi knew well enough by now.

It took only a few seconds for Marconi to follow up with "That Viola's probably being framed. Just like you were."

This was why Gretchen had regretted her nice thoughts about Marconi almost as soon as she'd had them. "You seem quite insistent that I'm not a killer."

Marconi hummed. "You seem quite insistent that you are."

Gretchen paused, her finger stilling against the spine of one of the classic novels.

"Shaughnessy sure is convinced," Gretchen murmured, her search continuing.

Marconi laughed outright at that, and it startled Gretchen enough to get her to glance over her shoulder.

When Marconi caught her expression, her own sobered. "You really think he'd let you work on active cases if that were true? You think he would have vouched for you to other detectives?"

It was rare someone could surprise Gretchen, yet Marconi seemed to have the ability. Gretchen filed that little observation away in the many folders she kept neatly cataloged in her head. That was for later, this was for now.

Her fingertips brushed against ribbed wood just as she had the thought. She closed her eyes in silent thanks to Lena's predictably paranoid soul, and pulled what, to the casual observer, would look like a book from behind a pile of old sci-fi classics.

Gretchen tapped two knuckles against the cover, and the knock came back hollow. Marconi was at her elbow in an instant, and Gretchen didn't fight the impulse to shoulder her out of the way, out of her space.

"What do you have?" Marconi asked, not put off in the slightest by being shoved around a little.

Gretchen hesitated a moment before pulling out her phone and finding the "Break glass" email Lena had sent.

"'He who dies gains; he who sees others die loses.'" Marconi whistled low. "Well. That's quite the epitaph."

"It's Alexandre Dumas," Gretchen said, waving the fake book a little. Something rattled inside it, and she quickly righted the thing. She found the seam, prying the box open as she said absently, "*The Man in the Iron Mask.*"

"Her insurance," Marconi said with quiet understanding as they both stared at the thumb drive that was the only thing in the fake Dumas. Gretchen snatched it up and tossed the "book" back on the shelf.

"You know I read that monstrosity after she sent that message. I bet she didn't even read it, that cunning—" Gretchen said, cutting off when Marconi bumped her shoulder, probably to remind her that they were standing in the place Lena had died and that it wasn't actually appropriate to call her names just now. But the small smile Marconi offered along with the nudge told Gretchen she'd heard the admiration in Gretchen's voice as she'd said it. Gretchen cleared her throat. "Lena was wicked smart."

"Seemed it," Marconi said without a trace of sarcasm.

Gretchen shook herself. "Enough of that. Give me your computer."

Marconi patted the pockets of her jeans and then, with a deadpan expression, snapped her fingers. "I must have left that in my other pair."

"Unprepared is what you are," she scolded, and Marconi's laugh trailed her through the apartment. "Well, you're lucky I was a Girl Scout once upon a time. My laptop's in the Porsche."

"*You* were a Girl Scout," Marconi said as they waited for the elevator. It wasn't a question, but Gretchen heard the doubt beneath the words.

"I beat the rest of the little crybabies every year in cookie sales," Gretchen informed her.

"By any means necessary, I'm sure," Marconi murmured. But it didn't sound barbed like it could have. Rather it seemed to fall into the same banter-like rhythms Gretchen shared with Shaughnessy.

Gretchen hid her own smile as they stepped out onto the street. She slid into the Porsche and twisted around for her bag.

Marconi shook her head as she eyed the expensive computer Gretchen had left in her unlocked sports car. "You're just begging for something to be stolen, aren't you?"

The laptop whirred quietly between them as Gretchen booted it up and signed in.

"It's like a release valve, isn't it?" Marconi said after a minute of contemplation.

That got Gretchen to look up.

"It is," Marconi continued, nodding as if she'd just solved a complex riddle. "You have this impeccable control over yourself, over your desire to self-destruct, over your impulses. You have to loosen the reins in areas of your life where it doesn't matter."

"Someone's gone too far down the Wikipedia rabbit hole," Gretchen chided.

"You're not saying I'm wrong," Marconi pointed out.

Gretchen ignored but didn't contradict her, as the thumb drive's innards burst onto the screen. "An audio file," she told Marconi.

"Play it."

"Oh, thank you for the direction," Gretchen drawled. "I was going to stare at it, hoping it transcribed itself."

Marconi waved a hand dismissively. "Yes, yes, you're quite biting and clever. Now play the damn thing."

A part of Gretchen didn't want to do it out of sheer contrarian stubbornness, but she was desperately curious, and that always—always—won out.

She hit play.

# CHAPTER THIRTY-TWO

## REED

*Two and a half years before Claire's death—*

"You're tense," Claire noted as she took out her earrings.

Reed realized she was watching him in her mirror, realized he'd been staring out their bedroom window at the rain-slicked road below for far too long, his hand at the knot of his tie.

He shook his head and shrugged out of his blazer. "Just tired."

Claire laughed, a delicate sound so at odds with the way she looked at him. "From what exactly?"

If this had been five years ago, or even a year ago, the remark might have drawn blood, enough to get him to lash out. But he was *tired*. A soul-deep exhaustion that weighed like lead in the hollow places in his body. "I'm going to go check on the kids."

They both knew that by "kids" he meant Sebastian and Milo. They didn't poke at Viola when it wasn't absolutely necessary.

Claire's eyes narrowed in the mirror, but finally she nodded, crossing over to her jewelry box to retrieve the necklace chain that held a single key on it. She didn't wear it when they went out. Someone might ask questions neither of them wanted to answer.

When she pressed the metal into his hand, he tried not to flinch. He walked out without another comment, Claire's eyes hot on his back.

The boys' bedroom was only a few steps from their own, as far away from Viola's as possible. He stopped in front of their door, rested his palm against the wood of it, could swear he could feel their beating hearts against his skin, in his bones, in his chest.

This is what kept him going, even when he knew that he failed them every day.

Reed slid the key in the lock they'd had installed for the room—for the boys' protection, Claire had insisted.

The click of metal and tumblers made him sicker each time he heard it.

The lights were off, the boys tucked in their bunk beds. Sebastian on the bottom, so that he'd be the first to fight off the monsters should they come.

None of them talked about how the most likely shape that monster would take was that of a ten-year-old girl.

Reed ran a gentle hand over Milo's shaggy hair, smiled at the drool crusted at the corner of his mouth. Then he knelt down.

Dark eyes stared back at him.

His breath snagged against his throat. "Hey, buddy. You're awake?"

Sebastian just blinked and then pulled his blanket up farther until it was nestled beneath his chin. His voice came out as just a rasp. "Couldn't sleep."

"Oh yeah?" Reed ran a thumb along his son's little furrowed brow, wishing he could smooth it out for good.

"What if she comes?" Sebastian asked, so serious with those big eyes. A sour taste sat at the back of Reed's mouth.

"You have the lock."

Sebastian nodded and leaned forward, his jaw set, his mouth in a tense pout. "But there's always a key."

It took all of Reed's control not to let the little broken sound that pressed against his lips escape. Instead he sat down fully, shifting so that his back was against the wall. "It's time to sleep, buddy. I'll keep guard."

"You'll stop her?"

"Yeah," Reed said, his throat thick with emotion. "I won't let anyone hurt you tonight."

"Or Milo," Sebastian said, always stubborn, always too brave.

"Or Milo," Reed agreed, knowing he had no ground to stand on. In the light, the bruises on the boys' arms proved him a liar. But in the dark, they could pretend he meant what he said. *I won't let anyone hurt you. Tonight.*

Reed counted each inhale, each exhale as Sebastian finally relented, his tiny, tired body giving in to the false security that Reed offered.

Reed counted each inhale, each exhale, as the silver moonlight slid into the gold of dawn, painting the plush carpet in pinks and purples.

Reed counted each inhale, each exhale, memorizing the quiet whimpers that gave away the nightmares behind the boys' closed eyes.

Reed counted each inhale, each exhale, knowing every night spent just like this was one more tally against his soul, one more weight he'd have to carry for eternity. It was all right, though. He already knew what hell would look like.

He was living it.

# CHAPTER THIRTY-THREE

## GRETCHEN

*Now—*

A crisp voice drenched in upper-class Bostonian filled the small confines of the Porsche.

"Thank you for meeting with me." The greeting was awkward.

"Of course," Lena replied on the recording. Gretchen mouthed her name to Marconi.

"This . . . I know this is highly unusual," the first woman said. Marconi lifted her brows in a silent question, and Gretchen shook her head. She didn't recognize the voice.

"It's been a long time," Lena said. Her tone was neither warm nor cold, but rather perfectly controlled and neutral. It made Gretchen think that this was not exactly a joyous reunion. For all that Lena was a complicated soul, she loved deeply. If this had been a dear friend, she would have sounded less stilted.

Gretchen also couldn't discount the fact that Lena'd had the foresight to record the conversation for whatever reason. Nor could she ignore that there was no agreement on the tape from the other woman.

That meant it was unlikely Lena had been planning to use whatever this was for court.

So why take the precaution?

"I won't waste your time," the unidentified woman said. "Do you remember Tess Murphy?"

"Yes, of course."

"I know that—" The woman cut herself off with a forced, brittle laugh. "You're going to think I'm crazy."

"I won't," Lena promised.

"I . . . I found this the other day," the woman said.

Lena was smart, so smart. She was recording this for a reason, and so she narrated what was happening.

"A bracelet," Lena said. "That's Tess's, right?"

"I think so."

"What does this mean?" Lena asked.

"There's blood on it," the woman pointed out.

"Ah," Lena said softly. "So there is."

"I want to be wrong," the woman said, sounding quiet and beaten down and sure that more than anything in the world she was right. What that meant Gretchen still didn't know.

"Claire . . . ," Lena finally said.

*Claire Kent.*

Gretchen met Marconi's eyes. She wasn't surprised by the identity of the woman, but it was still a jolt to the system to hear it confirmed. Marconi's face reflected a similar unsettled resignation.

"You think it was Reed?" Lena spelled it out when Claire didn't continue. "You think he hurt Tess back then?"

"I think he did more than that," Claire said, her words tumbling out like she'd been holding them back for too long. "You don't know him anymore."

"What do you mean?" Lena didn't sound defensive, just curious, willing to listen. She was a good lawyer. *Had* been.

"Reed seemed so different back then," Claire said. "Different from the other boys."

Lena murmured a little sound of agreement.

"And he's like the sun, you know?" Claire's voice had gone a little dreamy, nostalgic. "When he shines on you, it's the most beautiful summer day."

"And when the clouds come?" Lena prodded, clearly knowing the answer.

"It's so cold it hurts," Claire said.

"I always thought it was different with you."

Claire laughed, and even through the recording, Gretchen could hear the resentment beneath it. "Don't we all tell ourselves that?"

"Claire," Lena started gently, and Gretchen could almost see her touching the other woman's hand to offer comfort, a gesture Gretchen had seen countless times. "I have to ask . . . Why now?"

In the pause between the words, Gretchen heard the question that must have been obvious. *Is this a woman seeking revenge on a cheating husband?*

"I'm under no delusion that my husband is faithful to me. But that's not what this is," Claire said with a twist to the words. She'd likely heard the suggestion of a hidden motive layered underneath. "I was in the attic the other day."

"He kept this bracelet in the attic?"

Claire huffed out a disbelieving breath. "Can you believe it? In a box of old baseball cards. He must have thought I'd never look there."

Which actually seemed like a fair assumption. Why had Claire Kent been in her attic? She seemed the type of woman to hire someone to bring her the boxes she wanted. Marconi's brows had gone up a notch.

"This could be nothing," Lena said. "Maybe she gave it to him before she left, and neither noticed the blood."

"I know you and Reed go back a long way," Claire said, more tentative than she had been earlier, someone who knew they were pressing on bruises. "I know I'm not your favorite person ever."

"We're not kids anymore," Lena said.

"But I get where your loyalties lie," Claire said. "I understand that."

Lena didn't agree or disagree. "Why do you care about Tess? You never did back then."

"I'm not a kid anymore," Claire said quietly, some of that veneer wearing thin again. "But I don't care about Tess, you're right."

Gretchen shifted in her seat. That was a smart strategy. There was no way to convince Lena of something she was certain was false. And from her voice just then, Gretchen knew Lena wouldn't believe any argument that Claire actually cared about the missing girl.

"Then what's going on?" Lena asked.

"Reed has become . . ." Claire hesitated, cleared her throat with a delicate precision. "He has these panic attacks . . . He's angry so much these days. He thinks I'm—"

Claire didn't continue, but her implication was obvious. In it Gretchen heard echoes of their conversation with Penny.

"What does Tess have to do with any of that?" Lena asked, though she must have seen where the woman was going. If Claire could prove Reed had done something terrible to Tess Murphy, she could rid herself of a husband who seemed to scare her. But once again Lena was smart—and she was still recording.

"I just want to know what I'm dealing with," Claire said after her longest pause yet. It was a lie. Claire must have known Lena knew it was a lie.

But what was Claire going to say otherwise? Even if she didn't realize she was on tape, it would have been foolish to admit she was digging up dirt on someone she was likely about to threaten with divorce. They'd been young when they'd married, too. Gretchen wondered if there'd been a prenup. Thought about how Claire had been about to revise her will, directing most of her inheritance to the foundation.

"I'll pay you for your time, of course," Claire said.

Lena laughed lightly. "I know you can afford it—that's not the problem."

There was a loaded silence that Claire broke. "You're afraid of what you're going to find."

"What if Reed isn't guilty?" Lena asked, instead of denying that. Which seemed just as damning. "What then?"

"Honestly?" Claire asked. "I'll be relieved. If he's capable of murder . . ."

The fact that both women in the recording were now dead made the unfinished thought all the more chilling. Marconi shifted in the passenger seat, clearly uncomfortable.

"All right," Lena said. "I'll look into it. But I'm not a PI."

Gretchen again wished there was video of the conversation. There was something unreadable in Lena's voice, but Gretchen couldn't pin it down, not without her accompanying expressions and body language. What had been going on in that head of hers?

"I know, I know. Thank you," Claire said on an exhale, the audio saturated with her relief. There was some shuffling, a scraping of chair against floor. "I started to investigate her disappearance myself, but I really had no idea where to start."

"You made a file?" Lena asked, for the tape's sake, Gretchen guessed.

"Yes," Claire confirmed, though they must have been both staring at it. "You were everywhere a few weeks ago. All over the TV for that big case. And I thought . . . I thought maybe you'd know what to do at least. Maybe you had some police contacts or something."

Like Gretchen. Wasn't that interesting?

There was a tapping that sounded like Lena drumming her fingers on the table too close to the phone. "I'll take care of it."

The audio ended abruptly, the women and background noise cutting off, as if someone had sliced it just so. It would have been odd for Lena to hit stop in that moment, especially if Claire didn't know she was being recorded. Gretchen wondered how their goodbyes had gone.

"Well," Marconi said. "I guess we know why Lena didn't get the second half of her payment."

Gretchen was about to agree but was cut off by Lena's voice.

Another audio clip had started playing.

# CHAPTER THIRTY-FOUR

## REED

*Two and a half years before Claire's death—*

The first animal bones hadn't come as a shock. Not because Reed had been expecting to see them, but because his brain hadn't realized why they were there. What they meant.

Viola had hid her obsession with torturing the poor creatures at first. Then that car had backed into their stone wall, and the secret was out. The bird had been missing a wing, and that had been the least of its injuries.

Both he and Claire tried to keep her contained, tried to keep her away from anything with a heartbeat that would race too fast beneath a knife. But they weren't perfect.

After she'd been discovered, Viola still hoarded some of her little experiments, hiding them away. But she had also turned some of them into psychological weapons, riding the fear-induced high from animal to human with ease.

It had started when she left a bloodied rabbit in Milo's bed, and again Reed had been late to putting the dots together. He'd stared at the soaked sheets and had wondered how on earth a dog had gotten into their house to leave such a mess.

There had been no dog.

Viola didn't as often go after him and Claire with her games. She'd long ago realized that it hurt the most when she went through the boys.

Sebastian joined Reed that night in the backyard, shovel in hand. This was a routine Reed had down, but it was the first time Sebastian had come out.

They'd had many conversations in recent years, though. About how life was precious, that animals deserved respect, deserved burial, maybe even more so because their deaths had been so ugly and brutal.

Fireflies held vigil as Reed and Sebastian broke the earth.

The only thing that disrupted the quiet night was the sound of Sebastian's occasional sniffle that neither of them acknowledged.

When they were finished, Reed dropped to his knees, pressing a flat palm against the slightly raised ground.

The soft weight of Sebastian knocked into him, and he wrapped his free arm around the boy's thin shoulders, taking extra care with any potential tender spots.

"Can we leave?" Sebastian asked, his voice so small, so tentative that Reed almost missed the question. Reed heard the tremble beneath and knew it had taken Sebastian a while to work up to asking it.

But Reed didn't know what to answer. Of course, he'd thought about it; sometimes he'd thought about it once an hour, once a minute, once a second.

Claire wouldn't let them leave without a fight, not if she was being left behind to deal with Viola and the fallout from their departure.

But he'd opened his own bank account years ago, had quietly been putting money into it every month just in case. He had a bag filled mostly with Milo's and Sebastian's things stashed in the garage behind boxes of crap they never used. He'd scoured domestic abuse websites for tips—knowing that such violence wasn't limited to the narrow scope everyone thought it was. His boys had the bruises to prove it.

His marriage with Claire was but a ghost, and not even memories of the good times seemed to be able to get them through this rough patch.

And there had been good times, he knew that. Reed could still see her bright and laughing, fingers laced with his, challenging him and soothing him, making him burn with want so that he'd thought he was going to catch fire from it.

Maybe she'd been Viola's first victim; maybe it had been the moment the eerily silent baby had been placed in Claire's arms that Viola had taken her first life. And when she'd blinked up at Reed, she'd taken her second.

But could he leave them? What would happen to Claire, who too often refused to see Viola for what she truly was? What would happen to Viola, who was his child just as much as Sebastian and Milo were?

What would happen to his own soul if he were forced to make that choice?

When Reed didn't say anything, Sebastian knocked their knees together. "Aunt Ainsley said we could stay with her."

Sebastian said it with such forced casualness Reed knew it had taken all his courage to put that out there.

If Reed left, Claire would just find him. Ainsley's would be her first stop.

Maybe . . . maybe the boys could go there. And then Claire and he and Viola could just continue on the inevitable path toward destruction until one of them was dead. He didn't even have a guess as to who that would be.

But that meant giving this up, this soft weight against him, the smell of boy and summer, the quiet eyes that watched him with such trust. It was the only thing that pulled him back from the brink some days.

He would think about it. If he could convince himself to stop being so selfish.

One more day. He was allowed this for one more day.

Reed ignored the fact that he'd had that very same thought many times before.

# CHAPTER THIRTY-FIVE

## GRETCHEN

*Now—*

When the audio clip started up again, it was just Lena talking. It didn't take long to realize it was a voice memo to herself rather than a taped conversation.

"I think Starbucks will be the best place to initiate contact with Reed," Lena said. "He goes every Monday, Wednesday, and Friday like clockwork."

There was a pause full of low-grade technological static. "I haven't been able to locate anything on Tess Murphy, dead or alive."

A second of silence followed. And then: "I think she's dead. Not that I believe Claire Kent or trust her further than I could throw her."

Marconi's quick grin flashed and faded at that, like a lit match.

"But there's a reason she's bringing this up now," Lena continued. Static again, until Lena, more softly, said, "I always wondered why Tess never called me."

The audio cut off again, like it had after the conversation with Claire. Gretchen raised her brows at Marconi in a silent question that was answered almost immediately when a new clip played.

"He's so skittish," Lena said. "I made contact, pretended I had run into him out of nowhere. Can you believe he bought that? I've been avoiding the man for two decades. Do you know how hard that is in this city? When we run in the same circles?"

Gretchen could all but see Lena shaking her head, laughing in disbelief at some foolish thing. Gretchen pressed a palm to her sternum, her chest aching.

"He probably thinks he's fooling everyone," Lena continued. "He puts on this act that might have worked years ago, but it's worn so thin you can see everything beneath. Like one of those clear, plastic masks that distorts your features but doesn't really hide your face. Is it guilt? Does he know Claire thinks he killed Tess? Did he?"

"Fiona Murphy thinks he did," Lena continued. "I love her, but I'm not convinced. This is going to sound like something Gretchen"— Marconi glanced over sharply—"would do, but I think the fastest way to get Reed to crack is to put more pressure on him. I asked Fiona if she'd put on a show if I brought him back. You should have seen how giddy she was about playing a role in the investigation."

The audio cut off, and Marconi shifted the computer to show her there was still more on the file. Lena must have edited them together at some point.

When the sound came back up, it was somewhat muffled. Another conversation instead of a memo.

"You know he didn't do it, Lena."

The voice, it sounded like . . .

"Ainsley Kent," Marconi whispered.

"And how do I know that?"

"It's Reed." Like that was an answer. "Once upon a time you knew him."

"I think I did," Lena said.

Ainsley made a little distressed sound. "What happened between you two?"

Lena laughed. "You know what happened."

There was a pause. "Will you tell him? That you don't think he's guilty? He thinks you hate him, thinks you're about three seconds from calling the cops on him."

"No body, no crime," Lena said. "You think cops are going to go arrest Reed freaking Kent over a teenage girl everyone thinks was a runaway?"

"Why are you acting like this?" Ainsley said after a moment. "Like you really think he killed her?"

"Who says I'm acting?" Lena countered.

"You forget that once upon a time I knew you, too," Ainsley said.

Lena's inhale was shaky, coming through even over the recording. "Ainsley . . ."

There was a long silence then, not like the audio cut off but like they were both waiting for the other to break.

Gretchen wasn't surprised that it was Lena. "Can you just trust me?"

"Give me a good reason."

"Give me a few more weeks," Lena said instead. "Just stay there, watch him. But don't tell him you know anything."

Ainsley sighed, deeply. "You're asking a lot."

"I know," Lena said, sounding solemn and sincere. "I know . . . I just." A pause, a pivot. "God, do you remember Tess at all?"

"You two were so close," Ainsley said. "I do remember that."

"I want to know what happened to her."

"You want justice," Ainsley said, a sour note slipping into her voice. "Which means you'll take Reed down if that's what it takes to get it."

Lena didn't argue that. Even Gretchen knew it would be pointless for her to have tried.

"Ainsley?" Lena prodded.

"A couple of weeks," Ainsley said, clipped and rushed. "Then I'm telling him you've been playing him from the start."

On that, the clip cut off.

Next up it was Declan Murphy, his booming voice recognizable almost before he spoke due to the inhale before his practiced politician voice.

He greeted Lena, and it gave the impression they were together in person. From the shifting quality of the audio, Gretchen guessed Declan wasn't aware he was being taped.

"You're really buying into that whole conspiracy theory?" Declan asked. "The one Fiona peddles."

"He left Tess a message to meet him that night, Dec," Lena said, in a voice that was different from how she'd talked to Ainsley, Claire, and herself. It was . . . suggestive? Sultrier, definitely.

"Kids," Declan said, in that kind of fond, exasperated way adults reflected on their teen years. "They were in puppy love."

"Except Reed was messing around with Claire," Lena cut in.

"Can you blame him?" Declan shot back, and Marconi's lip curled back in a half-disgusted snarl in response.

There was some shuffling and then: "What's that?"

"Her bracelet," Lena said. "Claire found it in a box of his things."

"There's blood."

"Yeah."

Silence. And then the scrape of chair on floor, quick movement, and a slamming door. "Wait, Declan, calm down."

The rustle of clothes and limbs and feet. And then quiet. Just Lena's breathing.

The final second of the file was just Lena's barely audible "Shit."

# CHAPTER THIRTY-SIX

## REED

*Three years before Claire's death—*

"Did you see Declan Murphy is running for city council?" Claire asked from across the long dining room table. They always breakfasted here, formally, and so far apart. Claire gave him the sports section, though he didn't care much for games these days. She took the rest of the paper.

Every day the same. The same coffee, the same oatmeal and fresh fruit. The same empty places where the kids should have been if they weren't relegated to eating in the kitchen with their latest nanny.

"What?" Reed hadn't had enough caffeine for this conversation.

"Declan. Murphy," Claire repeated with deliberate emphasis, just in case her facial expression didn't quite convey how angry he made her just by existing. "City council. We should donate."

Reed couldn't think of anything he cared less about than Declan Murphy's city council race. "Sure."

Claire wedged the folded paper beneath the edge of her plate, looking like she did when she tried to appear casual. "Didn't Ainsley have a little fling with him at some point?"

"Weren't we all sleeping with each other back then?" Reed said without thinking. Claire's shoulders went taut.

He had not had enough caffeine for this. Reed took a swallow that burned the roof of his mouth, knowing it was too little, too late anyway.

"*You* might have been," Claire said stiffly, the words going sharp at the edges. "The rest of us were decidedly not."

Reed squinted down the length of the table, trying not to point out that if he had been sleeping with them then that meant they had been sleeping with him, too. Logic was on his side. He took another gulp of coffee and realized that might not be a smart thing to say.

"I'm sure he'll appreciate any donation," Reed said as carefully as possible. Claire didn't like to be steered, but sometimes she would let him do it anyway. If she wasn't in the mood for a battle.

Every feature on her face—her lips, her eyes, her brows, her forehead—tightened, and he prepared to have something flung at his head. But then it all smoothed over until she was polished porcelain, not a crack in sight.

"Have you ever heard from Tess?"

Adrenaline did a much better job than coffee ever could. He always felt that same kick whenever her name was mentioned, the pulse of it echoing through his body down to the soles of his feet.

"Tess Murphy?" Reed asked to buy time.

"No, Tess my friend from down the street," Claire shot back. "Don't be deliberately obtuse."

Reed gave her a look. "I haven't heard from her."

"Like you would tell me," Claire said like she was trying to keep it under her breath. But she always said those bits loud enough for him to actually hear.

Maybe on another day he would have rushed to reassure her. But the name had come like a slap, one that had caught him off guard when he'd been drowsy from a terrible night of sleep and scratched up from Viola's most recent temper tantrum.

"Didn't you use to keep a little box with mementos of her?" Claire asked, and it was so unexpected that Reed actually answered.

"Not of her," Reed said. "Of stuff from when I was a kid."

"But I remember, I remember seeing it one time," Claire pushed. "Wasn't there something in there of hers?"

Reed licked his lips. Swallowed. Stared at his empty coffee. There was no help to be found there.

When he looked back up, she was watching him, her eyes predatory until she noticed his attention. Then she relaxed, smiled pleasantly, like this was idle chitchat and not an interrogation.

He lied because he always lied. "No, not that I . . . Nope, nothing of Tess's."

"Oh," she said on a delicate exhale. "My mistake."

Then she went back to the paper as if she hadn't just pulled his life right out from under him.

# CHAPTER
# THIRTY-SEVEN

## GRETCHEN

*Now—*

The silence inside the Porsche pressed against Gretchen's eardrums, but neither she nor Marconi said anything through some unspoken agreement to make sure the file was actually over.

After a few minutes, Marconi blew out a breath. "Well."

"I wonder if there was going to be another tape," Gretchen said. "And she just never got around to it."

"That would have been helpful," Marconi noted dryly. "Right now I just have more questions than before."

"What a slacker, our Lena," Gretchen said, amused. "Dying before she could finish the job."

"All right, here's what we know," Marconi said, closing the laptop before shifting toward Gretchen. "Claire Kent hires Lena Booker to look into the disappearance of Reed's childhood sweetheart. Lena and Ainsley are in on some pact where no one tells Reed anything. Declan thinks Reed killed Tess because Lena showed him the evidence that Claire brought in."

"They should hire you to do those little summaries at the top of TV shows," Gretchen said. Marconi wasn't wrong about anything, but it felt like there were several thousand layers they were missing, and Gretchen knew she would be listening to the audio clips the rest of the night, trying to peel at least some of them back to see what was underneath.

"Har, har," Marconi intoned, dry as dust. "To be fair, I'd probably at least make more money than I do now."

"You've missed your calling, clearly."

Marconi snorted and then sobered. "So, what if Reed Kent found out Claire was onto him, and he killed her to shut her up?"

"Or he thought the reason she was digging around in the past in the first place was because she wanted to get rid of him," Gretchen suggested. "If he kills her, he gets to keep her fortune and get rid of his little psychopath along the way."

"You know what?" Marconi asked, sitting up straight in a sudden, abrupt movement. "Maybe we've been thinking about the reason Lena took the case wrong."

"As a favor to Reed," Gretchen said more to herself. "Or guilt, of course. If she's the one who actually killed Claire."

"What if she knows Reed's guilty?" Marconi countered. "What if she took Viola's case in spite of Reed Kent, not because of him?"

*I messed up, Gretch.* But what did that mean now?

*She's like you.*

Gretchen pulled out her phone and didn't bother with greetings when Shaughnessy picked up. "I need to speak with Viola again."

"You realize how much of a pain in my ass you are?" Shaughnessy grumbled on the other end. "You know I actually have a real caseload that doesn't involve chasing conspiracy theories."

"Thanks," Gretchen called out, singsongy and overly cheery, as if he'd agreed. "You're the best, darling."

Marconi was smirking when Gretchen hung up. "He's wrapped around your finger. And you still think he's convinced you're a killer."

"I think he has a healthy appreciation of what I'm capable of," Gretchen bit out. "As will you if you don't let that topic drop."

Marconi held up her hands as if surrendering, though she didn't seem nearly cowed enough for Gretchen's tastes.

Before Gretchen could put her in her place further, Marconi shook her head and laughed a little in disbelief. "What if this was just about money? Can you imagine, I've been thinking in terms of evil kids and affairs and lurid secrets."

"Most times it's about money," Gretchen said on a half shrug. "Or brain chemistry gone wrong, as would have been the case with Viola."

"Revenge," Marconi countered.

"Mm-hmm," Gretchen hummed absently. "I'm guessing we just heard the conversation that provoked Declan Murphy into punching Reed."

"Not an affair gone sour, then," Marconi said, echoing Gretchen's earlier suspicions that there had been more to the altercation.

"Ainsley Kent keeps coming up."

"Maybe she's the accomplice?" Marconi suggested. "Penny Langford seemed to suggest there was some tension between Ainsley and Claire."

And Penny had made it seem like Ainsley would take care of Reed's problems for him if he asked her to.

*My money? It's on someone who bought tickets to Reed's pity party.*

That could certainly be Ainsley Kent, who was so clearly protective of her brother.

"Reed somehow convinces Ainsley to kill Claire in her sleep?" Gretchen suggested, wanting to hear how it sounded.

Marconi's fingers tangled in her lap. Nervous, Gretchen thought. In a way Gretchen hadn't seen her yet.

"Spit it out," Gretchen demanded.

"It's harder to kill someone than most people think."

And Gretchen got it, nearly laughed. "You think I don't realize that?"

"I get that you consider yourself nonviolent," Marconi said, and her voice had taken on a placating, patronizing swing to it that grated against Gretchen's skin. "I'm just saying, for empaths even in the exact right scenarios, a lot of people can't go through with it."

"But I would?" Gretchen clarified, not in actual disagreement, but just to see how awkward she could make Marconi. It was the first time she'd seen the woman this uncomfortable, and considering how much Gretchen had tried to push her off-center, that was saying something.

"Yes," Marconi said. And it sounded strong and certain again. "I think you would. Without hesitating. Ainsley, on the other hand, I think she would need a damn fine reason." She paused. "Am I right?"

Gretchen hummed a little in agreement. "Maybe we're looking for the wrong thing then."

"What should we be looking for?" Marconi asked, almost hesitant.

"That 'damn fine reason.'"

"You don't think it's money, then?" Marconi clarified.

"Sometimes it can be difficult for me to judge character," Gretchen admitted, teeth clenching around the words. "Power, social dynamics, sure. But character . . ."

"You don't think Ainsley Kent seems the type to kill to secure a fortune," Marconi finished for her.

Gretchen hated it. Hated that she had a gut instinct that relied on "the type." She spent her life lecturing people about how anyone was capable of anything. But still . . . "Exactly."

"Maybe she just really hated Claire," Marconi suggested.

"There's no indication that she was there that night, correct?" Gretchen asked. "And if so, how strong is her alibi?"

Marconi shook her head. "I'd have to check."

"You're waiting for an invitation?"

A rude gesture greeted her when she glanced up, but then Marconi started texting as Gretchen navigated out into traffic.

"No alibi, Shaughnessy says," Marconi reported. "And also says this is the last favor of the day."

Gretchen rolled her eyes because that was so far from true. Shaughnessy melted like butter when the favors were legitimate. It was almost like he had integrity or something. "Nothing about her being there in the initial days after the murder?"

Marconi relayed the question, then the answer. "Neither she nor Reed mentioned it."

"What's going on do you think?" Marconi asked.

Gretchen just shook her head. "I don't know. But I'm starting to think Ainsley Kent does."

# CHAPTER
# THIRTY-EIGHT
## REED

*Four years before Claire's death—*

Ainsley was the one who gave Reed a gun.

Reed hated the thought of having one in the house. The thing was midnight black, and sucked the light out of the room just like Viola's eyes did.

It had been after the third hospital trip in eighteen months. If Reed and Claire had been anyone other than the Kents, they probably would have had child protective services called on them. They never went to the same ER, but medical files were often connected these days. It worked in their favor that people assumed boys were naturally rambunctious and that old scar tissue went unnoticed in favor of new injuries.

For the suspicious doctors, the ones who knew how to look for the secondary signs of abuse, it helped that the boys never flinched away from Reed, always sought comfort. As someone who'd researched domestic violence extensively, Reed knew that didn't really indicate anything, but he'd seen more than one set of shoulders relax when Milo buried his face in Reed's neck or Sebastian clung to his leg.

He knew he was pushing it with this third trip, but Sebastian had fainted dead away, cracking his head on the marble in their lobby.

The doctor, an older man with drooping jowls and pale, watery eyes, had stared at Sebastian for a long time, before pulling Reed aside to ask if the boy had had a stomach bug recently. "He's dangerously malnourished."

Reed had tried to shake his head, and the doctor had reached behind him for an informational pamphlet.

"I've seen this before," the doctor had said, pushing something glossy into Reed's hands. "It's about control for these kids, having control over something in their lives." He shook his head. "All that social media at such a young age. It's not good for anyone."

*Disordered Eating*, the pamphlet had whispered in soft, italicized lettering.

Reed had cursed softly, knowing his voice came out ruined, broken. The doctor had placed a hand on his shoulder, squeezed. "It's not just happening with girls anymore."

When Reed had glanced up, the doctor gave him one more pat, signed discharge papers, and then swept out of the room.

No authorities had been called in. Reed wondered how many times similar scenes played out throughout the country for other reasons—biases, societal norms, manners, manipulation. Reed wondered what would have happened if he hadn't been wearing a thousand-dollar watch, if he hadn't played the part of concerned—and privileged and wealthy—parent so well.

On the way home, Reed had stopped at a burger joint, ordering several days' worth of food, using the couple of twenties he always kept in the car.

Sebastian had eaten too much and too fast and thrown up in the bathroom, his pulse racing dangerously. Reed had kept his fingers on his wrist, as he'd sat on the dirty floor, cradling him, both their faces wet with tears.

Now he sat with Ainsley outside the town house in her stupidly large SUV that looked like a tank in their elegant neighborhood.

"I don't want that," he said, refusing to take the gun she was holding out to him.

"It'll make me feel better," Ainsley said.

"But Viola . . ." What if she got a hold of it? He didn't want to think about what she'd be capable of with such a powerful weapon.

"Lock it up," Ainsley countered as he knew she would.

Reed knew the statistics. If he brought a gun into the house, it was more likely one of them would end up accidentally shot than stopping something that shouldn't be happening. But he also knew the jut of Ainsley's chin. The protective set to her shoulders.

He took it.

"Thanks for coming up again," he said, his eyes on his lap.

There was a moment when the only sound was the low-level hum of the cello music she kept on a constant loop in her car. "Reed . . ."

It was plaintive, begging. A plea maybe.

He cleared this throat. Ainsley would never understand his life. Reed barely understood it.

"Hey." She stopped him when he shifted to open the door. "This isn't a way out."

Reed glanced over, not sure what she meant by that.

The weak overhead light must have caught the confusion on his face, because Ainsley jerked her chin toward the gun.

"For you," Ainsley said, as if she was only realizing in that second how dangerous it was to offer him such a temptation. "That isn't a way out."

Reed nodded once, as if that hadn't been his first thought.

When your life was built of lies, what was one more?

# CHAPTER THIRTY-NINE

## GRETCHEN

*Now—*

Ainsley refused to come to the station or even talk to Marconi and Gretchen at the Kent town house. Shaughnessy, meanwhile, warned them that there wasn't enough evidence to convince a judge to force the issue.

"And Viola?" Gretchen asked. "Can I get in with her again?"

"Tomorrow."

With nothing else to do Gretchen slid Marconi a look. "Want to go to my favorite place?"

"Oh God," Marconi muttered. "Why do I feel like you're about to drive me to a body farm?"

Gretchen laughed. "Close enough."

Not only was the medical examiner's office one of Gretchen's favorite places, but Dr. Leo Chen was perhaps Gretchen's favorite person in the entirety of the Boston Police Department. Not because he was professional or kind or smart—though she noted objectively that he was all of those things. Instead it was because he shared her morbid fascination with dead things.

"Gretchen," Dr. Chen called, swanning out from behind a pillar, with arms outstretched, blood on his gloves. "Oh, ha, silly me."

He stripped off the latex as he beamed at them both, his glasses covered by bug-eyed microscopic lenses. When he stopped beside Gretchen, he kissed the air beside her cheeks and then nodded cordially at Marconi after she'd taken a notable step back. That was fair, as Dr. Chen still had a smear of something that smelled like bile on his work apron.

"Dare I hope this is a social call?" Dr. Chen asked, putting himself to rights and pushing his glasses up onto his forehead. By "social call," Dr. Chen meant poring over old historic photos of medical oddities while drinking a glass of port, as they sometimes did on Friday nights.

"Sadly not," Gretchen said, genuinely disappointed. Conversations with Dr. Chen often proved to be the highlight of her week, as he never shied away from such questions as, *What does a spleen actually feel like in your hands?*

"Ah, blast." Dr. Chen punched the air in disappointment. "A boy can dream."

Gretchen laughed at the idea that the man who was both nearly old enough to be her grandfather and gay would be hitting on her. But she did so love flirting. "You act as if I wouldn't run off to Vegas with you at your word."

"But how would I keep you in the lifestyle to which you've grown accustomed?" Dr. Chen countered.

"And by that you mean, how could you keep me sourced on all things related to dead bodies, I presume?" Gretchen asked. She was outrageously rich thanks to a family trust that no one had figured out how to keep out of her hands. Even though she frequently gave in to her impulse to spend large quantities of the money, her vast wealth would be nearly impossible to deplete. If her car was stolen once a week, she could afford to replace it with a new one.

"What else?" Dr. Chen said with a flourish. Then he glanced toward Marconi. "I suppose that's partly why you're here today?"

"Claire Kent," Gretchen said, not bothering to ease into it. Dr. Chen didn't like minced words when it involved anything other than pointless flirtations. "I've read the report, but I wanted to hear from you."

Dr. Chen had a magical way of describing the murders that professional words in a file could never do justice. Gretchen knew empaths didn't like the stories as much as she did, that they tended to avoid coming down here when at all possible. But Dr. Chen wasn't violent, nor was he a sociopath, so she thought that was fairly narrow-minded of them.

You could learn so much if you simply listened to people, even when—or *especially* when—they scared you.

"I can only put so much in there," Dr. Chen agreed, his eyes a little dejected and resigned as he pouted at the file. "Such is life." He brightened. "And death."

Gretchen and Dr. Chen laughed at that, and Marconi simply shoved her hands in her blazer, looking distinctly uncomfortable. Most people did in the cold, sterile room filled with corpses and light that was too bright.

"Claire Kent," Gretchen said again. She didn't mind repeating herself with Dr. Chen. He rarely made her do it. "Your take?"

Dr. Chen sucked his front teeth, his gaze going a little unfocused. "Claire Kent, stab wounds, no signs of a defensive struggle. Murdered at night in her bed with a butcher's knife—"

He broke off when Gretchen slapped him lightly with the file on his shoulder, his attention drawn back to her face.

"You're telling me facts I could read and already know," Gretchen complained. "Tell me what you think."

When Dr. Chen's eyes slid to Marconi, Gretchen waved a hand in his face. "She's okay."

That also seemed to shake Marconi out of the strange mood she'd sunk into. She brought a hand to her chest, and she swooned a little dramatically. "Be still my heart."

"That's a high compliment from this one," Dr. Chen informed Marconi, who, from the small smile she was now wearing, already knew that.

"Who did it?" Gretchen pressed.

"Inexperienced," Dr. Chen finally said on a little bit of a sigh. "There were hesitation marks, near her ribs."

That could certainly mean Viola, but it could mean a lot of people. "Personal?"

"It was overkill, certainly," Dr. Chen said. "The number of times the knife went into the body . . . I would say anger was likely driving the attack. Or a strong emotion."

"Like?"

Dr. Chen considered that for longer than she would have expected. "Fear. Possibly."

"She was asleep," Gretchen countered.

He nodded. "Rage is far more likely then."

Which meant there had to have been a trigger. This was a blind spot for Gretchen, and she realized it. Often when she was consulting on an investigation, she'd get lost down a path, unable to see a way forward because no matter how she unraveled the mystery of a killing, it was nearly impossible for her to account for the complex emotions that might be involved.

Motive, she understood. Greed, power, revenge, money. At the core of a motive was human psychology, and Gretchen was a well-studied expert on that.

But emotions, those were different. They were sticky and confusing, and she was never sure if they didn't make sense to just her or if they didn't make sense to the killers themselves. This was a perfect example.

Reed Kent had every motive in the world. Gretchen could stick the reasons on a dartboard and land on a believable motive for him murdering his wife.

Gretchen hadn't been thinking about the killing itself, though. Why would a premeditated murder aimed at securing a fortune look like the scene in Claire's bedroom?

Perhaps the excessive violence was meant to further implicate Viola, in case there were any doubts. But perhaps it revealed something else, something they couldn't yet see.

"Why weren't there defensive wounds?" Marconi asked. "If she was stabbed in her stomach and then bled out through there, why didn't she fight back after the first strike? It would have been a slow process, surely."

Dr. Chen eyed her, but it was with consideration, not contempt. For all his lighthearted manner, Dr. Chen didn't suffer fools—just one more reason Gretchen gravitated toward him. It was easy to lose his respect, but a good question could earn you lifetime points.

After a second of silence, Dr. Chen held out his hand for the file. Gretchen turned it over without a word, and they shivered slightly in the cold room as he flipped through the pages.

"The tox report isn't here," Dr. Chen said slowly.

"Was one ordered?" Gretchen asked, delicately, careful not to imply that Dr. Chen had made a mistake.

He blinked up at her, but she got the impression he wasn't seeing her. "Patsy."

"No, Gretchen."

Dr. Chen wagged his finger at her. "Don't be smart. Patsy, she's my assistant. She sent the tox off, but I told her to mark it low priority. The labs are always backed up."

"For months?" Gretchen asked.

"We are not a TV show," Dr. Chen scolded her. "Yes for months. For years even."

"And it was marked low priority because of the obvious cause of death?" Gretchen asked.

"Yes," Dr. Chen agreed, but he'd slumped, a little of his natural glow dimmed.

"Do you think that could account for it?" Gretchen tried to distract him, going for hypotheticals now. "She was drugged, then stabbed?"

"Yes," Dr. Chen said slowly. "This is not my area of expertise, but I believe the prevailing thought was that she didn't want to fight back against her daughter."

Gretchen pictured Viola. "Correct."

"Those are two different things," Marconi commented, a bit distantly, like she hadn't meant to say it out loud. But when both Dr. Chen and Gretchen looked over, she nodded once, twice. Firmly. "The drugs would suggest premeditated murder."

"And the stabbing suggests a heat-of-the-moment killing," Gretchen finished Marconi's thought for her.

"Unless . . . ," Dr. Chen said. "The rage was performative."

"Can someone really make that seem convincing?" Marconi asked.

"Oh, darling," Gretchen drawled, even though she'd just been wondering the same thing. "Any emotion can be faked with enough practice."

# CHAPTER FORTY

## REED

*Five years before Claire's death—*

Reed kept a PO box that he had never told anyone about except for Ainsley. It felt powerful to be able to have a secret, for it to be such a big one.

He couldn't check it often. Sometimes he went months between visits. Once, it had been two years.

When things got bad, though, he went more often. The very act of checking the box felt like he was exerting control on an admittedly tiny part of his life.

This was a rough patch they were going through. Viola's teacher had called him in for a special meeting with the school psychologist and the vice principal as they explained how Viola had been systematically teaching another child to dissect frogs outside class. They hadn't managed to catch them in the act, but they'd found a scalpel from the science lab hidden in the child's desk.

Reed wasn't worried about the other kid. Probably, he wasn't a psychopath and had just fallen under Viola's spell. A little distance and discipline should sap the bloodlust right out of him.

Viola had a way of picking the weakest members from the herd. He used to watch her sometimes, before it made him too sick to his stomach to do so, when they were at the playground or a birthday party. Any social gathering was ripe with promise for his little psychopath.

She'd always stand back, just off to the side, not enough to be noticed by a concerned parent, but not in the mix, either. It would take all of a minute before she'd identified the hierarchy unspooling before her.

And she always, always, went for the easy prey.

The attacks weren't actual attacks every time. Like with how Viola treated Ainsley, sometimes none of them—Reed, Viola, or her victim—knew what the endgame was until it was too late. With those kids, Reed imagined Viola was essentially setting up a testing laboratory for years to come.

Sometimes the attacks were fast and vicious, though. It was terrible to think, but Reed actually preferred those outbursts. Quick pain instead of prolonged fear.

Her brothers were the ultimate long game. And Reed didn't go one day where that knowledge didn't paralyze him with terror.

So when Viola's pretty teacher, with her concerned eyes and gentle hand laid on his forearm, had asked if he needed water, he'd nodded, followed her, flirted with her, and then nudged her into the storage closet. For ten minutes, he'd been able to do something other than drown beneath the crushing weight of his own life.

Afterward, the teacher whose name he couldn't even remember now had been so flustered that she hadn't pushed the issue much further beyond handing him some pamphlets. Reed had nearly laughed at those. What were they going to give him? *How to Manage Your Sadistic Psychopath in Three Easy Steps?*

That had been two days ago. Now Reed took the last stop on the T's purple line. There weren't many riders who got off with him, but he hung back on the platform anyway, strolling instead of rushing for the exit.

When it was clear there was no one following him, he walked the four blocks to the post office and pulled the key from his wallet.

He had to admit he was a little surprised when he saw something waiting for him. A postcard this time, like most times.

The image on the front was ridiculous. A cow wearing big novelty sunglasses and a photoshopped grin. No location was featured.

He smiled back at the silly cow for longer than he would admit. Then he flipped it over to see the familiar scrawl.

When he got outside, he glanced both ways, then ducked into the alley, crouching behind the closest dumpster.

Then he pulled his lighter out and burned the postcard, watching as the silly cow was consumed, watching until the message was nothing but ash in the wind.

# CHAPTER FORTY-ONE

## GRETCHEN

*Now—*

Gretchen dropped Marconi off and then locked herself in the room in her apartment that she'd converted to an office. She sat on the floor, the notes from the Kent case fanned out in front of her.

When she realized what was wrong with the file, it was past 3:00 a.m. She called Shaughnessy almost absently as she stared down at the papers, and he answered before the second ring, not even sounding groggy.

"This better be good."

"Please, don't act like you aren't sitting at home brooding over a glass of something with a high proof," Gretchen said. If she'd really woken him up, he wouldn't have picked up so fast.

"What do you want?" Shaughnessy asked, not denying the accusation. She wondered if he'd had a night of peace in all his years on the force. He was the type of man who felt the weight of the job like it was a cross to bear. Gretchen didn't understand it, but she knew it to be true.

"Lena didn't take the case because she was feeling guilty," Gretchen said with every bit of confidence that she now felt. *I messed up, Gretch.* "She took it to make sure Viola was charged."

"Come again?" Shaughnessy said after a minute.

"The rest of Lena's files are detailed and incredibly thorough," Lena said. "Viola Kent's has almost nothing but the facts in it."

"A separate file maybe?"

"Perhaps," Gretchen conceded, though it didn't sit right. "But why would she need to hide it if it contained her arguments that would become public in a month anyway?"

"Do you know if she was usually prepped a month out?" Shaughnessy asked.

Gretchen almost laughed at that. "Lena came out of the womb prepared."

"Got it," Shaughnessy grunted, presumably put off by the image, and Gretchen swallowed a smirk. "Well, I hate to say it, but it makes sense."

"Lena acts as the accomplice, kills Claire, frames Viola, and then takes the case to make sure the plan isn't thrown off by some scrupulous lawyer," Gretchen summed up.

"You sound impressed."

"I am," Gretchen breathed. "And it lets Reed Kent off the hook, too. If he hadn't hired a fancy lawyer for his daughter, people would have been suspicious."

"But a fancy lawyer might have pushed for a lighter sentence." Shaughnessy's tone wasn't quite as reverent as hers, but there was some satisfaction in it that Gretchen could relate to. Good planning should always be appreciated. "So you think Lena could have really killed Claire Kent?"

*A damn fine reason.* Gretchen was just about to answer when his laugh cut her off.

"Look who I'm asking," Shaughnessy said, almost to himself. "You think anyone could murder anyone."

"And you don't?" Gretchen challenged, not in the mood to be poked at.

"Yup," Shaughnessy said, easily as ever. But there was an odd pause Gretchen didn't rush to fill. "Hey, can I ask you a question?"

"You can ask—I won't guarantee an answer," Gretchen said. "And don't make it stupid."

"Why do you do this?" Shaughnessy asked. "Not . . . not this case. I get that—I know it's personal. I mean the rest of this."

"Consulting?" Gretchen rarely couched her words with Shaughnessy. He expected the worst out of her, so she didn't bother wasting energy pretending to be anything other than who she was. She supposed that made him her closest remaining friend. And wasn't that a goddamn sad thought for another day. "Well, partly you, of course."

"Me?"

"Mmm," Gretchen confirmed, though slightly annoyed for having to do so. She'd thought this obvious. "I was quite . . . put out by your obsession with me."

"I wouldn't call it an obsession," he grumbled.

She would *absolutely* call it an obsession. Not a sick one. She'd been a young girl after all, and she knew how people could spin things. But he hadn't wanted her to kill anyone else, and adopting that responsibility and placing it on his own shoulders had resulted in the dynamic that had followed them into adulthood.

"Conviction of my guilt," Gretchen corrected anyway. Empaths preferred euphemisms to hard truths. "You were so annoyingly insistent I had murdered Rowan. And, well, you kept hanging around making sure I didn't kill anyone else."

Shaughnessy choked out a small cough at the phrase "hanging around," but he didn't interrupt.

"I thought, what better way to get further under your skin than to become a police consultant? And not only a consultant, but one whom you would have to work with," Gretchen said, trying not to sound too smug about it. This was her violence, this impact that she'd had on him, the impact he'd had on her. There was something undeniably visceral about two lives intertwining like theirs had, something so brutal and beautiful.

"I know you don't believe me, but not every sociopath has the desire to kill someone," Gretchen continued. "Yes, we have flashes of impulses that we need to learn to control, and we don't have that . . . intrinsic feeling for right and wrong that empaths seem to be born with."

"Exactly—"

"But." Gretchen cut him off. "Moral codes don't need to be innate to be effective."

He didn't even need to say anything for her to be able to hear his doubt.

"All right, take religion," Gretchen said, decidedly climbing on her soapbox. Empaths were no better than anyone else just because of their particular brain chemistry. "There are plenty of moral codes built into religion that are far from innate. Mormons aren't supposed to drink coffee. Jewish people aren't supposed to get tattoos. I don't think any person, empath or not, was born with such outstanding moral fiber as to think that maybe they shouldn't indulge in lattes or get inked. Yet millions of people abstain because a book written thousands of years ago tells them to."

"Because they want to be good," Shaughnessy argued. "It's not just about the codes and where you can find them. There has to be the desire to follow them, because they believe that's what makes them good people. Without that, why follow those rules?"

"Nope." Gretchen waved a finger in the air, though she knew the gesture to be nonsensical. He couldn't see her. "They want some promised heavenly reward, or they want to avoid hell. It's like Santa Claus.

Be good and you'll get presents. Be bad and you'll get coal. When really those books are just telling people how to operate in a society because otherwise it would be chaos. That's not nearly as convincing."

"So you're saying—"

Again she stopped him because he was about to put words in her mouth. "I'm not saying that people aren't born with this conscience thing that you all hold up above all others. Atheists are just as moral as Christians."

"Then what is your point?"

"Just because I wasn't born with some magical feeling that tells me it's wrong to kill people doesn't mean I am *going* to kill people," Gretchen said, exasperated.

"You're not Mormon," Shaughnessy said.

"If anyone ever questions your detective skills, you send them my way," Gretchen said, lightly, leaning back against her coffee table. "I like my life, my home, my career. I understand enough about my diagnosis that, due to my penchant for boredom and my lack of concern about consequences, I could easily ruin all that. So, long ago I accepted a moral code into my life that wasn't exactly religion but seems to have worked."

"Do I want to know what this 'moral code' is?"

Gretchen grinned even though he couldn't see her. "Proving you wrong."

"Are you shi—messing with me?"

"Not even a tiny bit," Gretchen said. "Anytime I get the urge to stab someone in the neck because they're walking too slow in front of me, I think of how much you'd gloat about it."

"Well, I'll be damned." Shaughnessy sounded genuinely surprised. "That can't be all of it, though. Why you devoted your life to this."

And here was the part where she really could tell Shaughnessy about the dark parts of her. He would trust her more for it anyway. "It gives me an outlet."

There was a second where he seemed to be trying to follow the implications behind that. "The bodies."

The bodies. And the blood and the bone and all the ways humans tore into each other, all the ways they hurt each other and destroyed each other while leaving a bit of their own souls behind. Just like her and Shaughnessy.

She thought it was perhaps the most fascinating thing in the world.

"I get my fix, if you will," Gretchen admitted.

Shaughnessy was one of the shrewdest cops she knew, despite—or because of?—his penchant for believing the worst in her. "And if that got cut off?"

"There are plenty of outlets," Gretchen said. "Oh, unbunch your panties, Detective. I meant crime shows and the like. We're living in a golden age, if you haven't noticed."

"I did," Shaughnessy said, like the cantankerous grump he was. "Do you think it would ever escalate? Your need for . . . that."

"Of course," Gretchen said, not even hesitating. "Everyone has the capacity to kill."

"Where exactly do you fall on psychopaths like Viola?" Shaughnessy asked. "Do they fall into your beloved gray area of relative morality?"

"They're all terrible and can burn," Gretchen said with a deadpan voice.

He laughed at the hyperbole as she'd meant him to, but underneath that was a warmth that felt something like understanding.

"All right, so what's your best guess on the Kent thing?" Shaughnessy said, all business again. "You still think Reed Kent instigated it, though? What if it was just Lena?"

"The casino keeps throwing me off," Gretchen admitted, and then paused. Remembering why she'd wanted a warrant for Ainsley Kent, remembering that short audio clip. *Do you trust me?* "But what I could believe is Ainsley Kent is involved somehow. Maybe she and Lena plotted this whole thing out."

"And Reed isn't involved at all?" The doubt came through loud and clear.

"Not necessarily," Gretchen said. "I bet whatever the motive turns out to be, if Ainsley Kent is involved, it's because she thinks she's protecting her brother from something."

"Which means what for us?"

"Claire Kent hired Lena to look into the disappearance of Tess Murphy," Gretchen said. "There's audio that shows Lena and Ainsley were in communication behind Reed's back, behind Claire's back, too."

Shaughnessy hummed thoughtfully. "Might help with the warrant to bring Ainsley in if we make that argument. Would help if we had motive, though."

Tess Murphy.

Her disappearance was what had sent these people on a collision course toward each other after decades of silence. But there wasn't even proof that she was killed, as far as Gretchen knew. Not more than an old bracelet that supposedly had some blood on it.

Maybe . . .

Maybe that meant there was still someone out there who needed protecting.

Maybe Lena hadn't found a *damn fine reason* to kill someone when she'd gone digging around in the past.

Maybe Lena had found Tess Murphy.

# CHAPTER FORTY-TWO

## REED

*Twenty years before Claire's death—*

Soft, warm hands covered Reed's eyes, lips brushing his ear. "Boo."

Reed laughed and reached up to snag Tess's wrist, tugging her around and down onto his lap. "Hi."

He hadn't had to wait long at their place. A park just six blocks south of Fiona Murphy's house. It was usually deserted at night, save for a few college-age guys drinking in the fake tree house near the slides.

Tess smiled up at him, moonlight caressing her face, tangling into her hair. Objectively, he knew she was beautiful, knew she was kind and lovely and way too good for him. But he didn't want that, had never wanted it, he realized too late.

He wanted ice-tipped lava, sharp features, and a little bit of meanness that could match his own.

The happy welcome slipped from Tess's expression, a small, sad smile in its place as she studied him. "You were never quite mine, were you, Reed Kent?"

He picked his words with rare care and precision, already consumed with guilt for hurting her. "I'll always be here for you."

One corner of her mouth ticked up. She was far too nice to say, *I wish I could believe that,* though they both knew what she was thinking. They'd really been together for only two months before Claire had entered the picture. Reed couldn't deny that in the two months since, he'd been far more distracted than he should have been, considering he'd yet to actually tell Tess the truth.

But, like always, she didn't make him do the hard thing. Sometimes he wished she would, and then he realized that's why they would never fit.

"You have enough money?" he asked instead of saying, *I'm sorry.* Instead of saying, *I should never have let us be more than friends.* Instead of saying, *I never wanted to hurt you and so I did anyway.*

Those were empty words. Pointless. They were words meant to soothe the burn of shame that Reed figured would scar his soul for the rest of his life. If he'd actually been a good man, he wouldn't have needed those words in the first place.

Tess deserved a good man. A good life. Something better than this.

"Yup," she said and climbed out of his lap, probably for the last time. They were a tactile bunch, he and Lena and Tess. But Tess was keeping a careful distance now, her hands shoved into the pockets of the summer jacket she wore. "Have my new ID, too."

They knew a guy at school who knew a guy who knew a guy who had been able to hook Tess up with a believable-enough driver's license to get her by for a while.

"You're just going to disappear then?" Reed asked, though he'd heard the details of her plan enough times. It still felt like there was something she wasn't telling him. The reason she startled sometimes when someone moved too quickly toward her.

"There's nothing left for Tess Murphy. Let her die here," Tess said, lifting one shoulder. She kicked at the duffel bag half slumped near his feet. "Thanks for bringing this."

He shook off the gratitude. "Whatever you need."

At that, Tess looked up, and it was only when their eyes met that he realized she'd been avoiding his gaze. Her voice, when she spoke, was urgent, near-on desperate. "I need you to keep your promise."

Reed almost stood to grasp her shoulders, to pull her into a hug, to reassure her. But she flinched back when he moved. He stopped, hands up. "I won't tell anyone. I swear."

*Who are you afraid of?* is what he wanted to ask. Because if she was just running away to get a new life, she would have told Lena, would have let him reassure Fiona sometime down the line. Tess didn't just want to get out of Southie. She wanted to hide.

He'd almost forced the issue countless times, had swallowed the question to the point that it had become rough against his throat.

A coward. Always a coward.

"No one," Tess iterated, and the moonlight was no longer kind to her pretty face. Rather it threw it into sharp relief, her skin made all the paler, her eyes dark, her brows pinched. "Not the police. Not Fiona. Not Lena." She paused, licking her lower lip. "Not Claire."

"Not even Declan," Reed promised, and she nodded, like it was an afterthought.

"Not even Dec," she murmured, eyes on the ground. "Okay, good."

An ambulance screamed in the distance, a car backfired, the group of kids at the far end of the basketball court hollered something unintelligible.

"Where you gonna go?" Reed finally asked, still tense, still caught somewhere between sitting and standing, between friend and ex-boyfriend.

Tess lifted one shoulder, and when she looked up, she grinned. "That's the beauty of it, isn't it? I don't have to know."

"Somewhere better," Reed said, parroting the words she said weeks ago when she first brought up the idea. She'd been planning long before that, had been saving money for years.

*Nothing holding me here,* she'd said then, her head on his shoulder, her leg tossed over his thighs. Neither of them mentioned that he might be a reason for her to stay. Her words were mean and they were meant to be, and Reed hoped he hadn't twisted something in her irreparably.

That was probably giving himself too much credit. But there was a tiny part of him that liked the idea, that wanted to have made his mark on someone else, that wanted to have this power over her.

He wondered if she was starting to realize that. Wondered if she watched him and Claire together and realized she was far more suited for the light.

When she stooped to grab the duffel, he noticed a smudge on her wrist where her jacket had been pushed up a little. Without thinking, he caught her arm and brought it closer for inspection.

The smudges were bruises, finger-shaped, like someone had gripped her hard and yanked. They were fading, but noticeable still. Gently, he ran the pad of his thumb over the ghost of the violence. "Who?"

Tess made a small sound. "You know who."

If Reed were a better man, he would have nodded. Instead he just cradled her arm, like an apology that wasn't even his to give until after several long, silent minutes, she finally stepped back.

She slung the duffel bag over her shoulder and threw him a lazy salute as she went to turn away.

"Hey," he called.

Tess stopped, listening, but now with her back to him.

"Do me a favor?" he said.

Her shoulders went taut, like she expected the worst from him. He didn't blame her.

"Forget me," he finished.

She shifted just a bit, so that he could see her profile, the long spill of blonde hair, the small smile. "Nah, never. I'll even send you a post-card when I get there."

And with that she was gone.

Headed toward somewhere better.

# CHAPTER FORTY-THREE

## GRETCHEN

*Now—*

Gretchen redialed Shaughnessy, realizing only belatedly that she'd hung up on him.

"One of these days I'm going to enroll you in a class on manners," Shaughnessy said. But he'd answered, so he couldn't be too riled up about it.

"You'd have to be right there next to me," Gretchen shot back.

An idea was beginning to form, but she didn't want to look straight at it, not yet. She still wanted to talk to Viola. And, more important, Gretchen didn't want to get sidelined from the investigation if she told Shaughnessy her suspicions too soon.

But she wondered if assumptions and confirmation bias had trapped her just as much as they had Shaughnessy.

She'd been operating under the premise that Tess Murphy's death was some mystery Lena had been digging into, one that had tipped over a set of dominoes that had led to Claire's murder.

What if, instead, the catalyst that had led to all this was rooted in the fact that Tess Murphy had never died in the first place.

Dead bodies didn't tell secrets.

Vengeful women on the other hand? They did.

"Tell me about that night," Gretchen said. "The night Claire was murdered."

"A bedtime story for you then?" Shaughnessy asked. But then he continued. "The 9-1-1 call was made by Reed Kent at 4:11 a.m. He sounded . . ."

"Distraught?" Gretchen guessed. She'd thought him a good actor.

"Genuinely so," Shaughnessy agreed, almost reluctantly. "Seems like he called right away, right when he got home."

"Did you map out the time he was last seen on the videos in the casino to when he arrived home?" Gretchen asked.

"You think you're dealing with an amateur?" Shaughnessy said and then quickly added, "Don't answer that."

Gretchen laughed because softballs like that weren't fun anyway.

"Time checks out," Shaughnessy said. "About a missing forty minutes, and if you account for finding a taxi, everything adds up."

"Did the cameras record him getting any phone calls before he left?" That might answer the accomplice question.

"We didn't check," Shaughnessy said. "You think we have limitless resources?"

"For a murder?" Gretchen asked. "Yes."

"For a murder with a suspect that might as well have had 'guilty' stamped on her forehead?" Shaughnessy countered. "No."

Gretchen pivoted. "What happened after the 9-1-1 call?"

"Police got there. Kids were together in the living room, first responders tried to resuscitate Claire Kent while Reed Kent watched," Shaughnessy said. "Reed said he hadn't turned on the lights when coming into the room. Didn't know anything was wrong until he felt the damp bedsheets."

"When did they start to suspect Viola?"

"Officers asked if he had any enemies, anyone he suspected who could have done this." Shaughnessy sounded like he'd refamiliarized himself with the file recently. "And Reed said, 'Check my daughter's room.'"

"Well." This was far from Gretchen's first case dealing with children who displayed antisocial personality disorders. When the behavior escalated to the point of violence on the level of the Kent case, the parents, almost without exception, tried to hide it first. She'd asked a colleague about it once—confused as to why the parents wouldn't be the first to hand over a child who must have been nothing but, at best, a headache, at worst, a nightmare.

The colleague had shaken her head. "Loving children defies logic," she'd said, and had left it at that like it was an explanation.

The fact had held true even if Gretchen had never wrapped her head around it. If this were a typical case, if it was exactly what it looked like, Gretchen would have expected Reed Kent to do anything in his power to delay the police from finding that weapon.

Instead he served it up on a silver platter.

When it came to violence like this, few things were hard-and-fast. But the odds were looking like Reed Kent at least had a role in implicating his daughter in his wife's murder.

"I guess you're probably right," Shaughnessy admitted, as if he'd needed to hear that part out loud. "They framed her from the start. But we still have nada to prove that."

Gretchen bit at the skin on the inside of her mouth. "What happened to the blood?"

Silence greeted her question.

"On Viola," Gretchen clarified, though she knew he'd realized what she was asking. She just couldn't resist pointing out when he'd missed something big at a crime scene. "Was she checked for physical evidence?"

"Of course she was," he said, and somehow it didn't come off as defensive. Maybe in his younger years he would have snapped that at her, but now he just sounded tired. "She's used to hiding her killings, Gretch. You know that."

"Did she deny it?" Gretchen asked instead of agreeing to that. A thirteen-year-old girl might know how to hide a small, dead bird that didn't have much blood in it in the first place. To conceal the spatter from a violent stabbing seemed far less likely, even for someone as practiced as Viola was in her young age.

"She didn't say a word," Shaughnessy said. "Not one word."

"And no one really thought to ask her why she did it," Gretchen murmured. "The picture was already painted."

"Don't tell me you're feeling sorry for the psychopath now," Shaughnessy said.

"Our justice system is a funny thing, isn't it?" Gretchen said, idly flipping through the papers once more. "It's set up to prevent biases, and yet every step of the process relies on human judgment in all of its flawed glory."

"Oh, another lecture from our sociopath," Shaughnessy snarked, but didn't actually shut her down. Being able to rant at will was one of her few perks, and she took advantage of it.

"Like you," Gretchen pointed out. "Your white hat is oh so clean, but—"

"You want me to say I don't think you killed Rowan?" Shaughnessy cut in, his voice thick with something she'd call emotion but was probably just exhaustion.

"I want to know why you don't care that Viola Kent is being held for a crime she didn't commit," Gretchen countered, furious that he'd brought up Rowan. It wasn't that Gretchen even cared about Viola, but she was tired of the holier-than-thou, sanctimonious attitude about who was the decider of guilt and innocence. That same attitude had ruined her life.

"Because not all of us live our lives in black and white," Shaughnessy said without a trace of shame. Just like she knew he would. Empaths on high horses rarely saw when their own knees were buried in the muck.

"But who makes you the judge and jury of everyone else's soul?" Gretchen pressed, because it was late and her mind was desperately trying to put pieces together that wouldn't fit. Like with a blue sky in a puzzle, she knew she was in the right area but couldn't get the edges to align.

"Not everyone's," Shaughnessy protested. "Just Viola Kent's."

"And mine," Gretchen said quietly in a way that she knew would have more impact on Shaughnessy than if she'd raged at him. He didn't know how to handle her when she sounded hurt, because she so rarely did. But that was the point. You didn't deploy powerful weapons all the time; you did it when you wanted it to make an impact.

He didn't say he was sorry, and she didn't expect him to. He'd die before apologizing to her.

"Dr. Chen thinks Claire might have been drugged," Gretchen said, knowing Shaughnessy would keep up with the conversational pivot.

"Meaning, the person wouldn't have had to overpower her."

Lena had been short and curvy, petite but not bird-boned. From what Gretchen could tell from pictures and the news coverage, Claire had been on the willowy side. Maybe Lena could have fought her, but if Gretchen were going to kill someone taller than herself, possibly stronger, she would take the advantage where she could get it.

"Right," Shaughnessy echoed in her same condescending tone. "Which supports the idea that Viola was her killer."

"You have zero creativity in your thinking."

Shaughnessy huffed out an amused breath. "And you have too much."

"Can I get in with Viola again today?" Gretchen asked without acknowledging the weak comeback.

"Yes," Shaughnessy said, but it was slow and hesitant, like he was nervous about what she was planning.

"Fantastic," Gretchen murmured. "I think it's time we ask Viola who killed her mother."

# CHAPTER FORTY-FOUR

## REED

*Twenty years before Claire's death—*

Lena had invited Claire Brentwood to the party on a whim driven by cruelty.

No one in their little group of friends had any tolerance for rich kids gone slumming in Southie, and all three of them were dead set on hating her. Maybe not Reed. He still remembered the way the shorts she'd worn at the baseball game had clung to long, supple thighs that he had already pictured wrapped around his waist too many times to count.

Still, when Lena had railed against all the ways she thought Claire was some prissy, stuck-up bitch, he'd nodded along, Tess doing the same.

He didn't know quite how he'd ended up on a beer-stained couch that smelled of weed and cat piss with Claire sitting a little too close to him, her hand on his thigh. He tried not to stare at it, but from her pleased smile he could tell he hadn't been successful.

"You're with Lena," Claire half shouted into his ear. The music was some god-awful pop thing that had been playing nonstop on the radio for months. Someone stumbled into them and dumped most of their drink on Reed's arm.

Neither of them took their eyes off each other. God, she was pretty. He knew he was supposed to be drawn to girls with big boobs and plush bodies, puffy lips and narrow waists. But he liked Claire's angles, the way her eyes reacted even if her face didn't follow suit.

"Nah. Not Lena," he said.

"Really," Claire asked. "You guys seem . . . close."

He leaned in, his mouth brushing her earlobe, clumsily, he could tell, but he was drunk and turned-on from the way her breast pressed against his forearm. "She's like my sister."

"You don't think she's in love with you?" Claire pushed, and Reed wanted to stop talking about Lena and start talking about . . . shit. Tess.

"With Tess."

There was a moment where she pulled back, stared at him, then leaned back in. "What?"

Reed scratched at his nose. "Tess is my girlfriend."

The words tasted wrong ever since Tess had kissed him two months ago.

Claire leaned forward, her elbow on her knee, her chin resting against her fist, a contemplative smile working its way free from the serious set of her lips. "You're madly in love with her, I suppose." She paused. "She seems . . . nice."

Reed slumped against the couch as he watched her. "Are you nice?"

Claire's smile twisted into an amused smirk. "Never."

# CHAPTER FORTY-FIVE

## GRETCHEN

*Now—*

After hanging up with Shaughnessy, Gretchen dived back into the files she had stretched across the carpet. When she was done poring over those, she turned to the texts and emails between her and Lena both around the time of Claire's death and also a year ago, looking for hidden, subtle clues.

There was nothing. At least nothing that Gretchen could pick up on.

She glanced at the clock on her phone: 4:17 a.m.

Too late to bother sleeping, too early to be productive. There were years in Gretchen's early twenties that she'd loved this time of day. The in-between hours. Like any good sociopath, she'd tried mindless sex, she'd worked her way through most drugs imaginable—though had drawn the line firmly at meth as she liked her skin healthy looking. She'd found open stretches of highway and pushed the Porsche to its limits, the wheel vibrating beneath her fingers, everything blurry and wonderful and one hairbreadth away from catastrophe.

Gretchen considered that now, but by the time she made it out of the city, there would be too many cars for it to be any fun.

Instead, just for the sheer lack of anything else to do, Gretchen yanked her laptop closer and pulled up a few gossip sites.

This case felt like one of those images that actually contained two separate pictures—a vase and also two women's faces looking at each other, the wife and the mother-in-law, a rabbit with its ears tucked back and also a duck with its bill tipped up. Ambiguous images, they were called.

It didn't matter which figure you saw first. It was almost impossible to get your brain to recognize the other picture. If you saw a rabbit, you would not easily see the duck, and vice versa.

But if you were told just one thing to look for, the whole picture shifted like magic. And then all you could see was the image you had never been able to recognize three seconds earlier.

That's how Gretchen felt now. She was seeing the rabbit and she needed to see the duck. She knew it was there, knew there was a layer running beneath this whole investigation that she couldn't make her brain recognize. Yet she still couldn't see it.

She just needed that one thing, that one clue that would shift the entire image like magic so that she would never believe how she hadn't been able to see it in the first place.

When she'd first found the audio file Lena had left behind, Gretchen had thought that might be the right hint. It had given them plenty of information, so Gretchen's irritation that it hadn't been quite enough didn't seem justified.

She knew Tess Murphy's old disappearance had brought Claire and Reed Kent back into Lena's life after decades of silence.

She knew Lena was trying to get Declan Murphy to think Reed was the guilty party for Tess's presumed death.

She knew there was no hard evidence Tess had ever died in the first place.

She knew there were millions of dollars involved and Claire had been thinking about changing her will to cut Reed out.

She knew, or suspected, that their marriage wasn't quite the picture-perfect fairy tale that it looked like from the outside.

And she knew Lena and Ainsley Kent knew something the rest of them didn't.

Perhaps Viola would say the right thing, with or without meaning to, that would make those separate pieces come together into a cohesive image.

For now, Gretchen typed "Reed Kent Tess Murphy Boston murder" into her search bar. The first page of results were either irrelevant or crime blogs that offered no insight on the old case. A few had entries from six months ago when Claire Kent had been buried, speculating if the husband was the same Reed Kent who was a player in the "Tess Murphy cold case."

Most people scoffed at the suggestion, pointing to Reed Kent's supposed upper-class background that had led him straight into Harvard. Whomever Reed had paid off to bury his past had done spectacular work. She guessed that it had helped that his name was fairly common—in Massachusetts alone there were three other Reed Kents—but she still found it impressive what Claire's money had accomplished when it came to erasing any trace of Reed's roots.

Gretchen idly skimmed through the next several hundred results and wondered how many people really made it that far in when most stopped before page two.

That's when she saw the highlighted comment on the Google page. "Anyone ever looked into Reed Kent?"

She clicked on the link. The blog wasn't about Tess Murphy, but Gretchen found the reference in the comments.

The *Boston Globe* article attached to the mention of Reed Kent was dated from the summer Tess Murphy went missing.

World's End park.

Gretchen bit the inside of her lip, the implication obvious. This was Tess's burial site.

According to the other commenters, someone was trying to plant these seeds in multiple places.

Once again Gretchen tried to make the pieces fit. Was this Tess Murphy's doing? Back from the grave to haunt Reed Kent? But this accusation was so insubstantial as to land on page twelve of a fairly specific Google search. And it didn't even substantially link the Reed Kent known as Tess Murphy's boyfriend to the Reed Kent known as Claire Kent's husband.

If this was Tess's work, she was doing a poor job of it.

What would be interesting was if Tess's body was actually found near the site in the article's picture. The crime blogger themselves had commented on the response. If the body's discovery made news, the blogger would surely remember this exchange.

The person commenting would look like someone with insider knowledge, and would gain instant notoriety in the community. Enough to get buzz going. Enough to get the attention of the police even?

Because if Tess had died, who would know where she was buried other than the killer?

But had Tess died? Gretchen kept coming back to that, and she didn't have an answer.

She decided to switch tacks and pulled up a popular gossip site that usually proved more accurate than others. The Kents had long disappeared from the front pages of the digital rags. Six months might as well be six years for sites like these. But a simple search turned up dozens of articles, mostly quick hits, a bunch of photo galleries of Claire and Reed at various events compiled solely to inflate site traffic numbers. There were a few longer pieces, with actual bylines, too. Gretchen found one about the boys, and opened that first.

Objectively, she realized it was distasteful. She knew it was the kind of thing that she would have to pretend disinterest in if it had been sprung upon her by surprise. In the privacy of a locked apartment, though, Gretchen let herself look.

There were a few staged family photos, both from events where there'd been paid paparazzi, and more private ones that looked like they'd been bought from either a friend of the family or a housekeeper with sticky fingers and an eye on the prize.

At first glance, both Milo and Sebastian looked like normal boys, pampered, rich ones, of course, but normal.

Then came the photos from the day after Claire's death, where police had swarmed in and out of the town house. Someone with a long-range lens had been able to capture pictures of the boys, their faces no longer flushed and chubby with youth like in some of the earlier ones. The pictures were high-enough quality that you could see the bruises on Sebastian's arms, the cuts. There was a particularly compelling image of Sebastian looking away, his too-skinny body curled into itself, as Viola was led from the house between two officers.

The photographer must have struck gold with that one. She made sure to jot down the name of the guy. Gretchen made it a point to collect information about people who were particularly skilled at their jobs. You never knew when they could come in handy.

On that thought, Gretchen found a contact in her cell, ignored the fact that it wasn't even 5:00 a.m., and hit call.

The phone rang through to voice mail. Gretchen didn't bother to leave a message, simply texted:

Have a job.

It took three seconds to get a reply, which meant the person on the receiving end had simply been refusing to pick up.

If you ever call me this early again, I'll block your number not only for my phone but for every halfway decent hacker in the city.

Gretchen rolled her eyes at the empty threat. Then waited.
It took another five minutes.

What job?

Gretchen touched the last photo of Milo from the day after Claire's death. He had a cast on his arm. Instead of replying, Gretchen hit call once more. "CPS records."

"Sure, local government's easy." Fred's voice didn't hold any of the animosity of her earlier text.

Gretchen had few friends, but she did have a network of people who tended to be helpful when she was consulting on a case. Ryan Kelly, the tabloid reporter, was one of them. Lena had been another.

Fred was probably the most valuable. Fred's full name was Winnifred James, but she had told Gretchen once that she'd stab a sharpened pencil into Gretchen's carotid artery if Gretchen ever called her that. Fred fell high enough on the antisocial spectrum that Gretchen knew the threat was legitimate.

Not only was Fred useful enough for Gretchen to make the monumental effort of keeping her somewhat happy, but she also aligned closely with Gretchen in terms of rational thinking and ethics. If Fred weren't such a misanthrope, Gretchen thought they might have been something like friends. Or drinking partners, if nothing else.

"Anything on Sebastian and Milo Kent?" Gretchen asked. The number of times the boys must have been taken to the hospital because of Viola would be enough for any doctor to call the authorities.

"You gotta give me time."

"I'll come by today," Gretchen said, her eyes still locked on Milo's little face, flushed with tears. "Later."

"It's going to cost you," Fred warned.

"Sure, sure," Gretchen murmured. There wasn't a price she wouldn't pay for this information.

"And I wasn't joking before."

"Never again," Gretchen promised, and if she believed in that kind of thing, she would have had her fingers crossed. It wasn't like Fred kept normal hours anyway. She couldn't be pissed if someone woke her up.

Fred hung up with a disbelieving grunt.

Gretchen tossed the phone to the side, still considering the picture, and wondered why Milo's cast hadn't been included in any of the official reports.

To be fair, Gretchen knew she must have seen the pictures, too, back when the case had broken. She'd paid attention enough because psychopaths were interesting, and it was rare that it had been a girl, rare that she'd been so young. It fell enough into Gretchen's purview that she could pretend her curiosity had been professional.

Plus, no one would blame her for watching the case closely. The echoes from her own past so clear they could almost be seen in the air as tangible ripples.

Still, she could not for the life of her remember noting the cast. Not apart from the list of the boys' other injuries.

And as she stared at the image, everything shifted. Like magic.

Because she thought she might have just found the duck.

# CHAPTER FORTY-SIX

## REED

*Six months after Claire's death—*

When some people came into your life, the ground shook. For others it was a blip, tripping over a crack in the sidewalk and forgetting about the whole thing two seconds later.

Tess had come into Reed's life with a sweet smile and an offer to share half of her peanut butter sandwich on the playground.

Lena had come into his life when she'd faced down a bully, hands on her hips, the kid who'd been teasing Tess knocked flat on his ass, crying on the ground.

Ainsley had come into his life a screaming, red-faced blob whom he hadn't been allowed to hold, but who had, when he'd reached out one shaking hand, curled her little fingers around his thumb and gripped tight, unwilling to let go.

And then there had been Claire. An earthquake, a wildfire, a frost that covered the scorched earth, and everything in between.

When Milo had come into Reed's life, he'd whimpered and blinked up at Reed with liquid eyes that always seemed full of tears. A gentle soul that got all the kindness that neither Reed nor Claire possessed.

Sebastian came despite predictions that he wouldn't. His hands balled into fists, feet kicking, lips blue but parted on a battle cry. Reed's little fighter.

Viola came into Reed's life silently, refusing to wail like she was supposed to, that calm interlude when the air and the earth got quiet before the storm.

When some people came into your life, the ground shook. And it left nothing but devastation in its wake.

# CHAPTER FORTY-SEVEN

## GRETCHEN

*Now—*

Viola looked no more the monster the second time around. She smiled sweetly at Gretchen from the other side of the table, and neither of them mentioned the crude, long gash on her arm.

*Shank,* Shaughnessy had informed Gretchen before she'd entered the room. *Self-made.*

He'd told Gretchen so that Viola couldn't use the wound to manipulate her. As if Gretchen would roll belly up at the first sign of the girl being injured.

"My father hasn't visited me yet," Viola said right off the bat. "Yet *you* can't stay away."

"Why do you think your father hasn't come?" Gretchen asked, knowing she was playing into the girl's script, knowing she was laying out a space for Viola to lie, knowing Shaughnessy would likely be huffing about bad interrogation techniques behind the silvery glass. She was still curious. As Viola had intended.

That innocent smile wavered, wobbled, disappeared, and then came back too bright. It was a pitch-perfect imitation of someone putting on a brave face. "He's . . . I think he hates me sometimes."

"Because he hasn't come to visit?"

Viola hunched a bit, glanced up and back down at her lap. Then her shoulders lifted in a weak shrug.

Gretchen wanted to laugh. "Who are you performing for?" she asked, looking around as if she were really going to spot someone else in the room.

"I'm . . ." Viola blinked too fast, as if holding back tears. "I know . . . I know what they say about me."

"That you're a psychopath who murdered her mother," Gretchen said without any sympathy. She could all but see Shaughnessy slapping a bearlike palm to his forehead.

Something shivered across Viola's face, and just like that she dropped the act.

"But you think I'm innocent," Viola singsonged. "You said you weren't going to tell a single soul."

"You know better than to trust the word of a . . ." Gretchen waved at herself and Viola stiffened, her eyes darting to the mirror and then back to Gretchen.

The girl was valiantly fighting down a reaction, but she hadn't quite done it yet.

"You want people to think you killed her," Gretchen said, and it wasn't even a question. In their first interview, Viola had made it seem like the attention was what she wanted. But that couldn't be all of it. Gretchen tipped her head, considering. "You're not protecting someone—you're incapable of that level of attachment."

"Rude."

"Why else would you stay silent?" Gretchen asked out loud, not expecting an answer. "You are a narcissist, so the attention is a draw."

"Yup, that's definitely it."

"Bribery, of course," Gretchen mused. "But I can't imagine a thirteen-year-old, let alone a psychopath, being bribed into taking the fall for murder."

"Blackmail," Viola suggested, almost eagerly getting in on the game now that Gretchen hadn't let herself be deterred. She was leaning forward, engaged with the conversation as if they were talking about a TV show and not her life.

"What would be worse than jail, though?" Gretchen countered. "If someone were blackmailing you, what could they threaten you with that was worse than this?"

Viola pursed her lips, plucking at them absently before dropping her hand flat on the table. "A long con?"

If Viola herself hadn't put the idea out there, Gretchen actually might have been intrigued by the concept. Depending on her sentencing, there was a chance Viola could be released when she turned eighteen. Holding that secret over someone would be powerful indeed.

"Too many variables," Gretchen concluded. Because why would Viola tell her the plan, looking for all the world like she just thought it up?

But then . . . a smug lip twitch gave her away. That was pleasure right there—pleasure that Gretchen had dismissed the idea as implausible. So far Viola hadn't been able to manipulate Gretchen like she no doubt could others, but the smile told Gretchen she'd accidentally taken a misstep like so many before her.

Which meant . . . *a long con*.

Whom would Viola want to hold power over? Enough so that she was willing to keep silent about a murder.

Reed Kent was the obvious answer.

"Does it upset you that your father hasn't come to visit?" Gretchen asked, without any attempt to smooth over the abrupt topic change.

Viola seemed caught for a moment, like her foot was halfway through a dance step when the music had been cut off. Her eyes narrowed. "Yes. I miss him."

The delivery was stilted and dry, deliberately so, Viola having completely shrugged off any attempts at playing like this was all a big misunderstanding.

"What would you say to him if you could?" Gretchen asked.

Viola watched her for a long moment, the room quiet. Gretchen wondered if she was choosing a strategy or simply letting the tension ratchet up. The victory of a moment earlier might make Viola reckless, reckless enough to give something away she didn't want to while thinking she was being clever.

Gretchen almost wished that she could take credit and say she'd planned that moment of weakness in front of the girl. Complacency was a beautiful thing, after all. What better way to get a psychopath to talk than to let her think she's winning?

"I'd say, 'You're welcome.'" Viola's feral grin stretched across her face until Gretchen could see the sharp points of her incisors.

"For killing your mother?" Gretchen clarified.

Viola tilted her head. "But you don't think I killed her."

"So what should he be thankful for?"

"For not killing them," Viola said, eyes bright. She thought she was getting away with something here.

*Them.* Gretchen made the logical leap. "Your brothers?"

"Mm-hmm," Viola hummed in agreement. "But Daddy was always so worried about the wrong things anyway. They were too fun to kill."

"What should he have been worrying about?" Even as Gretchen asked the question, she realized she had slipped into Viola's current, getting pulled along out to sea. If she wasn't careful, she'd lose total control of this conversation.

"He wanted to leave me for good, you know," Viola said without answering Gretchen. "But Mommy would never have let him do that."

"Leave you and your brothers?"

Viola barked out a laugh, a rough, unpracticed sound. "Daddy would never leave them. He'd do anything for them."

Like kill Claire and frame Viola so all his problems would be taken care of in one fell swoop?

But Reed Kent had an alibi, and it was a good one.

Still, this wasn't the first time the Kents' relationship had been called into question. If Viola were to be believed, Reed Kent wanted to take the boys and leave Claire to deal with Viola. If Gretchen's suspicions were right, Claire was cheating on Reed with Declan. Even Penny Langford had mentioned couples counseling and hinted at a woman at the end of her marriage.

Had Ainsley taken stock of the situation and offered Reed a way out?

If so, where did Lena fit in to all this? And Tess? It couldn't be a coincidence that her brother was Claire's lover.

That thought prodded at something that Gretchen hadn't even realized had been hovering at the edges of her mind.

The bracelet with the blood on it.

It was the only evidence that anything nefarious had happened to Tess Murphy. And from the audio Lena had recorded, they were supposed to think Reed Kent had been keeping it as some kind of serial killer–esque token in his attic.

But how had Claire even found it? What had she been looking for to have stumbled over something so damning? Why would Reed keep the souvenir in a place that could be so easily discovered if it really had been evidence of a crime he'd gotten away with?

On that note, what did twenty-year-old blood on a bracelet look like? Gretchen assumed the bracelet had been a light-colored one, like the woven-rope kind that had been so popular with teenagers those days. From how both Lena and Declan reacted to it, the blood must have been easily distinguishable from faded mud or some other stain.

Maybe Gretchen had been right. Maybe Tess Murphy hadn't been killed that summer she'd disappeared.

But that didn't necessarily mean she was alive to tell her secrets.

"Would your mother have done anything for you?" Gretchen asked, the question slipping out before she had given it permission.

It seemed to catch Viola off guard, but the girl quickly righted herself, her tone more amused than anything else when she asked, "What do you think?"

It was déjà vu, back to their first conversation about how the boys had been kept in their room, safe from Viola.

*"There was a key,"* Viola had said.

*"Locked away from you,"* Gretchen had repeated.

Amusement had flickered across Viola's face. *"What do you think?"*

The obvious answer to both questions was yes.

But wasn't that their problem? They all kept stepping into the space left open by the obvious answer.

It was always the husband, except when it wasn't.

*He wanted to leave . . . Mommy would never have let him do that.*

This whole time, Gretchen had been thinking of this as the perfectly plotted murder, thwarted only by Lena's unexpected overdose.

But what if, instead, this had been a poorly plotted frame job that had never fully played out?

Gretchen stood, ignoring Viola's distressed call when she stepped out of the room. As she dug her phone out of her pants, she tried to remember the exact date on that entry in Lena's financial records.

Marconi took far too long to answer. She'd missed the interview with Viola because of a meeting with the chief that she had sworn she hadn't been able to reschedule. But Gretchen didn't care about that anymore. When Marconi finally picked up, Gretchen didn't bother with niceties. "Tell me your meeting's over."

"My meeting's over," Marconi repeated back obediently. "And it actually is, in case you're wondering."

Shaughnessy popped his head out of the observation room, and Gretchen put the phone on mute just in time so that it wasn't obvious.

"Got a hunch about something," she told him. "I'm going to have Marconi put a uniform on it. I'm going back in—just one second."

He stared at her, suspicious—with good reason, though he didn't know that.

But then he nodded with a gruff "Be quick about it, you're wasting time," before ducking back inside.

Gretchen exhaled and unmuted the phone. "How fast can you mobilize a search team?"

"Uh, for what?" Marconi asked.

"Tess Murphy's remains," Gretchen said.

Marconi's startled pause was so loud Gretchen could almost picture her rocking back on her heels. "You have an idea where they are?"

Gretchen pictured that *Boston Globe* article, the picture. "Wompatuck State Park."

"You want us to search the whole thing?"

The section featured in the *Globe* article had been about a specific area of the park. "World's End. Focus on that," Gretchen said.

"Okay," Marconi said, a bit more tentative than usual. "Are you coming?"

"No, I'm going to try to get more out of Viola," Gretchen said.

Marconi hesitated at that, and Gretchen silently cursed. Why did Marconi have to be astute? Why couldn't Gretchen have been saddled with one of the dull bulbs Shaughnessy seemed to attract?

"Shaughnessy's with me," Gretchen said on that thought. "You don't have to worry that you're neglecting babysitter duties."

"All right," Marconi said, but it didn't sound like she thought it was all right. "I'll keep you updated."

"Oh, and Marconi," Gretchen said before the woman could hang up. "You're not looking for a twenty-year-old grave."

"How fresh are we talking?"

"If I'm right?" Gretchen ran the timeline in her head. "I think about a year."

# CHAPTER FORTY-EIGHT

## Reed

*Seventeen years before Claire's death—*

The first time Claire hit him was so startling Reed didn't feel the pain.

It had been a slap, one that carried enough strength to surprise him, but not enough to leave bruises behind.

Pink stained his cheeks, from humiliation, from arousal, from the ghost of her handprint.

It was rare that she used her hands, he later learned. She was small and he was big and sheer force wouldn't cut it. She could punch down when the occasion called for it. But Claire didn't like the brutality of closed fists or even the weakness implied in a slap.

Instead she employed a tool belt of weapons. Lit cigarettes, scissors, hot metal in various forms. A knife, a threat, both just as sharp and deadly as the other.

Claire liked control more than anything, and what screamed control more than a cowering man, all six feet two inches of him, his muscles straining, the unrealized ability to break a neck there in his big, calloused palms?

He could never quite bring himself to kill her. No matter how many times he'd imagined it.

That first slap hadn't been playful, like he tried to tilt it while he explained it away as normal behavior later. Convincing himself, always convincing himself.

The thing that drove him crazy in the years to come was that he couldn't—*just could not*—remember what he'd said. He couldn't remember the offhand remark that had provoked that first glimpse of violence.

It had been completely unremarkable, like tripping on the sidewalk. And yet it had changed both of them forever.

# CHAPTER FORTY-NINE

## GRETCHEN

*Now—*

When Gretchen sat back down across from Viola, the girl watched her with that smug little smile. But before Gretchen could say anything, Viola leaned forward.

"Did you see Lena Booker's body?" Viola asked, eyes greedy as they scraped over Gretchen's face.

Gretchen considered answering, but that's not how negotiations worked. "Do you know who killed your mother?"

Viola sat back, arms crossed over her chest with the hint of a pout. "I already told you what you need to know."

"But that's not what I asked."

"Would you believe anything I answered?" Viola shot back. "I'm a pathological liar, aren't I?"

That part was tricky. But just like with everything else about Viola—and, in truth, most people—it wasn't necessarily hard truth that Gretchen was after. What she wanted to see was *how* Viola would lie.

"An answer for an answer," Gretchen proposed. "I think that's a fair deal, don't you?"

Viola's eyes narrowed as if searching for a trap. "You'll go first?"

"Of course."

"And why do you think I'll tell you the truth?" Viola pressed.

"I don't."

If Gretchen pointed out Viola's habit of chewing on her lower lip when uncertain, she was sure the girl would cut it off. Vulnerability was not something Viola would tolerate within herself. But Gretchen just stayed quiet until Viola sighed, long and deliberately obnoxious.

"Deal," Viola said.

Gretchen raised her brows in silent invitation.

"What did her body look like?" Viola rushed out, as if she'd tucked the question right behind her teeth for safekeeping.

Gretchen thought of the outstretched limbs, the shadows, the hollows, and the points. "Pale."

Viola waited a second for Gretchen to continue and then stomped her foot against the linoleum tile when nothing came. "That's bullshit. I want more or the deal's off."

"Empty," Gretchen said. She heard a thud behind her and could all but picture Shaughnessy's forehead dropping against the glass in exasperation. From the outside looking in, it probably wasn't the best idea to light the match for this future serial killer. But from what Gretchen could tell, Viola was already consumed with flames. A little more fuel wasn't going to hurt anyone. "It was like she was a doll. Positioned just so."

"Were her eyes open?" Viola asked, enthralled, swaying toward Gretchen slightly.

Gretchen knew in that moment she would have lied to the girl, but she didn't have to. "No."

"Oh," Viola slumped, chin dipping down. "I like watching their eyes."

"But you didn't watch your mother's," Gretchen noted, despite the fact that they both knew Gretchen didn't think she was the murderer.

"I watch the boys' sometimes," Viola said, eyes still cast toward the floor. But there was something about the way she had gone still that grabbed Gretchen's attention. "Sebastian and Milo."

"You watch their eyes?" Gretchen clarified.

"I like to find the places where the skin is the thinnest," Viola went on as if Gretchen hadn't spoken. "Then I pinch it together until I can feel my fingertips on both sides."

When it came to shock tactics, Viola was a battering ram who thought she was a fencing blade. She was clever, of that Gretchen had no doubt, given her propensity toward organization in her crimes. But she seemed to rely on vulgarity and offensive ideas and language to get a reaction conversationally. Gretchen guessed that lack of finesse could be chalked up to age.

"Their pupils dilated?" Gretchen guessed. The problem with using a battering ram on a sociopath was there were no refined sensibilities to trample upon. Viola could do her worst; Gretchen had entertained plenty of vicious thoughts in her life.

Viola's own eyes snapped to Gretchen's at that. "And get small, too."

"Constrict," Gretchen supplied absently. "Do you miss your brothers?"

The question might sound odd to someone who didn't understand people like Viola.

"They were locked up all the time," Viola said on a comically exasperated sigh. Like it had been the world's biggest imposition to her that she couldn't torture them at will.

"From you?" Gretchen asked, though she thought she knew the answer now. She wanted to see if she was right.

Viola laughed a little at the question, her gaze going to the ceiling, to somewhere else. When she looked back at Gretchen, there was something hard in the jut of her chin that hadn't been there before. "If you think so."

Again with the déjà vu. "What do you mean by that?"

A pause as Viola's gaze raked over her face. "They call us evil, you and me."

"Yes."

"Do you ever think they're wrong, though?" Viola asked. "That maybe it's not us who are the awful ones."

She paused, but Gretchen didn't rush to fill the silence.

"Or maybe we are, but at least we wear our true faces," Viola mused, and Gretchen didn't comment on the fact that both of them were probably far too comfortable with wearing masks. Viola was attempting to make a point, as clumsy as it might seem at the moment. "I think it's the people who pretend they're not as ugly as the rest of us that are worse."

"Humans are terrible creatures held together by the illusion of civility," Gretchen agreed.

"People like to hurt each other," Viola said. "They just don't like to think they like it. But you and I, we know different."

"Give them justification," Gretchen murmured. "And they'll rip each other to shreds every time."

There was darkness at the edges of even the brightest soul, and empaths just didn't like to think themselves capable of it. The monsters knew different.

Viola full-on smiled, a youthful, easy thing that was far more startling than any other expression the girl had worn and discarded like dress-up clothes. "Does that answer your question about why I killed my mother, Dr. White?"

*She's like you.*

"No," Gretchen said, because Shaughnessy was listening. She didn't add, *I didn't need you to in the first place.*

# CHAPTER FIFTY

## REED

*Eleven years before Claire's death—*

"You embarrassed me," Claire said as they returned to the town house after dinner with her parents.

Reed was hardly paying attention. The nanny had thrust Viola into his arms and fled without speaking to either of them. Reed sighed and wondered if the woman would show up the next day at all or if he should just repost the job listing.

Viola wasn't even a bad baby. Quiet mostly. When she threw tantrums, they were loud and tearful, and she could do a decent amount of damage if she got a hold of your hair just right. But wasn't that every kid? They were called the "terrible twos" for a reason.

Now, Viola blinked up at him with her pretty pale-blue eyes and smiled so that one little dimple popped out. He placed his lips against it and blew a raspberry that never made her giggle like he'd hoped. But she didn't smack him with her tiny fist, either, so he considered it a win.

"You're not even listening to me," Claire said, kicking off her shoes. She hadn't glanced at Viola once. Reed sighed and set the girl down.

"How did I embarrass you this time, Claire?" he asked, exhausted. "By existing?"

Viola headed toward Claire, arms outstretched, babbling something indistinguishable but that included "Mama" every so often. Claire still didn't look down, merely stepped past her own daughter. When she did, her leg caught Viola's shoulder, sending her back onto her diapered butt.

It hadn't looked intentional. But there must have been a quiet rage already flickering beneath his skin, because Reed actually felt the last of his control snap. He picked up Viola, who had been sadly yowling on the floor, more surprised than hurt, it seemed.

"What the hell?" Reed said once he reached the kitchen. Claire hadn't even stopped to check on Viola after knocking her down. By the time they got to her, she had a glass of wine poured already, her hand resting on the swell of her belly. Reed eyed her drink. "You've already had a glass tonight."

Like she needed reminding.

She didn't even pause. "Yes, and now I'm having another."

Reed's jaw clenched, and he pictured crossing the room, slamming the fine crystal against the wall so that the shattered pieces would cut into Claire's skin. Then Viola sniffled. He exhaled, doing his best not to imagine slamming the bottle down on the back of Claire's head instead. It was a bad night; they were just having a bad night. That was often the result of any time spent with Claire's judgmental parents.

"You knocked Viola over," Reed finally said when something other than nasty, derisive insults came to mind.

Claire's eyes finally dropped to her daughter, her expression impassive. "She'll live."

Reed inhaled sharply, then turned to walk out of the room. If he didn't, he wasn't sure if he'd be able to stop himself from, at the very least, putting his fist through a wall.

He buried the anger, not deep down because he wanted to be able to access it later, but enough so that he could give Viola her bath and then put her to bed. He rubbed his cheek against her hair, the chemical strawberry scent from her shampoo making him sneeze. "I'm sorry your mama is a psycho," he murmured, though he knew he shouldn't.

Viola just blinked sleepy eyes. "Mama?"

Reed pressed his lips together, gave her one more good-night kiss, and then went to find Claire.

She was waiting for him in their bedroom, wearing a lacy negligee that was tight enough to pull taut over her pregnant belly. Reed knew she'd picked that one on purpose. It wouldn't be the first or last time she used his kids against him.

"You embarrassed me," she said again like the past hour hadn't happened. She was at her vanity, applying hand cream. "Why didn't you just accept my father's offer? You think anyone else is going to hire you?"

Now that he was no longer holding his daughter, Reed tapped into the anger that he'd been keeping tenuously in check. "He offered it to me to humiliate me, and you know it."

There was no way he'd ever work for Claire's father; both Claire and her father knew that. Hell, even the Brentwood family's servants knew that at this point, as often as the argument came up at dinners.

"What's this really about?" Reed asked, because, knowing Claire, she was pissed about something else entirely.

"Someone saw you out with your whore," Claire said, the words sounding so strange in that richly polished Boston accent of hers.

He flinched, and she was too close all of a sudden, her eyes dark and her mouth pinched.

"You're not even going to deny it?"

Reed knew when she got like this it was pointless to try. He didn't even know whom she was talking about, but his best guess was the friend of a friend he'd met for coffee a week or so ago. The woman had been new to town and looking for suggestions on where to buy a house. But the explanation didn't matter.

Claire crossed back to her vanity, toyed with a bright orange prescription bottle resting there among her pretty perfume collection. "I think you should accept my father's offer."

Reed shook his head once, twice to clear it, his attention slipping to the bottle. Probably as she'd intended. He couldn't keep up with the disjointed conversation.

"What?" was all he could come up with.

Claire's palm pressed against the baby growing in her womb, as if he needed a reminder that she shouldn't be holding that pill bottle. She began rubbing at her belly while staring at the prescription instructions. Slowly, she repeated, "I think you should accept my father's offer."

And then it hit him, far harder than a slap ever could.

Swallowing at the implication, the threat that he knew she would carry through, Reed managed a hoarse, shaky "I will."

"Wonderful," Claire said, looking up with a bright smile. She tossed the bottle to the back of her vanity like picking it up had been an accident. "I'll tell him to expect you tomorrow."

# CHAPTER FIFTY-ONE

## GRETCHEN

*Now—*

Shaughnessy was waiting for Gretchen in the hallway, probably because he knew she'd try to slip by him if he wasn't.

"You have that look on your face," he said, pointing at her rudely. She slapped at his hand. "What look?"

"The cat-that-got-the-canary look," Shaughnessy accused. "The look that says you just solved something."

"I would be flattered you know my face so well if you were right," Gretchen said lightly as she started down the long hallway of the detention facility. "But that's what happens with obsessions, I suppose."

"Deflection," Shaughnessy called from behind her, not quite able to keep up with her pace but trying.

Gretchen stopped, turned. "I guess you really do know me well. Because you tried to wrongly arrest me for a crime when I was eight years old."

"Oh stop it." Shaughnessy shoved by her. "You're better than that. A guilt trip? What is this, amateur hour?"

It had been worth a shot. She'd even considered dredging up a few tears, but that definitely would have tipped Shaughnessy off. "I'm distracted," she said with an unapologetic shrug.

"Yeah. I know," Shaughnessy said with deliberate emphasis. "Why?"

Her heels clicked against the cheap linoleum tile as they crossed through the lobby. "I don't think Tess Murphy was murdered twenty years ago."

"Okay."

"I think she was murdered last year," Gretchen said. "Last spring to be precise."

Shaughnessy stopped at that, but she kept walking, digging for her Porsche's keys. "What?" he said, loud enough that two security guards and a visitor turned to look at them.

"Really?" Gretchen drawled at the scene he was making. He flushed a little and hurried to catch her as she signed out. He demonstrated impressive patience as they went through the administrative process.

It wasn't until they were back outside in the parking lot that he grabbed her arm. "Okay, what?"

She stared at his hand. "I have a gun, you know."

He rolled his eyes but let her go. "Tell me what you're thinking."

"Didn't you hear Viola?"

"I heard a few things that convinced me we locked up the right girl," Shaughnessy said.

Gretchen smacked him on the forehead and ignored his grunt of displeasure.

"If that's all you got out of that performance, I am, with no exaggeration, deeply disappointed in you," Gretchen said.

"All right," he shifted back. "What did I miss?"

"Reed wanted to leave Claire," Gretchen said. "Claire wasn't going to let him do that."

Gretchen thought back to that moment on the tape, the conversation between Claire and Lena.

*"I have to ask . . . why now?"*

"Claire hired Lena to look into Tess's disappearance," Gretchen said. "After twenty years of everyone just thinking the girl ran away. Why would she do that if she wasn't confident that something would be found?"

"Wait, wait, wait." Shaughnessy threw both hands in the air like a flustered cartoon character. "Don't tell me you think Claire Kent killed someone just to keep her husband from leaving her."

Claire hadn't been just a normal person, though; she hadn't been an empath. She must have thrived on violence, on power, on the little kingdom she'd created, able to blame everything on Viola if anyone started throwing questioning glances her way. It wasn't just about her husband leaving her. She needed to reestablish herself as the one in control. "Yes, that's exactly what I'm saying."

Shaughnessy squinted into the sky. "Or she covered for Reed all those years ago and had been sitting on the evidence until it worked in her favor."

That . . . actually seemed plausible. But in that case, why hadn't she just gone straight to the cops? If Reed had killed Tess, there was no reason to do any more groundwork. But this way, Claire could let Lena put everything together, make the case for her.

Gretchen thought about those other clips on Lena's hidden thumb drive.

It had been Lena who had convinced Declan Murphy that Reed was guilty.

It had been Lena who had scripted that exchange between Fiona Murphy and Reed.

It had been Lena who had made Reed so paranoid his sister had called Lena to ask that she come clean about her suspicions.

*I messed up, Gretch.*

"You know what? You're right," Gretchen said to Shaughnessy, deciding it wasn't worth the time to argue. She didn't want him tagging along anyway. "I'm going to go meet Marconi at World's End just to check."

"What if the psychopath is just toying with you?" Shaughnessy asked the obvious question as if it hadn't occurred to Gretchen.

"Of course she is," Gretchen said as she opened the car door. "But she's thirteen, in case you've forgotten."

*Just a girl.*

"Point," Shaughnessy acknowledged. "I'm coming with you."

"No, you're right, it's probably a wild-goose chase," Gretchen said, waving him off.

His eyes narrowed on her face. "Didn't say that."

"Marconi's going to be there if you're worried about babysitting duties," she pointed out. "That's what I called her about earlier."

Shaughnessy's attention didn't leave her face as he pulled out his phone and put it on speaker. She rolled her eyes but didn't push it further.

When Marconi answered, Shaughnessy barked out, "Where are you?"

"Organizing a search team for Tess Murphy's body," Marconi answered. Gretchen raised one eyebrow, a skill it had taken years to perfect but that she'd never once regretted learning.

Shaughnessy's mouth pursed as he disconnected. "You really think it's only been a year?"

"In what universe does Claire Kent stumble over a bracelet soaked in blood and then go to Lena Booker—whom she hasn't spoken to in twenty years—to get her to investigate Lena's former best friend?"

"The universe where Claire Kent is as much a psychopath as her daughter," Shaughnessy said, finally catching up.

*She's like you.*

"I'm thinking the blood on the bracelet has to match Tess's," Gretchen said. If Claire's ultimate plan was to take this to the police, that part had to be solid. "And I think Claire made sure it would be."

Shaughnessy exhaled, running a hand over his head. "Well, goddamn."

"Which also means," Gretchen continued, watching him carefully, "that we have another possible motive for Claire Kent's death."

"Revenge," Shaughnessy said. "Declan Murphy?"

Perfect. "That is the obvious suspect," Gretchen said. "And he's the one who suggested Reed go to the fight. Maybe you should talk to him?"

Shaughnessy studied her, and she cursed her own impatience. Usually she was better at tricking him. "You don't want to come?"

"Marconi," Gretchen reminded him. And hesitated long enough to make it obvious. "And I've spoken to him already."

"You think he'll be more flustered by me," Shaughnessy concluded.

Gretchen lifted one shoulder like it didn't matter to her either way, and for the first time since they'd left the detention facility, Shaughnessy looked like he believed her, starting to pat down his pockets for his keys, no longer watching her with suspicious hawk eyes.

"All right, go get me some solid evidence," Shaughnessy directed a bit absently now.

The salute she tossed off, and the sarcastic "Aye, aye, Captain," sealed the deal.

Gretchen peeled out of the lot, but she didn't go far. The Porsche was difficult to hide—its only downside—but eventually she turned down an alleyway that she thought would give her cover. She waited until Shaughnessy's dark SUV flew by her, and then finally relaxed enough to thumb back to that one voice mail that Lena had left.

*She's like you.*

Gretchen thought about Milo's cast, thought about each and every person who had become tangled up in this mess, thought about Viola's petulant *"I already told you what you need to know."*

Gretchen tossed the phone on the seat beside her, Lena's message playing through the speaker.

"You have to fix it for me, okay?"

"I'm trying, darling," Gretchen murmured as she hit the gas.

# CHAPTER FIFTY-TWO

## REED

***Seven years before Claire's death—***

"What's that?" Ainsley asked, leaning over the kitchen island to grab Reed's arm. He nearly flinched away when she brushed against the edges of a burn.

The question had been casual and easy, like Ainsley had thought it was a marker smudge or a stray bit of food coloring.

Everything about her stilled when she got a good look at it. Then very slowly and while holding on to his wrist like he would bolt otherwise, she rounded the island to stand in front of him. Her eyes were still locked on the burn, and he cursed himself for pushing his sleeves up. She'd been there for three days, and he'd gotten complacent, thinking that the kids would distract her enough that she wouldn't notice.

Nobody else did.

"Reed?" Ainsley asked, her voice small. "What is this?"

"I burned myself cooking the other day," Reed said without even the slightest hesitation. "It's not as bad as it looks."

"It looks like someone took a curling iron to your skin," Ainsley said, and Reed couldn't help but stiffen at the accuracy of that guess. "You're really going to tell me that's not exactly what happened?"

Reed licked his lips, shame burning in his gut. He knew, he *knew* it wasn't his fault. But it still felt like it. And the way Ainsley was looking at him now wasn't helping. Her expression was both stricken and building toward the kind of unparalleled anger he knew she could unleash.

In that moment, he didn't see Claire's face, the impassive expression as she brought the searing hot metal down onto his arm, but rather he saw Sebastian and Milo, their vulnerable skin and their breakable bodies.

And he knew he had to lie.

"Viola got a hold of it, okay?" Reed said, keeping his voice pitched low. Claire wasn't the only one who could use their kids. "We're dealing with it."

Ainsley didn't let go, didn't look like she believed him. But when he refused to say anything else, she sighed, her thumb brushing against an uninjured patch of skin as if she could offer comfort. "You need to take her to see someone."

"I'm working on it."

Reed didn't breathe again until Ainsley had circled the island, going back to whatever magazine she'd been flipping through.

It was the first time he'd blamed Viola for Claire's violence. Something told him it wouldn't be the last.

Maybe Ainsley hadn't really believed him. But most people would. They looked at him, and even if they'd seen the bruises for themselves, they'd never make the leap. He was tall, strong, confident. If he actually told anyone what was happening, they'd laugh.

Men who were abused by women were never taken seriously. He would become the butt of their jokes.

It was a good thing that no one guessed the truth, though. Claire would get the children in a heartbeat if he ever tried to leave. And that was the best-case scenario.

And it wasn't all bad. It didn't happen often; a lot of the time he brought it on himself, anyway. At least she hadn't done anything deliberately malicious to the children yet.

Some part of Reed knew that the *yet* was getting ever more certain with each passing day.

# CHAPTER
# FIFTY-THREE

## GRETCHEN

*Now—*

Although Gretchen knew Fred could afford a much swankier place, she lived in a dank basement beneath a town house on the edge of a sketchy neighborhood because she never wanted to become one of those "richy-rich jag-offs who wipe their butts with hundred-dollar bills just because they can." Gretchen never pointed out that there was a happy middle that Fred could surely find acceptable. It wasn't *her* life, after all.

Once Fred let Gretchen in, she crossed back to her seat in front of what Gretchen had always called command central. It was just one ten-year-old monitor with a fancy laptop docked to it, but Fred could work miracles with the setup, and so Gretchen always showed the proper respect when she was in the inner sanctum.

"Find anything?" Gretchen asked, knowing Fred, like her, hated small talk and wasting time.

"No CPS records." Fred shrugged, slumped in her computer chair, lazily swinging back and forth.

"Nothing?" Gretchen asked, knowing she shouldn't be startled. But startled just the same. The scar tissue documented in the reports was enough that they should have had a dedicated file to each of the Kent children. Gretchen had guessed it would be thick.

"Nada," Fred repeated.

Gretchen pressed her lips together for a moment. "Can you get hospital records?"

That was a bigger ask. Medical data was protected to the teeth. But considering the leaks that occurred on what seemed like a monthly, if not weekly, basis, Gretchen was hoping there was a back door Fred would know about.

She was excellent at her job, after all.

"Depends on what you want," Fred said, cracking her gum. "You have a social?"

"Name and approximate date of hospitalization, but no social," Gretchen said. "And a guess at the health system."

"We might get lucky," Fred said, the low light from her desk lamp glinting against the metal dot tucked into her dimple when she smiled sweetly. "But it'll cost you. A lot."

Gretchen waved that off. "That's fine."

Fred swiveled to look at her fully, her thumb running over the tail of the fox tattoo that Gretchen knew ran from her collarbone over her shoulder to her back. The fox's grin was as sharp and cunning as Fred's own. "That's a dangerous thing to say to a hustler, Dr. White."

It wasn't respect that had Fred only ever calling her Dr. White. When Gretchen had first introduced herself, Fred had laughed for a solid minute about the irony of her last name. *Just like your soul, huh?*

"How much?" Gretchen asked, only because she knew Fred would take her to the cleaners if she reiterated that she really didn't care about the cost. When Gretchen became obsessed with finding answers, she wouldn't hesitate to sign over her entire bank account. It wasn't something she was proud of, but considering she mostly worked with cops, few actually took advantage of that particular weakness.

Fred would, though.

"Six thousand," Fred tossed off without any shame. Like that was a reasonable amount to confirm something that Gretchen already suspected. Still, Gretchen was loaded. Six thousand was a mere drop in the bucket of her wealth.

Gretchen only countered because Fred would think less of her if she didn't. "Four."

"Six or nada, lady," Fred said. "And you have five seconds to decide."

"Brat," Gretchen accused. "I'll take it."

Fred tapped her phone, and Gretchen knew the drill. She'd get nothing until she'd transferred the amount to Fred. "These apps make it so easy these days," Gretchen said as she did so, and Fred ignored the small talk like expected.

But when Fred got the notification that the money had gone through, she was quick to ask, "What do you need?"

"Last April, in the week prior to April 6," Gretchen said.

"Mass General?" Fred asked.

"No, somewhere else, maybe smaller, near Beacon Hill," Gretchen said. "Can you search on more than one system?"

"Sure." Fred snapped her gum. "Ritzy area."

Gretchen hummed in confirmation. "It would be emergency room and . . ."

Fred stopped typing at her pause, glancing up over her shoulder, a red curl bouncing into her face.

"A kid," Gretchen said. "It would be a kid."

Whistling low, Fred shifted her attention back to the screen. "Name?"

"Kent."

A few minutes passed as Fred worked, and Gretchen tried not to fidget. Finally, something leaped onto the main screen. "Bingo."

Gretchen leaned forward, resting a hand on the small amount of free space on Fred's desk. She figured Fred would be lenient enough to overlook it since she was six thousand dollars richer thanks to Gretchen.

"Tufts Medical Center," Fred read. "Milo Kent. Broken arm, broken ankle."

Stairs, Gretchen thought. "And CPS was called?"

"Wasn't marked down if they were," Fred said, a bitter edge in her voice that made Gretchen think Fred knew what those injuries meant just as well as Gretchen did.

*Easy prey.*

Gretchen's eyes found the date. Two days before Claire Kent was killed.

Two days.

Long ago, Gretchen had learned there *was* such a thing as coincidence. Like she'd told Marconi, the brain loved finding patterns where none really existed.

But Milo Kent having to be taken to the emergency room two days before his mother was killed wasn't one of them.

# CHAPTER FIFTY-FOUR

## REED

*Two weeks before Claire's death—*

Lena kept texting and calling after that night at the auction, where she'd asked if he loved Claire, that night that she'd looked crushed when he'd lied and said yes.

It had been a couple of weeks since then, and now the log on Reed's phone would be damning except that he never responded, never answered. He didn't block her number, though.

Reed didn't know why he was surprised when Lena finally tracked him down in person.

"If you didn't kill Tess, help me figure out who did," Lena said without preamble as she sidled up next to him at the playground.

"Christ," Reed whispered, darting looks at the parents around them. They were clustered in bunches far enough away not to have over-heard Lena. That didn't stop Reed's hands from going clammy anyway.

"Unclench," Lena said on a laugh. She was dressed down again, like how she'd been when they'd interviewed Fiona Murphy. It seemed so long ago now. "No one is listening to us."

That was probably true. Most of the parents kept a careful distance between their families and his. Even if people didn't explicitly know about Viola, they could sense the rot at the edges of all of them. Even the boys were left to play with just each other. It ached in a way Reed didn't know how to fix.

Ainsley was across the park, spotting Milo on the monkey bars, and she hadn't seemed to notice Lena's presence yet.

"Why do you think I didn't?" Reed asked.

She slid him a side-eyed glance. "I don't want you to have."

Reed looked away toward Sebastian, who was waving from the top of the slide. Reed waved back, faking a smile like he could always do so well. "Wanting has little to do with reality."

"You know that too well, don't you?" Lena asked. He didn't respond. He didn't need to.

"It wasn't an accident, was it?" Reed said. "That first day. At Starbucks."

"Of course not," Lena replied easily. "You figured that out long ago." She paused, glanced at him. "What do you really want to ask me?"

"Who hired you?" he asked instead.

Lena shook her head. "No, not that, either."

Reed bounced on his toes to stay warm. "Did you ever think it was me?"

"In the dark of the night sometimes," Lena said. "It made sense." She paused. "Sorry."

"Don't be," Reed said. "It's not like I ever gave you any reason to trust me. The opposite in fact." It was his turn to let the silence fall. When the air stretched thin between them, he nudged her shoulder. "I owe you an apology."

Lena's lips pressed into a straight line. "Get outa here."

She'd never been comfortable with sappy displays. But Reed didn't let that deter him. He did stare at the ground instead of her, though. "I threw you away. I'm sorry."

Lena's throat worked as she swallowed hard. "I let you."

Reed shook his head, but Lena turned so she could full-on glare him into submission. Then she ran a hand that looked not quite steady through her hair. "You know it didn't matter, right?"

"What?"

"Any of it, all of it?" Lena said, squaring up for real, meeting his eyes. "I loved you like you were blood."

Reed looked away, ashamed but also numb.

"Tess was alive, wasn't she?" Lena asked, sounding like she knew the answer.

Reed ran his tongue over his teeth, thought of the post office box. Thought of how the cards had stopped coming, thought about swing sets, and childhood, and bruises on pale skin and wondered why he was still protecting a monster. "Up until a year ago, at least."

"Oh, thank God," Lena muttered beside him.

He turned in his surprise, and she winced.

"Not that she's dead," Lena said. "But that you admitted it."

Reed swiveled his jaw, annoyed with himself for walking into that one. Lena had been trying to get him to confess to Tess's murder for months now. "That wasn't a confession."

"No, I know," Lena said. "I didn't need a confession."

Before either of them could say anything else, Ainsley was in front of them, the boys still over by the slides.

"I told you," Ainsley said to Lena, sounding smug.

Reed looked between them. "What's going on?"

"Lena didn't trust you with the truth." Ainsley glanced his way. "To be fair, she's learned the hard way before that you're easily blinded by Claire's—"

"Ainsley"—he cut off whatever vulgarity she'd been about to utter—"it's a playground."

"Winning personality," Ainsley drawled instead. "I told her she could trust you, but she didn't believe me."

And, *ah*. The night of the auction finally made sense. "You asked me if I loved her."

Lena shrugged, not looking guilty at all. "And you said yes."

"He says a lot of bullshit," Ainsley pointed out.

"I didn't want to lose seven months of work because Reed was whipped by Claire," Lena said, not at all apologetic. "I didn't want him reporting our theories to Claire and getting her spooked. She's good at hiding evidence."

He huffed out a visible breath that he watched turn to nothing, thinking about the knife he kept in the back of his closet. With Viola's fingerprints on it. "I would have helped you."

"Your past behavior—"

"Proved otherwise, yes," Reed acknowledged. Claire always had made him stupid. At that thought, he touched the very edge of his cheekbone. "You convinced Declan you believed that I killed Tess because you know he's sleeping with Claire."

Lena did look sorry at that. "She can't know I'm onto her."

The way she phrased that . . . "You're working with her?"

Ainsley and Lena exchanged a glance before Lena winced. "She hired me. To find Tess."

Find Tess's body. That's what Lena really meant. Reed thought about the missing bracelet, those comments on the crime blogger's website, the way Claire had been laying the groundwork for Declan.

*He punched a wall.*

What other evidence had his wife planted? The note at Fiona Murphy's? He hadn't remembered writing it, and who was to say that Fiona had actually found it the day after Tess had left?

Reed swallowed. "You took the job."

"I had always wondered why Tess hadn't written me," Lena murmured, her eyes on the boys. Ainsley shifted like she was about to step in front of Reed, but Reed shook his head.

"She was scared of Claire even back then."

That got both of them to look at him, and he forced himself to meet their eyes. "I thought it was just . . . I don't know, Tess being irrational or jealous or something."

Ainsley swore ferociously. "You're an idiot."

"Why didn't she tell me?" Lena asked, but not like she expected an answer.

"She wanted a new life," Reed said, face hot with mortification for his younger self. He knew enough now to know he wasn't to blame for staying with Claire all these years—she was a classic abuser who'd isolated and manipulated him into thinking he was trapped. But he hated himself for not knowing then, not realizing that the bruises on Tess's wrists that night weren't something to shrug off.

That maybe when Tess had asked questions like, *"Do you think there's something . . . off about her?"* he should have actually listened.

"And Claire got her in the end, anyway," Ainsley said, all bitter frustration.

Reed chanced a glance at Lena, who still looked about one wrong word away from throwing him to the wolves. "You sure? That Tess is dead."

He'd suspected but hadn't been sure. The postcards had never been frequent, and if it had just been that they'd stopped coming, he wouldn't have thought anything about it. But when Lena had started asking questions six months ago, when he'd discovered that bracelet gone—then remembered Claire asking about that box all those years ago—he couldn't help but worry that Tess hadn't survived whatever Claire had been planning.

Lena's anger flickered into grief. "As sure as I can be. Fiona Murphy let me compare the blood on the bracelet to her own. The results came back that it was a high match for a relative."

"But it could have been Declan's," Reed said.

"And it doesn't mean that Tess is dead, anyway, if it was hers," Lena said with a little shrug, as if either of them were really considering those possibilities. "That's why I haven't been able to do much with what I have yet. It all could be explained away."

"You need the body," Ainsley said.

"Working on it," Lena gritted out.

Reed studied her face, her clenched hands. "How did you figure it out?"

At that, Lena actually relaxed, rolled her eyes. "Claire's not as clever as she thinks she is." She paused. "And neither is Declan."

"Declan?"

Lena waved away his surprise. "He's not involved." She paused. "I don't think, at least. But he's got some seriously loose lips when he's been drinking."

"He gave Claire up?" Reed asked.

"Not in so many words," Lena said. "But once I realized she was cozying up to Declan, making him think you were some kind of violent, abusive husband, I started asking more questions. There're emails, things that can help build a case once we actually have a case."

Reed pressed his fingernail into his scarred knuckle. "How did you know I wasn't abusive?"

"I didn't," Lena said, the answer landing heavy in Reed's gut. "But I am actually good at my job. I talked to people, all the nannies who cycled in and out of your house."

He could only imagine the stories they'd told. Lena must have seen something in his face.

"They didn't say much—they seemed scared," Lena said. "But not of you. And I started poking around the foundation, too."

"I'm sure Penny Langford gave you plenty of material," Reed said. The woman had never liked him, not that he blamed her. But he had guessed Claire was painting quite a different picture of their marriage than he would have.

"Yeah, she doesn't like you," Lena said easily. "But I don't talk to the bosses. I talk to the workers. And Claire might be good at manipulation, but when enough people say the same thing . . ."

"You start to believe them," Ainsley finished for her.

Reed glanced at her. "You were in on all this?"

Ainsley had the good grace to flush. "Just when I realized Lena was trying to make you think that she thought you killed Tess."

"Claire couldn't know I didn't believe her," Lena said again. "I couldn't care about your feelings. Claire couldn't know. That was the most important thing."

He understood, he really did. After two decades of marriage, he knew the only way Claire would be stopped was by playing as dirty as she did. He also wondered what Lena would say if she knew about the knife, about the desperate plan he'd hatched that one afternoon at the baseball game, feeling like a wounded animal backed into the corner.

What Reed couldn't guess was if Claire really ever wanted to go to the cops with the information. Had she been setting up Lena to do all the work, raise the red flags for the police, take on the brunt of any questioning that followed? Or was Lena's investigation just a way to get leverage on Reed without having to drag them all into the public eye?

"Okay, now that we've established Claire's the devil and killed poor Tess, what are we going to do about it?" Ainsley cut in.

They both looked at him, and he shook his head. "I can't prove anything. I can't even prove that Tess was still alive a year ago. She stopped sending me postcards, but I burned all the evidence that she ever did in the first place."

Ainsley huffed out an annoyed breath, but Lena cut her off. "I'm working on that part. I think I'm narrowing in on the town where she'd settled." She crossed her arms, like she was defensive she hadn't made more progress. "I just need a little more time, a few weeks at most. If we can establish that she was alive, we can establish she went missing. After that, it should be easier."

A little flame flared in Reed's chest, and he almost didn't recognize it for what it was. Hope. It had been so long since he'd felt anything other than crushed that it scared him, the possibility that he might get out of this.

"Just . . ." Lena trailed off, and when he looked up, she was staring at him, her brows drawn, her lips tight. "Just keep your head down until then, okay?"

When Lena walked away, he slumped against Ainsley, letting her take his weight. "What if Claire manages to wiggle out of this?" he asked. Having hope—even if it was a delicate, fragile thing—was almost worse than the total darkness of endless despair. "You know how she is."

"That's not going to happen," Ainsley said, her chin jutting out, her shoulders rolling back. "This is going to end. No matter what."

# CHAPTER
# FIFTY-FIVE
## Gretchen

*Now—*

Gretchen stood outside Fred's depressing little apartment and stared down at her phone. She'd been rooted in the same spot for five minutes now, and she knew if she lingered longer, Fred would come out waving a gun or a machete.

But Gretchen couldn't move. All she could hear was Lena's voice from that message she'd left as she was dying.

*You have to fix it for me. You're always able to fix things.*

Almost without her own consent, Gretchen found herself searching for Ainsley Kent's number and hitting call.

"I know what happened," Gretchen said as soon as Ainsley answered.

There was a startled silence. Then: "How long do I have?"

"An hour."

Gretchen wondered if the soft "Thanks" she heard before the line went dead had been real or imagined.

If someone subpoenaed Gretchen's phone records, she wasn't certain she wouldn't be hauled to court to explain that call. But when had she ever worried about consequences? She wasn't about to start now.

Her cell blared out a cheerful jingle of notes just as she had the thought.

Marconi.

Gretchen let it ring and crossed the street to where she'd parked her car.

An hour might have been too generous.

Marconi would likely call Shaughnessy when she couldn't get a hold of Gretchen. Shaughnessy would call her when he realized she wasn't with Marconi. And they'd circle the wagons if they both knew she was out investigating this alone.

She turned off her phone just in case Shaughnessy decided to get tricky for once in his life and track it.

It wasn't long before she found herself in front of Lena's apartment, parking in the same spot she had three days prior when she'd walked in expecting the worst.

After she let herself inside, Gretchen began to pace from one end of the apartment to the other, eventually ending up in front of Lena's desk, staring down at the stack of folders she'd so arrogantly told Marconi were worthless only yesterday.

Lena was nothing if not prepared. She'd told Gretchen about that book months ago. She must have known she was slipping out of control, must have known she'd need to have backup just in case she spiraled.

Maybe she'd thought Viola deserved to be in jail—as her lackluster defense efforts seemed to show—and she'd had to self-medicate with opiates to numb the guilt.

*I messed up, Gretch.*

Lena knew exactly how that could affect a young girl's life, had watched Gretchen deal with the stigma for years. Lena also knew Gretchen didn't have that pesky conscience that empaths were saddled with. She'd left behind audio that in a short amount of time laid bare the dynamics of this twisted group. She let Gretchen know she didn't fully trust Reed, let her know she was fooling Declan Murphy.

Most important, though, she'd let Gretchen know she trusted Ainsley Kent. If pressed, Gretchen would have to say that was the reason Gretchen had called Ainsley. Gretchen didn't necessarily care what happened to the woman, but she thought Lena might have. If this was one parting gift Gretchen could give to her friend, she would.

A tiny part of her whispered that it might be deeper than that, might have something to do with *Gretchen* and not Lena. But she ruthlessly silenced that voice.

On an impulse, Gretchen checked the stack of files on Lena's desk for Claire Kent's maiden name—Brentwood. Gretchen had looked it up last night after realizing she had never learned it.

She found it exactly where it should be, alphabetized in its proper spot with the other cases.

Hiding in plain sight.

Torn between annoyance that she hadn't thought of it earlier and a fond sort of affection for Lena's brains, Gretchen decided to ignore her feelings altogether and flipped through the pages.

In it was everything anyone would need to build a case against Claire Kent. There was the prenup that stipulated Reed would be entitled to half of everything after twenty years of marriage, the phone records that showed Claire contacting one number several times in the month that Tess Murphy—otherwise known as Fiona Declan—went missing from her new life, and printed emails between Declan Murphy and Claire that were so obviously laying the groundwork for framing Reed. Gretchen couldn't have asked for better evidence.

Well, other than a full confession.

At the very end of the file was an envelope with Gretchen's name scrawled on it.

It was simple, just one line, one last plea.

Lena's actual last request.

Gretchen stared at it until the alarm she'd set on her phone went off.

She tucked the note in her pocket and then started for the stairs.

Ainsley had had enough time.

# CHAPTER FIFTY-SIX

## REED

*Two days before Claire's death—*

Reed knew he should shut up and take it.

He knew that he should just play his part and hang in there a few more weeks, wait for Lena to come through with more evidence against Claire.

He'd known hope was a dangerous, dangerous thing. But he hadn't realized it would give him the push he needed to fight back for once in his life.

"She's not changing doctors," Reed said for what felt like the twentieth time. "This problem isn't going to magically go away, no matter how much you pretend it's not real."

Claire continued to run a brush through her hair, barely even acknowledging Reed's protests, which grew louder with each passing minute. "Mary Beth Schaffer uses Dr. Sloane. If she comes across us in the waiting room, well, you know what kind of gossip she is."

"Screw Mary Beth," Reed said, and barely recognized his own voice. "Screw them all, this is our *life*. This is our daughter's *life*."

"Stop being so dramatic," Claire said.

Reed scrubbed his palms over his face and told himself *two weeks*. That's it. Two weeks. But they might not have that long.

"Viola was with Milo the other day," Reed said, quietly this time so that maybe she'd listen.

Claire paused, her arm still raised, brush in hand, and Reed almost wept with it. The first true reaction that he'd seen from her since the start of the conversation. Even Claire knew how serious that was. "In the house?"

"In the garage," Reed confirmed.

"Why weren't you watching them?" Claire asked as she came back to life. But there was a rigid frigidity to her voice that belied her impassive expression. "It's not like you have anything worthwhile you're doing."

A familiar tactic—turning it back on him, getting a dig in while she was at it.

"They're not babies anymore," Reed said, so exhausted. Two weeks stretched in front of him, distorted so that he couldn't see the end of it. Would never see the end of it. "You can't control them all the time."

Claire's fingers twitched toward the key for the boys' room. She used to keep a lock on the refrigerator, too, until she realized it provoked too many questions from the various nannies they had in and out of the house. The lock on the bedroom door was far more discreet and let her limit the boys' freedom in ways far beyond what they ate.

Control. Claire loved it, craved it, needed it beyond anything else.

He should have known not to say anything, not now, not when they were so close. But that hope burned in his throat, threatened to consume him.

"They're going to realize they can fight back, you know," Reed said, conversationally now. He'd gotten a reaction, and it was like a drug to him, always had been. Even when he'd hated her so much he nearly couldn't breathe with it, even on the worst days, even during the most degrading of the humiliating jabs, he'd always been hungry for her attention. "How long will that lock hold?"

"Shut up," Claire said, the slightest tremble in her voice. He heard it, though. *He heard it.*

"Do you think it will be Viola who kills you?" Reed asked. "She's the safe bet, of course."

"Shut up," Claire said again, and it was the closest he'd ever heard her come to a shout.

"Or do you think—"

The vase hurtled toward his head, and he'd been expecting it just enough to duck. The fine crystal shattered against the wall, tiny pieces raining down on him. Claire panted where she stood, her eyes calm, but her hands curled in fists.

It had been so long—*so long*—since he'd pushed back like this it hadn't taken much to get her to the end of her tether. She had to know it was more than this one argument, bigger than just this fight. Had to know something had given him the confidence to fling this at her, as unexpected as that crystal vase.

He grinned down at the broken glass on the floor, wrecked just as easily as her control had been, revealing a startling fragility underneath.

It could be destroyed.

She might have pretended not to see the smile. But the laughter was too much.

Reed knew it as soon as it slipped out of him, knew it was the kind of mistake he'd regret the rest of his life—however long that was.

Claire went rigid, and then lightning quick she grabbed the key to the boys' room. Before he could react, she was out the door, across the hallway. The boys had been locked in an hour ago, and would likely be asleep. But Claire didn't pause.

They were tucked in the bottom bunk together, and it happened so fast. Claire grabbed Milo's arm, dragged him from his sleep onto the floor. Reed went for them, blind with rage, but Claire anticipated the move, spinning away from where Reed charged so that his shoulder hit the bunk beds with a sickening crack.

Milo sobbed as she dragged him behind her.

"We're going to show Daddy what happens when he's a bad boy," Claire told Milo, her voice sickeningly sweet. "Stop crying, baby."

And then before Reed could reach them, Claire gave Milo a nudge toward the stairs. Unbalanced, disoriented, and distraught, Milo's little body went easily, a tumble of limbs and a terrible, awful silence that almost took Reed to his knees.

Then Ainsley was there, hovering over Milo on the second-floor landing, protecting him. She cradled Milo against her chest, singing a gentle lullaby as she rocked to her feet, the boy still in her arms.

Reed took the stairs two at a time on his way to help her, but she flinched, and a tiny part of Reed died. This *was* his fault, this was absolutely his fault, and Ainsley was justified in her repulsion. He nodded once. "Go."

"You psycho bitch," Ainsley screamed at Claire, who stood halfway down the stairs, pressed against the wall from where Reed had brushed by her, a small, crooked smile on her face. "You're never getting near him again."

Then Ainsley was gone.

The laughter when it came again wasn't from him. He looked up to find Viola at her bedroom door. But she wasn't staring at Reed, nor was she watching Ainsley as his sister carried Milo down the stairs.

Instead her attention was locked on Sebastian, devastation and fury written into every line of his body.

And Reed knew then that it had been a mistake to ever hope.

# CHAPTER
# FIFTY-SEVEN
## GRETCHEN

*Now—*

Gretchen climbed the outside stairs of the Kents' town house and wondered how many times Marconi had tried to call her.

She pushed the thought aside and tried knocking. When no one answered, she reached for the doorknob.

It was unlocked.

The house was the kind of quiet that descended when no one was home, but Gretchen had seen the curtain on the third floor twitch, like it had every time she'd been there. She knew where to find Reed.

As she made her way up the three flights, Gretchen considered going back to the Porsche for her gun.

But Lena's note sat heavy in her pocket. Gretchen had a guess how this was going to end. She paused outside what she figured to be the right door.

Inhaled, exhaled.

And then she stepped into the room.

# CHAPTER FIFTY-EIGHT

## REED

*The night of Claire's death—*

Reed didn't sleep the night Milo fell—*was pushed*—down the stairs. He didn't sleep the following night, either. He wondered if he'd ever sleep again.

Ainsley found him in his study in the evening of the third night. She kicked his legs from the couch so that he was forced to sit up, forced to meet her eyes.

"Claire's pretending like nothing happened," Ainsley said without preamble. Her eyelids were red and puffy, and for some reason he couldn't imagine her crying, but she must have been. "I gotta tell you, Reed, I don't know if we can wait until Lena works her magic."

Reed shook his head, though he knew she was right.

"Just let me take the kids, Reed," Ainsley said. "We'll leave, and you guys can sort it out."

The door flew open, slamming against the wall.

Both Ainsley and Reed jumped to their feet, Reed shifting so that he stood slightly in front of Ainsley.

But it was Sebastian and not Claire who stood in the doorway, his face splotchy, his lower lip wobbly, but his stance mirroring theirs, his fists at his sides.

"No," Sebastian said. "She'll get away with it."

Reed edged toward him like he would approach a wounded animal. Because that's what Sebastian was—wounded, broken, and still fighting. Just like he'd been when he'd come into Reed's life eleven years ago.

"No, she won't, buddy," Reed murmured, though it tasted like just another lie, and by now Sebastian could recognize them well.

"You always say that," Sebastian screamed. "You never *do* anything."

Thick tears rolled down Sebastian's cheeks, and he swiped at them with angry little jabs. When he tried to speak again, a sob came out.

Reed took two strides over and bundled him in his arms, holding him close, the boy's face pressed just below Reed's heart. Sebastian's body heaved with every single ounce of his grief and pain and betrayal, and he held on to Reed even though Reed knew his boy hated him right now in this moment and maybe forever from here on out.

He swallowed around the knot of emotion in his throat, the room silent except for Sebastian's wrecked hiccups that preceded silent tears.

Then as suddenly as Sebastian had come, he was gone, tearing himself out of Reed's arms, running back up the stairs toward his room.

Ainsley watched the space where he'd been, her eyes distant. "Go to dinner with Lena tonight."

The suggestion was so out of place it took Reed a moment to process. "What?"

"Go to dinner with Lena tonight," Ainsley repeated, but she wouldn't meet his eyes. "Get an update on where her investigation into Tess's death stands. Then we'll figure out what to do tomorrow."

Reed knew his sister. Knew her better now since she'd become a semipermanent guest in their town house, disrupting her own life to help him, protect him, offer him a shoulder to cry on and a drink when he needed it. Maybe she would have gotten away with this little subterfuge when he'd thought of her only as "sister" and not a person unto herself, but those days were long gone.

The calculation behind her eyes was obvious. If he left the house, even for an hour, she would take the boys even if that meant losing his trust forever, even if it meant hiding them from him for as long as it took to get rid of the threat of Claire.

With that one suggestion, he knew she'd decided the risk involved with essentially kidnapping them was worth the potential pain the betrayal would bring. He pictured her holding Milo against her chest two nights ago, looking like an avenging angel about to go into battle. Pictured the way she touched the back of the boys' necks at dinner, lovingly, as if she could press tenderness into their bodies with just her palm. Pictured the way she read to them, spoke with them, took them for ice cream and bandaged their hurts.

He and Claire were meant to burn each other to the ground along with Viola. But Milo and Sebastian didn't have to be destined to that fate. They had someone who loved them beyond measure, someone who would stab her brother in the heart if it meant getting the boys out safe.

Maybe it was crazy to be reassured by the fact that his sister wanted to kidnap his children right beneath his nose. But he was. For the first time in a long time it felt like there was someone in the room who cared the most about Milo and Sebastian. Not about themselves or about what Viola would do or about what their friends would say.

But who actually cared about the boys.

He crossed the room before he could think about it. She almost recoiled—maybe thinking he was going to hit her, shake her, try to convince her not to take them. But she must have seen something in his face.

Relief. That's all he felt. Unending waves of relief.

Reed gathered her in his arms just as he had Sebastian, though Ainsley was tall enough that she could tuck her face into his neck. He held her close. A port in the storm, a real one this time.

"There's a go bag in the garage," Reed said, so quietly that there wasn't a chance anyone but she could hear. "I'll get you access to my bank account once I can."

She squeezed him once to let him know she understood, and then her grip loosened.

Reed didn't let go right away. "Thank you," he whispered against her temple, felt her nod once, and then he finally stepped back.

This had been inevitable. He'd always known he wouldn't be the one who could pull the trigger. Milo and Sebastian would never be safe here. They needed to leave, to escape. And it was his fault that he hadn't been strong enough to do so before this.

Ainsley, though. She'd always been strong enough for both of them. She would do what he couldn't.

In that moment, he didn't know if he loved her or hated her for it.

# CHAPTER FIFTY-NINE

## GRETCHEN

*Now—*

Gretchen didn't look at Reed Kent's gun, though she knew it was there.

He stood plastered against the wall, the weapon resting against his thigh, his finger on the trigger. His eyes were pools in the dark room, backlit as he was by the window, but she could still see his face. There was no fear there, just quiet resignation.

"Why did you do that?" Reed asked. "Will you tell me?"

Why warn Ainsley, Gretchen guessed. "Lena was a friend of mine."

He nodded once, but didn't say anything else.

"She left me a note."

Gretchen telegraphed her intention when she slowly dipped her hand into the pocket of her blazer. "Would you like me to read it?"

Reed's eyes were locked on the paper. He nodded again, just a dip of his head, but enough.

Gretchen smoothed a hand over words she already had memorized. "Please let him do it," she read. "Because I can't."

A small, wounded sound escaped him, and Gretchen looked up.

"What can't she let you do?" Gretchen asked, though she knew what Lena had meant.

"It was me," Reed said, and it came out strong and steady. "Viola didn't kill Claire. It was me."

"We both know that's not true," Gretchen said, not taking her eyes off Reed's face, though she knew the gun had twitched on her words.

"It's a confession," Reed countered. "You can't prove otherwise."

Gretchen considered that. She might be able to if she really wanted to. But she was far more curious for the details of the truth than some kind of pursuit of justice. Claire Kent had clearly deserved to die, and even if she hadn't, Gretchen wasn't the type to get tangled up in some kind of universal grief for lost innocence.

Lena had known that.

*Please let him do it. Because I can't.*

She'd needed Gretchen to let Reed confess to Claire's murder, and to let the confession stand.

Needed Gretchen to do her dirty work.

"I'll make you a deal," Gretchen said, and had such strong déjà vu from her interrogation with Viola she lost her sense of place for the stretch of a heartbeat. "You tell me what actually happened, and we'll both pretend your confession is enough."

Reed didn't hesitate. "Deal."

# CHAPTER SIXTY

## REED

*The night of Claire's death—*

Once the decision was made for Ainsley to take off with the boys, Reed didn't linger in the study. He turned and left the room, texting Lena as he did.

Lena wrote back with a readiness that seemed to confirm his suspicions that Ainsley had gotten her on board with the plan first. That was fine with Reed.

There had been a time when he wouldn't have even suspected he was being manipulated by the pair of them. But life with Claire, life with Viola had taught him better. They were clearly trying to buy Ainsley a window of time where Reed wasn't in the house so she could be long gone with the boys before he even figured out they weren't in their room.

Still, he couldn't imagine feeling anything other than relief, even if he had been unsuspecting, even if he'd come home to find them gone. He'd resigned himself long ago to burning to the ground with Viola and Claire; all he wanted now—all he'd really ever wanted—was for Sebastian and Milo to get out.

Reed stopped outside the boys' room, pressed a palm to the door, pretended he could feel their heartbeats. Saying goodbye would be a bad idea. Milo was too young to keep a secret, and Sebastian too volatile these days. Viola might overhear and pull some stunt. Saying goodbye would be a bad idea. But something in his heart ripped apart at not doing so, and he knew that he'd never be whole again after this very moment.

This was too important to be selfish. So he pulled himself away and didn't look back.

Claire had been keeping to her own office for the past few days, perhaps for once heeding the tensions in the house, perhaps knowing his control was frayed to the point of snapping with one wrong look.

He didn't see her when he got dressed nor when he went to meet Lena at the restaurant a few neighborhoods away.

Lena was waiting for him, beautiful as ever. She smiled, stood, and kissed him on the cheek like this was normal, like they were two old friends getting dinner.

"Smile," she told him through clenched teeth after the waiter shot him a nervous look. "Your face screams 'serial killer' right now."

Reed tried to laugh, tried to relax, but his knuckles were white where they gripped the menu, his hands shaking when he tried to set it down, enough to rattle the silverware.

"You're about to give yourself an aneurysm," Lena said after she'd ordered the wine for them.

"How is Ainsley going to get the boys out of the house without Claire noticing?" Reed asked, knowing he wasn't being slick or smooth or anything an accomplice should be, but unable to stop from voicing the one question he couldn't quite figure out.

Lena's eyes widened and she glanced around. But he'd pitched his voice low enough that they were safe. "God, Reed, no wonder you weren't able to do this earlier."

Shame flickered in his chest, but he snuffed it out. It wasn't like it was anything he hadn't heard before. "How?"

She sighed. "She switched Claire's sleeping pills with Milo's painkillers. The higher dose should be enough to knock her out for a few hours at least."

Reed blinked at that. He would never have considered such a thing. The thought of her waking up tomorrow, the boys gone, her leverage, her power stripped away, and realizing that she'd slept through the whole thing was so deeply satisfying that Reed almost did relax just then.

Lena studied him for a long minute. "I wouldn't have told you if you hadn't guessed," she admitted, like the confession had been a heavy burden she wanted off her shoulders.

"I don't blame you," Reed said. He thought about Sebastian's tearful prediction. *She'll get away with it.* "Tell me, are you going to nail her? For Tess?"

"Yes," Lena said, but she looked away, took a sip of her wine. They both knew how powerful Claire's family was, how influential. There was no guarantee that Lena could make the charge stick.

But just like every time Reed promised the boys it would get better, he let himself believe her. Because it was the only way he could walk back into that house tonight.

Lena carried the conversation through the rest of the meal, with Reed contributing a grunt or one-word response when necessary. She didn't seem bothered by the fact, and he was relieved he didn't have to put energy into something other than breathing right now.

It was just when she finished signing the check that the call lit up Lena's phone.

Her hand paused on the last letter of her name, her brows wrinkling together in confusion. "It's Ainsley."

Everything around them slowed so that Reed could feel the rush of blood against his eardrums, feel his pulse thrumming against his throat, feel his stomach heave, just once.

He knew.

Then the world snapped back into motion, and he had the phone in his hand before he even realized he'd reached for it. "What's wrong?"

"You have to go somewhere you'll be seen," Ainsley said, her voice tight but almost calm, sounding every inch the ex-soldier she was. "But not with Lena. Right this second. Hang up and go somewhere you'll be seen."

"What happened?" But he was already moving his body, following the clear command in the words.

There was a beat, and he knew, *he knew* before she said it. "Claire's dead."

Reed cursed, trying to keep a smile on his face as he did. People would be asked about how he acted right now—the waiters, the other diners. They'd be interviewed. He slowed his pace and glanced back toward Lena with a forced smile that he hoped read as real to anyone who didn't know him.

Lena's smile was just as awkward, but she made a point of detouring to the hostess stand and thanking the woman there for a lovely evening.

They stopped on the sidewalk, and only then did Reed ask Ainsley, "How?"

But he knew. *He knew.*

Again, that same pause. "I was in the foyer with Milo, and . . . Reed, I'm sorry . . ."

Reed squeezed his eyes shut. "Sebastian?"

"He's covered in blood," Ainsley said, and like a switch had flipped, the composed soldier was gone and it was just his sister, her voice trembling, her inhale shaky. On a sob, she said, "He stabbed her. God, Reed."

*Stabbed her. Stabbed her. Stabbed her.*

"Reed, you have to go." Ainsley was almost yelling now. "You'll be the prime suspect. I'll take care of it."

"He can't . . ." His throat closed over the words. "He can't . . ."

Lena snatched the phone from him. "I'm coming over."

Then she hung up, gripped his shoulders. "Reed, you're not taking the fall for this."

Reed blinked at her, swayed, wanted to collapse into her arms despite the fact that there was no way she'd be able to hold him up. "Sebastian."

"We'll figure something out," Lena said, but her gaze slid sideways like it had in the restaurant. A lie. "We'll get rid of the clothes, get rid of the evidence. It's going to be okay."

Get rid of his clothes because he was bloody. Because he'd *stabbed* his own mother.

And in that moment, *he knew* what had to happen, the words slipping out before he'd even processed them. "There's a knife in the back of my closet. In a shoebox."

His skin was too tight against his bones, his tendons stretching and pulling every inch of him apart. Was he going to do this? Was he really that person?

Yes. *Yes.* He would sell his soul to the devil without hesitation, would gladly live out eternity in hell if it would just save Sebastian. This was his fault, his failure, his responsibility. Sebastian shouldn't have to pay for Reed's mistakes for the rest of his life.

"There's a knife in the shoebox," he repeated slowly, clearly. "It has Viola's prints on it. Put it in her room, bury the one Sebastian used. They'll be close enough the cops won't notice the difference."

Lena recoiled as if he'd slapped her. He didn't care; he needed her to acknowledge what he'd said. He gripped her arms, his fingers digging in too hard. "Lena."

He could no longer read her expression, but she shrugged out of his grip. "Go."

"Where?"

"Video, you need to be on video," Lena said. "That's the gold standard for alibis."

Reed inhaled. "The casino. The fight tonight. Declan said I could use his tickets anytime."

Lena shook him, pushing him toward the end of the block. "Grab a cab. Go."

He stumbled back, ready to run. But then he stopped. "Will you do it?"

Lena licked her lips. "Go."

There was no point in asking her again, no point in trying to convince her.

Reed ran for a taxi that had just passed by, not even knowing what he hoped her decision would be.

Because it wasn't just his soul he was selling to the devil. It was both of theirs.

# CHAPTER SIXTY-ONE

## GRETCHEN

*Now—*

"How did Lena get the knife into Viola's dresser?" Gretchen asked, and she guessed that shouldn't be her first reaction to hearing the whole recounting. But it was.

"Ainsley gave her half a painkiller at dinner," Reed confessed, and it was saying something that drugging a child wasn't the worst part of this particular story.

"Are they gone now? The boys and Ainsley," Gretchen asked. She assumed so—she had given Ainsley plenty of warning—but some people were too incompetent or too emotional to do the right thing.

Reed nodded once. "Everything was set up already. We just thought . . ."

That it wouldn't be necessary with Claire gone.

"Sebastian, he's not like Viola," Reed said, eyes wide and pleading like he wanted her to confirm it.

Gretchen tilted her head this way and that. "Well, he's a little like her."

"No," Reed said, not quite lunging at her but jolting a few steps forward. "He was doing it to protect his brother."

"By stabbing an unconscious woman thirteen times?" Gretchen didn't know why she was provoking him. The gun was half-lifted now, but in a way that seemed to imply he'd forgotten he was holding it rather than intending to use it.

"He's not like her." Reed shook his head. "Neither of them are."

Gretchen wasn't going to argue the point. Not all killers were psychopaths, and she guessed growing up in a house with two of them gave you a warped enough sense of morality that stabbing your mother might actually seem like a viable option when you're an abused and traumatized eleven-year-old.

"I take it not all of those injuries splashed across the TV were from Viola?" Gretchen guessed.

"Some were," Reed admitted. "A lot weren't."

People saw what they were told to see, what they expected to see.

He swallowed, and it was loud in the quiet room. "You knew."

"Suspected," Gretchen corrected. Though it had been a strong enough guess that she called Ainsley. Something had stuck with Gretchen from that first interview with Viola, buried by every other chaotic detail of this case, but there, lodged in some corner of her mind.

*"Sebastian I would have gutted slowly,"* Viola had said.

*"The older one?"* Gretchen had asked. *"Why Sebastian? Not Milo?"*

Viola had never answered. But then during that second conversation: *"I already told you what you need to know."*

Gretchen had narrowed down her suspects to either Ainsley or Sebastian Kent. And she'd decided to take Viola at her word. The girl hadn't mentioned Ainsley once.

When Gretchen didn't say anything more, Reed shifted. "What now?"

"A deal's a deal." Gretchen slipped Lena's note back into her pocket. "I keep my promises."

Reed's shoulders relaxed, but then his eyes flew to a point over her shoulder, his gun coming up a little higher.

"Maybe so," Marconi said, stepping into the room, her weapon trained on Reed. "But I didn't make one."

# CHAPTER
# SIXTY-TWO
## REED

*Now—*

Detective Lauren Marconi.

That was the name of the woman who had a gun on him now, Reed remembered. She was pretty, with Italian features, small but sturdy. She held the weapon like she'd used it before and wouldn't hesitate to shoot.

Dr. Gretchen White had stepped to the side in surprise when her partner had entered the room, enough shock and irritation crossing her face that Reed didn't think it had been a setup from the start. That didn't stop the panic that crashed against him in unrelenting waves.

"What did you hear?" Reed managed to get out, his fingers tightening compulsively around his own gun. *He probably shouldn't have the weapon.*

"Enough," Marconi confirmed. "Your son Sebastian killed your wife, and you framed your daughter for it."

"No."

But Gretchen was already nodding. "Well summed up."

The look Detective Marconi shot the woman was exasperated and almost affectionate, out of place in the moment.

How many bullets did he have?

"No, that's not what happened," Reed tried again. They wouldn't be able to find Ainsley, she had enough of a head start. But what if they did?

*No.* That couldn't happen.

He wouldn't *let* it happen.

The weak attempt at denial earned him a contemptuous stare from Gretchen. "Oh, please don't say you're going with that angle."

The disdain was too similar to how Claire had always talked to him, and he tried to steady his hand. *He shouldn't have a weapon.* "You made a deal."

It was only when Marconi stepped in front of Gretchen, blocking her partner with her body, that Reed realized he'd shaken the gun at her. Threateningly.

*He shouldn't have this, he shouldn't have this.* It was too tempting to use.

The easy out.

"Mr. Kent, I need you to put down the weapon," Marconi said in that voice Reed often used with Sebastian and Milo. Like when he was soothing wounded animals. "Then we can talk it over, everything. But first I need a show of good faith from you."

Gretchen took a deliberate step around Marconi, brushing off the sleeves of her jacket.

"If I could successfully persuade empaths to do my bidding, I certainly wouldn't waste the power on holding up our deal," she said, responding to Reed's earlier plea as if Marconi weren't there.

The contempt, the clear dismissal, it rubbed on his sore spots, picked at scabs that were barely formed. His lungs felt curiously empty, his head heavy. And still he knew he shouldn't have the gun. "You're no better than Claire," he said. "No better than Viola."

Marconi took a half step forward, and he wondered what he'd sounded like just then, how he had been almost yelling before. How that last bit had come out quiet and controlled.

And he realized it was the exact same tone Claire used before she brought a lit cigarette down on his thigh. It was the exact same tone Viola used when she'd told him how she'd skinned the rabbit alive.

It was the voice of a psychopath. And it had come from him.

But Gretchen recovered swiftly, waving her hand at him like he wasn't about to kill her in cold blood. "Will you put the gun down? Marconi is going to pop a blood vessel."

Marconi huffed, but her eyes were locked on Reed, her stance battle-ready. He lowered his weapon but didn't drop it. It wasn't just the easy out. It was his only out. One way or another.

"What's going to happen?" he asked.

"You are going to put down that gun before you accidentally shoot your foot and embarrass everyone," Gretchen said. "And I am going to convince Marconi here that she came into the house five minutes later than she actually did."

Reed didn't blink, didn't react. But his lungs filled with air, his head stopped pounding. And deep in his chest, a tiny spark flared to life. He knew that spark was dangerous, and yet it was there anyway, waiting to catch fire.

"No," Marconi corrected. "Mr. Kent is going to put down his gun, and then we're all going to go down to the station and figure this out."

Which was why hope was dangerous. His fingers tightened around the grip.

Gretchen's hand twitched. It was the tiniest movement. But it was then that Reed realized some of her flippant poise might be an act.

They met each other's eyes across the room. They both knew that Reed wasn't going into the station. Gretchen's lips moved, and Reed thought she might be cursing beneath her breath.

"You really want to waste resources finding an abused kid who snapped?" Gretchen asked, shifting her attention to Marconi, who still hadn't looked away from Reed. "You think that's justice?"

Marconi didn't answer, didn't move. But there was a hesitation.

Again, again, that spark. It whispered promises to him that he couldn't yet believe.

"No one knows you're here," Gretchen said, her full focus still on Marconi. "They don't know you heard the real story."

It had been the wrong thing to say. When Marconi spoke again, it was with more conviction than before. "I know I did."

"Lord save me from empaths," Gretchen muttered, tipping her head back toward the ceiling like she was actually pleading to a higher power. "I'm not saying we should keep Viola locked away." She paused. "Although, for the record, I think we should."

Reed knew better than to agree with that. The knife in Viola's drawer—the one he had orchestrated to be found there—spoke volumes without him needing to say anything else.

"I'm saying, maybe we shouldn't ruin a young boy's life," Gretchen said. "After he'd been tortured for months."

When Gretchen hesitated and looked toward him, Reed corrected her. "Years. Most of his life."

"And he snapped when Claire sent his brother to the hospital," Gretchen continued with a little nod of acknowledgment. "It's practically self-defense. Just . . . a little delayed."

Marconi's eyes flicked to Gretchen before coming quickly back to Reed. "What do you care about any of this?"

Gretchen's hand went to the pocket where Reed knew Lena's note sat. "Lena wanted it."

"Lena," Marconi said with deliberate emphasis. "Who overdosed because this messed with her head so much."

That news had come like a gut punch. Lena, his brave, magic Lena. All she'd wanted to do was find justice for Tess, and like with everyone else in his life, Reed had managed to drag her down into the depths of this writhing, irredeemable mess.

When Viola had gone along with the arrest, when the cops closed the case, when Lena announced she'd be running the trial so there wouldn't be any surprises—they'd thought they'd gotten away with murder.

Sebastian had been quieter these days, kept to his room mostly, and wouldn't meet his or Ainsley's eyes. Reed had been coaxing him out of his stupor little by little, with plenty of setbacks. And Milo, finally free from relentless terror, had blossomed in just six months into a sweet, funny kid.

Reed had almost been scared to breathe. He knew it was fragile, knew it was a house of paper cards. But those six months had been the happiest of his life, even if they were lived on what he now realized was borrowed time.

At least the world knew what Viola was. No longer was it a hidden secret, a dark look shared between her teachers and other parents. When she was let out of custody, her first victim might not be found, but her second might be. Or her third, at least.

Gretchen White wouldn't let her go on killing forever. Reed trusted that, could go to his grave easier now.

"Lena made her choices, too," Gretchen said with a shrug. "It seems to me that she didn't have to relay Reed's instructions about the knife to Ainsley."

If the cold assessment shocked Marconi, the woman didn't show it. "There's a difference between making a plan and following it."

Gretchen took a step closer to Marconi. "What do you think this is going to accomplish?"

Marconi shook her head. "You don't get it."

"Explain it to me," Gretchen said, shifting a half step closer. It was interesting that it was Marconi she was worried about and not Reed.

*He shouldn't have this gun. He shouldn't have it.*

"You don't just get to decide who is guilty, who's not," Marconi said. "You can't just tell pretty stories and call that justice."

"I'd call this anything but a 'pretty story,'" Gretchen countered.

"When I or when you or when he"—she flicked the muzzle of her gun at Reed—"decide who takes the blame for a murder that was committed by someone else, that's us deciding we're the moral center of the universe."

From the way Gretchen narrowed her eyes, Reed guessed Marconi was tossing Gretchen's own argument back at her.

"You, more than anyone, can see the problems with that," Marconi said. "You're basing your decisions on emotions even if they're not your own."

Gretchen chewed on her bottom lip. "And you're being too rigidly rational. How did our stances switch like that?"

"We clearly spend too much time together," Marconi said. "I'm not being rigid."

"You are," Gretchen countered easily. "The question is why."

"Because I'm sworn to uphold the law," Marconi shot back.

"No . . ." Gretchen drew out the denial, long and considering. "You don't mind bending the rules. It's one of the things I like about you."

Marconi's eyebrows lifted in surprise. "There are things you like?"

"Of course." Gretchen waved that away. "And one of them is that you aren't an extremist in either direction, emotional or rational. Yet you're acting like an extremist. Why?"

Reed didn't know either of them, but he ran the conversation back over in his mind. The way Marconi had spit out *you framed your daughter* struck him harder this time.

"You don't like that I framed Viola," Reed said, and only when he spoke did he realize how quiet he'd been throughout the exchange. Both women turned toward him.

"What?"

But Gretchen's expression had shifted, had become thoughtful. "Oh, I was wrong."

"Mark the calendar," Marconi murmured, but her weapon was back to pointing directly at Reed's chest.

"You're being too emotional," Gretchen said, a bit of glee in her voice. "You're conflating Viola and me and getting confused about who's who."

"I know who's who," Marconi snapped.

Gretchen smiled, and it was strange and too wide. "You don't. But let me tell you, Viola is not me. She's dangerous and she will kill someone."

"You can't know that," Marconi countered. "You're finding her guilty before the fact."

"She will," Reed said, taking a chance. There were two options here. He could kill both of them before turning the gun on himself. If the cops found the three of them dead, they'd make certain assumptions that would still end up protecting Sebastian. He didn't want that ending. There was perhaps a single shred of his soul left, and he didn't want to dirty it beyond repair.

Marconi had to agree to let his confession stand. "Viola takes pleasure in hurting others. In hurting them in violent ways, in slow, torturous ways. She will kill someone, and I am only thankful one of her brothers wasn't first."

Marconi shifted on her feet. "Shaughnessy thought that of you, too, Gretchen. That you would kill someone someday."

Reed didn't know who Shaughnessy was, but Gretchen rolled her eyes like she wasn't in the middle of a standoff.

"Shaughnessy saw a knife in Viola's drawer and didn't think to ask a single question further," Gretchen commented. "Do not take your cues from him. God bless the man, but he's blinded when it comes to little girls he thinks are killers. He must have a phobia from watching too many horror movies."

When Marconi didn't say anything, Gretchen glanced Reed's way. "Reed tried to do the world a favor, Marconi. It's only a pity that it failed."

*Because of Lena.* Reed hated himself for having that thought. But had she not killed herself, would anyone have looked deeper into this case that was so obviously already solved?

Would he have ever truly been able to live with himself, though? Would he ever have been able to look in the mirror and not shatter it with his fist as the years passed and Viola rotted away in a maximum-security detention facility?

Lena and Marconi were both onto something. The minute he'd decided to frame Viola was the minute he'd sealed his own fate.

"So . . . let's say I came in five minutes later," Marconi said slowly, and the relief of it almost took Reed to the floor. Instead he sagged back against the wall, his eyes landing on the stuffed bear that Milo had always carried everywhere.

There hadn't been time to find it in the haste to pack.

He knew his family was forever indebted to Dr. Gretchen White for calling ahead, for giving them warning. He knew his family was forever indebted to Lena for making sure he had the chance to take the blame for the murder.

An hour wasn't much, and it might not have been enough had they not already had everything planned. Ainsley had run for the go bag while Reed pulled each boy into a hug, marveling at the fact that he was getting the chance to say the goodbye that he'd denied himself six months earlier.

When it had been Sebastian's turn, Reed had knelt by his son. In the six months since Claire's death, the remaining softness that had clung to his face had melted. His eyes were harder than they'd ever been before, and he no longer fell into Reed's arms just for comfort.

Reed had looked him in the eye, forced him to hold his gaze.

*"You did good, buddy,"* Reed had told him. *"But now it's time to rest."*

"We have a confession," Gretchen said. Marconi hadn't caught on to where this was headed. Or maybe she had and didn't want to admit it. "And Reed has your promise that you'll honor it, yes?"

The long pause that followed stretched to the horizon and back, and in it he saw his life.

Every mistake.

Every love.

Every tragedy. Every bruise, every laugh, every hesitation, every time he'd turned left instead of right.

Drinking on the floor in Ainsley's new house. Sitting in the cheap seats at Fenway with Lena and Tess. His first kiss with Claire. Their last.

Milo's warm weight pressed against his side. Sebastian clenching his little jaw as he tried not to cry.

And Viola's quiet, watchful eyes that looked so much like his own.

Finally, Marconi, without lowering her gun, sighed out a quiet yes.

The last of Reed's tension bled out of his body, the hope rushing in like wildfire. He met Gretchen's eyes, and she nodded slightly.

He smiled at them both.

"Now," Reed said quietly. "Now it's time to rest."

And then he brought the gun to his own mouth. In the split second before he pulled the trigger, he saw Sebastian's tear-soaked face when he'd nodded and promised, *I will.*

# CHAPTER SIXTY-THREE

## GRETCHEN

*Now—*

Marconi slid into the booth across from Gretchen, her thighs dragging across the cracked red vinyl so that it squeaked. Gretchen hid a grin.

"You eat pizza?" Marconi asked, her expression incredulous. She was staring at the large, greasy pepperoni pie that Gretchen would certainly not be sharing.

"Yes, and if you touch it, I'll stab you with my fork," Gretchen warned. Pizza was the one indulgence she allowed herself after solving a case; it was sacred, and Marconi was treading on thin ice even by being here. But she'd come bearing ice-cold bottles of beer, so Gretchen would allow her to watch.

Marconi rolled her eyes but then went to order a couple of slices of her own. When she returned, she was quiet, seemingly content with just drinking her beer in silence and staring at Gretchen.

"Don't be creepy," Gretchen said around a mouthful of sauce and cheese.

"Do you think we did the right thing?" Marconi finally asked, the question somehow layered with every emotion ever felt by an empath in the eternity of the universe.

Gretchen tipped her head back, laughing until her eyes were damp. "Oh, how far we've come in only a handful of days."

"You mean me checking my moral compass against a sociopath's?" Marconi said with almost as much humor, dry as it was. "Yeah, I may have fallen into an alternate reality somewhere along the way."

"Welcome to the dark side, darling. We have so much more fun over here anyway," Gretchen purred.

Marconi tossed a grease-stained napkin at her, and Gretchen batted it away, her lip curling in disgust.

"Don't get complacent," Gretchen said, adding a little snap to the warning so it came off as threatening and not lighthearted. "Just because we've made some morally questionable decisions together doesn't mean I won't—"

"Stab me with a fork, yes, I know," Marconi said with a, quite frankly, impertinent eye roll. "You called Ainsley *before* you read Lena's note."

Gretchen hummed in agreement but didn't answer because she'd been hoping Marconi hadn't picked up on that.

"Does that mean you're not really a sociopath?" Marconi asked, the slice of pizza hanging out of her mouth.

"Don't go giving me a white hat," Gretchen scolded. "You empaths can build a redemption arc off the slightest hint of feelings."

"Your life has been one big redemption arc," Marconi pointed out. "Maybe it's not driven by right and wrong, but you've still helped more people than you've hurt. You still looked at the situation with the Kents more clearly than I did. Made a decision based on something other than the strict letter of the law. Isn't that emotion?"

"The problem with you all is you're so tied to your emotions you can't even fathom that there are other reasons to make decisions,"

Gretchen said. "I wanted one thing from this investigation. And I got it."

"Oh, do tell," Marconi said, something teasing in her voice.

"Answers," Gretchen said with a grin. "You will soon learn that I care about that above all else."

"Well, I still think you're a better person than you think you are," Marconi said, waving her slice around until a pepperoni slid off and landed on her nearly transparent paper plate.

"Yes, and that belief will get you killed one day," Gretchen countered, but she couldn't help but preen slightly. "So you're really not going to raise a fuss about Sebastian Kent?"

"I said I wouldn't," Marconi said, sitting back against the vinyl.

"Yes, but you could have been lying to try to get him to drop his gun."

Marconi shook her head. "I realized when he didn't try to shoot me when I walked in that he was planning on killing himself."

"That gives you more incentive to have lied," Gretchen pointed out.

"What can I say, I'm a woman of my word."

Gretchen studied her. "You have no moral pangs?"

Marconi laughed at the phrase. "A few. I always do. That's the curse of being an empath, I suppose. But we found Tess's body in the park. That, together with the evidence Lena compiled, was enough to give her justice." Marconi shrugged. "And all the adults paid for their crimes. Lena and Reed are dead. Claire's very dead. Declan doesn't seem like the best human, but he didn't really play a role in any of it, either."

Marconi held her hand up, clearly reading Gretchen's next question in her expression. "I'm not about to go hunt down Sebastian Kent. He's a victim in this."

"What about Ainsley?" Gretchen asked, genuinely curious.

Marconi squinted at her. "It's going to be an empath kind of answer."

"I expect nothing less," Gretchen drawled.

"Everything she did was to protect those kids," Marconi said. "She went along with the plan to frame Viola to protect Sebastian. It's not like she hid the knife in the first place. And on top of all that, she's giving up the life she knows to go into hiding with those boys."

"Reed was right, wasn't he? That's what got to you?" Gretchen said, seizing on the little tidbit. "The knife."

"The premeditation, yeah," Marconi said. "Lena and Ainsley, they were acting in the heat of the moment. Reed had planned for it."

"And who knows what he was thinking when he saved that knife with Viola's fingerprints on it," Gretchen agreed. If she had to guess, she would say he'd been plotting something like this in the back of his head, and the moment just happened to fall into his lap.

"He was abused, too," Marconi said, and Gretchen laughed because of course Marconi had to be fair to the man she didn't even like.

"Six months more and he probably would have killed Claire himself," Gretchen mused, and Marconi nodded with a grimace.

They both ate another slice, Marconi eyeing Gretchen's pie when her plate was empty. Gretchen toyed with the knife so that it caught the light, and Marconi backed off, her hands raised in surrender.

"So what's going to happen with Viola?" Marconi asked.

"She'll be let out," Gretchen said, mournfully washing down her last bite with the dregs of her beer. "Put in the foster system unless Ainsley comes back to claim her. I'm sure that will do wonders for her developing psychopathy."

Marconi raised her brows in silent agreement, and Gretchen wondered what steps the woman would take to monitor Viola. They couldn't really justify it legally, but Shaughnessy had done it to Gretchen for three decades, so she guessed they'd find a way to keep an eye on Viola.

Gretchen also wondered how long it would take Viola to disappear off the grid, get a new name, find a new city. A year? Two? Certainly by the time she turned eighteen.

Marconi watched her for a long time. "Be honest."

"I try never to do that," Gretchen countered.

"If I hadn't been there, would you have made up some story for Reed?" Marconi continued as if she hadn't interrupted. "That he hadn't confessed, that he'd simply shot himself?"

"And let Viola rot in prison?" Gretchen surmised. The answer of course was yes, but Gretchen didn't want to break Marconi's little empath heart. "I guess we'll never know."

Marconi seemed to see through her anyway. "Even though you were falsely accused?"

Gretchen looked away. But contrary to what Marconi seemed to think, Gretchen didn't see herself in Viola.

She saw herself in Sebastian.

"You don't know that," Gretchen said.

"You're right," Marconi agreed, and there was the slap of a heavy file landing against the laminate table. "But don't you think it's time to find out?"

Heart pounding, palms suddenly sweaty, Gretchen didn't allow herself to look. When the silence dragged on, she realized Marconi wasn't giving up. Slowly, ever so slowly, her eyes slid from the wall, to her half-empty pizza tray, to the discarded plates, to finally land on the folder.

She reached out a shaking hand to spin it in her direction.

On the tab was a name.

GRETCHEN ANNE WHITE.

# ACKNOWLEDGMENTS

Many, many thanks to my editor, Megha Parekh, who didn't hang up on the spot when I said, "So I think my next main character is going to be a sociopath." Thank you for always being clearheaded, thoughtful, and smart about our projects, for supporting my weird ideas, and for knowing when to nudge me away from disastrous ones.

And thank you—always, always, always—to Charlotte Herscher, who has been helping make my books the best they can be since my very first thriller. I am endlessly grateful for your guiding hand and spot-on edits.

It takes so many people to get a book out to readers, from the fantastic copyeditors—to whom every writer owes their life!—to the production editors, to the proofreaders and the marketing team. Thank you all so much for your hard work and dedication. It is truly a pleasure to work with such a wonderful team.

Thank you to Abby McIntyre, my first reader extraordinaire, for being gentle and encouraging and extremely helpful all at once.

To my family and friends—and then all of their friends—who have offered support over the years, I cannot thank you enough. I have been consistently blown away by the sheer amount of love and encouragement I have received from all of you.

I'd also like to acknowledge some of the experts whose work on sociopaths and emotional intelligence I drew upon while writing this book, including Robert D. Hare CM, M. E. Thomas, Dr. Martha Stout, and Dr. Daniel Goleman, among others.

And, as always, thank you, dear readers. Thank you for trusting me with your time and energy—both of which are at a premium these days. It is an honor and a privilege that I don't take for granted.

# ABOUT THE AUTHOR

*Photo © 2019*

Brianna Labuskes is the *Washington Post* and Amazon Charts bestselling author of the psychological suspense novels *Her Final Words*, *Black Rock Bay*, *Girls of Glass*, and *It Ends with Her*. For the past eight years, she has worked as an editor at both small-town papers and national media organizations such as Politico and Kaiser Health News, covering politics and policy. She was born in Harrisburg, Pennsylvania, and graduated from Penn State University with a degree in journalism. Brianna lives in Washington, DC, and enjoys traveling, hiking, kayaking, and exploring the city's best brunch options. Visit her at www.briannalabuskes.com.